Dear Reader,

Do you judge your *Scarlet* books by their covers? Or do you choose your romances by the 'blurb' on the back of the book? Perhaps you pick a particular novel off the shelf because of its title, or maybe because of the author's name? You'll notice that each month we provide a list of forthcoming *Scarlet* books, with short outlines giving you a taste of each new story. Does *that* help you to make your selection? Of course, I hope you are buying all four titles each month, but I'd love to know how *you* make *your* reading decisions.

And by the way, how do you feel about sequels? A number of readers have already written to ask if we are planning to publish new books featuring popular characters from already published *Scarlet* novels. If you'd like to see a spin-off of your top-of-the-pops *Scarlet* romance, why not send me a letter for the author in question and I'll be happy to pass it along.

Till next month,
Best wishes,

Sally Cooper

SALLY COOPER,
Editor-in-Chief – *Scarlet*

About the Author

Chrissie Loveday was educated in Staffordshire and gained her teaching certificate in Leicester. She taught in secondary schools for many years, and worked in Special Education and at further Education Colleges.

She is currently a part-time lecturer at Cornwall College, working with students who have learning difficulties and physical disabilities and she also runs a new course for ancillary staff in schools and colleges.

Chrissie adores travelling – anywhere she can manage! She's already visited much of Britain and Europe, Singapore, Thailand, New Zealand, Australia, Kenya and many other exotic locations.

Her main interests, apart from writing include, people, crafts of all sorts, walking her two dogs and generally living life to the full. She has three sons and one grandchild, and has recently remarried.

Other *Scarlet* titles available this month:

LOVE BEYOND DESIRE – Jessica Marchant
TIME TO TRUST – Jill Sheldon
LOVERS AND LIARS – Sally Steward

CHRISSIE LOVEDAY

THE PATH TO LOVE

Enquiries to:
Robinson Publishing Ltd
7 Kensington Church Court
London W8 4SP

First published in the UK by Scarlet, 1997

A copy of the British Library Cataloguing in
Publication data is available from the British Library

ISBN 1–85487–924–3

Printed and bound in the EC

10 9 8 7 6 5 4 3 2 1

CHAPTER 1

This was really the start of her new life. Kerrien held her breath as the undercarriage of the big plane creaked down. Brisbane's airport rushed up towards her. It had been a long, long flight and she felt almost light-headed from lack of sleep. She had never travelled so far before in her life.

'This is it then, love,' said the large, comfortable woman who had sat next to her on the flight. 'You've got my address safe, just in case you need a friend?'

'Yes. Thanks very much. It's good to know there's one person at least who will know me,' Kerrien replied. 'So, this is Australia!'

'It's so good to be back,' Margaret smiled. 'Gives you a real buzz to see the sun and the water again. Don't think anywhere is quite like your own home town.'

'No, I guess not,' Kerrien said in a small voice.

'Oh sorry, love. Just listen to me will you? Rabbiting on like that. No feeling nor nothing. I'm sure you'll be fine. Lovely looking girl like you. Bet you'll have all the fellas rushing to your door. My Brett will certainly be in line, once he's met you. I think you'll like him too . . . great tall thing he's turned out and quite a looker too. But then, you'd expect me to say that, being his mum and all.'

Kerrien smiled at the woman's enthusiasm. If she had any preconceived ideas about Australians, Margaret confirmed the lot. They had only met around twenty-four hours ago but here she was, treating Kerrien as if she were family. Perhaps it was something to do with spending a day and a night in a plane, sharing confidences with the stranger sitting next to you.

Everything had happened so fast. Kerrien could scarcely believe what had happened to her. Never again would she knock fate. It was all so weird, she had trouble coming to terms with the situation. Just a couple of months ago, she had been working at the nursery back in her home town, living with Mum just as she'd always done. Margaret had prised the whole story from her during the flight. It had started when Margaret saw her wiping her eyes. Whatever she thought about leaving the UK, she still felt huge pangs of homesickness and that was almost before the plane had taken off. The Australian woman soon drew out the whole story, tutting and shaking her head whenever she felt Kerrien's story reached a particularly poignant phase.

'You can get up now, love,' Margaret was saying. Kerrien jerked back to the present. 'Come on. The lights have all gone out. Brizzy . . . here we come.'

With surprising speed, she was out of her seat and was pulling Kerrien's bags out of the overhead locker. 'Come on love. I want to see this doctor of yours is here to meet you. I'm not leaving you at the airport until I know everything's OK.'

'Thanks,' Kerrien murmured gratefully. Her knees were feeling quite weak and it was not entirely due to the long flight.

The passengers gradually pushed forward, everyone trying to be first off the plane and out in the warm air of the Australian city. Clutching her papers, passport and hand luggage, she followed her new friend along the narrow aisle; nodded at the flight stewards, who formed a reception line of set smiles. She gasped as the heat struck her. The contrast between the November gloom she had left behind in Britain and this blaze of light, was almost too much. Thank heavens she had taken Margaret's advice and shed several layers of clothing during the flight. The stream of passengers went into the terminal, into the luggage hall and, at last, she was assuring the customs officer she had nothing in the way of foodstuffs, banned goods or excess duty free allowance. Margaret was at another table, convincing the officer that she had only brought presents back for her family. She was about to give them the whole saga of her sister's illness and her only niece who was, in her opinion, neglecting her duties, when the officer thought better of it all and sent her on her way.

'Always works,' she grinned. 'Tell 'em what they don't want to hear and they can't wait to be rid of you. Right, love. Where's this doctor of yours?'

'Hardly my doctor!' she protested, looking round anxiously. She had no idea who she was looking for. She assumed he couldn't be all that old if he had young kids, but then who could tell these days? She had built her own fantasy of a good-looking young doctor who would be waiting to sweep her off her feet. Some fantasy! There seemed to be hundreds of people waiting at the barrier, a great sea of faces and most of them smiling. People waved as they spotted the awaited familiar faces. She couldn't even begin to tell if it was a wave at her or someone behind her. The whole crowd appeared as a blur.

'Brett . . . Lennie . . . oh it's so good to see you.' Margaret had evidently located her family and practically vaulted over the ropes. She flung herself at a huge man, about her own age. 'You're looking thinner. I hope you've been eating properly? This is Kerrien. New friend of mine. Moving to Brisbane to work for some doctor . . . other side of town but we shan't let that stop us seeing her, eh love? Here, Kerrien, come and say hi to my two lads. Brett, you mark my words, you should make sure you get her phone number. You could do a lot worse.'

Kerrien stared at the tall, strikingly handsome man holding out his hand to her. He was so different from his plump, comfortable parents. His hair was sun-bleached at the tips. As for the tan . . . he looked like a refugee from *Baywatch*, or a typical Aussie soap hunk. His light blue eyes had an intensity that made Kerrien feel he was looking right inside her. Her knees felt like jelly and she wished she didn't look quite so travel stained.

'God, you just never change do you Mum? I apologize for her. Back on Australian soil for less than five minutes and she's already trying to get me married off. I'm Brett,' the good-looking young man said. Courtesy of Margaret, Kerrien knew he was twenty-four, just two years older than her.

'Kerrien,' she said a little shyly, holding out her hand. 'Pleased to meet you.' She didn't miss the slight flicker that crossed his face and wished she'd said something witty or at least less boring than *pleased to meet you.*

'You did well to survive the flight and Mum,' he laughed. 'She's quite a case but she means well.'

'Oh no, I mean she was lovely . . . most kind to me. I was feeling very, well odd, I suppose, about leaving home. She listened to all my moans.'

'Bet she just loved it,' Lennie put in. 'Give her a story and she'll soon have you sorted. Now love, where are you heading? Need a lift or anything?'

'Someone's meeting me, thank you. At least, that's what the telegram said.' Again she looked around, hoping to spot her new employer. The crowd was rapidly disappearing, as the new arrivals met friends and families. Kerrien could see no one who fitted her mental image of Doctor Ashton Philips. One or two chauffeurs were still standing, clutching neatly printed boards with the names of their clients and looking hopefully at each new collection of people. She followed Margaret and her family towards the main doors of the terminal.

'I refuse to leave the poor girl here alone,' her travelling companion was saying loudly. 'If they aren't meeting her, she'll just have to come home with us.'

'Oh no, I couldn't,' Kerrien protested. 'They're probably held up in traffic or something. I'll wait over there on those seats. Go on, I'll be fine.' As she looked at the handsome son, she was more than a little tempted to take up their offer, but she felt it might be foolish.

They argued for a few moments and would only leave when she promised faithfully to telephone them later in the evening. If her employer failed to show, she agreed that she would take a taxi straight to their house. However much she protested that she was all right, Kerrien was grateful to have someone who cared in this new, strange city she had flown round the world to make her home.

The automatic doors suddenly opened and a woman rushed in, dragging two small children behind her. She looked around for a few moments and then her eyes settled on Kerrien.

'You must be Miss Clark? Kerrien? Hi. I'm Kate, Kate Philips. I can't tell you how sorry I am not to have been here when you landed. But, if I'd had notice, I might have been better prepared.' She held out a hand that was rather damp and sticky, having disentangled it from the clutch of the small boy, who looked up with huge scared eyes.

'Hallo Kate. You're Doctor Philips' sister, I gather?' Kerrien was slightly confused but Kate nodded.

'Yes, I'm sorry. Ashton sent his apologies. He was called out to a birth, about half an hour before he should have left for the airport. These new babies, they never obey clocks and convenience do they? Anyhow, by the time he knew he wouldn't make it, I was already up to my neck in baking and the kids were, well as you see, playing in the sandpit and filthy dirty.'

Margaret caught Kerrien's arm.

'Looks like you're OK now love. We'll be off. Just you make sure you keep in touch. I shall come looking for you if I don't hear from you.'

'Yes. Thanks. Goodbye and . . . well . . . thanks,' she finished lamely, as the family swept out of the airport, Margaret's head nodding frantically as she chatted away nineteen-to-the-dozen. From the look of resignation on Brett's face, it was obviously quite normal for his mother to talk non-stop. He followed his parents but just as they went through the doors, he turned and gave her a grin, a special grin that seemed to hold an unspoken promise. He was nice, she thought to herself, nice as well as the best looking male she'd seen in ages. She made a mental note to get in touch very soon. It could be interesting to have a bloke like that to show her round a bit. He'd be sure to know all the best, fun places. This was, of course, assuming that he was, as his mother thought, totally unattached. Somehow, with looks

and personality like his, she doubted that very much.
'I'm Jodie,' said a small voice and a hot little hand
was held out politely.

'Hallo, Jodie. I am pleased to meet you. I'm Kerrien.'

'Ben, shake hands with Miss Clark,' instructed
Kate, the little boy's aunt. In response, the child
hid himself behind her and flatly refused to budge.
'Come on Ben,' she urged. 'What will Miss Clark
think of you?'

'Kerrien. Please call me Kerrien,' said the English
girl.

'Well, Miss Clark, Kerrien, we should be getting
home. Is this all your luggage? You didn't bring much,
did you?' Kate sounded somehow less than friendly,
Kerrien thought, or was it just her imagination? She
pushed the trolley with her two suitcases on board and
the little group set off for the car park. Once again, the
heat struck Kerrien with a blast as they went out of the
building. It was blistering and she felt as if she was
entering a sauna. She would need to take care not to
get burnt, her fair skin was quite unaccustomed to
such intense sun.

'Wow,' she breathed. 'Is it always this hot?'

'It is in summer,' Kate answered. 'But it's cooler
where we live. We get a bit of breeze from the ocean,
even though we're some distance away.'

'This is our car,' Jodie announced, stopping beside a
fairly elderly yellow Ford. 'Daddy has the best car but
he's at work. He's always at work.' Her voice was flat
and unemotional and her face didn't look as if it was

used to smiling much. As for Ben, he seemed unnaturally subdued for a child of four. His eyes were dull and showed none of the sparkle she was used to seeing in small boys. She hoped that would all change soon, once they got to know her. They climbed silently into the back and waited for Kate to strap them into their seat belts. Kerrien sat stiffly beside Kate and fastened her own belt. It felt like something of an anti-climax after meeting Margaret and her son. They swept out of the car park and into the busy morning rush of the city. Kate was a competent driver and soon they were making their way over the spectacular bridge and into the suburbs. Kerrien had little idea of what to expect and was pleasantly surprised when at last they turned into a quiet cul-de-sac with large houses, surrounded by very large gardens. There were trees everywhere, providing plenty of shady corners. She fell in love with the house immediately and the garden was a dream.

'Oh, this is just gorgeous,' she breathed. 'It's all so spacious and light everywhere.

'Can I show Kerrien . . . I mean Miss Clark, my room?' Jodie asked.

'In a while. Let her get inside first,' Kate told the little girl.

'I'd rather everyone called me Kerrien. Miss Clark is much too formal.'

'The Doctor would prefer a little formality. For a while, anyhow. We'll see later whether it is appropriate to become more familiar.' If Kerrien felt uneasy, she managed not to show it.

'I expect you'd like a shower and a rest for a while.

9

You two, go out and play quietly in the garden. I don't want any arguments and no noise. Understand?' Kate was rather brusque with the two small children, Kerrien thought, but she made up her mind that she should not make judgements at this early stage. Reluctantly, the two wandered out of the kitchen and into the garden.

'Please may we have a drink?' Jodie asked, sounding almost frightened.

'Really . . . you two are always wanting something. You can have something in a little while, when Miss Clark has been shown her room.'

Kerrien, too felt desperately thirsty, in all this heat and sympathized with the children. They sat quietly on the step, obviously knowing it wasn't wise to pester their aunt.

'Come along Miss Clark. Your room is this way, next to the children's rooms.'

Kerrien followed, glancing back at the waiting children. She gave them a quick smile, as if promising that things would be changing, very soon if she had her way. The house was a bungalow style with a long internal corridor and rooms opening off it. The two children's rooms had pottery signs on the doors, with their names on. Kerrien's room was simply furnished but beautifully light and airy. The flowered curtains were the only patterned things in the room and the feeling of spaciousness was very welcoming.

'This is lovely,' she said gratefully.

'You have your own shower room and toilet, so you won't need to share the children's. Doctor Philips had it put in specially for you, so I hope you will appreciate it.' Kerrien hated the formality that Kate was showing and wished she would relax and settle down to calling her Kerrien. It was odd when she had expected Australians to be easy-going and relaxed. Perhaps it was because they were not naturally Australian. Kate's English accent was still very obvious.

'I'll leave you now, to settle in. Is there anything you need?' Kate sounded polite, rather than solicitous.

'I could do with a cold drink. I'm not used to such heat,' she said tentatively, not wanting to get the same response as the children.

'Very well. I'll bring you something.'

'There's no need. Show me where things are and I can help myself. I could get something for the children too, to save you the bother.' She noticed the flicker of annoyance cross Kate's otherwise quite pretty face, but she made no comment. She turned silently and went back towards the kitchen. Rather uncertainly, Kerrien followed. Kate went to the large refrigerator and took out a container of fruit juice. She poured four glasses and added ice cubes to two of them. She took the other two and called the children, who rushed over immediately, grabbed the drinks and gulped thirstily.

'I don't allow them too much juice and it must be home-made. The additives in the commercial stuff are quite unacceptable. Chilled things are not good for them either, hence no extra ice in theirs.'

Feeling rather disconcerted, Kerrien took the drink to her room and undressed for a shower. The cool

11

water revived her and with fresh clothes she felt more human. She lay on the bed to relax for a little while, hoping that Doctor Philips would be a little more friendly than his sister. What would he be like? The two children were adorable but so unnaturally sub-dued that she longed to play with them and see the smiling faces she knew must be hidden beneath the surface. She must have dozed for some time and when she awoke, she could hear voices. She got up from her bed, ran her fingers through her short blonde hair and crossed to the door. Something made her stop, before opening it.

'For God's sake Kate. Stop trying to mother me. Save your worries for the children, not me. I'm quite capable of looking after myself.' It was the voice of a man, presumably, Doctor Ashton Philips himself. She was about to go into the corridor, when Kate's voice, raised in anger, began to speak.

'Oh yes? Then why am I here, wasting my life and slaving away to look after your kids that your precious wife couldn't be bothered to stay and care for? Do you think I wanted to give up my life for you? It's always been the same. Whatever dear Ashton wants, Ashton must have. Everyone else's lives included.'

'Please Kate. You know how grateful I am for all you've done. Surely this is why we've tried so hard to get someone to look after the children? I'm sure that this one is going to work out. Let's give her a chance, eh?'

'She's nothing more than a namby-pamby girl. No better than the last one. She'll never cope with them and I know she'll never bother with proper diets and keeping them off harmful junk foods.'

Oh won't she, Kerrien muttered under her breath. Perhaps this was the reason for Kate's lack of friendliness . . . understandable in a way, if she'd given up her own life to look after her nephew and niece. But surely that was all going to change, now that she had arrived?

'Please, Kate. Let's give her a chance. After all, the references were good and it's not as if she has anything much to go back for. The agency said she's suitable in every way. Besides, I've forked out a lot of money one way or another, to get her here.' He had a nice voice, Kerrien decided. And he sounded a lot more reasonable than his sister.

She opened the door, making as much noise as possible so that her arrival was announced.

'Welcome,' said the man standing next to Kate. Even if she hadn't heard the argument, it was evident from the expression on Kate's face, that this particular conversation was far from over. 'Ashton Philips. I hope you will be happy here with us. I'm so sorry that I wasn't at the airport to meet you but the life of a doctor is nothing, if not unpredictable.'

'Thank you and please don't worry about not meeting me. After all, Kate and the children arrived, before I had time to get myself together.'

'Miss Clark had met with some people, so she was not inconvenienced,' Kate said, emphasizing the *Miss Clark* pointedly.

'Kerrien, please. I'd like you all to call me Kerrien. I hope the children and I will soon become friends.'

13

'Great. Kerrien it is. And please call me Ashton. Can't all live under one roof and be starchy and formal, can we Kate?'

His sister said nothing but the glare spoke volumes. There was definitely a problem here that Kerrien needed to sort out, if she was to make a success of this new job. After all, she had taken a huge gamble, travelling round the world, leaving everything she had known. When Mum had died, there seemed to be nothing to keep her there, in the little English Midlands town where she had lived all her life. Mum's illness had always made it impossible for her to move away before. Memories of her father, who had left them when she was only eighteen months old, were non-existent. Her mother had coped single-handedly. When Kerrien had seen the job advertisement in a specialist magazine, the idea of a completely fresh start had seemed appealing. Not really expecting to hear any more, she had been pleased to get an interview at the rather exclusive agency. She was even more surprised when a couple of days later, they telephoned their offer of the job. She would be nanny to two small children in Brisbane, Australia, all fares paid. She had given in her notice and wham, here she was!

'We'll sort out your duties later. First, let's show you around,' Ashton said. He held the door open for her to follow him out into the garden. He pointed out its main features, explaining what was allowed and what he expected from the children. The small swimming pool seemed to pose the greatest problem. She

14

stole a few surreptitious glances at her new employer, hoping he wouldn't notice. He was around thirty, she decided. He was quite good-looking, and there was one feature she couldn't fail to notice – his gorgeous eyes. She couldn't decide whether they were brown or green, a depth of colour that you could melt into. Long lashes shaded the expression but she sensed reserve, as if he covered them to keep his feelings to himself. His hair, unfashionably long, was the same fair shade as Jodie's and they both had the same, shy smile. Ben was totally different. He had dark, curly hair and the clearest of blue eyes. Kerrien assumed he must take after his mother, wherever she was. There was also a strong family resemblance between Ashton and his sister but her mouth was narrow and had formed hard little lines at the corners. Obviously, she had some huge chip on her shoulder. She seemed determined that everyone should know how generous she was, giving up her life to look after her brother's motherless children.

'How long has Kate been living with you?' she asked, hoping to hear some explanation of the set-up.

'She came down about three years ago. Jane, my ex-wife, was finding things a bit much with Jodie and the new baby, so it seemed like a perfect answer. Kate came to help and then, after Jane decided she couldn't face life in Australia any longer, she took off and I was left with two kids and a built-in baby minder.' His voice was steady but Kerrien sensed a deep pain beneath the words and she tactfully waited for him to say more. He remained silent.

'You certainly have a lovely house and garden,' she said lamely. 'The trees make a perfect shade for the children to play in. And the little wildlife area . . . it's super.'

'I started it when we first came but I don't get much time now. There are some great birds around here.' A slight flicker of enthusiasm crossed his face, lightening the strain lines that wrinkled the corners of his eyes.

'I shall have a lot to learn!' Kerrien said. She was a town-girl and knew little of the countryside in England, let alone Australia.

'You must watch yourself in the sun. You have very fair skin. When you've seen as many cases of skin-cancer as I have, you wouldn't think twice about sun block.' Kerrien was well aware of the problems, after the constant coverage in the UK.

'Lunch is ready,' Kate called from the house. 'Get the kids organized Ashton. Miss Clark can start work properly, tomorrow.'

'Jodie, Ben. Lunch. Come on you terrible two-some,' he shouted, grabbing Ben round the waist and tossing him in the air. The little boy screamed in delight and laughed as he was flung over his father's shoulder. Kerrien was relieved to hear him sounding more like a normal child. Six-year-old Jodie bounced along behind and shyly slipped her small hand into Kerrien's. She looked up at her new nanny and smiled. Kerrien grinned back and gave the hand a small squeeze.

'I hope you're going to like us, and that you won't

want to leave too soon,' she said. Kerrien felt it was a curious thing to say, especially after she had travelled so far to be here.

'Ashton, really. You shouldn't get them all excited just before they eat. Go and wash your hands, quickly now.' Obediently, the pair did as they were told.

'I thought we would all eat together, just for today,' Kate announced. Kerrien wondered how else they would eat but said nothing. 'I thought Miss Clark might prefer to eat with the children in future, so you can be left in peace,' she added to her brother.

'Nonsense. We shall all eat together. It's often the only time I see the children all day, so I hardly want them isolated somewhere else. Honestly Kate, I sometimes wonder where you get your ideas. This is the twentieth century you know. Australia. Not some *Upstairs Downstairs* set-up in Victorian England.'

Kate made no reply but her sniff of disapproval was unmistakable. They all took their places and Kate served the cold chicken and salad.

'You'll thank me for a well-established routine when Martine moves in,' Kate said stiffly.

There was total silence round the table, Ben looked down at his plate and Jodie's eyes filled with tears. As for Ashton, he turned scarlet with fury and glared at his sister. He glanced at Kerrien and obviously fighting his temper deep inside, he chose to say nothing. The tension was becoming unbearable. Kate had a smirk on her face, pleased with the result of her comment. Who was this Martine she'd mentioned? What was it with Kate? Kerrien wondered.

She was looking after her brother's children, being cook and housekeeper rolled into one, had presumably given up whatever career she had and seemed, on the surface, to be doing a good job. But her attitude was distinctly hostile and she seemed to be more intent on disciplining the children than giving them the love they so obviously needed. Kerrien looked forward to spending some time alone with the children, helping them towards the high spirits and fun that they lacked in their present lives. Every moment, she became more and more determined that this was going to work.

After lunch, the children were ordered to their rooms to rest. While she approved of small children taking a rest, surely these two were a little old for that? Kerrien said nothing but made a note of another change she would initiate at the first opportunity.

'I'll help with the washing up,' she offered.

'We have a dish-washer and I'm used to loading it, thank you. I suggest you take a rest now and then perhaps you might like to accompany us for the afternoon walk, when the children wake again.' It seemed whatever move she made to be friendly, Kate was intent on rejecting her and trying to make her feel uncomfortable. Still, perhaps the idea of joining them for a walk was an olive branch to be grasped.

'I'd better get back to work. See who has done what while I've been away. I'll try to be home early this evening and we can have a good chat about life here in Brisbane.' Ashton left the table and Kerrien watched him drive away, still speculating on who Martine could be. Why had the name caused such a reaction in the family and why was Ashton, Doctor Philips, so angry at Kate's comment? She went into her room, intent on unpacking and arranging her few possessions. She had brought a few pictures and ornaments, things that held memories too precious to be parted from. Apart from that, her clothes had taken up the rest of the space in her suitcases. She'd left most of her stuff in the local Oxfam shop at home. There had seemed little point in bringing a mass of thick winter clothing to a climate that was nearer to an English summer for most of the year. She had some savings and planned to buy herself lots of new clothes and see something of the country when she had time off. She hung her few dresses in the wardrobe and stowed the rest in the drawers. She wondered how long the children would sleep and how much time she would have to spend in her room. She lay back on the comfortable bed. It all seemed very strange and the long journey had taken its toll. She drifted off into a light sleep and eventually slept so deeply that she didn't wake again until it was nearly dark.

'Heavens,' she muttered sitting up. She switched on the light and looked at her watch. It was nearly nine o'clock. Quickly, she leapt off the bed, splashed her face with cold water and went through to the large family room, where Ashton was watching television.

'Hallo there,' he said. 'Feeling better for your rest?'

'I am really sorry. I didn't feel particularly tired when I lay down but I must have gone right off.'

'Kate's left you some supper in the microwave. Heat for four minutes, she said.'

'That was kind of her,' Kerrien said gratefully.

'Have to keep your strength up. Put it on a tray and bring it in here,' Ashton suggested. 'I'll pour us a glass of wine and we can relax in front of the television.' His words sounded friendly but there was tension in his eyes and his body was taut. With restless energy, he sprang out of his chair and went to open a bottle of wine.

She was soon sitting in the comfortable chair and tucking into the casserole. She felt extremely hungry and was grateful for the delicious meal.

'Has Kate gone out?' she asked.

'She's gone out to one of her clubs. She has many interests and likes to be away from the house most evenings. That's partly why you're here. It becomes a real problem when I'm on call and as she spends all day with the kids, I can hardly expect her to do evenings as well. Baby-sitters are hard to come by. Besides, the possible changes ahead mean that Kate won't be staying forever.'

Kerrien was now intrigued.

'Was that the reference to Martine?'

Ashton sighed.

'You know, there are times when I could cheerfully strangle my sister. Then I remember how grateful I am and have to bite back my thoughts. Sorry . . . that sounds disloyal and I don't mean to. Trouble is, I think Kate wants to see me married off again and I suppose I can understand why. She'd be able to leave with a clear conscience. Martine is a friend of mine. We met through medicine, at a seminar, earlier this year. We've spent quite a lot of time together, mostly because of shared interests. Kate has somehow got it into her mind that I'm about to bring her here to live with me. I should tell you now, I have no such intention. But, when Kate thinks she knows what's going on, she expects it to happen.'

'You don't have to explain anything to me. I was just wondering about my role here and exactly what you want me to do.'

'Kate decided she wanted to get back to her own career and fair enough, why should she look after me and the kids? She was a physiotherapist and feels she'd lose any chance of a decent job if she doesn't move soon. A nanny seemed like the answer.'

'Why advertise in England? Aren't there any nannies here?'

'Of course, but the last one we had didn't stay for long.'

'Why not? The children are gorgeous and very well-behaved.' Kerrien was curious. The whole set-up seemed ideal. Lovely house, lovely garden and a super room.

'I suppose she couldn't cope with Kate interfering. I shouldn't be so ungrateful, I know, but Kate can be trying at times. Look, I don't want to put you off but there are a few things you should know. She can be very demanding and jealous, too.' His face was etched with the strain from many years of coping with his

21

work and family and evidently, very little fun or social life.

'I see. It sounds to me like she doesn't want anyone else to be able to fill her role. Yet she resents the fact that all her time is taken up in a job she doesn't really want.' It made sense, she thought.

'She is loyal to the end and would never let the children or me suffer. Old habits die hard. Our parents died when we were young. She looked after me and pushed me to go to medical school. I was all for giving up education and getting a job. But, we came out here to Australia together, thinking the medical service here would open up many more chances. I met Jane and we got married. Kate disapproved of the marriage and eventually we moved out of Sydney, partly so that we could have lives of our own. It was tough on Jane. After Ben was born, she found things difficult. Then her parents in England became sick and she went over to stay with them, leaving the kids here with Kate and me and a girl who came in daily. Jane came back but she had begun to hate Australia. The rest is history. She went back soon after. Kate had to bale me out once again.'

Kerrien listened, eating her meal as she did so. Much was now clearer. Perhaps Kate was not unfriendly after all but just wanted to be sure that her nephew and niece would be properly cared for. When she was satisfied, she could go back to work herself. She had a career and wanted to return to it. It all seemed very reasonable, she thought and planned to reassure Kate that she was quite able to care for the

22

children, just as Kate would want. She would begin the very next day.

'Shall I make some coffee?' she asked, when she had finished eating.

'I'd rather have another glass of wine,' Ashton replied. 'How about you?'

CHAPTER 2

Despite her long sleep during the evening, Kerrien slept soundly that first night in her new home. She awoke early to the sound of a strange hammering noise. It was not quite that, but she couldn't decide what else it could be. Looking out of the window, she saw the noisy creature. It was a kookaburra, a beautiful bird sitting in the tree outside her window, making its strange noise. She smiled and went for a shower. She dressed in a pair of shorts and a tee-shirt that had, in truth, seen better days. They would have to do until she could get to some shops and replace them. She went through the house towards the kitchen. Kate was already there, preparing breakfast and, seemingly, lunch as well.

'Good morning,' Kerrien said brightly. She was going to remain cheerful, whatever disapproving looks were sent in her direction. 'Oh and thank you for the delicious meal last night. I did enjoy it and it was very kind of you to leave it for me.'

'Well, don't think it's going to become a habit. Usually, meals are served at set times and anyone who is not present doesn't eat. Doctor Philips said I should make an exception as it was your first day and you were tired from your journey.'

Why did she persist with this stupid formality? Calling her brother Doctor Philips all the time!

'Yes. Thank you,' Kerrien said a little uncertainly. 'Shall I get the children up now?'

'Oh no. They don't come through for breakfast until eight o'clock, after the Doctor has left for work. He needs peace in the mornings, otherwise he'll not be able to give of his best at work. It's a demanding life you realize, being at everyone's beck and call.'

'Quite,' agreed Kerrien. What a misery the woman was! She wondered whose idea it had been to leave the children in their rooms. From what she had seen, there was nothing Ashton would like more than his children around when he was at home, however demanding his job.

'Morning,' Ashton said as he came through from his room. 'Sleep OK?'

'Fine thank you, despite my long sleep yesterday.'

'You'll be over the jet-lag after today. Mind you, with my two monsters, it could be a good idea to keep it going a little longer . . . a chance to get off on your own for a spell!'

It was obvious from the glare that Kate did not approve of his comments.

'Have you time to discuss my duties now, or would you prefer to leave it till later?' she asked, She would much prefer to hear it from Ashton rather than Kate, who would doubtless make things sound very complicated.

'Grab some coffee and we'll talk while we eat.' He helped himself to the breakfast Kate had set out. It was toast and cereals and there was some fruit in a basket on the side. Kerrien took an orange, and some coffee from the machine, all the time aware of Kate's disapproving glare. Furiously, she was scrubbing at some potatoes and banging saucepans around, evidently to make some point.

'I thought you should take charge of the kids completely, dressing, washing and everything. For the time being, Kate will continue with the cooking and shopping and so on. We'll review things once Jodie is back at school next term. Then you might be able to take over the cooking? I believe the agency mentioned it? You'll also have to be available for up to four evenings some weeks, when I'm on call, but you can have time off a couple of afternoons a week in lieu. Saturdays and Sundays we shall have to alternate, again to cover my duties. How does that sound? You can use the car, of course.'

'Not when I have shopping to do,' snapped Kate. 'I can't be expected to walk everywhere.'

'I'm sure you will come to some agreement,' he said, munching his toast, as if trying hard not to be drawn into an argument.

It was not going to be easy, Kerrien thought, but she was determined to make a success of her new life. She would be understanding and try to make the lives of the two children happier, and that of the doctor easier.

26

'I'll go and get the children up now,' she said as she finished breakfast and she left the room before Kate could think of any new objections.

Poor Jodie had never managed to show Kerrien her room, the way things had turned out. She knocked gently on the door, pushing it open as she did so.

'Morning sleepyhead,' she called. But the room was empty. She turned and went to Ben's room, glad of the identifying labels on the door. Again, she knocked and pushed the door open, calling out good morning as she went into the room. Jodie guiltily leapt off Ben's bed and stood, as if waiting to be scolded.

'I . . . I'm sorry,' she said, looking as if she might burst into tears at any moment. 'I didn't think it was time yet.'

'That's OK,' Kerrien reassured her gently. 'Did you come through to play with Ben?'

'Yes, only Aunt Kate gets very cross, if we don't stay in our own rooms.'

'Very, very cross,' agreed Ben sitting on top of his duvet looking so adorable that Kerrien wanted to hug him.

'I won't say anything,' Kerrien promised, 'if you get your clothes on quickly and don't forget to wash your hands and faces first. Off you go now, Jodie. Come on Ben.' The pair leapt into action and were soon standing ready with shiny damp faces and dressed in the clean clothes Kate had left out for them the previous night. She led them through to the kitchen, where Ashton was putting last-minute things into his brief-case.

'Hallo you two. Come and give me a hug. Don't often get to see you before work, do I?' They rushed over to their father and he picked them up, one on each arm. He hugged them and closed his eyes briefly, as if somehow trying to make the moment last longer. Then, business-like, he let them down and became the impassive doctor again.

'Come along now. Your father has to leave and you'll mess his clean shirt,' Kate snapped. It was quite unnecessary, as he was so obviously pleased to see his children and Kerrien wondered why he allowed himself to be so dominated by his sister. Kerrien promised herself that very soon, they would all have breakfast together, as a family should. After all, it was not beyond anyone to get a few cereals out and make toast.

Saying nothing, Kerrien put the dirty breakfast dishes in the machine and took the children through to the bathroom, where teeth were cleaned, hair brushed and they were ready to go out to play. Kate watched every movement, seemingly waiting for the chance to criticize. Kerrien was determined there would be nothing for her to complain about and kept them right away from the house. Promptly at ten-thirty, she went to collect mid-morning drinks and a snack, returning the cups to the kitchen when they were finished. So far, so good, she thought. She asked about lunch . . . did Kate need help? Help was declined and an uneasy truce seemed to be forming.

At twelve-thirty, Ashton returned. His practice was only a few minutes drive away, so he usually came home for lunch. Jodie and Ben rushed over to him and he swung them up once more to give them a hug.

'We've had a brill morning, Daddy,' Jodie began.

'Brill, brill,' Ben echoed.

'Well, you can come and tell me all about it,' he said, smiling at Kerrien, as he went inside the house.

'. . . and Aunt Kate didn't get cross with us, not once . . .' she heard, as they disappeared. She felt pleased with her first morning and went inside, confident that she would be given a favourable first report. Even the way Ashton greeted his children suggested that things were beginning to change.

After their rest, Kerrien took Ben and Jodie into the swimming pool and their gleeful shouts and yells soon made them seem more like ordinary, happy children. Kate's disapproval at the noise was evident from her glare, as she left the house to go shopping. While she was away, Kerrien allowed them to make even more noise and thoroughly enjoyed herself in the cool water.

The day set the pattern for the future and after a week, small changes were beginning to creep into the routine. She felt settled and much happier. The smiling faces of the two children told her she was succeeding there too. The tension between herself and Kate was the only thing that marred her new life. Anything she could find to criticize, she did. Even when Margaret had phoned to make sure everything was going well, Kate said she hoped the phone wouldn't be constantly engaged with her friends as *The Doctor* needed access at all times. Kerrien had not risen to the bait and said nothing. Margaret invited her over for the day on Sunday, her first day off since her arrival. Kerrien told the family her plans at supper that evening, preferring to tell them when Ashton was present.

'Great,' he said. 'I'm very pleased you have some friends already, aren't you Kate?'

'Naturally,' she replied, obviously begrudging her the day out. 'I hope she isn't planning to take the car. I shall need it later in the day and I don't expect Miss Clark will be back very early.'

'Brett's coming to fetch me, around ten. I'll have time to see to the children before I go, so there shouldn't be any extra work for you, Kate.'

She looked forward to meeting the friendly family again, not to mention their handsome son, Brett. She had so far spoken to no one outside the household, so it would make a nice change to get to know some other locals. Sunday was another scorching day and she put on her only decent dress for the occasion. She stuffed swimming togs and a towel into her bag and the inevitable tube of sun block, thoughtfully provided by Ashton. He obviously didn't want her custom in his surgery!

Promptly at ten, Brett drew up in his sports car. He was wearing a blue shirt that exactly matched his eyes. Her heart gave a leap of anticipation as she looked at the picture he made . . . he was almost too good to be true. He was wearing shorts and Kerrien was immediately concerned that she might be over-dressed.

'You'll be fine,' he assured her. 'Mum's done her usual thing and invited half the neighbourhood to a barbie. She says it's to welcome you and give you a few friends to be going on with. Actually, you mustn't mind Mum. I guess she's got us halfway married already.'

'I'm sorry,' she laughed. 'Promise I won't hold you to anything!'

Though her words were light, she felt her heart racing at the closeness of this powerful man. He had an aura of good health and seemed to fit the outdoor lifestyle, a complete contrast to her new boss, the over-worked doctor. Today was going to be fun and the thought of 'half a neighbourhood' to meet was OK by her. They joked and laughed all the way through the hour-long drive. Brisbane was a large place. Nearer the centre, the houses were much closer together and it looked more like an English suburb. There was, however, a distinct lack of the larger, old houses seen in most British towns.

'Have you been into the centre yet?' Brett asked.

'No. I've been settling in and getting used to my new life.'

'When's your afternoon off? I'll take you to see the sights and show you around a bit.'

'Thanks, that would be great. I'll have to phone you as we haven't decided on times off yet. It varies, depending on Ashton's surgery and Kate's moods.' She had told him a little about the sister who was giving her a few problems.

'Sounds like she's a screwed-up old spinster. Needs a good man, that's all that's wrong with her!' Brett's diagnosis was probably correct and she laughed at the

31

thought. Somehow, Kate and sex didn't seem a natural combination. The thought of Kate's obsession with hygiene made her giggle at the idea of someone being intimate with her. Brett grinned, unexpectedly liking the English girl. His mum had the habit of match-making, introducing him to the daughters of old family friends whom he found immensely boring. She couldn't wait to get him married off and provide her with a hoard of grandchildren to spoil. But he could get to like this one a lot, he thought, given half a chance. She was a little shy at the moment but she'd come round, once she'd experienced a full-blooded Aussie male.

Kerrien apologized for not bringing flowers or wine but Margaret brushed it aside.

'You're in Australia now,' she chirped. 'No form-ality here. Come on young man, get the poor girl a drink, she must be gasping after an hour stuck in a car with you. Now, come and tell me all about things. What's the Doc like and the kids?'

Despite her good intentions to keep things light, Kerrien found herself pouring out the minutest details of her new life. It must be something to do with Margaret's ability to get people talking. The older woman looked concerned.

'Sounds to me like they're taking advantage of you, love. You should get things sorted properly, terms and conditions . . . the lot. Get a contract, as soon as possible. Mark my words, you'll be glad you did.'

Kerrien felt the slightest stirring of apprehension at Margaret's words. Had she been foolish, not to say unprofessional, in her flight across the world to her new life? Perhaps she should discuss it with her employer, preferably at some time when Kate was out of the way.

'Here you are girls,' the ebullient Lennie called, arriving on the patio with a tray of drinks, topped with fruit and chinking with ice-cubes. Kerrien took one gratefully.

'Have you got all the stuff ready for the barbie, Mags? The first crew are coming round the back right now.' As he finished speaking, a crowd of people came into the garden laden with bowls of salad, bottles and cheerful good humour.

Kerrien was in something of a daze by the time the folks started leaving at the end of the afternoon. She had laughed and joked, been teased about her Pommy accent and had a little too much to drink. The younger ones had formed a group and the mood was quite hilarious. She had enjoyed her best day in ages. Life in England had not been pleasant during those last weeks. It had taken its toll, seeing her mother reach the end of her tether until finally, awful as it was, it had been a relief to everyone, Kerrien included, when she died. Now it really was the start of a new life and Kerrien was ready for it.

'Do you fancy a trip to the beach?' Brett asked, as they sat and relaxed in the cooling evening garden. 'We could take a look on our way back to your place. Show you where I learned to surf.'

'Do you mind?' she asked Margaret.

'No love. You young ones go and enjoy yourselves.'

Kerrien hugged her and thanked her for making her feel so at home. With calls of come again soon, ringing in her ears, she and Brett drove off to the beach. It was her first sight of the sea, except what she'd seen from the plane. Brett knew the area like the back of his hand and they were soon walking across the cooling sand, sniffing the sea breeze which kept the bay less oppressive than the rest of town. Casually, he slipped his arm round her shoulders and they walked easily together. She liked his tallness and the obvious strength in his body. She snuggled against him. It felt good. As dusk was falling, he turned her face towards him and very gently kissed her soft lips. She responded, letting her long loneliness evaporate into the warm embrace of a new friend. Suddenly, he drew back. She stiffened.

'What's wrong?' she asked.

'I think we should go now.'

'I see,' she murmured. Suddenly, she felt hurt and a little angry. Was there something wrong with her?

'Don't get me wrong,' he said softly. 'If I stay here any longer, so close to you, I may regret the consequences . . . my mother would never forgive me!'

'I don't see the connection,' Kerrien replied, puzzled.

'Mum has you all lined up in a white dress, veil and the lot. Don't worry. I share none of those thoughts. I'm having too good a time, But, for Mum's sake, I won't get into trouble by scaring you off. Who knows, I might possibly spoil the future.'

Kerrien was silent. Her body was rippling with a

heat she could not control. The closeness of Brett's hard, muscular body had the power to melt her but she knew that, for him, she was just a bit of fun. Someone to enjoy briefly, when she was presented to him, on the proverbial plate. She could imagine exactly what Margaret might have said, though it seemed slightly out of character for Brett to take any notice of anything his mother might say or think. Margaret might be hearing future wedding bells, but for the two of them it was ridiculously soon. Besides, she'd noticed the easy way he flirted with every female he encountered. He was a totally physical man, touching and putting his arm round the girls' shoulders whenever he was near to them. Kerrien had had several boyfriends in the past but none of them serious. She was not in the least ready to begin some intense relationship with a relative stranger so soon after her arrival, even if his kiss might have stirred her feelings. Besides, there was something about Ashton. Every time she thought of him, she felt a slight thrill run through her body. She began to feel extremely confused. Brett was staring at her, expecting her to say something. She pulled herself together.

'I see. Well, I like your mum a lot but I agree with you. She's certainly pushing things a bit. It is all too soon. But, I do like you.' She blushed slightly in the darkening twilight, and added, 'I enjoyed the kiss. If you think you can control yourself, we could try again?' He laughed and pulled her towards him.

'You're my sort of girl,' he whispered. 'Mum may be right about some things.'

Hand in hand, they wandered back to the car and he helped her in. He drove her home in almost total silence. When they arrived, he leaned over and kissed her again, gently but very thoroughly. 'Call me when you're free and we'll do a spot of sightseeing. I only need short notice. Dad is pretty cool about time off.' Brett worked in the family electrical business and, as with most things, seemed to be very free and easy about their lives.

As she was getting out of Brett's car, she noticed a light go on in Kate's room. Obviously, she had been looking to see who was outside. She turned back and leaned over to plant another kiss on Brett's cheek. He looked surprised.

'That one was for Kate's benefit,' she chuckled.

She awoke early the next morning and collected the children for breakfast before Ashton himself was ready. The two children sat quietly at the table munching their cereal. Kerrien had put the coffee on and was making toast when Kate came through.

'Conscience pricking is it?' she asked.

'I don't know what you mean,' Kerrien said calmly. 'I am entitled to a day off and Ashton said he didn't need me to be home for the evening.'

'Just you understand this, my girl. I won't have these two exposed to your nasty little goings on. You will not bring men back here, under any circumstances. Do you understand?'

Kerrien was boiling with rage but controlled herself, as the children were present.

'My day off is my own, to do with as I choose,' she

said, a good deal more calmly than she felt. If Kate was going to criticize anything, she would first have to admit that she'd been spying on her last night. Further conversation on the subject ended, with the arrival of Ashton. Kate tried never to let him see her in less than her best light, though he was obviously aware of the tension in the air.

'How's my best girl?' he said to Jodie, and to Ben, 'And you young man, how's your world?'

'Good,' the pair replied in unison.

'You sound like a real pair of Australians,' he smiled but the smile never reached his eyes. They were as usual, almost clouded, as if looking at the world was painful to him.

'I wonder if we might discuss a few things this evening,' Kerrien ventured.

'Nothing wrong, is there?' Ashton asked in some alarm. There was a loud sniff from beside the sink. Kate rarely sat down to meals, especially breakfast, with the rest of the family. She preferred everyone to see how busy she was and how little free time she had.

'No. But I do need to get things clear . . . my duties . . . days off and so on. I think it would be better for us all if it was clearly set out.'

'That seems reasonable, don't you think so, Kate?' he asked.

'I was planning to go to my art seminar tonight. But obviously, Miss Clark's needs will have to take priority,' she said, not missing the chance to try and score.

Kerrien remained puzzled as to her motivation. Surely, the whole point of her being here was to remove the pressure from Kate? Ultimately, wouldn't she be free to resume her own career? Perhaps it was martyrdom that appealed to Kate. Perhaps she felt put upon and taken for granted but, perversely, enjoyed the suffering it caused and wanted everyone to know how bad things were for her. It was all very strange. Further speculation was interrupted by the phone. Kate was there, almost before the first ring was completed.

'Doctor Philips' residence. How may I help you? Who? Oh. Yes, I suppose so. This is an important line and must not be engaged for long. I'll call her to the telephone. It's for you,' she said ungraciously to Kerrien. 'Don't waste time in idle chatter please.'

'Hallo,' Kerrien said curiously. Who could be calling her at this time of day? 'Oh, Brett. Hi. I don't know yet. Look, I'll have to let you know OK? Yes. Tonight probably. Bye for now.'

'Who was that, Kerrien?' asked Jodie.

'Just a friend,' she answered blushing slightly, hoping no one could hear how painfully her heart was thumping at the sound of Brett's voice.

The little girl was puzzled since Kerrien had told her she didn't know anyone here, except for them.

'It isn't someone who wants you to leave us, is it?' she asked anxiously. Their sense of insecurity was something that needed to be overcome, as soon as possible.

'No, of course not. Come on, if you've finished breakfast, let's go and get those teeth cleaned. We've a busy morning ahead, sorting out the cubby house.'

'Oh goody,' Ben squeaked. 'I like your sorting things out games, They're cool.'

'She seems to be doing a good job,' remarked Ashton, after they had left the room.

'I don't like what I saw last night, not one little bit,' was Kate's reply. 'Disgusting behaviour when they've scarcely met. All over that, that common young man, she was. A beach bum if ever I saw one. And there's the phone calls. You need to make it clear right at the start, or you'll have goodness knows what going on under your roof.'

'What did you see?' Ashton asked.

'That young man brought her home and they were up to all sorts in that car of his. Then she practically climbed in through the window, trying to push herself all over him. Nasty. Disgusting. Not the sort of thing we want in this street and especially not in front of the children.'

'I'm sure you're exaggerating Kate. Anyway, what were you doing looking out at that time of night?'

'I just happened to glance out before I went to bed. Couldn't miss the performance she gave. You have trouble ahead with that one, mark my words.'

Ashton looked thoughtful as he left for work. Kerrien was certainly a pretty, perhaps even beautiful girl but surely not the type his sister was suggesting? Still, perhaps he needed to be on his guard. He wondered what she wanted to discuss with him that evening and hoped it wasn't trouble looming. She'd seemed so right for the job and the children already loved her, that much was obvious. He had high hopes of restoring a little normality to the children's lives and giving them a better time. They had taken the loss of their mother remarkably well, but then Ben had been just a baby when she left and Jodie could scarcely remember her. The pressure of his work and virtually no social life, was getting to him. Why was life so complicated?

There were more complications awaiting him at work. His receptionist had left him a message to call Martine, *urgently*, it said. He dialled her number.

'Thanks for calling, love. Listen, how's the new girl settling in?'

'Fine, I think,' he replied. 'Why do you ask?'

'There's a conference next week on the use of alternative therapies in degenerative diseases. How do you fancy coming? It's only four days and it would be great to spend some time together, especially now your Mary Poppins is established. There will be plenty of free time for us to . . . well, socialize. Do say yes, darling.'

Ashton thought for a moment. It was certainly a subject that interested him greatly. He liked Martine, liked her a lot. She was beautiful, accomplished, intelligent and what was more, seemed keen on him. He couldn't understand why, as he was committed to raising his children and she didn't seem the type to enjoy a family life. But, if she was making the offer, why not? Now Kerrien was there, he could indeed be a little more flexible in what he could do. He was sure he could rely on her to look after his children and Kate wouldn't complain, not if it was *business* and *Martine* combined. She had positively encouraged them to get together, even down to her remark the other day about Martine moving in. That, he did admit, was totally wishful thinking on her part and doubtless made to make Kerrien feel uncomfortable.

'Perhaps I'll be able to arrange things. How soon do you need to know?'

He agreed to call her the next day, when he'd had time to sort out his work and home life. Maybe he should offer to pay Kerrien a little extra, as a sort of responsibility bonus, though he would need to do it without Kate's knowledge. After all, she had been doing the job for a couple of years with very little reward for her efforts. The sooner she went back to work, the better for us all, he thought.

Once the children were in bed and the evening meal over, the three adults sat together in the family room, drinking coffee.

'Right. You wanted to discuss something?' Ashton asked Kerrien.

'Well, I don't want to sound pushy, but I need to know exactly what you want me to do and what are my limits. I think it would be a good idea if we had some sort of contract . . . you know, a sort of job description.'

'What nonsense,' Kate snorted. 'We are talking about children here. Not some inanimate machine, churning out parts all day long. Are you going to stand there with a child who's . . . who's fallen down and not clean the wound because it isn't in your job description? You're pottier than I thought if you listen to this garbage, Ashton. I said it was a mistake to be too friendly. Miss Clark has obviously seen you for the mug you are.'

'Have you quite finished?' Ashton asked, his voice dangerously calm. Kate looked away and said no more.

'As a matter of fact, Kerrien, I do think it's fair to give you a more concrete job description. You are a professional and deserve to be treated as such.'

'I will not stay and listen to this. She's no more than a little tart. See a man and she'll set her cap at him. She'll be after you next, mark my words!' Kate got up and flounced out of the room, slamming the door shut behind her. Kerrien looked distraught.

'I'm sorry. I didn't mean to cause trouble. But why should she say such awful things about me? I know she saw me come home last night but all I did was kiss Brett goodnight. He'd been kind to me and we had fun. Actually, I have to admit, I had the feeling she was watching me and I leaned into the car to give him another kiss for luck. Specially for Kate's benefit. I assure you, it was nothing more than a bit of fun. You don't mind, do you?'

'What, that you kissed someone? Why should I? I assume you know what you're doing. You're not a kid after all. Lucky bloke, that's all I can say.' Unexpectedly, Kerrien blushed, not unnoticed by Ashton.

They talked through Kerrien's proposals and Ashton agreed to get his secretary at the practice to type it up the next day. Her afternoons off would be flexible, to allow for emergencies. If she had to work in the evening, she'd have time off in lieu, when Ashton or

Kate could look after the children. He asked if she would be willing to take charge for a few days the following week, while he went to his conference. She could have another weekend off, to make up for it. That meant she'd be able to meet Brett again and soon. She didn't relish the idea of Kate being in charge and bossing her around, but she felt sure she would cope, if only for the children's sake.

'I think we've found a star in you,' Ashton said, his normally serious face relaxing into a warm smile. Kerrien wished he would smile more often; it suited him. She was pleased with his words of praise. Pity Kate couldn't be so easy going, she thought. Perhaps once she found herself a job, things might change.

'May I use the phone please?' she asked as she followed him into the kitchen.

'Course you can. There's no need to ask . . . unless you plan to phone England every five minutes!'

'No ties there, any more,' she smiled.

Ashton looked at her quizzically. 'And here? Is your new friend a serious contender? Sorry. Don't answer that. I have no right even to ask.'

'I shouldn't think so for a minute, but it's nice to have someone else around, just to go out with.'

'Please take care, little Kerrien,' he said, sounding surprisingly gentle and concerned. 'Life is tough at times, especially in Australia. Men are never as sympathetic or understanding as they ought to be.' He reached out and touched her cheek, almost paternally, but the touch seemed to burn like fire, and her heart was racing. What could be wrong with her? First she was burning with fire from Brett's kiss and now Ashton's slightest touch on the cheek sent her heart racing all over again. She must be suffering from delayed reaction to her mother's death and any gesture of friendship must suggest something more significant.

'I shall take care, no worries,' she smiled.

'Now *you* are starting to sound like an Aussie. I don't think Kate will approve.'

CHAPTER 3

A couple of days later, once she had settled the children for their afternoon nap, Kerrien left the house to meet Brett. They had agreed it would be best to meet a little distance from the house to avoid any further problems with Kate. She stood waiting at the roadside for him to pick her up. She felt a thrill of anticipation at the thought of seeing him again. She was longing to see the city centre and hoped to do some shopping. She desperately needed some new clothes and knew she could afford to splash out a little now that her money had all been transferred from the UK.

'Hi,' Brett called out, as he drew up beside her. 'Sorry I kept you waiting. Traffic was awful.'

Kerrien climbed into the car beside him and sat awkwardly, unsure of whether he expected her to lean over and kiss him. That degree of informality was not really in her nature but she didn't want to give the wrong impression. She needn't have worried. He touched her hand and gave it a slight squeeze.

'Good to see you again,' he said, engaging the gear and pulling off. His eyes suggested he meant it.

'Me too,' Kerrien murmured. He was wearing designer jeans with a white open-necked shirt. The pale blue eyes stared at her, approvingly.

'Where do you fancy going?' he asked.

'Anywhere you like,' she replied. 'Seeing as I don't know anywhere, it's impossible to know what there is.'

'Well, there's the art gallery, one of Australia's finest; or the coast; harbour sort of area up the river a little way; botanical gardens; or we could just do the shops.'

'Could you bear that? I mean the shops? I'd love to buy some new clothes. I've hardly got anything to wear. I planned to buy a new wardrobe when I got here. That way I can be in fashion here, not looking as I did back home!' she laughed.

'OK. I'm happy with anything you fancy. This is *your* afternoon out and I want you to be happy.'

Kerrien wondered if he was too good to be true! It seemed Ashton's warnings were rather unnecessary. Most of her other men friends had hated the thought of shopping and left that to her, at times when they were not out together. They parked in a rather scruffy multi-storey and walked out to the shops. It was extremely hot in the centre and she was glad to get inside where the air-conditioning gave a little relief. She browsed along the rails of clothes, dubious about the bright colours that she rarely chose to wear. Brett was enthusiastic about colour and had soon persuaded her to buy a selection of shorts, mini skirts and tee-shirts, that back home she would never have looked at twice. But, as she'd decided this was a new life, why shouldn't she dress to suit it? With a sudden pang, she thought how much her mum would have liked to have seen all this and how she would have chided her choice of such bright clothing. 'Ladies are never garish in their manner of dress,' she might have said in one of her primmer moments, only partly teasing.

'Old ghosts?' Brett asked suddenly and very perceptively.

'Something like that. Let's go and pay for this lot, before I change my mind,' she said. 'Look, I really ought to get something a bit smart, in case I need to look civilized at any time. You never know, living in a doctor's household. I mean, I might find myself dining with some high flying medico who needs to be impressed.'

Brett laughed. 'You'd probably be shut in the attic . . . kept out of the way in case you impress the visitors more than the embittered Kate.'

'She's not embittered,' Kerrien protested. 'Well, not very. She just needs a life of her own. Yes, that's it. She doesn't know how to live her own life because she's never really had one.'

'Very profound, for one so young,' Brett teased. 'Come on then, we'll find you a sensational outfit designed to impress doctors. We need the hospital gown department I guess!'

What they did find, was a boutique selling very expensive designer labels.

'I can't afford these prices,' Kerrien gasped, looking at the price tags in utter horror. But Brett insisted she try on a couple of dresses he particularly liked, just for fun. She fell completely in love with a tightly fitting scarlet dress with a long slit at the side.

'Kate could really call me a scarlet woman in this,' she laughed. She took it off and tried on a slinky black outfit, very simply cut and oozing expensive good taste. It clung to her slim body like a second skin. She felt very sexy in it, quite unlike her usual self. Amazing what effect clothes could have, she thought.

'I can't make up my mind which looks the most stunning,' Brett said quietly. He thought she grew more beautiful every time he looked at her. 'Go on. They were made for you. Get one of them at least.'

'But that's nearly a month's pay,' she said doubtfully. 'Besides, whenever would I wear either of them? Doctors' dinners excluded.'

'I'll take you somewhere, if only so I can be seen with the most glamorous woman in Queensland.'

'Glamorous? Me?' she said smiling. 'In my entire life, no one has ever even hinted at me being glamorous. I'm your original homely type. No, this is silly. I just need a simple cotton dress to look smart in. Not anything like this.' Firmly, she went back into the changing room and nothing Brett or the assistant could say would change her mind. They went back to the car with her various bags of bright clothes and one carrying a nice, safe blue linen dress, plain and the sort of good taste her mother would have approved of.

'Fancy a pizza?' Brett asked as they were driving away from the town centre. 'There's an excellent place down the coast a little way. They specialize in sea-food pizzas, all cooked to order.'

'I didn't say I'd be out for dinner,' Kerrien said doubtfully.

'Ring them, if you think it's necessary,' he suggested, handing her his mobile phone. 'Dial the number and press send,' he added, seeing her look of doubt. 'Go on, do it.'

She dialled the number and waited for Kate to answer. It took ages and she knew Kate must have been in the garden and would be even more cross at being called into the house.

'Doctor Philips' residence. How may I help you?'

Kerrien gave her message and listened to the flow of words with the phone held away from her ear. She sighed, having gained the expected response about inconvenience, thoughtlessness and taking everything for granted. At last it was over and she handed the phone back to Brett.

'She sounds worse than my mother on a bad day, when I tell her I'm going out of state for a month. Honestly love, I wonder if you're doing the right thing staying there.' But she had given a guarantee that she would stay when she agreed to take the job. After all, Ashton had spent a considerable sum on her flight and doing up the room for her. Besides, already, she loved the children; Ashton was super and Kate might eventually either go back to work or better still, leave the house altogether.

They ate their pizzas in relative silence, Kate's outburst having quite spoilt the occasion. Brett did his best to cheer her up, making ridiculous suggestions of ways they might try to get rid of Kate. Kerrien felt guilty, joking like this about the woman who had given up everything to care for her brother and his children. Even if she wasn't very good with them, they all owed her a great deal.

Exactly what did she give up?' Brett asked suddenly.

'Her career. Her own independence. Her home and her life in Sydney.'

'But, from what you told me, Ashton and his wife had to move to get away from her interference. Doesn't that tell you anything? She couldn't have had much of a life to leave behind.'

Kerrien considered his words. He was probably right. Maybe Kate's air of martyrdom was her own defence for a life with little to commend it. In her defence though, she was always attending classes and going to meetings for something or other, so she must have something to interest her with all that going on.

'Perhaps she's having a fling with some married man,' Brett suggested wickedly. She laughed, remembering her earlier amusement at the possibility of Kate even thinking about sex.

'Sex and Kate just don't go together,' Kerrien said firmly.

'All right. Maybe she had a fling with someone and the wife found out and that's why she came up to Brizzy.'

'You don't know what you're talking about. Anyway, enough of Kate and my problems. How's your mum? I did enjoy my day last Sunday.'

'Nice to see you smiling at last. Mum's fine. Quite over the moon with today, our meeting. I think I've

50

managed to stop her ordering the flowers and her wedding outfit but it's a close run thing.'

Kerrien smiled. She hoped he was as light-hearted as he sounded about this relationship. He was really nice, as well as being the best-looking man she knew and maybe, given time, she could grow to like him a lot. She was in no hurry and he was definitely not the settling down type. She knew she would never be able to trust him completely, given the easy way he talked to other women. Besides, she intended to make some-thing of her life, however simple, before *she* settled down. That she *would* settle down eventually, she took for granted. She had always intended to have a family of her own but just now, she considered herself much too young to even think about it.

'Penny for them?' Brett asked after several moments of silence.

'Just thinking about your mum I guess. I do want to settle down but it will be some years before I'm ready. How about you? Aren't there any other women in your life?'

'Dozens,' he boasted. 'There's old Mrs Smith down the road. Thinks I'm a hero since I fixed her leaky tap. Then there's Sally Norman . . . she's a bit of all right. Fancies me rotten too. Big Norm is too much of a challenge for me though. That's her husband, all one hundred and twenty kilos of him. Teresa's all right. But I think she's a bit too old for me.'

Kerrien giggled helplessly. He was such an idiot but he was fun and made her laugh. Her own life had lacked fun for too long.

'Perhaps you should come and sort out Kate for me. Mind you, if you smiled at her, she would probably accuse you of two-timing me. But then, according to her, you are only one of the many I have in my harem. Can women have such things?'

'Not in Australia. Come on. It's time we were off. I'll be in trouble if I don't get you home in good time. Can't have your reputation completely shattered by an evil Aussie male.'

'Thanks so much. I've really enjoyed myself.'

Before they left the car park, he reached over to her. He placed a gentle, undemanding kiss on her soft lips. Despite her good sense, Kerrien felt herself respond, her body pressing towards his. She knew inside that she was playing with fire. His body responded to hers and the intensity of his kiss deepened. He forced her lips apart with his tongue and she welcomed the intrusion. She felt herself swimming through the waves of passion created by their closeness and felt his desire hardening and pressing against her. Just as she felt she might drown completely, she made herself draw back.

'I'm sorry. This isn't what I meant to happen,' she forced herself to say.

The look on Brett's face was a mixture of disbelief and anger.

'You're a tease, do you know that? I don't like women playing with me. What is it? See how many men you can lay in your first month here? Don't try your games on me lady. I'm not the type. Make up your mind what you want and don't pretend to want one thing and lead me into something else.'

Kerrien was angry. It had been his need just as much as hers. Why should he think it was her fault alone that things got slightly out of hand? They drove home in almost complete silence. She opened the car door and collected her parcels from the back seat. If Kate was watching, she could have no complaints about her behaviour on this occasion.

'Can I see you at the weekend?' Brett asked, unexpectedly. She stared at him, amazed at his apparent change of mood.

'Why?' she asked stupidly.

'I'm giving you the benefit of the doubt. Besides, maybe I like being teased . . . as long as there is a resolution to follow,' he said enigmatically.

'I'll have to think about it. I'll phone you. Thanks again for today. Bye.' She tried to sound light, as she turned and went into the house. Inside, she was in a turmoil. She wanted to be friends. She wanted just a little physical contact . . . the occasional kiss or hug. She'd missed out on affection for too long. But with a man like Brett, that seemed to be quite out of the question. Did he behave this way with all the women he knew? One kiss was an open invitation for the rest. If he was really like that, should she even consider going out with him? These days, one heard so much about unprotected sex. Somehow, she couldn't imagine him taking time to use precautions. No, he was just a good-looking stud who was doubtless out for everything he could get. If she decided she would see more of him, then she'd be as casual as he was. There would definitely be no more intimate meetings and no more opportunity for things to get out of hand.

In the family room, Ashton was sitting alone, watching TV.

'Sorry to cause problems over dinner,' she said, after dumping her purchases in her room. She tried to sound light and casual, not wanting her inner turmoil of emotion to be allowed to surface.

'I didn't realize you had,' he replied. 'Kate was going out anyway as I arrived back and she just left us something cold. I didn't think she expected you home anyway.'

Kerrien smiled cynically. All that fuss she had made, her own evening almost ruined, when Kate had never intended to feed her in the first place.

'Did you have a good time? I gather you went out with your man friend, as Kate calls him.'

'Among other things, I expect,' Kerrien muttered. 'I had a good time, mostly.' She paused, not wanting to give anything away. 'I've actually bought some new clothes so you won't have to see me in my scruffy shorts any more. Genuine Aussie clothes this time. Though you might need sunglasses to look at me!'

'No complaints from me! You always look nice. I must turn in now. I have a busy day tomorrow, to make up for this afternoon off.'

'I thought Kate was minding the children today, only she asked me to make sure they changed their clothes, to go out somewhere.'

'No. She went out around two, on her own. She came back for early tea, when you phoned I expect, and then she went off again. She's still out now.'

It had obviously been another point-scoring session, Kerrien thought and dismissed it from her mind. She made some cocoa and took it to her room. She looked in on the children to assure herself all was well. They were both deeply asleep. She gazed at them for several seconds. They looked so adorable, peaceful little souls with no worries. She would do all she could to protect them from whatever unhappiness the future held.

Having finally agreed to see Brett again at the weekend, she was forced to change her plans at the last minute. Ashton had to be on call, as one of the other doctors in the practice was off sick and it was too late to call in a locum. Kate was unwilling to help, as she had made plans to go out for the day on Saturday. She was surprisingly cagey about her plans and for a moment, Kerrien wondered if Brett could possibly have been right, maybe she was having an affair with some married man.

Brett was angry when she called to change the plans. They had decided to make a fresh start and he offered to take her to the beach for the day. He complained bitterly about the inconsiderate attitude of her employers but she chided him, pointing out that children were not a nine to five job. They were not files to be left on her desk to work on the next day, or whenever the mood took her.

'When do you get time off instead, then?' he demanded to know.

'Not next week, as Ashton is away on his conference. I should definitely have the next weekend off. We could do something then, if you like.'

He was not pleased. He promised to call during the next week, just to make sure she was all right. Ashton was most apologetic and promised to make it up to her as soon as he could. In fact, he only had one call during the morning and he was away for just over an hour. The rest of the time, he joined in the games with the children. They loved every minute of the precious time their father spent with them, especially away from the watching, disapproving eyes of their aunt. Even Ashton seemed more relaxed with her out of the way.

'Now I feel even worse,' Ashton said as they all sat down together for an early tea. 'I've done you out of a day off, being taken somewhere really nice, I don't doubt, and I've hardly been out all day. Still, I must say, I've really enjoyed myself.'

'And me, Daddy,' piped Ben. 'I've really enjoyed yourself as well.' They all laughed.

'I've never played swimming cricket before, have you, Daddy?' Jodie asked.

'It's a strange old British custom,' he laughed. 'It rains so much in England, they've had to invent a form of cricket they can play all through the Summer.'

'Do they play it with a balloon and a blow up bat?' asked the little girl.

Kerrien assured them she had made the game up, rules and all, just for them. They were delighted and shrieked with laughter when they remembered getting Ashton run out. In fact they were all laughing and enjoying themselves so much, they failed to hear Kate come in. She stood at the door, watching the happy group at the table. When she was in charge, there was never any laughter allowed at table. It could only lead to indigestion, and lack of discipline. Really, that girl was leading them all on. Even Ashton seemed to have forgotten his responsibilities as a father, an important doctor and head of the family.

'Aunt Kate,' Jodie said suddenly. Everyone turned round and became silent.

'Come and join us, Kate,' Ashton called. 'There's still some tea in the pot. Or I'll make some fresh if you like.'

'No thank you. I had a cup of tea at tea-time. I'll start dinner, once I've changed out of my good things.'

'Don't bother,' Ashton told her cheerfully. 'We've decided to have a take-away, haven't we, Kerrien?'

'We have?' asked Kerrien quietly. Ashton winked and grinned.

'Junk food, rubbish,' Kate snapped. 'I have got proper food available. Something healthy, not the sort of mess they serve up in the shops.'

'Pleeeease can we have some take-way, Daddy?' Ben asked.

'Certainly not,' Kate said. 'You will eat proper food and not be influenced by . . . by . . . new ideas.' It was obvious that she did not say what she was thinking.

'Aren't you going out this evening?' Ashton asked his sister.

'I am planning to go out but thought I'd better come home first to prepare the meal. No one thought fit to tell me their plans. I didn't want the children to have some awful snack to go to bed on and then keep us up half the night.'

'You needn't worry,' Kerrien said. 'I am quite capable of giving them a meal and getting something for us as well.'

'It's obvious that if I hadn't come home when I did, you would all be eating some totally unsuitable rubbish and probably you'd all be ill tomorrow.' Silence followed her words. She glared at them all.

'It's also quite obvious that you don't want me around. I shall go to my room until it's time to for me to go out again. You can sort out your own meal.' She turned and stamped off into her room and everyone left the tea table, a miserable gloom taking over from the happy mood of a few minutes earlier.

'I'll pop out and get a take-away while you're bathing the children,' Ashton said softly. 'If Kate is going out, she'll probably leave by sevenish. If the kids are still awake, they can always come and have something with us in their night-clothes, Don't say anything to them though as they'll never keep it from Kate.' He was grinning like a schoolboy arranging a midnight feast. It was infectious and Kerrien found herself grinning conspiratorially with him. She wondered why he always allowed himself to be browbeaten by his sister. He didn't seem like a wimp in most ways, so why didn't he stand up to her?

She sent the children out into the garden to clear up the toys and other things left around and loaded the teacups into the machine. She wiped down the kitchen surfaces and tidied round the family room. She quite enjoyed being in charge. In fact, if Kate did ever move away, she would enjoy looking after them all single-handed. There wasn't so much to do, with washer and drier, dishwasher etc. Once she had her own routine, she knew she would manage, without neglecting the children at all, especially once Jodie was at school. She made up her mind to tell Ashton, when they were alone so that he would be prepared, should Kate ever spring a surprise on them.

Later, feeling slightly guilty, the family and Kerrien sat on the floor of the family room, sharing their picnic of Chinese take-away. Ben and Jodie were eating with an enthusiasm rarely seen at normal meal times. They stuffed spring rolls, fried rice, chicken and noodles into their mouths, both eating twice as much as usual. Ashton warned them not to dare to wake their aunt in the night, however bad they might be feeling. Kerrien was giggling at the thought of what Kate would say if she could see them now. She would be ceremonially drummed out of the *Nannie's Corps*, on far too many counts to number. Sitting on the floor to eat; feeding unsuitable food; allowing the children to eat, wearing their night-clothes . . . the list went on. Somehow, she just didn't care. After all, it was the children's own father who had suggested it all, so how could Kate complain?

'Right you two,' Ashton told them fiercely. 'Listen carefully. Have you enjoyed yourselves this evening?'

'Yes,' they both screeched in unison.

'Good. Then just remember what I'm going to tell

you. On no account will you say anything to Aunt Kate about what we've done. No mention of Chinese take-away, nothing. And if you ever laugh at me again when I am trying to use chop-sticks, I shall personally see to it that you never have a fork or spoon to use, ever again. You will eat everything with chop-sticks, including jelly and ice-cream. Is that clear?' The children rolled about on the floor laughing and at last, Kerrien thought it was time they calmed down and went to bed. She took them through to clean their teeth and read them a story, Jodie sitting on Ben's bed to listen. When she had finished, she sent Jodie to her own room and tucked Ben in.

'You won't ever leave us, will you Kerrien?' the little boy whispered. 'You're better than a real mummy. Can I have a kiss now?' With a huge lump in her throat, she bent over him and hugged him.

'I don't plan to leave you darling,' she said, hoping she was allowed to keep the promise. 'Night, night. Sleep well.' She crept out of the room and switched off the light. Jodie's thoughts were similar to her brother's.

'Why don't you and Daddy get married?' she asked a little more directly. 'Then you'd always be our mummy.'

'It's a little more complicated than that,' Kerrien answered. 'Come on now. Time for sleep.'

When she went into the family room, Ashton was sitting listening to some music. On the low table in front of him was a bottle of wine and two glasses. Of the illicit picnic, there was no trace.

'Whatever have you done with all the debris?' she asked.

'I got a bin liner and tipped the lot into it. It is now residing in the boot of my car and I shall take it to a suitable tip next time I go out. Now, some wine?'

'Thank you,' Kerrien smiled. 'What a performance over a simple take-away,' she added.

They sipped their wine, listened to music and chatted. Ashton explained how very grateful he was to Kate, for everything she'd always done. As the bottle gradually emptied, he admitted that he wished she would leave him alone sometimes. By the end of the bottle, he was suggesting there was something seriously wrong with Kate and that she ought to be seeking medical advice. Kerrien hoped that listening to him might help him. Talking was obviously something he needed and probably never had much opportunity to do.

'You are beautiful, Kerrien,' he murmured. 'You are so bright and happy. I've had a miserable few years but I think that's all over now.' As he tried to put his arm round her, she gently got up from the sofa.

'I think we both need some coffee. I'll go and put it on.' She went into the kitchen, carrying the dirty glasses and the empty bottle. She put the coffee machine on and stood staring out of the window. Poor Ashton. He seemed so self-assured and efficient, yet so much, he needed love. He had missed out for too long. She liked him, but there was her new relationship with Brett, whatever that was now. Besides, even if she wanted it, having a relationship with

Ashton could never work under the constant scrutiny of Kate.

He followed her into the kitchen area.

'Please Ashton, don't spoil things, not now.'

'You don't like me, not that way. No. I thought not. I'm too old. Too dull. And I've got a brace of kids to tag along. How could anyone half decent ever fancy me?'

'Have some coffee, Ashton.' Kerrien was uncertain what to do or say next. She didn't want to hurt him but felt certain he had only said those things because of the lovely day they'd spent, the relaxing evening, not to mention rather too much wine, drunk a little too quickly.

He drank his coffee and left the kitchen, calling goodnight as he went. It was an abrupt end to the day and she felt disturbed. She followed him through to the bedroom corridor and into her room. She shut the door and leaned against it, her heart pounding for reasons she couldn't explain. Ashton disturbed her. She was really attracted to Brett, felt there could be something special there in time, despite the unfortunate end to their last date. But Ashton . . . she had not considered him as anything more than her boss. He was the father of her charges. What was the real reason Jane had left him? Could it be that he drank too much? Or were they both simply too inexperienced to deal with their situation? They were both intelligent people . . . he was a doctor for heaven's sake, a good one, she believed.

'Damn,' she muttered to herself. 'I forgot to look in

on the children.' As quietly as she could, she opened her door and went across the corridor. Ben's door was open and she paused before entering the room. She heard Ashton talking, very softly.

'Oh little Ben. My poor little Ben. What am I doing to you? I do try so hard to give you a good life, yet again and again I fail you. I will make it up to you, soon, I promise.'

Silently, Kerrien drew away from the door and returned to her room, shutting the door. Poor Ashton. He gave so much to the world but his world didn't give back to him what he so obviously needed. She made a promise to herself that she wouldn't let the evening sour their relationship. She would not run away from the situation but would see it through, if nothing else, for the children's sake. They all needed defending from the doubtless well-intentioned domination by Kate. She had always controlled Ashton's life and now, her position was being threatened. Whether Kate liked it or not, Kerrien was doing a good job with the children. They liked her but she was professional in the way she dealt with them and whatever was lacking in their lives, she would never spoil them.

After a troubled night, Kerrien was late waking up the next morning. She could already hear voices in the kitchen. She dressed quickly, in one of her bright new outfits, red shorts and an orange, red and yellow top. She went into the children's rooms to find they had already gone through to the kitchen. She braced herself for Kate's sharp tongue, but was surprised to see Ashton preparing breakfast. He looked tired and had dark rings under his eyes as if sleep had eluded him.

'You like nice,' Jodie said smiling at her. 'You're all sunny.'

Kerrien laughed and thanked her for the compliment.

'I liked the chop-sticks meal,' Ben announced.

'Remember what I said about eating jelly with chop-sticks if you laughed at me again,' Ashton threatened and the little boy giggled.

'Have you eaten jelly with chop-sticks, Kerrien?' Ashton asked.

'Never,' she replied. 'I don't think I could even begin to try!'

'Right everyone. Breakfast. And no comments about my cooking.'

'Really, Daddy. You don't cook cereal. Or orange juice.'

The four of them sat round the breakfast table, like any normal family on a Sunday morning. It was comfortable and light-hearted. The slight tension that had developed last night had been forgotten. When everyone was nearly finished, Kerrien asked suddenly, 'Where's Kate this morning?'

'She must be sleeping late,' Ashton said but he looked slightly uncomfortable.

Kerrien took the children through to the bathroom and leaving them to finish off, went back to the kitchen.

'Don't say anything to the children yet, but Kate

didn't come home last night,' Ashton said softly. 'Don't worry though. It isn't the first time.'

'But where is she?' Kerrien asked.

Ashton shook his head.

'Don't know. She must be staying with a friend I guess. Someone from her evening class I expect.'

'Do they hold evening classes on a Saturday night in Australia?' she asked.

'I've never thought about it. I don't suppose they do. I never ask where she's going, just assume it's another self-improvement course.'

'Perhaps she has got a man friend after all,' Kerrien speculated.

Ashton said nothing and any thoughts he may have had were covered by his rather too enthusiastic loading of the dishwasher. He was spared further conversation by the telephone. His duty as a doctor was urgently required.

CHAPTER 4

Kerrien tidied round the house, humming tunelessly to herself. The children were playing quietly on the veranda, totally absorbed in their game. She was glad of this time alone, a space to think. In fact, she seemed to have spent most of the night thinking but had reached no conclusion about her feelings. She put down the half-peeled potato and stared through the window. On the surface, there should be no contest between the two men who seemed to be showing interest in her. Brett was young, good-looking, obviously available and his family seemed to run a successful business. Ashton was older and had two children already. Nor was he quite so devastatingly good-looking as the younger man but he had such hidden depths. His life must have seemed impossible for so long that it was little wonder he had forgotten how to enjoy himself. She sighed and went back to her potato peeling. She had been in such a reverie that she'd not heard the car draw up and Kate made her jump as she walked into the kitchen.

'Good morning,' she said cheerfully.

Kerrien jumped and turned with a start.

'Oh hi!' she replied. 'Have a good time?'

'Yes. I stayed over, at a friend's place. We had a few drinks and I couldn't have driven. Everything OK here? Ashton out on a call? I saw the children playing outside. Good as gold. Well, I must go and change.'

Kerrien's jaw dropped at the unexpected flow of pleasant words. She managed not to show her surprise and made no comment. Could that really have been Kate who passed through the kitchen? Where was the criticism? Where were the usual caustic remarks about the lack of attention she paid to the children? It was obvious that something had made her happy. Long may it last, Kerrien thought as she finished the vegetables. Could she really be having an affair with someone? Someone had cheered up her life, that much was certain. If so, why not be open about it and tell everyone, unless, she thought, it *was* an affair with a married man that had to be kept secret. Unlikely though it seemed, that must be the explanation.

Ashton returned from his call in time for lunch. The children enjoyed keeping their secret from Kate and grinned conspiratorially at Kerrien whenever supper was mentioned. If Kate noticed anything, she said nothing and her good mood lasted for the rest of the day. She even joined in with some of the games during the afternoon and everyone laughed and joked and the strain lines round Ashton's eyes seemed to melt away with the relaxed atmosphere.

'Let's have a barbie,' he said suddenly. 'It doesn't

look as if I'm going to be called out again. I've had a remarkably easy on-call weekend.'

For once, it seemed Kate had no objections to his suggestion and they delved into the fridge to find sausages and chicken legs, mixed some salads and toasted bread rolls. Ashton soon had a good blaze going and began the cooking. The children were excited at the unexpected treat and were soon laughing and shouting and chasing round the garden. Still Kate said nothing and Kerrien began to feel confident that everything was going to be all right. She knew she would even cope during the week, when Ashton was away at his conference. If Kate's good humour could only last, they might even become friends.

When the last sausage had been eaten, Kerrien told the children it was time for bed. Thoroughly tired, they made no protest and settled sleepily into their beds after their baths. In the cooling garden, Kate and her brother were sipping cold white wine.

'Grab yourself a glass and join us,' Ashton invited, moving along the garden seat to make a space next to him. It was a close fit and their bare legs were touching. Kerrien felt a surge of electricity between them. The strong, well-shaped calf muscles of the man flexed and she felt their hairiness brush against her. She jumped slightly, seeing a fleeting glimpse of reproach flash through his eyes at her movement. Feeling self-conscious at her every move, she attempted to restore the fleeting contact, hoping he wouldn't notice that it was deliberate. His body felt firm next to her and warm, so very warm. He wriggled slightly, reaching for the wine bottle to pour her drink.

'Looks like this one's dead,' he remarked, getting up to fetch another. When he returned, he made no attempt to sit by the girl and she felt strangely bereft of the contact. He gave her a quick glance, through eyes that were no longer soft, deep and melting . . . those velvety forest pools she almost felt she could sink into. Instead there was a cold hardness about them. Something impenetrable had covered their surface. He poured the wine, making silly jokes in a voice that lacked it usual gentleness. He was acting a part, trying not let anything show of the real man inside.

'Penny for them,' he said suddenly. Kerrien gave a start. She had been miles away, thinking about this complex man she was only starting to know. She wished with all her heart that she hadn't pushed him away last night, yet she knew deep inside that he had only made his approach because he was slightly drunk and she just happened to be there. What was it he'd said? *She couldn't fancy him?* After this wonderful, family weekend, he could not have been further from the truth. She was glad she had spent the time, here with him. Glad that she'd put off seeing Brett. In fact, she was now quite confident that Brett was no more than a tiny fling she had enjoyed while finding her feet in this new country. She smiled softly to herself, happy with her thoughts. She planned to phone Brett and tell him she wouldn't see him any more. She would do it as soon as Ashton had gone away to his conference. Once she knew that Kate was going to take up her own professional life once more, she felt certain that he would be more relaxed and who knew what might happen in the future? Not fancy him? Wine or no wine, he was an eminently fanciable man. She gave a loud hiccup.

'Sorry,' she giggled, 'I think I've eaten and drunk too much today.'

Kate smiled fleetingly. She looked quite pretty when she smiled, Kerrien noticed.

'I, for one, am going to bed. I'm quite worn out,' she said sounding unusually cheerful. 'Goodnight.' Making no attempt to clear away the dirty glasses, she went inside, pulling the screen door behind her, to stop the mosquitos from going into the house.

'Well, well. Whatever happened to my good sister last night has had a remarkable effect on her. She needs to do it more often.' Ashton sat back on his seat, smiling cheerfully. 'More wine, Kerrien?'

She gave another hiccup and decided that perhaps she had had enough.

'Sorry,' she smiled. 'I don't usually get hiccups. Not very romantic is it?' After she had spoken the words, she wished she could have bitten them back. What a stupid thing to have said! It was as if she'd been speaking her thoughts out loud and had expected him to know that he had been the subject of those thoughts.

'Good job you're not with Brett, then. Wouldn't he approve of you being human? I expect you have to keep him happy, don't you? Not to behave in an unladylike fashion. Or perhaps he's not too fussy about anything.'

She stared at him. He was being most unlike his usual amenable self and seemed almost offensive. Just when she was feeling quite softened towards him.

'Right,' he snapped suddenly. 'I have a busy week ahead and need some sleep. Goodnight. Leave the glasses till morning if you like.' With a spring, he was out of his seat and following his sister inside. Shaking her head slightly, Kerrien picked up the dirty glasses and the half empty wine bottle and took them inside. Thoughtfully, she re-corked the wine and put it in the fridge. The glasses she stowed in the dishwasher and set it to run. Unlike Kate to have left the small chore, she thought, remembering her comments about dirty dishes breeding germs. Sighing, she went through to her room. Why did she feel so despondent suddenly? Less than an hour ago, she was feeling happy and contented with her resolve . . . but that was before Ashton had suddenly gone so cold on her. Perhaps she had misunderstood his intentions last night and had read far too much into the situation. What could he have meant when he had whispered to Ben that things would soon be changing? She felt a little foolish and tried to settle down to sleep. Once more, it eluded her and she felt hot and sticky. She got up and took another cool shower, letting the water flow over her body until goose bumps rose on her arms. She was already looking browner and healthier than when she had arrived. Her hair had bleached even blonder in the little sun she had been exposed to. If only she didn't start complicating her life with unnecessary emotional entanglements, she could relax. She made a vow to herself. She would remain unattached and carefree for at least the next six months. No more complicated feelings and definitely no more men in her life. It just wasn't worth the effort. This time, when she lay down, she fell asleep almost at once.

During Tuesday afternoon, Ashton came home early to pack his suitcase for the conference. Kate's good humour had lasted reasonably well with few signs of her previous bad temper. She had dutifully prepared his shirts and packed one of his dark suits, anticipating he would need it for the more formal meals at the conference. She fussed round him like a mother hen, making sure he had everything he could possibly need.

'Give my best wishes to Martine,' she reminded him several times, obviously making sure that Kerrien was listening and was aware of the situation. 'Such a beautiful woman. So elegant and so intelligent. You should snap her up, Ashton. While you've got the chance. Can't think why she didn't marry years ago.'

'Perhaps she didn't want to get married. Perhaps she enjoys her career too much. After all, I'm not much of an advert for marriage, am I?'

'We're all allowed a few mistakes,' Kate said carefully. 'Go on now, time you were on your way. And you need have no worries about anything here. We can cope quite well without you. Enjoy yourself and make sure it isn't all work . . . spend time with Martine and relax.'

'Stop fussing, Kate. You are worse than Mum ever was, do you know that?' He was smiling as he spoke and seemed happy at the thought of a few days away from home. Kerrien wondered if he was happy at the thought of being away from her and the family or whether it was the beautiful Martine who was the cause of his pleasure. She felt a pang of sadness, a sense of loss at the thought of several days without his company. Then she remembered her resolve . . . no complications and definitely no men in her life for the present. After all, she had made enough major changes to her life in the past few weeks, so any thoughts of romance needed to be pushed right into the background. Despite the brave thoughts, she was going to miss Doctor Ashton Philips and she must make sure that the children were well cared for in his absence, whatever else she did.

The children clung tightly to her, as they waved him off. Ben had tears welling, she noticed and briskly, she caught their hands and marched them away from the gate almost before his car had turned out of the road.

'Come on,' she said firmly, 'we have a swimming pool waiting there, and it's getting lonely without us. I shouldn't be surprised if it didn't start splashing away all on its own.' Their father's departure quite forgotten, they rushed to get their togs from the laundry room and were soon waiting for Kerrien to lift them into the water.

The next morning, Kate was up early and had breakfast set out before Kerrien and the children came through. She was humming quietly to herself and seemed pre-occupied as they ate their cereals.

'Look,' she said softly, almost conspiratorially, to

Kerrien. 'I wonder if you'd mind if I was out this evening? I mean, can you cope without me? I had arranged to see a friend, before Ashton said he was going away and I didn't want to stop him. I wouldn't ask but it's important.'

Kerrien smiled. If it meant the continuance of Kate's good humour, she would deal with anything thrown at her!

'Of course I can cope. Don't worry about a thing. You go and enjoy yourself and don't give it another thought.' She was most intrigued at the thought of Kate and her mystery man and longed to ask more. But she decided Kate might think she was prying and she bit back the questions burning inside. She began to wish Ashton was home and that they would be able to spend a quiet evening, getting to know each other better.

'Thanks,' the older woman smiled gratefully. 'Actually, I wanted to go into town first, so I might go off after lunch, if you're sure you don't mind.'

'No problem,' Kerrien replied. Then she was struck by a thought. It would give her the perfect opportunity to contact Brett and tell him that she wouldn't be seeing him again. She was certain it would be no big deal to him as he was doubtless already going out with several different women. He was probably only being polite to her at his mother's insistence. Margaret had been determined to take the English girl under her wing and saw Brett as the perfect opportunity. She'd been pleased and flattered. After all, a hunk like Brett was not to be dismissed lightly. It felt good to be seen with someone like him and he was always fun. But, and it was a big but, he obviously expected more than she was prepared to give. He obviously enjoyed being with pretty women and expected them to respond to his charms in what he saw as an appropriate way. She was best out of that situation before anything got out of hand.

As soon as Kate had left, Kerrien put the children to bed for a short nap and she dialled Brett's number.

'Good to hear from you,' he said disarmingly. 'Look, I can't really talk now. I'll see you this evening, if that's OK.'

'I can't. I mean, everyone's away so I can't go out. Besides, I . . .' But she got no further, as Brett interrupted her.

'Right. I'll be over about eight. I'll get a take-out shall I? We can eat at your place and I'll help you baby-sit. Have to go now Bye. See you later.' And he was gone.

Kerrien stared helplessly at the receiver. She supposed it didn't matter. Kate would probably be out till late, which would give her plenty of time to give Brett his marching orders. She hoped she could carry it off without losing his friendship. After all, his mother, Margaret, had been her first friend in Australia and she would like to keep in touch, for a while, anyhow.

She felt restless as the children slept. It was hot, humid and very oppressive. There could be a thunderstorm. She wondered if the children were afraid of thunder and hoped they wouldn't react badly to a storm. She woke them and they played some games inside, not wanting to have toys all over the garden if the rain did start. It didn't rain very often but there could be massive downpours occasionally, which left everything sodden until the sun came out again. Ashton had told her about a small flood one year, before they'd built the veranda. The family room had suffered badly with a ruined carpet and tiles lifting. Hopefully, that couldn't happen now, with the additional building work.

The storm didn't break but as the children seemed tired and a little fractious, she decided to put them to bed early. A cool bath and a long story, all of them cuddled together on Ben's bed, settled them well. She heard the phone ringing, just as she reached the end of her story.

'P'raps it's Daddy?' Jodie said hopefully. 'Can we talk to him please, if it is?'

'Of course you can,' Kerrien allowed. 'But stay there until I answer it. I'll call you straight away if it's him.' She went through to the family room and lifted the receiver.

'Kerrien! Everything OK?' Ashton's voice came through.

'Fine. No problems. The children want to speak to you . . . I'll call them. They're having an early night as it's a bit thundery. I thought they might wake up if the storm breaks.' She called them through, and listened smiling as they chatted excitedly to their father. They squabbled slightly as to who was having the longest turn. At last, Ashton asked them to give the phone back to Kerrien.

'Isn't Kate there?' he asked. He was wondering how Kerrien had managed to get to the phone first as his sister usually dashed to answer, often making callers feel they shouldn't have bothered the busy doctor. She explained that Kate had gone out to see a friend but that everything was under control. They had been talking for a few minutes when Kerrien stiffened. Above the sound of Ashton's voice she could hear a deep and languorous female voice.

'Hurry up, darling. I'm getting lonely for you.' Martine! It must be Martine and from the sound of her voice, she must be waiting for him, most probably, in bed. A shudder ran through her. She felt an irrational surge of jealousy. If the woman was as beautiful as Kate said and was as keen on Ashton as had been implied, naturally they would be spending every spare moment away from the conference, together, possibly in bed.

'I have to go now,' she managed to whisper. 'Must get the children settled. See you soon.' Without waiting for his reply, she replaced the handset. She was shaking and felt as if her heart was beating somewhere in her throat, instead of its usual place. She pulled herself together. Ridiculous, she told herself. Just because he made a clumsy pass at you, doesn't mean a thing. A man like that could hardly be interested in his children's nanny. She was only here because she was being paid to do a job. He would scarcely have noticed her under other circumstances.

'Right you two,' she called as cheerfully as she

77

could, 'into bed with you. Anyone not in bed when I get there will be severely tickled.'

With squeals of alarm the pair scampered into their rooms and dived under the sheets.

'Will it be a storm tonight?' Jodie asked. Her voice sounded a little nervous.

'There might be, but don't worry. I shall be near. Are you afraid of thunder?' she asked, trying to sound as casual as possible.

'Only a little bit. Ben is though.'

'Settle down now and I'll come if you do wake up. Night night.'

'I love you Kerrien,' Jodie whispered as she left the room.

'I love you too, Jodie,' she whispered back and she knew she meant it.

She took a shower and changed into one of her new outfits. She wore blue linen shorts and another of the brightly coloured tops she had bought on her shopping trip with Brett. It was too hot to be more formally dressed. She brushed her short hair, forming a shining blonde cap on her head. She eyed herself critically, wondering how Brett would react to her decision to finish whatever relationship it was they had started. She felt another pang of jealousy, wishing *she* was the one being taken out to dinner by Ashton at some expensive hotel. She thought of the sophisticated Martine, doubtless dressed expensively and glamorously, flirting with her companion. She would gaze at him through lowered lids, looking seductive, her eyes suggestive of the pleasures to come during their night together. With tears trying to push their way out of her eyes, Kerrien made herself stop thinking, stop torturing herself. Ashton had made his advance towards her and she had rejected him. She had only herself to blame. She'd been unwilling to respond to the man, because at the time she had thought he was a little drunk. If and when she gave her heart to anyone, it would be when both parties felt the same way and were both fully in control of the situation.

Exactly at eight, she heard a car stop outside. She wiped her eyes, rubbed her cheeks to bring a little colour back into them and went to greet Brett. He leapt out of his car, clutching a carrier bag full of silver foil boxes.

'Hope you're hungry,' he smiled. 'I never asked what you like best so I've brought the lot. And some wine to go with it.'

'Thank you,' she said politely. 'Come on in.' She felt stiff and formal with him, knowing she must be strong in her resolve to finish with him. He looked striking in light denim shorts and shirt to match. Whatever else she felt about him, he certainly was devastatingly good-looking. He followed her through to the family room and dumped the packages on the table.

'Nice place,' he remarked. 'Can I put some music on?'

'Not too loud. I don't want to wake the children.'

'Quite the little mother figure, aren't you?' he remarked with a slight edge to his voice.

'It's my job. I'm just doing my job,' she replied with

an equal edge to her voice. This was not going to be an easy evening. She uncorked the wine and put out some plates. 'Do you mind if we eat here?' she asked.

He nodded and pulled up a seat. Kerrien had little appetite, dreading the moment when she had to tell him she would not be seeing him again, except if she came to visit his mother. He seemed unaware of her troubled thoughts and chatted about inconsequential happenings, customers who gave him trouble, his mother's earlier attempts to get him settled with a girl she could approve of.

'Actually,' he went on, munching his way through the curried vegetables, 'you are about the only one she's ever been right about. That must mean something, don't you think? I mean to say, for her to choose a real babe like you, shows she isn't all wind and blow.'

Kerrien choked slightly on the next mouthful. *A real babe*, was she?

'Look Brett, there's something I need to say to you . . .' she began.

'Nothing heavy while I'm eating. Save all the declarations of undying passion till we're more comfortable.' Kerrien sighed. He was impossible. His ego would never allow him to accept that someone, some female, she, could actually resist his charms. Well, she was different. She was most certainly not one of his so-called babes, ready to leap into bed with him at the first opportunity. She had heard him boasting at the barbecue the other day, to one of his friends. 'You just have to be determined. Keep trying and eventually, any babe comes round. Haven't failed yet!' Kerrien had thought at the time, she could just be the exception to prove the rule.

Toying a little longer with her fork, finally she stopped pretending to eat and pushed her plate away.

'There's stacks left,' he announced. 'Come on. You haven't eaten enough to keep a fly alive. Have I boobed? Don't you like Indian?'

'I like it fine but I'm not very hungry.' Ashton and Martine would be reaching their dessert by now. Then coffee and probably liqueurs and then . . . no. She would not think about it. Brett was rising from his place.

'Shall I put this lot in the fridge for tomorrow? I guess it'll warm up OK.'

'No. You take it. You can have it for lunch or something.' She didn't want to have to explain a whole heap of half-eaten Indian food to Kate. Her good mood might have evaporated by the time she found it and she would be quite nasty about Brett's presence. Putting off the dreaded moment a little longer, she went to make some coffee. Just as she was carrying the two mugs through, the first clap of thunder shook the house.

'I must make sure the children are OK,' she said, putting the cups down. Ben was just beginning to wail, as she reached his door.

'Don't like big bangy noises,' he murmured sleepily.

'It's all right, darling. Nothing to worry about. Try to go back to sleep. I'm just in the family room.' He seemed to settle and she left his door open while she looked in on Jodie. So far so good.

'They seem all right but I guess I'll have to sit with them if this goes on for long.'

'Meantime, come and sit by me,' Brett ordered.

Kerrien sat stiffly at the edge of her seat, trying to resist being close enough to touch him. She needed all the strength of her resolve if she was really going to tell him it was all over. Not that there had really been anything to be all over.

'Come on, Kerrien. What's wrong? I thought you liked being kissed. That was the impression you gave the first time we were alone together. I promise not to do anything you might object to. I learned that lesson after your last little outburst.' Feeling as if she might easily drown in her emotions, half of her desperately needed physical contact, half of her knew she should wait until Ashton was the man in her arms. But Ashton was probably making love to Martine . . . at this very moment. She gave in and yielded to Brett's kiss. The warmth of the male body, pressed close to her own, was comforting, exciting, healing. If she closed her eyes tight, she could pretend, imagine, it was Ashton. His hands held her firmly, the hard, lean body was making demands on her own body and, traitor to her own desires, she couldn't stop herself melding with his body. His tongue was probing the soft inside of her mouth and despite all her resolve, her own traitorous tongue responded. She could not know where it might have led, had the storm failed to gather momentum. A flash of lightning and the lights flickered and died out. The following crash of thunder shook the house and the children screamed out in terror. She shook herself away from Brett. She rushed out of the room, calling out that she was coming. Brett's eyes flashed dangerously for a moment. He was not used to being treated this way. Women liked him. Why, there were dozens of them he could fancy and who would not tease and play with him this way. Then he calmed down, his anger passing as quickly as it had flared. Kerrien had a job to do and no way could she leave frightened children alone, whatever she was doing. He could understand this and wondered just how far things would have gone if the storm had not interrupted. Whatever she might try to pretend, he sensed she was hot for him. He stretched his long body and slowly rose to his feet. Earlier, he had noticed a torch on the side and groped for it, taking it through to the bedroom area to take some light for Kerrien.

'Where are you?' he called. 'I've got a torch.'

'Thanks,' she called back gratefully. 'I'm in Jodie's room with both of them. Third door along, on the left.'

The thunder was moving away now and the rain lashed hard against the windows. A slight, cooling breeze blew in through the open window.

'I think the thunder has gone away now,' Kerrien said gently. 'Shall we let Brett light us to your bedroom, Ben? It's fun in the torch light, isn't it?'

'I want Brett to take me back. Can you really stand right up on a surf board?' he asked. Brett had been keeping them occupied with stories of surfing. They were both impressed as they only floated on their little body boards and rarely went to the beach to swim.

Kate didn't much like swimming and considered the little pool in their own garden by far the best option.

'I sure can and tell you what, next time Kerrien takes you to the beach, you get her to phone me and I'll meet you there. Then I can show you and maybe teach you a few tips.'

'Wow,' said Ben.

'That's enough now, Ben. He is only four years old Brett. He's too young to be fooling about with surf boards.'

'I had my first when I was about his age.' But Kerrien didn't want to be involved any more. She wanted the children back in their beds and fast asleep, as soon as possible.

'Night, night again, you two. Settle down now.' She closed their doors quietly and turned to walk back to the family room. Brett was standing silently waiting for her. He switched off the torch and reached out for her.

'Now, where were we?' he murmured softly, putting his strong arms round her. He pressed himself against her and started moving her towards the nearest bedroom door.

'Stop it. Brett. What are you doing? This is Ashton's room.'

'Show me yours, or this will have to do instead.' In the pitch darkness, she was disorientated.

'Please Brett, put the torch on again.' She felt confused, even more than before. She sensed the man's need and knew that her own needs were sending out the wrong messages. She desperately wanted someone to hold her, to comfort her and make her feel alive again. She wanted Ashton but he was no longer available. She had missed her chance but could she be content with second best? Was it fair to let Brett go on thinking that he was her first choice?

Suddenly, the power came back on, lighting the corridor. Brett's face was flushed with passion and he looked almost grim in his determination.

'Kerrien, my dear Kerrien. I do so want you. Please don't keep driving me away. I know you're in a strange country and it's early days yet, but you are very special to me. Just don't keep putting this wall between us.'

'Oh Brett, I do like you but I'm just not ready for all this yet. I thought we'd agreed not to rush into anything.'

'It's harder than you could possibly imagine. Yes, there have been several women in my life but never one like you. You are different. OK, OK, I know. Back off.'

They were spared further conversation when they heard a door bang suddenly.

'My God!' Kerrien exclaimed. 'Kate. She must have come back early. She'll go mad if she sees you here.'

'Too late now,' he murmured, letting go his hold on her shoulders. She turned to see Kate standing in the doorway, watching them.

'You are so right. It's too late now. I suppose you thought you would sneak him into your room before I came back and that I would know nothing about it. I knew from the moment I saw you that you were trouble. As for you, you mongrel, you can get yourself out of here before I call the police. Go on. Get lost.'

Tight-lipped, Brett looked at Kerrien for a word of encouragement but she was standing as if transfixed. She shook her head very slightly and he turned on his heels and went out of the house, slamming the door as he left.

'What do you have to say for yourself, Madam?'

'Nothing,' Kerrien said firmly. Why should she explain her actions to this woman? She had been left alone so that Kate could go out to do who knew what, for the whole afternoon and evening. Why shouldn't she entertain her own friends? The children had not been neglected in any way.

'Nothing is it? We shall see what Doctor Philips thinks of this little escapade.'

CHAPTER 5

The oppressive night gave way to a cooler dawn. Kerrien watched the strip of sky through her window, waiting for the day to arrive, so that she could get up. She had no doubt that Kate would want to spread her gossip to Ashton at the first opportunity. She also knew that whatever she said in her own defence, Kate's interpretation of what she saw would never change. She dressed and went through to the kitchen, desperate for some coffee to ease her burning, dry throat. The remains of last night's meal lay on the table and she bundled it into the waste bin. In his haste to leave, Brett had forgotten it. Automatically, she wiped down the surface while waiting for the coffee to brew.

'I'll go and wake the children,' she said as Kate came into the kitchen.

'I'd rather you left them. I don't want you to go near them now.'

'Whatever do you mean? That's what I'm here for . . . to look after the children.'

'Precisely. And what happens the moment my

back's turned? You bring in some beach bum and entertain him in the worst way possible. You are not fit to be in charge of small children.'

Kerrien stared at the woman. Feeling a surge of anger which she could barely control, she turned and left the room. Ignoring Kate's wishes completely, she went to dress the children. Their excited chatter proved there was nothing wrong with them, at least. Fortunately, Kate said no more about the previous evening, in front of them. The tension in the air could be cut with a knife and Kerrien hurried them through their breakfast, wanting to get away from the room as soon as possible. She took them out for a walk, preferring to avoid any chance encounters with Kate. If the woman didn't want to cook lunch, then Kerrien would do it herself. She knew she was within her rights to entertain her friends at the house and it wasn't as if anything had happened. In fact, if it hadn't been for Kate's early return last night, she would have sent Brett on his way, possibly for good. She had to admit, it might have been difficult, but she was determined not to be alone with him again. She smiled ruefully . . . it seemed unlikely she would even be given the chance to stay in Australia, if Kate had her way. What a mess. She had been so full of optimism and hope for her new life and after only a month, it lay in ruins. And it would be Christmas in just a few weeks. Christmas! No one had done or said anything about it, not in this household anyway.

When they got back to the house, Kate was out. It was a great relief to Kerrien to be able to act quite normally with the children. A note on the breakfast table said that Kate had gone shopping. There was food in the fridge for lunch and would she please empty the disgusting mess from the waste bin. Evidently the smell had made Kate feel sick. Kerrien smiled to herself, as she removed the offending food containers. Another of Kate's little jibes to let her know that she hadn't heard the last of it.

Ashton phoned again after supper. This time, Kate took his call and made sufficient hints about Kerrien's misconduct to give him cause to worry. She didn't tell him the whole story, making the excuse that she could not say more in front of the children, who had come through to speak to their father. Their chat was short and stilted, with their aunt supervising. Ashton was concerned and offered to give up his evening out with Martine, suggesting that he should drive straight back that evening, instead of waiting till the morning. The conference was over but he was staying on to have a social dinner.

'I won't hear of it,' Kate said firmly, making sure Kerrien was in earshot. 'I want you to have a good night with Martine. It would be such a pity not to make the most of your time together. Have fun dear, and don't worry. I can cope quite well here, whatever happens.' She put the phone down and turned to Kerrien. 'Seems he's having a marvellous time with Martine. He's taking her out to dinner again. I think he may have some news for us when he gets back . . . if you understand my meaning. So good for the children to have a proper mother again, poor little mites.'

The *poor little mites* were sitting on the floor, in front of the television, listening to every word their aunt was saying.

'Is Daddy going to marry Kerrien?' Jodie asked innocently.

'Don't be ridiculous child,' Kate snapped. 'She's only the nanny and she won't be staying here for long, if I have my way.'

'We want Kerrien to stay, don't we Ben?' Jodie said firmly. 'She's better than any mother.'

'Want Kerrien to be always, always here,' Ben affirmed.

'Don't be silly. Now, get yourselves off to bed. It's getting late. Daddy will be back tomorrow and I think he may even bring Martine to see you. That will be nice won't it? Such a pretty lady.'

From the look on their faces, Martine was the last person in the world they wanted to see and Kerrien smiled wryly to herself. Through her seemingly innocent remarks to the children, Kate had made certain that Kerrien knew exactly what she was thinking. What a pity the pleasant, good-tempered Kate had left them and the normal one returned. She obviously needed another night out with her man friend! Kerrien went through to the bathroom with the children and soon dispelled their miserable thoughts, wanting them happily settled before they went to bed. She insisted they went through to say goodnight to their aunt, while she waited in Ben's room to read them their story.

'You won't leave us, Kerrien, will you?' Ben asked anxiously.

as she showered and dressed. Whatever news Kate expected, whatever Kate told him about Brett's unfortunate visit, life with him here was so much better than without him. She dressed in her red shorts and colourful shirt, trying to appear the way he said he liked her, bright and happy. She held her head high as she got the children dressed. Kate would not swamp her, whatever she said. She vowed not to show any emotion, whatever insinuations were made and she promised herself that she would make whatever explanations were necessary to Ashton and to him alone. If Kate wanted to believe the worst, then let her. Her own conscience was clear.

'Come on you two, breakfast,' Kerrien said firmly and cheerfully.

When Ashton arrived home, late in the morning, Jodie and Ben rushed to greet him. Kerrien stood still where she was, looking to see if he was alone. The pounding of her heart must be reverberating round the entire garden, she thought. Her knees had become the consistency of jelly and she felt as if any sudden gust of wind would flatten her.

'I'm glad Martine didn't come back with you,' his daughter said, as soon as he got out of the car.

'Why should she?' he asked puzzled.

'Aunt Kate said you were bringing her back and that she might be our new mummy.'

'Whatever gave her that idea?' he asked. He got no further as Kate rushed out of the house, demanding to speak to him urgently. She looked so serious and angry that he moved the children to one side and followed her into the house. Kerrien had no doubt what the subject of the conversation would be. She occupied the children for the next few minutes, waiting all the time for the summons she knew was coming. At last, Kate called them in for lunch. Feeling anxious and rather defensive, she followed the children into the house. Ashton's face was quite expressionless. If Kate's evil tongue had worked its poison, he wasn't showing it.

'Did you have a good conference?' she asked tentatively.

'Excellent. It was most interesting. Some fascinating stuff. Did you know that . . .'

'Sit down please. The lunch will be ruined,' Kate snapped. She looked distinctly out of sorts and her tale telling had obviously gone badly. Kerrien felt the slightest sense of relief and wondered if possibly, there was a chance that she might not be dismissed after all. It was an uncomfortable meal but it passed relatively smoothly. It was after the evening meal before Ashton was alone with Kerrien and spoke about Brett's abruptly curtailed visit.

'I'd like your version of the events,' he said, sitting back comfortably. Briefly, leaving nothing out, Kerrien explained what had happened up to the point when Kate had arrived home unexpectedly. Ashton leaned forward and burst out laughing.

'And that's it? All of it?'

'Well, yes. What else did Kate say had happened?' she asked.

'Oh, you were practically naked, about to settle

down for the night or week at least and that she was afraid the children had been totally ignored for entire time she was out. I did point out that if she had been so worried, she shouldn't have left the house. She also recommended that you should be dismissed immediately. But, unless you have any objections, I should like you to stay on and, I believe, so would the children.'

Her heart lifted. She felt a relief more profound than she could explain. Whatever happened next, she knew she was safe and if nothing else, did not have to face returning to England, admitting defeat. She smiled at him, a dazzling smile which meant thank you, I love you and your beautiful children and I'm glad I'm staying; only he couldn't read all of that! She wanted to fling her arms round his neck; she wanted to hug him tightly; she wanted to . . . Instead, she asked if he would like any more coffee.

'I'm going to turn in now. It's been a busy few days and I have a lot of catching up to do for the rest of the week. Thanks for your help and cooperation, Kerrien. I appreciate it.' His warm smile bathed her in a glow of happiness which dissipated with his next comment.

'Oh Kate will probably tell you, I've invited Martine down for the weekend. She wants to get to know the children. She's only met them once or twice and we feel it's time she got closer. You can take one of the days off, if you like.' He walked briskly to the door. 'Goodnight.'

'Goodnight,' she mumbled. She remembered the deep, sultry-sounding voice she had overheard on the phone. Martine, coming here. It must mean they really were serious about each other, if she was trying to get to know the children.

'She smells all scenty and calls us dears,' she remembered Jodie's words. Soon, Kerrien would be able to judge for herself. 'Damn, damn, damn', she muttered to herself. How could she ever say now, what she truly felt for Ashton? Seeing him again after the few days break, she knew with even more certainty that he was the most attractive man she had ever met. Just being near him sent her heart pounding. There was a chemistry between them that was almost overwhelming. Could she cope with him and Martine under the same roof? Could she keep her feelings hidden? She was about to be put to the test.

'What do you want for Christmas, Kerrien?' asked Jodie at breakfast the next day. It was the first time anyone had spoken about the coming festivities.

'I don't know,' Kerrien replied. 'What do you want?' A long, comprehensive list followed, obviously well thought out. Kerrien laughed.

'I may not know what I want, but you certainly make up for me!'

'And Ben wants . . .'

'Get on with your cereal,' Kate commanded. 'There will be no presents for anyone who does not behave.'

'But Santa Claus *will* come, won't he, Kerrien?'

'Get on, I said. None of this Santa nonsense here, thank you very much.'

As Kerrien looked disbelievingly at Kate, their eyes met. There was a momentary flash of something in the older woman's face. She looked sad, almost as if she regretted her harsh words. After all, for children, the main pleasure of Christmas has to be the anticipation, the wondering whether the right presents will be there on Christmas morning. The look passed and Kate busied herself in her usual way.

'Perhaps Daddy will take you into town to see Santa Claus at the weekend,' Kerrien suggested.

'I shouldn't think he'll have the time. Martine is coming you know.' The children's faces fell. It was obvious to everyone that the prospect did not appeal to them very much.

'I thought the idea was for her to get to know the children better. Perhaps it would be the perfect opportunity, taking them to town.' Kerrien was not a little tongue in cheek at the idea. After all, shopping with small children in tow, was always something of a nightmare. If that didn't put her off, nothing would!

Kate spent the next day busily preparing for Martine's visit. She cleaned and baked and tried to make the house as nice as possible for the impending *royal visit*, which was how Kerrien was beginning to see it. So far, she was managing to control her feelings very well, she thought. She was slightly scared about meeting this woman, this doctor colleague of Ashton's, and not a little curious. She knew that she would compare badly with the glamorous woman, rarely having time to spend on make-up or generally titivating to make herself more attractive. She relied on her natural looks, clear skin and slender body. She had chosen a hair style that required minimum fuss, so she could swim with the children and not have to spend hours repairing the damage. But as for competing with this other woman, she didn't even make the starting block, she knew. Martine was arriving Saturday morning and they were to take the children out in the afternoon.

Sitting on the veranda as usual on Friday evening, Kerrien listened to the sounds of the creatures in the garden. There were frogs making small croaking noises; the drumming of cicadas; the occasional screech of a parrot. It was so peaceful, just what she needed before the anticipated emotional turmoil of the coming weekend. Ashton came to sit beside her. He carried the inevitable bottle of wine and three glasses.

'You'd like a glass?' he enquired, pouring one for her. Her fingers trembled slightly as she took it from him. He stared at her. 'Are you all right?'

'Fine thanks. No probs, as they say.' She tried to sound light-hearted but she knew she was failing miserably. 'Cheers,' she said, raising her glass. 'Isn't Kate joining us?'

'She's fussing round inside. Making sure everything is perfect for tomorrow.'

'Yes. Tomorrow. Here's to tomorrow,' and she lifted her glass again.

While they chatted about the coming weekend, it took a short time to empty the bottle. Unwittingly, Kerrien was drinking twice as much as Ashton. He rose to fetch another bottle, making the excuse that it would be needed for Kate when she came out. Kerrien was feeling more than a little tipsy, though very much more confident about the approaching weekend visit. After another glass, she began to feel a little weepy. Ashton watched her carefully, smiling gently at her growing intoxication. She got up and stumbled slightly. He put out strong arms to catch her and prevent a fall. She melted into his encircling arms and rested her head on his shoulder. It felt wonderful. Their bodies were a perfect height for one another, comfortable and close-fitting.

'Whoops,' she mumbled. 'Shouldn't have done that should I? Thank you for saving me.' Then she gave a loud hiccup.

'This is becoming a habit. Hiccupping, I mean. I think it may be time you went to bed yourself,' he advised gently.

'I'm sorry,' she said carefully, not wanting to make a fool of herself. He stroked her cheek, sending fiery waves of heat through her body. He smelt clean and masculine, his own unique scent which she had come to recognize and love. His grip on her tightened and she melted against him, knowing she was playing with a fire she didn't have the capacity or desire to resist. His lips came to rest on hers, gentle and yet demanding. It felt just as she had dreamed it; her wants, her needs were all here, melting into the body of the man she loved. She felt him grow hard beneath his shorts, his bare legs touching her own. Her body felt as if it was entirely made of warm fluid, nothing solid remained inside her. She was being held together by the love of this man. Her heart soared and she knew that this was where her own fulfilment must surely be found.

'You little tramp. You tart. Can't leave any man alone can you? I warned you Ashton. She'll try anything to get her own way. I hope you're ashamed of yourself.' Kate's strident voice shattered the momentary bliss. Ashton pushed her away, firmly but gently.

'I'm sorry, I shouldn't have done that,' he muttered as he strode inside the house. Kerrien followed, her moment of peace, of joy, of self-knowledge, was over. Reality was the unpleasant truth. Martine, soon to be his fiancée, was coming the next day and she, Kerrien Clark, Nanny, was treading on forbidden ground.

She lay on her bed, filled with longing and a hunger she could not explain. She felt warm tears trickling down her cheeks as she contemplated what might have been. She made excuses to herself for the tears . . . delayed reaction to the death of her mother, anything but the truth – that she had drunk a little too much and her defences had dropped. At least she knew now where her feelings lay; Brett was certainly not going to be a part of her future. She knew it for sure now and knew she could tell him with a clarity she had not realized earlier. She would have to learn to accept that she could never have Ashton but she preferred to be near him, even if he was with someone else. Besides, she needed to be certain that the children were properly looked after. She felt it was her duty, as well as her desire and her painful delight.

Kate had prepared the guest room for Martine, though she had made sure Kerrien knew that she had spent ages cleaning Ashton's room as well. She had even put clean sheets on his bed, *just in case*, as she phrased it. The flashy white sports car arrived at eleven. Kerrien's first impression was a mass of red hair being shaken out of a long emerald chiffon scarf. The car door was opened and long silk clad legs slid themselves out. The visitor stood up and Kerrien had to admit, she was indeed a strikingly beautiful woman. Her make-up was immaculate and her clothes completely unruffled, despite the drive. She was dressed perfectly, in a simple suit whose exquisite tailoring breathed expense. She wafted by in a cloud of expensive perfume and Kerrien was reminded of Jodie's phrase again, *'all scenty'*.

'Darling!' she exclaimed. 'I have missed you,' and she flung herself at Ashton. With Martine draped on his arm, he came over to Kerrien.

'You must be the little Mary Poppins,' she said and turned to greet Kate. 'So nice to see you again. Now darling, where are these delightful children of yours?' She towed him across the garden to where the delightful children were playing in the cubby house. They did not come out willingly, Kerrien noticed with a perverse pleasure.

'Mary Poppins!' she muttered angrily. 'Who does she think she is? Thank heavens she isn't *my* doctor.' This weekend was going to be tougher than she thought. She stared after the woman as she towed Ashton into the house, and shivered. A tight band clamped itself round her heart and she sensed an odd feeling of evil seeping into her mind. She shook her head as if to dislodge her irrational thoughts. It was simply that she felt threatened. She went back into the garden to find the children.

Ashton, Martine and Kate ate their lunch together in the dining room and Kerrien was relieved to eat hers in the family room with Ben and Jodie. At least the conversation was more fun, she thought. To her surprise, Ashton asked if she would accompany them on their trip into town. It seemed Martine would *love to be with the children on their visit to see Santa* but she *wouldn't know how to cope* if they needed anything. It was not a prospect Kerrien relished, but she agreed for the children's sake. Their fun must not be spoiled. Besides, it could be useful to get some ideas of suitable Christmas presents for them. As it turned out, she quite enjoyed the trip, which was more than could be said of Ashton. It seemed Martine's idea of shopping with the children was for Kerrien to take them off somewhere, while she and Ashton looked at jewellery and had tea in an expensive in-store restaurant.

They stopped off in the Myer Centre, a huge shopping complex with stores of every kind. Once Martine had dragged Ashton off to look at the more exclusive boutiques, Kerrien took the children to the fun places. They had a great time playing with the toys, seeing Santa and generally relaxing. They went up to Tops, high above the rest of the stores and set out as a children's world. The three of them drove dodgems, took the Dragon Ride and swung in a mock pirate ship. They spent ages looking round the different stores. It was a great treat for them to be in the town, as they rarely visited big stores. Shopping was not an option for children, as far as Kate was concerned. By the time they met Ashton and Martine back in the car park, their excitement had reached fever pitch. They were full of bright and lively chatter, as they drove home in the car. Martine made a grimace, as she said in her dulcet tones, 'My dears, are you always this noisy?'

They completely ignored her and carried on telling their father about the ridiculous things Kerrien had done to make them laugh.

'You should have seen her Daddy, sitting on a baby swing. The shop lady had to tell her off but she wasn't really cross.' Jodie giggled at the memory.

'And I went on the dragon and I wasn't even a bit frightened,' Ben added.

'Sounds to me like you had a lot of fun,' Ashton replied with a distinctly wistful tone to his voice. Kerrien hoped that he would rather have been with them than his beautiful woman friend. But, she decided, that was wishful thinking. Martine must have hidden depths and perhaps she was rather shy in front of the children. That she was bright and intelligent, there was no doubt. It was the unpleasant air of condescension that Kerrien resented.

Kate had stayed at home to cook a special dinner. She offered Kerrien a tray in her room, rather than inviting her to join them. It was not unexpected, as it had been her original suggestion that the nanny would eat with the children while she and her brother shared the adult meal. Before today, Ashton had never allowed that to happen. While Kerrien put the children to bed, Martine and Ashton shared cocktails on the veranda. He came through to ask the two women to join them and noticed only three places set at the table.

'You going out, Kate?' he asked wickedly.

'Me? No. Why?'

'You've only set three places.'

'You surely don't think the nanny is going to share our meal?'

'The nanny? Oh come on Kate. Kerrien will eat with us of course, unless she doesn't want to.'

'Of course she won't want to. She'll never stand the competition for one thing.'

Ashton glared at her warningly. Without saying a word, she collected another set of cutlery, a wine glass and place mat and laid them on the table.

'Do you want to change for dinner, as it's a special occasion?' Ashton suggested to Kerrien. 'We want you to join us, of course.'

'Oh. Well thank you. But Kate . . .'

'Kate has set your place, see? Go on, we'll wait. Come and have a drink when you're ready.' He turned and went back to Martine, who immediately draped her arm across his shoulder. She was very tall. Almost the same height as he was. The black cocktail dress she had changed into emphasized her slender body and a fresh cloud of perfume wafted into the air around her. Kerrien put on her new blue dress, wishing like crazy she had bought one of the two designer garments she'd tried on, the day she went shopping with Brett. That red one would have been perfect for tonight, a little too dressy maybe, but much better than this boringly safe little dress she was wearing. Angry with herself for always being cautious, she pulled the belt in tightly, emphasising her tiny waist. Her eyes stared back, bluer than ever, their colour enhanced by the simple blue linen and lit by the flashes of determination she felt inside. She would not be put down by all the Kates or Martines in the world. She brushed her shining hair, as she suddenly thought it boringly short and put on a pale pinky lipstick. In the short time she had spent, she didn't look too bad but how could she possibly compete with the other woman? She took a deep breath and remembered that she was not even going to try competing. She would somehow force herself to relax and enjoy the evening.

'Thank you,' she said as Ashton handed her a drink. 'You look lovely,' he murmured. 'That dress is perfect on you.' She smiled her thanks at his compliment and walked over to speak to Martine. She hoped the knocking of her knees was not too obvious.

Kate had certainly excelled herself with the meal. The delicious roast lamb was pink perfection, served with fresh young vegetables and the sweet, a delicate lemon souffle was quite mouth watering.

'I don't know how you manage it Kate, dear. You could get a job as a chef any day. Quite delicious.' Kate positively blossomed at the compliments.

'Perhaps you would clear now, Kerrien? Put the coffee on please. It's ready in the percolator. Now, shall we move somewhere more comfortable?' They rose and went into the lounge, which was rarely used.

Kerrien began to stack the dishes and took one load through to the dishwasher. Although she did not see Ashton, she sensed his presence behind her. He too was carrying a pile of dirty dishes and stood patiently waiting for her to finish loading the machine.

'Don't neglect your guest,' she said. 'I can do this.'

'Why should you?' he asked. 'You're entitled to a night off as well, you know. Go on. You go into the lounge. I'll finish here and bring the coffee through when it's ready.'

Uncertainly, she went into the lounge. The conversation stopped abruptly and Kerrien knew immediately that she had been the subject under discussion. Martine smiled encouragingly at her.

'Come and sit down dear. Tell us all about yourself. Have you travelled much? Or is this your first trip?'

Kerrien knew that no one was really interested in her and that Martine was only being polite. She made her decision.

'Actually, I only came to say goodnight. Thanks for a lovely meal Kate. Ashton will bring in the coffee in a moment. Goodnight.' She turned and fled. She couldn't take any more for tonight. She wanted to be sound asleep before the others went to bed. She didn't want to think about the sleeping arrangements. She couldn't stand the torture of knowing he might be making love to that artificial, superficial woman, so approved of by his sister. Mother to Ben and Jodie? Why, Martine had hardly said more than a few words to them and most of those had been critical. Thank heavens she would be going out the next day. By the time she returned in the evening, Martine would be well out of the way. If Kate's hopes did materialise and Martine did marry Ashton, there was no way Kerrien would be staying around. She remembered that she had not looked in on the children and went into the corridor. She opened their doors and crept in to see each of them in turn. Jodie's arm was flung back over her head and the hair, so like her daddy's, was strewn over the pillow. She stirred slightly as Kerrien tucked the arm in. She gave a little smile of recognition and mumbled goodnight.

'Goodnight little one. Sweet dreams.' She felt the now familiar sweep of love ripple through her body and at once knew, whatever the cost to herself, she had to stay with the children to make sure they were always properly cared for and, most of all, loved. She closed the door and turned round. Ashton had been watching her.

'Don't think of leaving us Kerrien, will you? We *all* need you,' he murmured softly.

'Of course you do,' she said as lightly as her breaking heart would allow.

CHAPTER 6

'You can take the car if you like,' Kate offered the next morning.

'Gosh, thanks,' Kerrien replied, surprised and pleased at the unusual offer. She had planned to take the bus to town and look round the Botanic Gardens. She had called Brett but his mother told her he had decided to go with some friends to Surfer's Paradise for the weekend. Some festival or other was on and it had seemed like a chance he couldn't miss.

'Come and see us soon, love. Everything OK with you?' Margaret had asked. How could Kerrien explain everything that had happened recently, in just a few words?

'Fine,' she answered simply. 'Everything's just fine.' She hoped Margaret was easily convinced!

As soon as she could, Kerrien made her escape. For once, she left the children for the others to organize. She would have liked to have seen Martine coping with dressing and washing them, but the temptation to leave before the other woman emerged, was too great. After she'd changed into a simple cotton dress, she said goodbye to the children and was about to leave, as Ashton's door opened. Wearing the shortest, most diaphanous negligee Kerrien had ever seen, Martine rested seductively against the door jamb. She blew a kiss back into the room and turned to smile at Kerrien.

'Isn't this just the most heavenly day?' She almost floated across the corridor to her own room and disappeared inside.

A dishevelled Ashton appeared at the door. He stopped dead when he saw Kerrien watching, her mouth slightly open with shock.

'Kerrien! It isn't what you think,' he began, moving towards her.

'What you do is your own business,' she snapped and turned quickly, so he shouldn't see the shock and disappointment on her face. She grabbed the car keys and rushed outside.

She drove carefully out of the suburb and into the town. It was still early and there was little traffic around. She parked easily as there were no restrictions on a Sunday. She desperately needed this time alone, to think. She had finally admitted to herself that she was in love with Ashton and it seemed that he too was in love . . . but with Martine. She was the obvious, natural choice for a successful doctor; another doctor who was also beautiful, sociable and worst of all, available. That they had slept together, both last night and doubtless at the conference, was patently obvious. Yet, several times, Ashton had led her to believe that he cared about her, Kerrien. She considered his situation. It had always been a sexist joke that husbands liked to have an au pair girl living in their homes. It was often joked that part of their duties seemed to include some sort of affair with the man of the house. It was probably little more than a silly joke of the nudge nudge, wink wink variety. But maybe, in Ashton's eyes it wasn't the same. She was a qualified nanny it was true, but her status was similar to that of an au pair. Obviously, her trust in and admiration for Ashton was quite misplaced. He saw her as someone he paid to be in his home and perhaps his expectations included her paying very personal attention to him, as well as looking after the children. She tried hard to convince herself, but secretly she knew it wasn't really like that. He was a caring person . . . must be, to be a doctor. Still, convincing herself of this idea might help her to cope. A little healthy anger could work wonders for her pride.

She had walked for miles, she realized, so deep in her thoughts, she'd barely noticed. Stopping at an ice-cream booth, she bought herself a large chocolate cone. She sat outside, under the umbrellas joining the rest of the Brisbane residents enjoying the beautiful December Sunday morning. How could it possibly be nearly Christmas, in this heat?

She walked toward the main centre of the town. There were open spaces between many of the buildings, creating the feeling of lightness. Everywhere was packed with people, looking at the Christmas decorations. A great tree, hung with parcels, was the centre piece, its lights diminished by the bright sunlight. She found a small craft market and wandered round the stalls, looking for little presents she could pack into a Christmas stocking for the children. She had decided that several small toys would be more fun for them. Had they ever had a Christmas stocking before, she wondered? She remembered her own childhood with sweets and oranges, silly plastic toys that broke very quickly but which were so cheap it hadn't mattered. Soon, she had a bulging carrier bag full and began to anticipate the happy family Christmas she would do her best to provide. She may have to cope with Martine; she may have to cope with a sulky Kate; but whatever else happened, this would be a Christmas for the children to remember. Ashton would surely not complain? She found a stall selling coloured paper of all sorts and bought several rolls. They could spend the next few days making decorations for the house. It would be fun.

By the time she had finished her shopping, she was almost melting in the heat. Inside, she felt considerably more settled. Kerrien returned to the car and drove home. The roads outside the centre were white with the dry dust, everything seeming very bright in the Summer sun. By the time she arrived back at the house, with any luck, Martine would have left and maybe Kate might have gone out. She hoped so, wishing that when the woman returned, she would have her earlier good mood restored.

'Kerrien's back. Kerrien's back,' she heard as she

111

reached the drive. The children were standing on top of the cubby house, waving their greetings. Ashton came out of the screen doors and smiled.

'Had a good day?' he asked cheerfully.

'Fine thanks.' She was calm and intended to stay that way. Nothing he could do or say was going to destroy the peace of mind, she had fought so hard to achieve. The children scrambled down and rushed to her for a hug. Somehow, she had to smuggle her purchases into the house without them seeing.

'You're back then,' Kate said, appearing from inside. 'I haven't cooked anything for you. Didn't know when you planned to return. I'll take the car, now she's back, Ashton. Then you won't have to do without yours if you need it.'

'Fine,' Kerrien said. 'I'll grab myself something to eat, later.' Fortunately, at that moment, Kate called the children in for their meal and she was able to unload her shopping in secret.

'Do you need a hand?' Ashton asked. 'Looks like you've emptied half of Brizzy!'

'I thought I'd make some decorations with the children and I've bought stuff for their stockings. Hope you don't mind?'

'Mind? It's a lovely idea. I usually rely on Kate to order whatever she thinks, from a catalogue. Don't like to give her too much extra to do. Hey! This Christmas could be fun. I'm looking forward to it already!'

Kerrien's enthusiasm was infectious. Everyone worked together to prepare for the festivities and

112

bad tempers were forgotten. Kate let the children stir puddings, help with icing the cake and generally behaved like the perfect aunt. The only unhappy moments for Kerrien, were the frequent telephone calls from Martine, which Ashton went to his room to take. Kate usually made some enthusiastic and pointed comment but she was determined not to let it bother her. For the most part though, Kerrien was able to enjoy life and somehow, she managed to push the torment of her love for Ashton right into the background. As for Brett, he seemed to have disappeared completely for the time being.

The heat of Christmas Day was a totally new experience for Kerrien. It was strange to have summery things for presents and instead of snow and cold for the children's stories and television programmes, there were barbecues and beach parties. It was too hot for the traditional Christmas dinner but they did have turkey for the evening meal. Once the children were in bed, the adults sat out on the veranda, enjoying brandies with their coffee, a rare treat in honour of the occasion.

'A toast,' Ashton announced suddenly, standing and raising his glass. 'To the women who have come into my life and made it worth living again. Thank you very much.' He sipped his drink and the two women smiled their thanks, though Kerrien felt a tug at her heart strings when she thought of that other woman who was now part of his life. It was fortunate that Martine had made other plans and did not join them to spoil the day for Kerrien and the children. But she would not let anything ruin this wonderful day. It was peaceful and harmonious and Kerrien felt as happy and contented with her life, as she could. The telephone shattered their reverie. It was Martine, spelling the end of the peace, as Ashton once more disappeared into his room. The others collected the glasses and cups and went into the house.

'I think she's coming over again soon, perhaps for the New Year holiday,' Kate announced. Kerrien's heart sank. She didn't want to face another difficult session with the woman she was growing to dislike intensely. Perhaps she could go away somewhere for the weekend? Perhaps Margaret might invite her over? Anything would be better than having to watch Martine drape herself all over Ashton and doubtless once more taunt Kerrien with her appearance at his bedroom door.

As it turned out, Brett resurfaced and invited her on a weekend camping trip with a group of his friends. Despite her many reservations, it seemed like the answer to her problems, especially if there was a group going together. Besides, she very much wanted to see something of the real Australian bush. She hoped to see some of the wildlife in its natural habitat and Brett had perfect timing.

Ashton remained tight-lipped about the whole affair, doubtless fed titbits of information by Kate's disapproving tongue. Ever since she had seen Martine leaving his room, there had been no physical contact between herself and her boss. She still cherished that wonderful moment when his body pressed close against her own, that moment when she had become certain that she loved him. But the pain of losing him was much worse. If she didn't allow herself anything more to remember, there would be less to lose, she had reasoned. But still her body ached for his touch, despite all her good intentions. This weekend with Brett might be just what she needed. If he was using her, as she believed, why should she not do the same? It wasn't as if anything could happen, not with a whole crowd of them together.

Early in the morning on New Year's Eve, Brett's car arrived at the house. She had packed a few clothes in a small bag and wore shorts, tee-shirt and a big shady hat. She had tubes of insect repellent and sun block provided, as usual, by Ashton. He wanted her taking no chances. The children waved, sad to see her leave. Kate had been trying hard to excite them about Martine's visit but it had not worked. They didn't like her and would much rather have gone with Kerrien and Brett. Camping sounded so much more fun than an entire weekend trying to be on their best behaviour.

The drive inland was long, hot and dusty. Brett was in good form and kept Kerrien entertained with anecdotes about his mother's exploits and the strange requests he had received from customers in his father's business. They stopped for cold drinks from the cold-box, the *Esky* as he called it.

'Where are we meeting the others?' Kerrien asked.

'Ah. Yes. I should have told you about that. They cried off. Sorry, but it's just you and me. Look, I know

115

what you are thinking. The others really were coming but couldn't make it in the end.'

'I see,' she said quietly. It wasn't what she had wanted and certainly not what she'd been expecting. Should she insist on being taken back immediately? Or was the alternative much worse? Was he anticipating that they would sleep together? If so, he would have a rude awakening.

'Well?' he asked.

'Well what?'

'Do I have to turn round and go back to Briz? Or can we continue with our trip? There's even a bottle of champers to celebrate the New Year. Mum gave it to us herself. Mind you, she did think there would be several of us at that time.'

'OK.' Kerrien had made her decision.

'OK what?'

'OK, we'll carry on with our trip. But it does not include sleeping together, is that understood?'

'Yes, Miss,' he replied, his grin reaching right across his handsome face. The blue eyes danced with mischief as they gazed back at Kerrien. His grin was infectious and she forgot her worries. They sang silly songs as they drove along and finally turned into a small site which had been fenced off to keep larger creatures out of the area.

'It's for their own good, really,' he explained. 'If they get in here, they can eat foods which might be dangerous to them or hurt themselves on the equipment.' Kerrien actually found it comforting. She had felt slightly nervous of what they might encounter, with her own background as a city-girl from England. She smiled, pinching herself to make sure she was really here. Who would have thought this time last year, that she would be out in the Australian bush with a handsome Aussie surfer? Her mum would never have believed it for one. She had always thought her daughter was such a home bird. But that was all in the past. It was the here and now that really mattered.

They set up camp, one small tent, she saw with some trepidation, but said nothing. She had made the terms of this trip clear. Besides, if it became necessary, she could always sleep in the car. They took a hike into the surrounding land, always making certain they knew exactly where they were heading and noting any diversions. Brett was an experienced bush walker and would take no chances of their getting lost. They returned to the little camp-site tired and dusty but Kerrien felt satisfied that she had seen a couple of kangaroos, her first in the wild. They had been some distance away but she had watched their graceful hopping as they cleared the ground covering yards at a time. She was even more excited to think it might have been a koala she saw in a gum tree, even if it may only have been a dark chunk of foliage. Conservation rights prevented them from going any nearer and disturbing this animal that was becoming an endangered species. Whoever could believe in an Australia without koala bears?

There were built-in barbecues round the site and some of the other campers using the place had already begun to cook. The smell of the food was wonderful and they soon took over one of the grills. Sitting on the ground, they munched steaks and salad, washed down with wine. The stars were clear and bright, millions of them dancing in the sky.

'Time to drink to the New Year,' Brett announced.

'But it's only ten o'clock,' she protested.

'It's New Year somewhere. We'll drink to that!'

They both laughed and opened Margaret's champagne. It was warmer than it should have been, despite the cold-box but enjoyable, nevertheless.

'Here's to New Year in New Zealand,' he chanted. They laughed and continued to toast various cities in the world, some of which would be celebrating even later than they were. When the bottle was empty, it was bed-time. True to his word, Brett had made no unwelcome advances, had not tried to touch her and she felt more comfortable. She tried not to think of the celebrations that may be going on back at home. She had been told by Kate that Ashton was taking Martine out to some dinner dance in town and they were staying over in one of the hotels, to avoid having to drive home after drinking. Despite herself, she felt a pang of jealousy at the thought of the two of them sharing some huge bed, probably complete with champagne and room service. She shuddered, hating the picture she was painting to torture herself. She looked at Brett in the moonlight. What was she doing here with him? He was devastatingly good-looking. He was fun. He had chosen to be here with her rather than at a party in town somewhere, with a crowd of

118

friends. She was being absolutely awful to him, using him. She was here simply to get away from Ashton's woman, whom she couldn't bear to be near. She knew that she was being grossly unfair.

'Come on. Time to turn in,' he was saying. 'You go first and get into your sleeping bag.' He was taking nothing for granted, making no demands, in fact being the perfect gentleman, as far as camping in the bush went anyhow!

Kerrien crept into the tent, pulling down the mosquito net behind her. Once she was safely inside the sleeping bag, she called to Brett. He had stripped off his clothes and knelt in the doorway, clad only in the briefest of boxer shorts. His tanned body rippled in the moonlight, as he crept in to find the opening to his sleeping bag.

'OK?' he asked, his voice husky with some emotion he seemed to be fighting.

'Yes thanks,' she said softly.

'Goodnight,' he murmured, turning his back towards her.

'Goodnight.'

'Oh hell, Kerrien. Surely I'm allowed a kiss?' He turned over and gently felt for her face. He raised himself up on one elbow and gently touched her lips. All the self-denial of the past days swept away from her. Her longing for Ashton and the hopelessness of it all washed any thoughts of control away and she responded. Brett may not be the man she loved but surely, he was a pretty good alternative? His kiss pressed harder on her soft lips and she felt his hot

119

tongue pushing for entry into her mouth. She fought back the feeling of revulsion that seemed to be growing inside her. Ashton would probably be doing exactly the same to Martine at this very moment. She tried to pretend it was Ashton pressing his body against hers but the scent of him was different. His mouth was a different shape. His tongue tasted different.

'Oh Kerrien, dearest Kerrien. Love me. Love me just a little.' Her own desperate needs pushed themselves foremost into her treacherous body. How much she needed someone to love her, to comfort her. She lay against his virile body, enjoying the pressure of the hard lean male shape close to her own. He pulled down the sleeping bag a little way, to expose the top of her body. She was wearing a thin tee-shirt to sleep in. He pulled open the buttons and cupped his fingers round her perfect breasts. The nipples became erect with his stimulation and he took first one and then the other in his mouth. Gently, as he circled the hard pink nub, her own desires filled her with longing. She felt hot pulses ripple through her body as the waves of passion swept down. Her most sensitive secret areas were longing to be touched.

'You are so lovely Kerrien. So very lovely.' He caressed her with his eyes, then with his hands. She closed her eyes, telling herself that it was Ashton lying close beside her, Ashton's hands exciting her body to new heights. She stiffened. She opened her eyes again. It wasn't Ashton at all, it was Brett. The same Brett whom she had heard boasting that he could get any woman he wanted. She refused to give her most precious gift to someone who only wanted an affair. He was not the marrying type and when she finally gave herself completely to anyone, it would be to a man she truly, totally loved.

'Brett . . . I'm sorry. I can't. I did warn you.'

'I'm sorry too. I'm only flesh and blood you know. Having you so close . . . so responsive. You *did* respond Kerrien. You know you did.'

'Maybe I *was* sending out the wrong messages again. I'm sorry Brett but I am just not ready for this.'

'Haven't you . . . I mean, well, had sex with anyone else?'

She turned her head away. Suddenly, she felt shy about admitting it. She had never slept with anyone. She was still a virgin. She swallowed hard.

'No Brett, I haven't slept with anyone. It may seem strange to you, especially these days, but I want to make love first with the man I love and intend to marry.' Her voice was a mere whisper, as if making her admissions out loud would somehow condemn her.

He fell back and laughed softly.

'So, our little Kerrien is still a virgin. If you intend to marry the first man you have sex with, looks like I had a narrow escape.'

'Right,' she said, her fears confirmed. She was no more than a casual affair to him. And the affair was all but over.

From outside the tent, there was a sudden commotion.

'Happy New Year' was being called from all around. Shouts and cheers from several other tents filled the night air. A cork popped out of a bottle and a fire cracker went off.

To Kerrien's immense relief, Brett suddenly started laughing.

'Good job we weren't in the middle of something else when this lot broke out. Come on. Let's join in the fun.'

They pulled on their shorts and went out into the night, where the occupants of the other dozen or so tents were joining together to sing Auld Lang Syne.

'Grab yourselves a tube,' someone shouted, indicating the box of lager cans lying on the ground. Soon, the still night rang with sounds of singing as they all celebrated the New Year. Stories shared, boasts of bravery and hardship shared, it was nearly dawn by the time anyone turned in.

'All things considered, I've never seen the New Year in quite like this before,' laughed Kerrien, a little the worse for wear.

'Quite a good bash in the end,' Brett agreed. 'Not quite what I'd planned, but not a bad party. Let's get some sleep now.'

Silently, she said in her head, *Happy New Year, Ashton, Happy New Year*. She wondered what the year would bring.

It was almost dark when they arrived back at her home the next evening. The children were in bed and once more, Kate was out. Ashton sat alone in the family room, watching TV He watched as she came in, making no comment.

'Happy New Year,' she said, as she put her bag down.

'Yes. Thanks. And you. Good trip?' he asked, seemingly without much interest.

'Yes, good. We had fun. A whole crowd of us saw the year in and sat singing most of the night.' Somehow, it was important to make sure he knew she and Brett hadn't slept together.

'Really,' he said in an off-hand way. 'And did you like camping? Sleeping in a tent was fun as well?'

She said nothing but picked up her bag and took it through to her room. He sounded chippy, as if he wanted to score points. She was not in the mood. Nor did she want to swap tales of their various exploits. She most certainly didn't want to know how his weekend with Martine had gone. Somehow, she felt as if she had remained loyal to him and wanted him, unreasonably perhaps, to feel the same way. So much for all her resolutions. She had broken them all: no more men; not to be alone with Brett; to stay and look after the children when Martine was around. A full set of broken promises, made to herself.

It would soon be her birthday. Coming so soon after Christmas, she often let it slip by almost unnoticed. There would be no little present from her mother this year. No little treat, somehow bought and smuggled in by a friend when her mother was no longer able to leave the house. She doubted any of the other distant relatives would remember now and she was resigned to no-one knowing about it. It came as a great surprise when the exclusive dress box arrived, the day before her birthday. With excited trembling fingers, she pulled the tissue paper off and gazed at a familiar, scarlet dress lying neatly folded inside.

'Wow,' said Jodie, who was standing close by, so as not to miss anything. 'It's beautiful. What is it?'

'It's a dress. One I tried on ages ago. At a shop in town. But, I don't understand. How could anyone know it was my birthday?'

'Is there a card with it?' Kate asked. She too was standing close, wondering who could have sent such a gift.

'Here. Here,' cried Ben. The envelope had fallen on the floor.

She opened it and read the card. *Happy Birthday from Brett.* Then it said, *I have a table booked at Domingues' for eight o'clock tomorrow evening. Formal dress required (scarlet!).*

She smiled. He'd promised to take her somewhere special if she bought the dress. Now he had bought that as well! It had been so expensive too. She shouldn't accept it. Not feeling the way she did about him.

'Try it on Kerrien, please try it on,' Jodie begged.

'OK. Wait there.' She went into her room and tried the dress she already knew fitted her like a glove. She slipped on a pair of high heels and stepped back into the family room.

'You look beautiful,' Jodie squeaked. 'Much better than Martine did when they went out.'

'It is very nice dear,' Kate admitted, much to Kerrien's surprise. A rare compliment indeed.

'Very nice indeed,' came a voice from the doorway. 'My, my, who's been splashing out then?' Ashton was home for lunch.

'I don't understand. However did he know it was my birthday?'

Ashton said nothing but his attitude seemed a little odd about her present and about the dinner date. When she finally challenged him about his 'funny mood', he said he was feeling disappointed. Evidently, he had also booked a table to take her out to dinner, not quite Domingues' but still somewhere nice. It was to have been a surprise but now it was spoilt. Kerrien felt her heart surge. How much more enjoyable it would have been to go out with Ashton, but she could hardly disappoint Brett, not now.

'I'm sorry,' she muttered. 'I didn't think you even knew it was my birthday.'

'Of course we did. You made a formal application for this job, so naturally we have your date of birth. Simple eh? Anyway, the kids and Kate are making you a birthday cake, so make sure you're suitably surprised.'

'I will, I promise. Perhaps we could go out another night?' she asked, pushing her luck a little, but she so wanted to spend time alone with him.

'We'll fix something, if an old man like me isn't too

125

boring after your exciting young friend.' If only he knew, she thought, if only he knew the truth.

Domingues' Restaurant was certainly expensive and exclusive. All the women were beautifully dressed and the men wore suits. As they entered the dining room, several heads turned to look at such a striking couple. Brett in a dark suit was a new experience to Kerrien. Even her hardened heart skipped a beat when he had arrived to pick her up. Kate seemed to have got over her objections to him and he had driven right to the door. Ashton remained in the background, not wanting to intrude on Kerrien's evening. She had promised to say goodnight to the children when she was ready to go, so that they could see how nice she looked. She was wearing the necklace that Ashton and Kate had given her, a pretty silver chain. She felt like Cinderella going to the ball.

Although she enjoyed her evening, each time she looked at Brett she was wishing it could have been Ashton sitting there. It was so unfair of her. Brett must have spent a fortune on her dress and the dinner and she was not really being grateful. She tried hard to entertain him and to enjoy the delicious food.

It was close to midnight when they got back to the house. Everyone seemed to be in bed and she asked him in for a final coffee. Kate had even suggested it herself, saying she would leave a tray ready, in case it was needed. She really seemed to be making an effort lately, a great relief to Kerrien.

'It's been a super evening. Thank you and for the

126

dress. You really shouldn't have been so extravagant but it is lovely.'

'I told you at the time. It was made for you. I went back the next day. I was going to give it to you for Christmas but never quite got round to it. Then Mum told me it was nearly your birthday, same day as my Dad's. She noticed it when you filled forms in on the plane. Actually, I think she was a bit alarmed when she saw the dress hanging in my cupboard. Thought I'd gone strange on her!'

Kerrien laughed.

'What you? Never in a million years!'

When he left, he leaned to her and kissed her lips tenderly. He didn't even try to hug her or put his arms round her. It seemed he had been scared off, well and truly. She was grateful. She liked him a lot but still didn't want more than his friendship. He seemed to understand that and respected her wishes. Her estimation of him rose, or perhaps he was scared of her suddenly demanding marriage if he did anything more!

'Will you wear your blue dress when we go out for dinner?' Ashton asked a couple of days later. 'It suits you. Makes your eyes look even more blue.'

'If you like,' she said doubtfully. 'But I thought I'd wear my new scarlet dress. It seems so glamorous.'

'I prefer to see you looking like Kerrien,' he said, implying much more than his words. She supposed that he was used to glamour when he took Martine out. Besides, perhaps he disliked the idea of seeing her dressed in another man's gift.

She was looking forward to her outing. It would be the first time Ashton had ever taken her out on his own. Although she knew that Martine was always lurking somewhere in the background, she was prepared to indulge herself in a little harmless fantasy. She dressed with care, brushing her cap of blonde hair to a shining crown. She used a little discreet make-up, sensing that Ashton preferred her to look natural. Funny really, she thought, when he's practically married to such a well-groomed woman.

Just as they were about to leave, right on cue Kerrien thought, Martine phoned. The conversation went on for a few moments without Ashton retiring to his room as usual to talk in private. Throughout the conversation, Kate was making pointed remarks to Kerrien about her brother's apparent devotion to the woman. She remarked how kind and thoughtful her brother was to be taking the nanny out to dinner for her birthday treat. She implied that it was purely selfless dedication that motivated him, making Kerrien almost want to hit her. She had been so nice lately as well. Then it struck her. Kate was only too pleased when it was Brett calling to take her out. That had been a complete turnaround, after the initial problems. It had all started after Martine had come on the scene and after the time when Kate had seen Ashton kissing Kerrien. *That* must be it. If Brett was keeping Kerrien busy, she was not going to spoil anything for Ashton and Martine. Once they were safely married, Kate would be able to leave and live her own life, maybe settle down herself, if her man friend was free.

'Don't you think so?' Kate was asking. Kerrien had been far too busy with her own thoughts to have any idea of what she had been saying.

'I said, they make a lovely couple don't they? Martine and Ashton.' Kerrien was spared from answering, when Ashton hung up the phone.

'When's she coming to see us again?' Kate asked happily. Kerrien's heart sank. She could well do without this to spoil her evening.

'There's some dinner and dance she wants to go to. Wants to make up a foursome with another couple. Do you fancy it, Kerrien? Bring your hunk with you?'

'Brett?' she asked in surprise. 'I don't know if it would be his sort of thing. I could ask if you like. Perhaps it might be fun.' The idea appealed in a perverse way. He was certainly a handsome partner to be seen with, the sort of man who would attract anyone's attention. It might stop Martine thinking of her as, what was it *little Mary Poppins*? But would she deign to be seen socially with a nanny and someone who worked in the electrical business? Come to think of it, she wasn't exactly sure what the family firm did do. She did know it must pay pretty well for Brett to be able to afford first the dress and then dinner at Domingues'.

'Ring him now, you've got time. The table isn't booked till half-past,' Kate suggested.

'OK,' she agreed and dialled the number. To her surprise, Brett seemed enthusiastic. She promised to phone him with the details later, as he was just about to have his dinner.

'Good,' Ashton said cheerfully. 'Right. Let's go and get some dinner ourselves. Don't wait up Kate. We shall probably be late.'

The restaurant was a small but popular one, with a reputation for excellent food and overlooking the sea. The dining room was crowded but their reserved table had one of the best views. She settled happily into her seat, planning to continue her fantasy that she was dining with a man who loved her as much as she loved him. His eyes were soft in the candle-light, deep dark pools. He smiled across the table and their fingers accidentally brushed, as he poured some water. She assumed that he did not share the feeling that shot through her own fingers like a bolt of electricity when they touched. She tried not to show it later, when heat flooded her already charged body, as he grasped her fingers and wished her happy birthday. His smile was always ready, always seeming to suggest something more, but he never said it. They had almost finished their main course when she noticed the extremely good-looking man enter the dining room. He had a pretty girl on his arm, one who gazed up at him adoringly. He moved his arm round her shoulder, protectively and kissed her fully on the lips, in front of the whole room full of people. Then Brett sat the girl down and moved his chair next to hers, clearly wanting to be as close as he could.

'Is that someone you know?' Ashton asked, watching her reaction.

'Yes,' she said miserbly. Brett really had been making a fool of her all along.

'It isn't . . .?' he asked. He had never actually met Brett.

She nodded.

CHAPTER 7

Although she tried to ignore the couple, Kerrien felt her gaze being drawn to them every few minutes. It was hard to accept that her fears were confirmed. Everything Brett had said to her, all his compliments, were designed only to seduce her. Once he had accomplished that, he would presumably have cast her aside and looked for his next conquest.

'Let's order a dessert, if you'd like one,' Ashton suggested.

'I don't think I could manage any more to eat. But you have one.' Her appetite had gone.

'Not on my own,' he answered. 'I'll just order coffee.' He stared at her, sensing her disappointment and her hidden anger. He thought she was suffering the blow to her pride that any woman does when she sees her lover with someone else. He could not know that she was angry with herself. She was angry that she had been taken in by Brett enough to spend so much time with him. But it did confirm that she'd been right to refuse him what he seemed to want so much. She'd been right to stop his love-making before it went any further. At least her sense of what was wrong for her had remained intact.

'Thank you for a lovely evening,' she said gratefully, as she and Ashton got into the car.

'I'm only sorry it was spoilt for you by seeing Brett with another woman.'

'It doesn't matter,' she mumbled. 'I would much rather have been with you. I just feel rather foolish.'

Ashton reached over and took her hand.

'Don't, little Kerrien. Don't grieve. He isn't worth it.' He slipped his arm round her shoulders and drew her towards him. He placed his mouth over hers and gently, firmly, kissed her. She felt her body turn once more to an aching fluid. This really was Ashton. No need to pretend this time. His hand caressed her neck, sending sharp thrills the length of her spine. His tongue played with her lips, forcing its way between her teeth and searching her mouth for its own response. Her body seemed to melt into his with sparks of unseen electricity flashing whenever they moved and touched. She desperately wanted him. Could she accept him on any terms? Could she give way to him and give herself to him completely, knowing it was one-sided? She loved him, of that she had no doubt at all. But he loved Martine. She couldn't allow him to use her, not when she felt so deeply for him. He was feeling sorry for her. He was offering his sympathy in his own direct way. However much she wanted him, she would not be driven by any man's lust – when he was obviously committed to another woman.

'Please, Ashton. Don't. Leave me alone.' It cost her all her strength to turn him away. The look on his face was awful to see. If she had hit him with all the force she was capable of, he could not have looked more stricken. His jaw hardened and his mouth tightened into a thin line.

'You are a tease,' he said coldly. 'You lead men on and when they almost reach the point of no return, you knock them back.'

With tear-filled eyes she listened to his words. Brett had said pretty much the same thing. *Was* she a tease? Surely not. Somehow the two men she had allowed into her life recently both seemed to mis-read the message she gave out. If only she dared tell Ashton the truth. The truth was that she loved him, deeply and passionately. But he was in love with another woman. Her own pride would not allow her to expose her innermost feelings until she knew for certain that he could feel the same way about her. She had ruined her chances with Ashton yet again. But despite her longings, she knew she had been right to refuse his advances, considering the terms on which he was making them. No one was ever going to have the gift of her love just because they felt sorry for her.

'We'd better get back,' he snapped, starting the car fiercely, almost bending the ignition key in his anger. 'Put your seat belt on.' There was no kindness in his voice. None of the earlier tenderness. She had hurt his feelings very deeply. She felt more miserable than ever and sat rigid and upright in the car. They exchanged not a single word during the journey and she was relieved when they finally stopped in the drive outside the house. She got out, still without speaking and went inside. Kate was still up and said she hoped they had enjoyed themselves. Almost unable to speak, Kerrien nodded and managed to mumble a few words as she went into her room. She shut the door and stood leaning on it, her eyes tight-shut, as if to blot out the world. She heard Ashton come in and speak to Kate. She couldn't quite hear what was being said and opened her door again.

'Did she try something on with you? I said you were taking a risk, dinner and all that.'

'You have to be joking! She's totally frigid that one. She's unresponsive, no sort of man-eater of any kind. No worries there!'

Kerrien didn't want to hear any more. She crept back into her room and shut the door tightly. Frigid? Was that her problem? He must be right. She thought she was being a bit old-fashioned maybe, saving herself for the man she would marry. Was it that, all the time, she was just frigid? If that was so, why did she feel such passion? How could she feel so much? Love Ashton and the children so much? Surely, the two things didn't go together? She pulled off her dress and looked at herself in the mirror. She wasn't glamorous, not like Martine or all these super models but she *was* attractive. She was slim, with long legs and her face was pretty, if not beautiful. She sighed and ran a shower hoping the sharp cold water could perhaps somehow wash away her turmoil. Why, when she was finally alone with the man she loved, did she have to knock him back like that? She felt certain now that had things been allowed to progress, the evening could have given her everything her body craved. Why did she have such sensibilities that deprived her of so many chances? Emotionally exhausted, she fell into an uneasy sleep. She woke several times during the night and each time, the memory of the evening came back to taunt her. She had held such high hopes and now everything was ruined. Her life was not turning out at all the way she had planned it. Perhaps this huge country was after all, more than she could handle.

The next morning was damp and miserable, somehow matching her mood. Ashton had left early for the surgery, which was a great relief to Kerrien. She didn't have to face him. Even the children were unusually grumpy. It was the last day of the school holidays and Jodie was far from happy at the thought of going to school again the next day. She liked school but would rather have stayed at home with Kerrien and Ben. He too, was starting kindergarten for a couple of mornings each week and Kerrien was to go with him until he settled.

Kate seemed pre-occupied and remote. Kerrien caught her staring at her once or twice, in an odd way, or so her heightened senses thought. As it was too wet to play outside, they decided to play at camping and soon the family room was covered in clothes airers, draped with sheets and other objects that were part of their make-believe camp. They even had lunch inside one of their tents, much to Kate's disgust. Ashton had telephoned to say he wouldn't be home for lunch and that he would probably be out for dinner as well.

'I think he's meeting Martine in town,' Kate told Kerrien cheerfully. 'You know, I don't think it'll be long now, before they announce their engagement.'

'I don't suppose it will,' Kerrien replied miserably.

'It will certainly make life easier once they are married. I expect they'll keep you on for a while at least. Martine is sure to want to keep working and the children will need someone here until they are both at full-time school.'

Kerrien sensed she was being goaded but felt so dispirited that she couldn't even be bothered to retaliate. The rain stopped during the afternoon and she decided to take the children for a walk, if only to get out of the house for a while. She looked down at the little boy and girl, of whom she had become so fond, and smiled at them. It was unfair to take out her unhappiness on them and she tried hard to cheer them all up with a silly game.

'Do you really think Daddy will get married to Martine?' Jodie asked suddenly.

'I expect so. Perhaps you will be able to be a bridesmaid,' she added in an attempt to cheer the little girl up. It hurt to say the words but if they all talked about it enough, perhaps she too would gradually come to accept it.

The week seemed to drag on and on. She saw little of Ashton and more happily, little of Kate as well. She had time to think and try to come to terms with things. Of Brett, she heard nothing. Perhaps he was too busy with his new ladyfriend. She felt rather lonely, with no one to talk to or confide in. What was it Margaret had said on their flight over? If ever you need a friend, someone to talk to? She really did need someone at the moment. She had a day off booked at the weekend and decided to go and see her friend. With any luck, Brett would be out and she could have a good natter with his mother.

Margaret was delighted to see her young friend again. Kerrien had made the long journey by bus this time and arrived rather late for lunch.

'Where have you been hiding yourself?' she demanded. 'You haven't been near us in ages. How did you enjoy your time with Brett and his gang over New Year?'

Kerrien stared. *His gang?* What had he been telling his mother about them? She tried to brush over it and lightly said it had been fun. She didn't want Margaret to start asking too many questions. But there was no avoiding it when Margaret wanted to know something . . . she was most persistent.

'So how are things going with you two? Really I mean. Truth time, my girl, you can't fob off an old hand like me.'

Suddenly, Kerrien broke down. The strain of the

past few days had been too much. She couldn't tell Margaret what she really thought of Brett's behaviour and nor did she say much about Ashton. She told her about Kate and the difficulties they had in getting on.

'Perhaps she's unhappy herself,' Margaret suggested. 'Perhaps she's living a life she doesn't want and can't get out of it.'

'But why does she always have to be so horrible to me? Surely, if I'm taking over the care of the children, she could be free to do her own thing, whatever that is? But all she does is criticize me.'

'But the children love her?'

'Sort of, I suppose. She is their aunt. But she's always too busy to do much with them. I love them, already. Very much.'

They chatted for most of the afternoon and Kerrien began to feel better. When Brett came home from his day out, he was surprised to see Kerrien sitting with his mother. He was obviously also rather uncomfortable. Margaret went to the kitchen to make some drinks.

'Look, I'm sorry but I've already arranged to go out again this evening. If I'd known you were coming over, I could have . . .' He tailed off his sentence, seeing the look on Kerrien's face.

'Enjoy your dinner the other night?' she couldn't help herself asking.

'You know I did.'

'I meant the one at the restaurant near the beach?'

His face coloured slightly. 'How do you know about

139

that? Mum tell you? I shall have to watch it. Spies in my own home.'

'It wasn't your mum. I happened to be there too. I couldn't help seeing you.'

'I didn't see you. Who were you with?'

'You were too busy with your new friend.'

'What new friend?' he asked, knowing full well what she was driving at.

'The very pretty girl who was draped all over you.'

'She's not a new friend, actually,' Brett snapped, wanting to end the conversation. Luckily, Margaret came in with a tray of tea and the conversation stopped.

'Why don't you stay over, love?' she asked Kerrien. 'You don't seem your usual self and you could do with the break I'm sure.'

'I don't know. I suppose I could, as long as I get back early in the morning.'

'How early?' Brett asked. 'Only I have to make a call on your side of town at eight-thirty. If you don't mind getting back around eight, I could drop you off.'

'Great, that's settled,' Margaret announced happily. 'I'll go and put some sheets on the spare bed. We'll grab ourselves a couple of steaks from the freezer and have a real girls' night. Lennie's away for a couple of days, so it's perfect. Why don't you phone that family of yours and let them know?'

'Thanks,' Kerrien said gratefully. Typical Margaret, organizing everyone's lives.

'I could maybe stay in too,' Brett said doubtfully. He was obviously torn, wanting to know what was going on but wanting to see his new love, Kerrien assumed.

'Any more details on that dinner dance thing?' he asked suddenly.

Kerrien had quite forgotten it. She couldn't possibly go ahead with it now and tried avoid the question.

'I'm really looking forward to it. I need to make a few new contacts for an idea I have. That sounds just the place I might meet the right sort of people. Must go and get a shower. See you later.'

Kerrien's thoughts began to whirl around her brain. How could she go to a dance in the company of Brett and Ashton, not to mention Martine? It sounded like the worst idea of hell but she had already asked Brett and, presumably, Ashton had passed on the news to Martine. It was already too late to wriggle out of it, she supposed.

She dialled the home number, praying that Ashton would answer. She was out of luck. Kate was baby-sitting while he was out on a call.

'You will give my love to the children, won't you? Tell them I'll see them early in the morning. And tell Ashton for me. I hope you don't mind.'

Kate said she didn't and hadn't planned to go out herself, so there was no problem and she needn't worry. Feeling reassured, Kerrien settled down to enjoy her evening with Margaret. It was almost like chatting to her own mother.

'I feel so much better. I never realized how much I missed my chats with Mum.'

Kerrien slept soundly in the strange bed, more peacefully than she had for some time. They had gone to bed before Brett had even returned home. Margaret woke her with a welcome cup of tea, just before seven.

'Thank you, Margaret,' Kerrien said gratefully. 'And I don't just mean for the tea. I feel so much more relaxed now. It was just what I needed, a bit of a break and the chance to talk to someone away from home.'

'I've enjoyed it, love. Come again. And don't worry your pretty little head about that son of mine. He isn't all bad you know. Just young and wanting to see a bit of life. He'll soon settle, mark my words.' She was a wise lady, Kerrien thought.

The journey back across town was comfortable and very much quicker than the bus. Brett seemed relaxed and they managed to talk. He told her that he was seeing a couple of other girls, nothing serious, but that he thought it was what she wanted. He hoped they could remain friends and go out together from time to time, no strings.

'That's nice of you, Brett,' she said gratefully. He really sounded as if he meant it, besides, if he was seeing someone else, it meant the two of them could simply be friends. He'd be someone to go out with casually and definitely with no strings. It was exactly what she wanted. Smiling happily, she leapt out of the car when he stopped in the drive. She waved as he turned and drove away. As she approached the porch, she saw Ashton standing waiting for her. She did not see the grim expression on his face.

'Oh Hi!' she said, cheerfully.

'Where the hell have you been?' he demanded. Her smile faded.

'To stay with Margaret. You know, I met her on the flight over. Didn't Kate tell you? I phoned to let you know.'

'Don't try to pretend to me. I've been up half the night worrying. I nearly phoned the police. No idea where you were or when you were coming back. How could you? You knew Kate was going out. I had to rush home to baby-sit; left no end of work at the office. I had planned to finish all sorts of things.'

'But I did phone. Kate said she was staying in and that I was not to worry.' Kerrien couldn't believe what she was hearing. She had spoken to Kate and been reassured that there were no problems.

'You lying little witch! Do you really expect me to believe that? I saw you drive back with . . . with that man. I thought you had stopped seeing him after you discovered he so obviously isn't to be trusted? Anything in trousers, that's what Kate said. How can you behave like this and then spend all day with my innocent children? I expect he gives you whatever it is you want. Does he manage to arouse you or do you keep playing hard to get with him as well?'

'What do you want me to say? You obviously don't believe *anything* I do say. OK! Yes. He is a fantastic lover. He can keep going all night. There. Is that good enough for you?' Wishing to heavens she had never said it, she turned and ran inside the house, angry tears coursing down her cheeks. How dare he? How could he make such assumptions about her? She was furious with herself, with Ashton and most of all with Kate. What on earth was the woman playing at? How could she tell such lies? There was a knock on her door.

'Kerrien? Please come out. I'm sorry. It was the relief of seeing you back in one piece.' His tone sounded conciliatory and she was tempted to answer.

'If you won't come out for me, then do so for the children. They need you. I really do have to go now or I'll be late for surgery.'

'Isn't Kate with the children?' she asked, through her tears.

'Kate stayed out over-night. That's mainly why I was so worried. In case I was called out. I was expecting you back.'

She went to the door, wiping her eyes. He was standing in the corridor, looking quite despondent. He really looked as if he hadn't slept much. She desperately wanted to fling her arms round him, to comfort him and feel his strength surround her. For a brief moment, he looked as if he might step towards her but he changed his mind and turned back to the kitchen.

'I did ring. Truly,' she said in a small voice. 'And I didn't sleep with Brett. I didn't mean what I said. I was angry.'

'What you do is your own business,' he said grimly. 'I just don't want you to get hurt. It would be quite against my interests, wouldn't it?'

Kerrien sighed. It was just himself he was thinking about, not her at all. He had to protect his children and so in turn, himself. The smooth running of his home life depended on her. Fixing her smile ready for Ben and Jodie, she went into the family room and began another week.

Despite her own doubts, Ashton and Martine were still expecting her and Brett to accompany them to the dinner and dance. They were all to meet at the hotel in town, as it saved anyone having to travel out to the suburbs. They took a taxi, Ashton and Kerrien sharing the rear seat. They had called an uneasy truce and he'd taken pains to ensure they were never on their own at any time. If he had challenged Kate about the telephone call she denied receiving, he had said nothing more. The subject had never been mentioned again.

Kerrien was wearing the scarlet dress again and Ashton looked most handsome in his dinner jacket. She tried very hard not to allow herself to think about him in any romantic way but it was extremely difficult when she was sitting so close to him like this. She could smell his after-shave, a musky smell that suited him. It mingled with his own masculine scent, his unique essence that sent her own senses reeling. She hoped the evening would be enjoyable, that they could all forget their differences and try to get on together.

In the foyer, Brett and Martine were standing

sipping drinks. Of course, they had never been introduced to each other and stood at either end of the bar. She was smiling provocatively at the good-looking man, a little younger than herself maybe, but for all that very attractive. For Brett, a stunning woman like Martine was equally not to be ignored. They had smiled and flirted with each other for nearly five minutes and he was about to cross the bar and speak to her. He could then pass the time pleasurably, while waiting for the others to arrive. It was most amusing, when they both stepped forward simultaneously to greet the new arrivals as Ashton and Kerrien came into the bar. They looked at each other and couldn't help bursting out laughing.

'What a time we wasted,' Martine commented suggestively. 'We could have spent it getting to know each other. Darling . . . how are you?' she asked Ashton. She pulled him towards her to kiss him on the mouth, before turning to Brett.

'How do you do? We haven't met before but I've heard so much about you.' Brett looked slightly disconcerted, but soon collected himself. Kerrien was impressed. She had only seen the surfing, light-hearted holiday version of the man. Here was a much more sophisticated Brett, a man of business who was capable of sophisticated small-talk.

'Come on. Let's find our table,' Martine said, tucking Ashton's arm under her own in a possessive gesture. She looked her usual gorgeous self, in a dress of midnight blue silk. Her hair was like burnished copper, twisted into a complicated knot high on her

146

head. Despite her own expensive dress, Kerrien felt she was completely outshone and almost dowdy. As if sensing her thoughts, Brett leaned over to whisper, 'You look quite sensational tonight. I'm a lucky man.' She smiled gratefully, wishing she could believe him. She hadn't missed the frank looks of admiration that passed between him and Martine.

It was a light-hearted evening. They laughed and joked together, superficially as companionable a group as anywhere. They danced between courses, swapping partners several times. Kerrien felt as if she were floating on air after her first dance with Ashton. He was a superb dancer, surprising her greatly with his prowess. He claimed it was down to his medical school back in the UK, an old-fashioned establishment with old-fashioned social standards. Wherever he had learned, Kerrien was glad she had the opportunity to share his expertise. Martine and Brett seemed to hit it off too. Surprisingly, he too seemed very much at home in this formal setting. Martine seemed to know everyone and was busily introducing him to people. He would be pleased with that, Kerrien thought, remembering his comments about making contacts and expanding the business. Besides, it kept Martine occupied and left Kerrien free to dream that she was there exclusively with Ashton.

If she had even dreamt of what would happen next, Kerrien would have never have agreed to come. To everyone's surprise, once the few speeches were over, Martine rose to her feet.

'My friends,' she announced. 'I wanted you, some

of my very good friends, to be the first to know. Ashton and I are soon to be married.'

There was stunned silence and someone called out, 'Congratulations! Well done, Martine. A toast everyone. To the Doctors, Ashton and Martine. Long life and happiness.'

All around, people were raising their glasses and calling out their congratulations. Ashton sat stunned. He said nothing, simply stared at the woman in front of him. Kerrien could neither move nor speak. It had happened at last. She would never have believed he could be so cruel. Why didn't he say something to her, on the way over, if not before? Perhaps he realized she would never have come if she had known. Then she looked into his eyes. They were dull, flat and filled with disbelief. Amazingly, she realized that he was as surprised as everyone else. The momentous announcement was news to him as well.

Martine brought them all back to earth.

'Well, darling? What do you say?'

'I don't know. Why Martine? Why say it like that? Here? In front of all these people?' His voice was controlled but they all sensed that he was far from calm.

'I didn't want you to say no. I knew you wouldn't, not in front of everyone. You're too much of a gentleman. Come on. Is it such a surprise? You know it's what I want. That it'll be a good move for both of us. Your sister certainly thinks so. She will be highly delighted. Come on darling. Let's dance.'

Everyone clapped, as Martine led her new fiancé on to the dance floor. The company formed two lines, applauding them as they passed along the middle and then stood aside as they took the floor. Ashton still looked uncomfortable but he managed a smile, as they whirled around the floor to the romantic music the band had struck up in their honour. Martine was leaning against him, in a manner suggestive of a close sexual contact that had become very familiar to her. Kerrien's heart felt as if it would finally break in two but she could not, would not, say a word. Brett was staring at her, his smiles of congratulation fading as the realization began to dawn.

'It's *him*, isn't it? You really care about *him*.' Kerrien made no reply. She was hanging on tightly to her emotions and would not yet risk speaking out loud. Without a word, Brett took her hand and led her onto the dance floor. Almost supporting her limp body, he held her closely, as the waltz ended. He took her back to their table and the four of them sat down again in silence. A waiter arrived with an ice bucket containing a bottle of champagne and popped the cork, pouring the golden liquid with a flourish designed to impress everyone around. Congratulations were being called from surrounding tables and they all smiled dutifully as the toast was drunk. Martine was positively gushing charm and looking happy and excited. Ashton too was smiling, but Kerrien noticed a grim tight line at the corner of his mouth. Brett was smiling his seductive smile at the newly engaged woman, while Kerrien sat silently in her world of quiet misery, wondering how she could possibly get through this evening of deepest torture. She wanted to escape somewhere, to be alone and let go of the flood of misery that was engulfing her. She had known it would happen. She had expected it to happen. Now it was here, she could think of no way of coping. Her unhappiness and her jealousy were threatening to overwhelm her. Brett understood. He knew.

'I'll take you home,' he offered.

'You haven't got your car,' Kerrien mumbled.

'No probs. I'll get us a cab.'

'But that's expensive. I can wait for Ashton.'

'Don't be silly. What's a few bucks? Besides, they may decide to stay over. I think you'd *prefer* to leave, wouldn't you?'

Gently, he bundled her into a cab and got in beside her. He put his arm round her shoulders, feeling her shiver. She nestled against his warm, protective shoulder, grateful for someone to support her. She despised herself. She hated herself for being so feeble. She had known all along that Ashton and Martine were lovers, that they would probably marry and that Ashton had never really cared for her, not deeply. She was the children's nanny and it was in his own interests to ensure that she was reasonably happy with her situation. His caring went no deeper than that. She sat, numb with the shock and made no protest when Brett helped her out of the cab back at home and gently propelled her towards the door. He paid off the cab driver and together, they went into the house. He put the kettle on and made them both coffee.

They sat side by side on the sofa, Brett with a gentle arm still resting protectively round Kerrien's shoulders. They talked, for the first time without any pretences, without either trying to impress the other. Kerrien, for the second time on that astounding evening, was surprised at this new side she saw to Brett. Perhaps she had been wrong in her judgement of him. He wasn't quite the stereotyped Aussie surfer she had imagined. With parents like Lennie and Margaret, how could he be just another playboy?

'Thanks, Brett,' she said gratefully, leaning over and kissing his cheek.

'I'd better go,' he said at last. It was way after midnight and they were both feeling shattered. 'Can I try for a cab?'

After several calls, he put the phone down in desperation.

'I cannot believe that a city the size of Brisbane can't produce a single available cab,' he said in disgust. 'It's pointless leaving a message on some answerphone in the hopes they might call back. Damn it. I should have asked the one we came in to wait for me, but I wanted to stay with you for a while.'

'Thanks for that,' Kerrien murmured, wondering what Kate would say if she let him stay on the sofa. She made up her mind. What the hell? Once she heard Ashton's news, nothing would matter again.

'I'll get you a blanket. You can sleep on the sofa if you like.'

151

'Thanks,' he said gratefully. 'What about the sister from hell or the doctor? Won't they object?'

'I shouldn't think anyone will even notice in view of the big news,' she said, a touch ruefully.

It was a tight fit on the sofa and his legs hung over the end.

'Don't worry,' he assured her. 'I've slept in worse places. Not much worse, I grant you, but there you are!' The small joke raised a little smile from Kerrien, as she said goodnight. In spite of everything, Kerrien fell into the deep sleep that often accompanies emotional exhaustion. She awoke refreshed the next morning and felt almost cheerful, until she remembered the events of the past night. With a start, she remembered Brett, asleep on the sofa and she dressed quickly, anxious to wake him before Kate discovered him and made all sorts of assumptions. When she went through, he was already up, dressed and making coffee.

'Morning,' she said. 'Hadn't expected you to be up yet.'

'How are you today?' he enquired, coming over to her and placing a friendly kiss on her cheek.

'What on earth is going on here?' Kate came into the room, looking accusingly at the pair.

'Brett came home with me last night and then couldn't get a taxi back to his place. He slept on the sofa. I knew you wouldn't mind.' From the look on Kate's face, it was obvious that she did mind and she was about to burst forth when Ashton himself came into the room. He glanced at his sister and took in the

152

whole scene. Brett with his arm round Kerrien's shoulder, her blushing embarrassment, the anger on Kate's face completing the story. Obviously, Brett had spent the night and Kate had discovered them both.

'I expect they told you the news,' Ashton said wearily.

'What news?' Kate burst out. 'Has Kerrien actually managed to persuade someone to marry her?'

'I'm not talking about Kerrien. Martine announced to the entire Brisbane social scene, that *she* and *I* are to be married.'

'Oh, my dear. I am so pleased for you. How wonderful. What a catch for you both! I'm sure she'll make you a wonderful wife.' Kate's gushing delight was increasing with every moment.

'I suppose so,' Ashton said. 'Mind you, I'd like to have had the chance to ask her myself. I don't think I have ever been so embarrassed in all my life. Blurting it out in front of everyone like that. I mean, what else could I have done but go along with it?'

Kate continued to burble on about weddings and the suitability of the match until Kerrien could have screamed. She had been standing as if frozen, with Brett's hand still resting on her shoulder. She turned to him and gave a wan smile.

'I'll see if there's a taxi available for you now, shall I?'

'Take him back in the car,' Kate suggested, unexpectedly. 'I don't need it today.'

'Well, thank you, but what about the children?' Kerrien asked.

'I'll see to them for once. Won't they be excited at the news? I'll go and get them up immediately.' She rushed out of the room as if she could wait no longer. Ashton looked concerned, but allowed his sister to go. He knew she would blurt out the news and wondered if they should have been told by him, perhaps a little more gently. He looked at the couple standing before him and said, 'I expect you two will be making an announcement soon, as well.' His eyes were cold and the hard line round his mouth indicated his displeasure.

'Who knows?' Brett answered, carefully avoiding Kerrien's direct gaze. He thought she would protest at his comment but he felt somehow protective of the girl, knowing her vulnerability where the doctor was concerned. Kerrien knew that she could do nothing; for one thing, she was afraid of making a fool of herself if she broke down again. She would not give Ashton the satisfaction of knowing that he meant so much to her.

'Right,' she said bravely, 'let's get you back to where you belong, Brett. Before Kate changes her mind about the car. See you later.' Ashton watched them leave and drive out of the road. He sighed. If things had turned out differently, if he hadn't spoiled everything, she wouldn't have fallen in love with Brett. He had never seen anyone gain his children's love so quickly, so completely. They would take it hard if she left them now. But then, so would he.

'Daddy, Daddy,' called out Ben, as he rushed into the room.

'Daddy . . . Aunt Kate says you're getting married to Martine. You're not really are you?' Jodie was shaking her head, as if that could somehow stop it happening.

'What do you think of the idea?' Ashton hedged.

'I think it's an awful, horrid idea,' Jodie said firmly.

'And me. I think it's horridy as well,' Ben's little voice piped.

Ashton went white. He knew his children were less than enthusiastic about Martine but had not suspected they would feel quite so strongly about her. It was just a matter of them getting to know her, he tried to tell himself. After all, she was a good doctor and must be able to make good relationships with her patients. Busy with his thoughts, he watched Kate organizing them and giving them breakfast. She was pouring out her excited chatter as she worked and he, busy with his own thoughts, let her get on with the practicalities of the morning. However beautiful and desirable Martine was, he knew the basic honest truth was that he didn't truly love her. His heart and mind were filled with a slender, lovely English girl who took such wonderful care of his children. But it was too late. He had lost her to an Australian. A very good-looking, younger man against whom he stood no chance. Besides, Brett was much more suitable for her, young, no responsibilities and ready to have fun. He, Ashton, had forgotten how to have fun, obsessed as he was with the need to look after his family. Brett was also a good lover, as Kerrien herself had made clear. Ashton's ex-wife had poured scorn on his own talents at love-making. So much so that he had lost his confidence completely. Martine had yet to discover that little truth, whatever she may have done to convince Kerrien that there was more to their relationship than there really was. What a mess. He had landed himself with a fiancée he didn't love, all because he hadn't got the guts to stand up to her. Living with Kate all these years, he had given in to her dominant regime through sheer self-defence. At the start, he'd fought against her constant nagging but the endless rows had unsettled the children, until he had finally been ground down. All he'd wanted was a peaceful life and as a result, he had allowed himself to become something of a door-mat. And now, he'd lost Kerrien because he had pushed *her* too hard, too soon. He knew very well that she was anything but frigid and bitterly regretted his accusation, made in a moment of frustration. Martine claimed she loved him and he supposed he might grow to love *her*, given time. He wondered about her own interpretation of the meaning of love. Probably little more than a few diamonds and a pleasant home and life-style. Why on earth had he allowed himself to go on with that travesty last night? But he had and now he must forget Kerrien and be grateful and happy that such a beautiful woman as Martine wanted to become his wife. He could certainly do a lot worse!

He came back to reality, as Kate was telling him to sit down and eat breakfast.

'I'm going to work,' he announced. 'See you later.' He rushed out of the house.

Breakfast over, Kate sent the children outside to play. It was Saturday and there was no school. She picked up the phone and dialled Martine's number. She had a plan in mind. Nothing was going to interfere with this marriage. She was determined that everything would go smoothly.

CHAPTER 8

It was nearly lunch-time when Kerrien returned from her trip to drop Brett home. A quick hallo to Margaret and a coffee before she had left, made her later than she intended. She'd then taken a couple of wrong turnings, her mind pre-occupied. The journey took longer and longer, it seemed. There was strange feeling of unreality about everything, as if she was in the middle some sort of dream that would end when she awoke. The house was quiet and Ashton's car was missing from its usual place. He must have gone to work, even though she'd thought he wasn't on duty this weekend. Perhaps he had gone out – to be with his fiancée she thought miserably. She had to keep experimenting with the words, so that she would get used to it. How could he want to marry someone who was so negative towards those two lovely children? It was obvious to anyone with half a mind, that Martine couldn't care less about them. It was equally clear that the children also felt the same way about their father's fiancée. Kerrien knew that whatever it cost her personally, she must do her best to make them accept their new mother-to-be. She planned various little things she would try to do, hoping to bring them round. She knew her heart wasn't in it, not one little bit, but for their sakes she had to try.

'Kerrien, dear, you're back,' Kate said cheerfully. Kerrien could hardly believe her ears. Dear? This must be a first! 'Martine's coming over this evening. A little surprise party in honour of the occasion. I thought it would be nice for the children to have the chance to get to know her better. Time alone together is so precious for Ashton and Martine. They hardly have any time to spend with the children. Still, once they're married, everything will be so much easier, won't it?'

'I'll go and see the children now myself,' Kerrien said, anxious to get away before she had to listen to any more of this. Kate in this sort of syrupy mood, she could well do without.

'Daddy's going to marry that smelly woman,' Jodie announced as soon as she caught sight of Kerrien.

'Yes darling, but you really mustn't be so rude about her. I'm sure you will get to love her once you know her. Just as your daddy does.' Kerrien's resolve had held firm at the first test.

'But we love you, not her. Besides, she doesn't want to know *us*. You know she doesn't. Like that time she was supposed to take us to see Santa.' Nothing Kerrien could say, was going to change Jodie's mind!

'It takes time to get to know someone,' Kerrien tried again.

'No it doesn't. Not always. We knew *you* in five

minutes flat. *And* we decided we want you to marry Daddy!' Some chance, Kerrien thought longingly.

'Daddy loves Martine,' she said, mentally gritting her teeth at the thought. 'You will grow to love her too, I promise you.' She knew her voice did not sound convincing but she was spared further conversation as Kate called them all in for lunch.

'There's a lovely surprise for you this afternoon. Martine's coming over for tea. Isn't that nice? Your new mummy. Aren't you lucky that you're going to have such a pretty lady for a new mummy?'

'She's not our mummy yet,' Jodie said with a look that contained rather too much venom for such a sweet little girl.

Ashton was late back from the surgery. Although he was not officially on duty, he had decided to catch up on some work, hoping to take his mind off things. He arrived home to find Martine sitting on the veranda, looking her usual cool, immaculate self, sipping tea with his sister. The children were somewhere in the garden playing hide and seek with Kerrien.

'Darling, where have you been?' she asked, as Ashton bent over for a peck on the cheek.

'Work,' he replied gruffly. 'What are you doing here?'

'Kate invited me for tea, to see the children. After all, I shall be seeing an awful lot more of them soon, won't I?'

'So where are they?' he asked, a cynical smile twisting the corner of his mouth.

'The girl has organized some game to keep them

160

out of the way. She is a treasure isn't she? I was most surprised at her young man. He is quite something. Can't think what he sees in such a dreary little thing.'

'You are being extraordinarily bitchy, my darling,' he said, emphasizing the *darling*, copying her own affected way of speaking. 'You should be grateful to her, or you would now have to be working hard to entertain the children yourself, while getting to know them better, of course.'

'My, my, you are tetchy. Sorry darling. Of course she is wonderful and I hope she'll stay on after we're married. I certainly couldn't begin to cope with the children on my own. I didn't take up working in paediatrics, for that very reason.'

'Look, Martine. We must talk. You did rather spring all this on me last night.'

'Couldn't resist. Well, it was inevitable that we should get married, wasn't it? We are so well-suited and I have lots of plans for our future together. A working partnership in every sense of the word. Besides, I find you madly attractive and quite irresistible. Come and give me a kiss.' In spite of himself, he smiled, leaning over and kissing her as requested. She was a gorgeous woman and he should be flattered that she was prepared to go to such lengths to snap him up. After all, a thirty-two year old man with two small children, was hardly the catch of the year. Perhaps the future needn't be so bad after all.

'Excuse me,' Kerrien said in a small voice. She had witnessed the fond kiss on the cheek and was trying hard to hide her hurt. 'The children are asking if you will come into the pool with them.'

'Sure thing,' Ashton drawled with a pseudo-American accent. 'You coming too darling?'

There was a flicker of horror on the woman's face. She controlled it and managed to say,

'Sorry, but I haven't any togs.'

'Kerrien could lend you something, couldn't you?' he replied.

'Certainly. No trouble,' Kerrien muttered, wishing like mad that she could see this woman in her own second best and rather ancient bikini. Not a designer label in sight.

'I don't think so, thanks,' Martine managed to stammer. 'I don't think anything Kerrien might own would fit me, do you? I have rather too much up top to fit into your bikini!' she boasted. Kerrien looked down at her own bust, doubting very much that there was anything to choose between their sizes. She smiled to herself, wondering if there were any other excuses she could force from her rival.

'I've got one top from which the elastic has gone,' she offered hardly able to control her giggles. 'You'd fit in that with no trouble. Shall I get it for you?'

'I think not, dear,' Martine answered coldly. 'The truth is, I hate swimming anywhere other than the Mediterranean. Greek Islands are one thing. Children's ponds in the back garden are quite another.'

'Right,' Ashton said when the exchange was over. 'You'll excuse me for a while won't you Martine? I'll have to go and play with the kids. Coming Kerrien?'

Martine watched the man and the girl racing over the garden and chasing the two children. Her eyes narrowed dangerously. She would not have any man fooling around with her. When it came to marriage, she was deadly serious. There had been plenty of men in her life but this one, he was someone special and besides, she knew it was time to settle down. Her career demanded it and he was exactly right for her. The only slight disadvantage was his children. Somehow, she had to make sure that there would always be someone to look after them. They were pretty enough children and gave an air of stability to a couple. She wouldn't mind being seen with them occasionally. Whatever the problems, she was certain they could all be overcome with a minimum of effort on her part.

Lazily, she rose from the armchair and wandered slowly across the lawn towards the pool where Kerrien and Ashton were playing a game of chase in the water with the children. Martine didn't like the way her fiancé looked at the children's nanny, nor did she like the ease with which the nanny dealt with the children. Still, it *was* her job and she must have had some sort of training. Why, she suddenly realized angrily, they almost looked like a family already! Martine wandered back to the veranda, bored with the afternoon. Ashton's bossy sister seemed to be messing around in the kitchen. Mind you Kate did cook like a dream. Idly, Martine wondered if she too could be persuaded to stay on after she and Ashton were married. With Kerrien to look after the children and Kate to cook, she would be able to carry on working without any worries. She planned to keep a neat little section of her life for her own independence, to follow her particular needs. And she would always have Ashton there for her. She settled back into her seat, happy with her plans, happy with her life and happy with what she could foresee as her brilliant future as Mrs Ashton Philips.

'All alone?' Kate asked brightly when she came out of the house.

'They are all swimming. Too energetic for me on my day off.'

'Can't say I blame you. Unpleasant business, getting wet. Now tell me, what plans have you made for the wedding? You know what Ashton's like. Tells me nothing.'

'I want a big wedding. Probably St John's. Long frocks, flowers, bells and choirs. The lot. I thought I'd go for oyster silk. What do you think? I'm such a traditionalist.'

'Sounds wonderful,' Kate enthused. 'I can't tell you how thrilled we are. I never thought he'd take the plunge again, not after all these years. He was becoming something of a recluse.'

'Tell me about the nanny girl. She looks at him with very moony eyes. Is there something going on?' Martine sat forward, eager to hear what the other woman had to say.

'She might wish it was,' Kate said darkly. 'A real madam that one. Looks as if butter wouldn't melt but you should see her in action. She has this beach type in tow, Brett is he called? Well, of course, you must know, you met him didn't you? She brought him here to stay the night, would you believe? Cool as a cucumber. Not for the first time either. Do you know . . .' and she spent several minutes recounting the various bits of scandal she thought she knew about, blackening Kerrien's name as much as she could.

'And what's more, as if that wasn't enough, I actually caught her doing her best to seduce poor Ashton. Can you believe it?'

'Well, hopefully, all that is over. I can't think she could possibly want to seduce Ashton now that I'm marrying him and certainly not with a gorgeous man like Brett around. I don't mean it like that, of course. Just that she will leave Ashton alone, while she persuades her own man to marry *her*.' Martine's face was a picture of innocence and Kate felt rather sorry for this woman. She must actually feel rather insecure if she was even remotely jealous of the little English girl, however much of a reputation Kerrien might have gained. Surely, she was no challenge to the beautiful older woman?

'Don't you think Brett's asked her to marry him yet then?' Kate asked curiously.

'Shouldn't think so for a minute. He could do better than that anyhow. Bright young man that one. He's got a good business sense as well as being extremely good-looking. He's ambitious. His parents own quite a sizeable electrical company. Make specialist electronic parts. We use them on some of our high tech medical machines. His family also owns at least a couple of retail shops.'

'Really? I thought they just had one store, on the other side of town. How do you know all this?'

'He told me last night. While we were dancing. He wanted to know if I could give him a few names, contacts, you know the sort of thing. Lucky Kerrien. She'll be marrying into money if she plays her cards right.' Martine's husky voice took on the slightest hint of peevishness.

Kate sat silent. She was astounded by all that Martine had said. So there was more to it even than *she'd* guessed. That little slut had been leading Ashton on, knowing all the time that she was going to marry into money! She wondered how Brett would feel when he knew about Kerrien's goings-on. Perhaps it was her duty to make sure he knew that Kerrien Clark was not Miss Pure and Innocent, after all. Frigid, was it that Ashton had said? Looked like he's really been taken for a ride. She would do her best to ensure that her brother was made aware of all the facts, knew all he needed to know. She wanted to make certain that his marriage to Martine went through as smoothly as possible, without any hitches caused by an unimportant children's nanny.

The rest of the day passed well enough, with Kate's delicious cooking once more delighting them all. Kerrien felt a mixture of emotions, jealousy, sadness and an occasional sense of unreality that the whole thing would end suddenly when she woke up. It was clear that the children adored their father and he them. The happy time they had shared in the little pool now seemed strangely out of place, with the elegant Martine sitting opposite her at the dinner table. Kerrien thought she was perhaps drinking a little too much wine but what the hell? She wasn't going anywhere. The children were safely in bed. Besides, it might make her sleep soundly, allowing her to forget the awful reality she knew was actually lurking beneath this superficially happy surface.

'So, when is the great day to be?' Kate asked happily.

'No point waiting forever, is there, darling?' Martine simpered.

'I suppose not,' came Ashton's unenthusiastic response.

'It will have to be at the Cathedral of course, St John's and as for the reception, how about seeing if we can use the University? Or maybe the Park Royal Hotel or better still, Lennons? Which do you prefer, darling?'

'I was hoping for something quiet. Registry office and then just a few friends back here. Not that I've had any time to give it much thought of course.' The jibe was not wasted and a flicker passed through Martine's clear green eyes.

'I'm going to have to take you in hand. It's time you came out of your shell and showed Brisbane what you're made of. You are a brilliant man but very few people ever see that. Things are going to be changing around here. I mean, no one who is anyone lives on this side of town. It's not as if you can't afford somewhere a bit more exciting.' Expressionless, Ashton listened to the woman's words. He made no comment and Kate excitedly filled the sudden gap in the conversation.

'You are so right, Martine. I've been telling him that for years. Someone with his talents should be seeking a much better post than he has. GP in a small suburb is hardly what we had in mind when we put him through medical school. I think, at last, you're just what he needs to shake him up, Martine.' The smirk on Martine's face, following this statement, made Kerrien feel almost physically sick. Martine seemed to want to marry Ashton just so that she could change him into the man she wanted him to be, or considered the most suitable husband to enhance her own career. The woman planned to turn Kerrien's beloved Ashton into someone else, simply to enhance her own social climbing and chances of promotion and one could only imagine what else. It was immoral, in Kerrien's book. People were what they were and should at least have the opportunity to remain so, if that was what they wanted. If Martine really loved Ashton, she wouldn't be talking that way. If she didn't and only loved what she might turn him into, then she should be stopped! Kerrien could stand it no longer and rose from the table, making the excuse that she needed to check on the children. Cathedrals, receptions with half of Brisbane's social scene in attendance, were things that she herself could never cope with.

'. . . And Jodie can be a bridesmaid and Ben can be a page. I have several young cousins who can also join in to make an even prettier picture. I shall have one of the children act as chief bridesmaid rather than another adult as Matron of Honour. I'll have them all dressed in shades of peach and cream with touches of green. What do you think, Kate?'

But Kerrien heard nothing of the older woman's reply. She was standing looking down at Jodie who was sleeping so peacefully. The little girl's long lashes rested on her cheeks and the thick blonde hair was spread over her pillow. A battered teddy was cuddled into one arm. Kerrien brushed the hair gently aside and planted a soft kiss on the forehead of the sleeping child. She went into Ben's room and smiled as the little boy turned over, plugging a thumb into the rosebud mouth. They were peaceful and happy as they slept. What would their future bring? She couldn't bear to leave them but she couldn't bear to stay to witness the changes Martine planned in everybody's lives. The lovely garden where parrots visited, rainbow lorikeets flashed brilliant colours among the trees and frogs croaked in the evenings; it was all to be replaced by a fashionable house in the middle of town.

Sighing, Kerrien returned to her room. She couldn't cope with any more of the falsely hearty celebratory party, going on in the living room. She lay back on the bed, trying to come to terms with everything that was happening. If the wedding was to take place in the next few weeks, she assumed she would have to stay on at least until after the honeymoon but then she knew she'd have to leave. She could never live in the same house as the man she loved, once he was married to someone else. She would stay just

169

long enough to make certain the children were settled. By then, her six months would be up and she would be free to look for another job, here in Australia. She would simply hate to have to go back to England and admit defeat.

With an aching heart, she undressed and climbed into bed. Through sheer exhaustion, she fell asleep. She awoke suddenly, hearing an unusual noise. She crept to the door and opened it a crack, straining to hear if it was one of the children. She heard voices, not clearly enough to hear the words, but she knew it was coming from Ashton's room. Martine must have decided to stay overnight again. She shut her door silently and leaned on it. The tears rolled slowly down her cheeks as once more, she began the self-torture of thinking of what might be going on in the next room.

The next few days were difficult. Kate had only one topic of conversation – the wedding – and seemed totally unaware of the discomfort of those around her. The children were silent and withdrawn, reminiscent of the time when Kerrien had first arrived in Australia. Kerrien herself was thoroughly sick of hearing about the fabulous designer wedding dress Martine was planning, and whether Ben should be dressed in green or cream velvet. Either was equally revolting, or so Kerrien thought and she instinctively knew that Ben would agree!

'I think you should start looking around for another job,' Kate suggested brightly one morning.

'I see. Your idea or Ashton's?' Kerrien asked.

'It must be obvious even to you that this situation

can't go on. Once they're married, I expect they will be starting a new family and Martine is sure to want someone of her own choice, to look after the new baby as well as Ashton's two. Besides, Ben will be at school and you surely wouldn't want to be hanging around all the time with nothing to do. Perhaps you might even meet someone yourself, if you haven't already!'

Kerrien stared. So, it was all planned was it? She was to leave after all, just as she had suspected she might be invited to do. She was slightly annoyed that she hadn't managed to get in her own resignation first. Saying nothing, she left the kitchen, almost falling over the two children who had been squatting on the floor outside the door . . . Both of them were sitting shedding silent tears. They clung to each other in the deepest misery and didn't stop crying even when Kerrien sat on the floor with them, her arms around them both. How could he do this to them? They had at last reached some sort of stability after the earlier years of their rather confused little lives and now everything was about to change once more.

'Come on my darlings. Cheer up. Martine will make you a lovely mummy. She will love you just as much as your daddy does. You'll have lots of fun and you might even have a new house. Think how exciting that will be.'

'Will Gluppy come with us?' Gluppy was a one-legged galah, one of the lovely pink and grey parrots that came to feed in the garden. The children had watched fascinated as the injured bird performed his

171

acrobatic feats, climbing down the tree with his one foot and using his bill to hang on.

'I think Gluppy will be happier here, where he knows his way around,' Kerrien explained.

'We would be happier here too where we know our way around,' Jodie insisted.

'But you're getting 'nuther job,' Ben wailed. 'You don't love us any more.'

'How can you think that?' Kerrien asked in horror. 'Of course I love you both. You are very special to me and I'll always love you, even when you are all grown-up.' How could she explain away the actions of the seemingly thoughtless adults who had up-turned their little lives? But she could not get through to them. Silently, they rose from the floor and hand in hand, went out into the garden. They shut the door of the cubby firmly, making it quite clear that grown-ups were not welcome.

Ashton seemed to spend less and less time at home during the next few weeks. He seemed to be attending more conferences and meetings and received constant summons from Martine to help sort out the complicated wedding plans. His hopes of a quiet wedding had been dashed and it was all set to be the social event of the year. One evening he did return early and after dinner, he and Kerrien sat out on the veranda, sipping glasses of cold white Chardonnay.

Ashton seemed distant and Kerrien tried to break the silence by asking about his day. He explained some of the cases he was dealing with, the patients that came to him for advice and help or just to be reassured.

After a while Kerrien realized that they'd never really talked about his work before and when he did his eyes lit up. Kate's earlier jibe about his lack of ambition in only being a small town GP seemed even more cruel to her now. She realized he loved his work and was a highly respected doctor.

'Not many more evenings like this to sit out. There's a definite autumn chill in the air, don't you think?' Ashton said, rather wistfully.

Kerrien nodded, thinking it was nearly as hot as midsummer back at home in England but a bit more comfortable than it had been in December. It was not the only cause of the chills in the air around them. She decided to broach the subject of her own future.

'Could I ask you to give me a reference please?' she asked in a slightly wobbly voice.

'What the hell do you want a reference for? Aren't you happy here any more? You looking for another job or something?' he snapped, looking unexpectedly shocked.

'I assumed that . . . well, Kate suggested I should be looking.'

'When did this happen?'

'A couple of weeks or so ago. She said you'd be having a new family and that once Ben was at school, I'd be wasting my time. Frankly, I can't afford to be out of work for long.' Kerrien would have given anything not to be saying this.

Ashton's face was white and his eyes were flashing angrily. The soft velvet was replaced by hard green flashes which almost sparked in their rage.

'This time, she has gone too far. When she comes back I shall have it out with her. She will not rule my every move. I don't want you to leave. Martine doesn't want you to leave. Most of all, the children don't want it. No one, not even, especially not, their own mother, has ever looked after their well-being as caringly as you have. There will be a job here for as long as you want it.'

'Thank you, Ashton, but I don't think it would be a good idea for me to stay. The children are already feeling unsettled and it might be better if I wasn't around. Give Martine a chance to care for them and for you to know you'll have a happy family life together.'

He stared at her. She couldn't mean it?

'But the children. Who will look after the children?'

'Kate will stay around for as long as she is needed, I expect.' Her voice faltered as she thought of the two, subdued little children who were being cared for by their aunt before she had arrived. They had come out of themselves so much under her own guidance and now behaved like normal, happy kids most of the time.

For Ashton, not to have her happy, pretty face around any more was something he hadn't foreseen. But it was understandable. It had been difficult for her to take over some of the duties from Kate, who never made anything easy at the best of times. But what Kerrien had established with the children was something very special. Then he remembered Brett. Of course, she was trying to let them all down gently. She was planning her own wedding and was trying to be discreet about it. It would surely be a much quieter affair than the one Martine planned. Brett presumably didn't have the financial resources available that the two doctors did and Kerrien, he believed, had very few savings of her own.

'How's Brett?' he asked suddenly, realizing he hadn't noticed the younger man around much recently.

'He's OK. I haven't seen him for a bit but he phones quite regularly. Everything's fine.'

'I think we work you too hard. You don't have enough time off. We should put that right. Now, pass your glass over and we'll have one more drink before we go in.' Their fingers brushed as she gave him her glass. The almost forgotten, yet painfully familiar bolt of electricity shot through her. She glanced up at him to see if he felt anything. His face was a mask. Perhaps it was the constant effusive praise from Martine, the confidence gained from having a glamorous fiancée on his arm but the soft corners of his mouth seemed to be permanently bracketed by hard lines. The sensuous lips were compressed tightly for much of the time nowadays. Whatever Martine had done to improve his self-esteem, some of the most precious part of his nature, his instinctive tenderness, had been lost, possibly forever. Anything he may have felt for Kerrien was obviously over, if indeed it had existed at all. She had lost him. She took her wine from him, carefully avoiding actual contact. She couldn't bear it. Suddenly, he leaned forward and took her hand. She felt pulses of heat rush through every part of her. Damn the man, why did she feel like this about him all the time? The kids on all the soaps talked about having the hots for someone. Wasn't this exactly what they meant? Crude it may sound, but she felt the most tremendous hots for this man who now belonged to someone else.

'You *are* all right Kerrien, aren't you?' he asked gently. He still held her hand in a tight grasp, as if he didn't want to let her go. She didn't want to be let go, not at all, but the pain of his touch inflamed her so much that she was afraid she would lose all of her hard-fought-for control. She felt herself boiling inside. What was he playing at? Almost a married man and he was teasing her. He made it sound like concern, his caring side showing but he must know the effect he had on her. Perhaps he was paying her back for the times she had seemed to reject him. She gritted her teeth.

'I'm fine,' she said as brightly as she could. Strengthened by the effects of the wine, she felt she was almost convincing. 'Everything is going well and Brett and we shall be seeing much more of each other soon, I expect.'

'And the other woman we saw him with on your birthday dinner? Is that all sorted out?'

'Of course. She was some old friend I understand.' He stared at her. He knew she was fibbing. Poor girl, she was obviously in love with the young man who was definitely not to be trusted. Still, she must know what she was doing and he should not interfere. He felt confused. His feelings for Martine were quite different

176

to his feelings for Kerrien. He thought he must love Martine, in some ways. Who could fail to be flattered, to love a woman like her? She was sexy in a blatant way and certainly very beautiful. Everywhere they went, heads turned to look at the striking couple they made. But Kerrien was beautiful too, in a very different way. Her beauty was more delicate and much of it came from within, her sensitivity and caring nature gave a soft gentleness to her mouth and to those clear blue eyes. He pulled himself together. What was he – practically a married man – doing, sitting dreaming about this lovely young girl in the twilight?

'So, do I get my reference?' Kerrien asked again.

'If you really feel you must leave, I suppose so. But it's your choice, you must realize. We don't want to lose you. I shall have more than a few words to say to my interfering sister when she gets back.'

'Thank you,' Kerrien stammered. She downed the remainder of her wine and rose from her seat. 'I think I'll turn in now. Goodnight.'

'Don't you want some coffee?' he asked almost wistfully.

'Not tonight,' she replied, mindlessly grabbing the telephone as it rang. It was Brett.

'How are things?' he asked. 'Haven't seen you for ages. Do you fancy a day out sometime soon?' They chatted for a while and she agreed that she needed a change. They made plans for one day the following week, Kerrien determined that she must pick up the pieces of her life and somehow, start again. As she and Brett now knew exactly where they stood with each other, he was as good as anyone to spend time with.

Ashton came into the kitchen and put on some coffee to brew. Kerrien tried to bring her phone call to an abrupt end, not really wanting to talk to Brett in front of the man she loved. Lightly, she said her goodbyes and see you soon, blowing a kiss down the phone for extra effect. Fortunately, Brett had hung up by then, so he never knew! It wasn't wasted on Ashton, who, now fully in control of himself, asked once more if she would like a coffee. She shook her head and went through to check on her charges once more. Her love for the two children was no longer joyous. Each time she looked at their dear little faces, her heart felt as if it might break. In a few short months, they had become as dear to her as her own life, as their father had become. Soon, she was to lose them all.

She heard the phone click, as Ashton made a call. She could hear something of what he was saying, obviously he was speaking to Martine. She heard her own name mentioned as Martine was informed of her decision to leave. There was some violent reaction, she assumed, as Ashton angrily said that it was all Kate's doing. After few more clipped replies to questions, he put the phone back on its cradle. It didn't sound too much like the happy, loving conversation of two people about to be married! Kerrien heard him banging about the kitchen and finally the television was snapped on and he obviously settled down to watch some sports programme. Kerrien pottered restlessly round her room, trying to read for a while but giving up when it proved to be impossible. She had read the same page over and over and still had no idea of what the story was about. She took a shower, hoping the warm water would calm her nerves. Subconsciously, she knew she was waiting for Kate's return from wherever it was she had gone. Kerrien had assumed that she was meeting her mysterious man friend but that was no more than supposition. As far as anyone else was concerned, Kate spent all her evenings at some class or other. Self-improvement seemed to be her main motivation in life and much good it seemed to have done her!

At last, Kerrien fell asleep, worn out with dealing with her overwrought emotions and the effects of coping with two energetic children. If Kate returned that night, she did not hear her. The next morning arrived with an almost autumnal chill. Suddenly the novelty of Christmas spent in the height of summer was blanketed by what should have been spring at home. Thoughts of daffodils and primroses blooming in quiet corners passed through her mind. Instead she only had winter to look forward to, albeit a considerably warmer winter than she had been used to in England. She pulled on a pair of leggings instead of her usual shorts and wore a long-sleeved blouse over her tee-shirt. She went through to the kitchen to put on the coffee. As she turned, she noticed Ashton, fast asleep on the sofa. He had obviously dozed off while waiting for Kate to come in. It was equally obvious that Kate had not returned last night. Her car was still missing from its usual spot in the drive. Kerrien gazed at the sleeping Ashton, his hair flopped over his forehead and long blond lashes rested on his cheeks. His little girl looked so much like him, especially when they were asleep. She hugged herself, loving the intimacy invoked by watching a loved one in deep slumber. His eyes opened and she quickly snapped into her role as nanny.

'You must have been tired to sleep there all night,' she said as lightly as possible. 'Time to get up now or the children will catch you out!'

He smiled up at her, approving the sight of her long, shapely legs with their covering of blue leggings. Then he remembered the reason for his unsuccessful vigil and the smile faded.

'I think Kate must have stayed out again. I wonder where on earth she goes?' he asked.

'Who knows?' Kerrien replied. 'I'll go and see to the children.' She was oblivious to the wistful gaze that followed her out of the room. Sighing deeply, Ashton hauled his stiff limbs from the uncomfortable sofa. He remembered the TV programmes ending and using the remote to switch off, but for the life of him, he couldn't remember why he hadn't gone off to his bed. Damn Kate. Damn Martine. Now he had to hurry or he would be late for surgery. What a mess he had allowed himself to get into.

CHAPTER 9

Once Ashton had left for work, Kerrien decided that she simply couldn't face another evening staying at home. She dialled Brett's number and swallowing her stubborn pride, asked if he was free that evening. She was taking a slight risk that she wouldn't have to baby-sit but as she hadn't taken any time off for ages, it was not unreasonable to expect a free evening. His response was very positive. If he had made other plans, it was not obvious. He suggested a movie and then a meal out. It sounded exactly what she needed to take her mind off things here.

When Kate eventually turned up, sometime after eleven, Kerrien had started the lunch preparations. She made some coffee for them both. Kate seemed edgy and moody. Things were evidently not going as well as she would have liked. But, she obviously controlled her wandering thoughts and agreed to mind the children for the evening, if Ashton was out. The woman seemed subdued and uncommunicative, so Kerrien left her alone and went to play with Ben. When Ashton came home for lunch, his own temper had not improved. Kerrien could only guess at the reasons and removed herself and Ben as soon as the meal was finished. Knowing that it was her own role now and in the future that was the subject of the dispute, she wanted to remove herself from the arena. She heard voices but was too far away to hear the words. Once Ben was settle for his afternoon nap, she went back towards the kitchen.

'I have to get back now,' she heard Ashton saying. 'But don't think this is the end of the matter. I have a whole lot more to say to you. Make sure you're here this evening and none of your all-nighters tonight please.'

'I promised that scheming little money grubber I'd be in. She's off to see her rich man friend apparently. Though how you can tolerate her, I shall never know. I am fully aware of what went on here last night.' Kate's voice sounded almost hysterical.

'What *are* you talking about, woman?' Ashton asked, his voice deadly calm in contrast.

'You didn't sleep in your bed and I know for a fact that you didn't go out last night. So I assume you must have slept in *her* bed. You should be ashamed of yourself. Nearly married and carrying on like that. I am quite disgusted with you.'

Listening outside the door, despite her reluctance to do so, Kerrien went pale. How could Kate think she would do such a thing? Whatever her innermost, secret longings, she would never sleep with another woman's fiancé! Really, she wondered, why must Kate always seem so bitter and twisted? She went quickly into her own room and closed the door firmly. She had overheard quite enough untruths. The sooner she could get away from this place, the better, before it began to affect her in other ways. But as always, she worried about the children. Somehow, despite all this mess and confusion, she had to know that they would be properly cared for.

Once she had heard Ashton drive off, she went through to the kitchen, where she made herself some coffee. She had been in too much haste to get out of the way before. Warming her hands on the mug, she stared out of the window. She was relieved to think that she would be out for the evening, right out of the way of any disputes that were about to erupt. What went on between brother and sister was best left to them to sort out. Besides, it was ages since she'd been to the cinema and she had a few things to sort out with Brett. She didn't want him saying anything to Ashton about the way he knew that she felt about him, should the two men ever meet again. Suddenly, she remembered something Kate had said. Something about her being a money grubber and going out with a rich boyfriend. Who on earth could she be thinking of? Brett certainly seemed reasonably free with his money, but could hardly be described as rich, she'd have thought. Besides, it was a family business, so if that was the case, Margaret and her husband, Brett's parents, would have been rich as well. True, they seemed comfortably off but not really rich, rich! Kate must have the wrong end of yet another stick. It seemed as if she specialized in jumping to conclusions. If they made it an Olympic event, Kate would win hands down!

Once Kerrien had left on her date, Kate paced the floor, waiting for her brother. She could not understand his attitude at all. She had surely made it clear that it was the children she cared about? She drew in her breath, suddenly afraid that things could go wrong. She was certain that he didn't suspect her own secret. Though he must often wonder where she went when she stayed out overnight, she deliberately held her tongue, feeling she was entitled to her privacy. She knew too, that if he suspected anything of her other life, it might cause problems with her role in his household. Where was he? Ashton should have been home long ago. Despite what she had said to Kerrien, she did plan to go out this evening, providing her brother was home in time. Besides, she didn't want to have the argument with him that he was clearly hinting at when he left at lunch time. 'I've kept your meal hot,' she announced when he came in. 'I'm going out now. Kerrien's already gone off with her boyfriend, so you'll have to baby-sit.'

'No you don't Kate,' Ashton growled in a voice like steel. 'I have cancelled my own evening out with Martine to talk to you. It's time we got a few things sorted out.'

Kate's mouth tightened and she folded her arms defensively.

'Get on with it then,' she challenged.

'Why did you tell Kerrien to look for another job?'

'I should have thought that was obvious. You can't

have a slut like that left in charge of small children. Besides, once Martine knows what she's like, that she will jump into bed with anyone, including you, Martine's brand new husband given the chance, she's hardly likely to want Kerrien Clark anywhere near her family.'

'You don't know what you're talking about. When is all this supposed to have taken place?'

'Last night. You obviously slept together. You haven't made your own bed since we were kids, so the fact that it's not been slept in suggests one thing only. Kerrien's been setting her cap at you since the moment she arrived. I bet it isn't the first time she's gone after her boss, either.' Kate spoke with venom in her voice, years of pent-up anger pouring out into the open.

'You really are an evil-minded woman,' Ashton said with unaccustomed harshness in his voice. 'You've always been jealous of me and any girlfriends I've had. Jane and I had to move all the way down here to get away from you but even then you had to follow us. Oh, Jane and I probably never would have lasted. We didn't love each other enough – but we might have survived if you hadn't always been there. Undermining her – encouraging her in her hatred of this country, my job. Why, she even began to hate her own kids in the end – thanks to your interference.'

'You ungrateful mongrel! I gave up my own life for you! Who took care of you when our parents died? Who did you run to when that silly little wife of yours couldn't cope with her own children? Who's done everything, yes everything for you since then. If it hadn't been for me giving up my own life, God knows what would have happened to you. I could never believe you capable of such ingratitude.'

'Kate, listen to me. Because I *was* grateful, I have never spoken to you like this before. I've put up with you bossing me around, organizing my life, controlling my own children, planning everything. When Kerrien came, the whole idea was for you to get back to your own career, just as you wanted. Once I saw that I could leave the kids in her safe hands, I got back a bit of my own social life and now Martine is about to change my future. Why then, have you done your utmost to get rid of Kerrien? Just as you did with Emma, the last nanny we had.'

Kate swallowed hard and almost gulped her next breath.

'Because Kerrien is not at all the sort of person who should be left with children. She's a slut, I tell you. Why can't you see it? A pair of pretty eyes and you fall for them. It's time you made something of yourself and stopped wasting time on some pathetic little tart. She'd just love to get you under her thumb and take charge of the household. But Martine's different. She really is someone. Snap her up Ashton. Quickly, before it's too late. You can't have them both under the same roof. That evil, deceitful little madam! Now I suppose it's come down to it. It seems it's her or me.'

'No contest,' he burst out, his control finally snapping.

'You're a bigger idiot than I could have believed

186

possible. If you think Martine will stand for this . . .'

'You can't resist always being an interfering busy body, can you?' he asked coldly.

Kate went white. She clenched her fists and turned to the door. She stopped and swung back to face her brother. With all the force she could muster, she slapped him hard across his face.

'You've gone too far this time. Don't you ever ask me to raise one finger to help you, not ever again.' She left the room and minutes later, stormed out of the house, carrying a suitcase. Ashton watched as she drove away. His anger was still firing his thoughts, stopping him from feeling the sense of loss that must surely come when the reality made itself clear. They would all miss Kate in many ways but deep inside, he knew it had been the right thing to do, if he was ever to regain control of his life.

Unaware of the dramas back at home, Kerrien was making the most of her evening out. Brett on his best behaviour, was charm itself and looked after her in every way she could wish for. He was attentive and full of fun. So why could she feel nothing for him? They laughed; ate vast quantities of popcorn; licked ice-cream cones and best of all, enjoyed the film. For a couple of hours, Kerrien didn't once think of all her troubles back at home. Afterwards, they went for a pizza at a sea-food place.

'Are you going to tell me why you wanted to see me, so soon after you said you hadn't time to go out?' he asked at last. 'Not that I mind of course. Seeing you, I mean.'

'I needed a break,' she hedged, not really wanting to go into more detail. But, she was no good at hiding things and soon, the whole story came tumbling out: of Kate telling her to look for another job and that she should leave. She found that it sounded much less serious when she talked about it and it didn't seem such a great blow.

'No worries,' Brett said after listening carefully to all she poured out. 'Mum will be wrapped if you come and stay with us. I shouldn't mind it either. You can look around for something else in your own time. Mum won't mind and I know she won't charge you anything for board and lodging or any of that rubbish.'

'That's terrific Brett, but I couldn't just dump myself on them. Not for free. I'd have to pay for my keep. But it's great to know I wouldn't be homeless.'

'We'll sort everything out later. But no more worrying. Relax and let me take care of you. OK?'

'OK,' she smiled gratefully.

'Now, eat up your pizza. You're losing weight you know. Being too slim won't help you to keep pace with a red-blooded Aussie male!'

When the evening was over, Kerrien felt more relaxed than she had done for several days. Brett drove her back home in his sports car. As the weather had got cooler, especially at night, he had put the hardtop on the car. It was cosy in the two seater but Brett made no move towards her. It was as if he was protecting her in a totally brotherly way and she was grateful. If he had tried to make love to her, she wasn't

188

sure that she would have found the inner strength to put a stop to it in her current emotional state. She desperately needed someone to cuddle her but that would open a can of worms she might never be able to close again. How she missed her mum at times like this.

They stopped in the Philips' drive and he leaned over to say goodnight. A peck on the cheek seemed to be all he wanted and she thanked him for the evening.

'Remember, whatever happens, we are your friends and are always here for you. Oh and did I mention, Mum sent her love? Bye now. See you soon.' And he was off, on his way back across town, speeding through the night.

When she went into the house, Ashton was waiting for her in the family room. His face was grave and drawn. Despite having spent a happy evening with Brett, Kerrien's heart was still bursting with love for this man. He looked so troubled that she wanted to fling her arms round him and hug him better, just as she might do to Ben or Jodie.

'What is it? What's wrong?' she asked. 'Is it one of the children?'

He shook his head wearily.

'No,' he replied. 'It's Kate. She's gone.'

'Whatever do you mean? Gone.'

'She's packed her bags and gone. Says she won't stay here any longer among such corruption and deceit. I don't understand what she's talking about and nor do I know where she's gone.' His eyes were heavy and the dark lines under them showed how much the strain of the past few weeks had been on him. He hardly looked the picture of a happy man about to marry a beautiful woman.

'I can't say I understand either. Will you tell me what happened?'

'I was late home and when I said I wanted to talk, Kate told me she was going out. I said I *had* planned to see Martine and had cancelled it, especially to talk to her. You were out anyway.'

'Sorry, but I desperately needed a break,' Kerrien apologized.

'No, no. That was fine. Kate really wanted to escape the inevitable row that she knew was coming. I guess she's been in charge for so long that it's hard for her to give up the reins. She seems to have been controlling my life for as long as I can remember.'

'And now, Martine seems to have the biggest say,' Kerrien stated. A look flashed across his face. It was pain mingled with perhaps, a sense of shame. No one likes to see themselves as a push-over and he hated to know that Kerrien could see how weak he had been.

'Kate and I had a terrible row. I was very angry with her for telling you to look for another job. She had no right to do it and I want you to stay, for as long as you are able. Martine wants it too. You are so good with the children and they adore you, as you well know. Kate gave me the ultimatum: her or you. As you see, she chose to leave. I feel dreadful that she should take this course after all she's done for us. But there's a limit to what I can take. I know I should have been stronger, sooner. But it was easier to let Kate take over.' His voice was controlled and steady but Kerrien sensed the underlying tension. It couldn't have been easy. She felt a sudden rush of gratitude towards Brett for giving her the chance to be away from the row that had taken place. She could think of nothing worse than having to sit and listen to the pair snapping and snarling at each other like a pair of angry dogs.

'So what do you say Kerrien? Will you stay with us, for as long as you can?' His deep, soft eyes were pleading with her. She felt again that urge to wrap her arms round him and hug him better but she knew that any physical contact with him would spell disaster to her own strength of purpose. 'Think of the children,' he added, knowing this was his trump card. She genuinely loved them and would never let them suffer. Besides, it would mean that she would still be around in his life and that meant a great deal more than he cared to admit.

'I need to think about it. I'll stay for a while, certainly. At least until you have made whatever arrangements you plan to make. Don't worry.' Her heart was near breaking as she spoke. She desperately wanted to be gone once Martine was living here. She couldn't bear to see the other woman doing all the things she wanted to be doing, having the exclusive love of the wonderful man she herself loved so much. If he should ever find out how she felt, she knew he would send her away immediately. If *Martine* found out, there would probably be an even greater battle and Kerrien would be out of Queensland, out of Australia faster than a hot knife through butter.

'Have you made any plans for your future?' Ashton asked. Kate's hints about Kerrien and Brett were still nagging at his mind. He knew he still wanted this woman wanted her desperately, but he wasn't going to interfere with her love, if love it was, for another man. A man who was clearly much more suitable. A man who was free.

'Yes,' she lied. 'I have all sorts of plans, so you don't need to worry about anything. I shall look after the children for as long as it takes for you to get over the wedding and honeymoon. It's for the sake of the children, and only them. I hope you understand that?' She hoped her acting was good enough to convince him.

'Of course,' he said gratefully. 'Martine will be delighted. She is actually almost scared of the children, the responsibility, at least. I'll give her the good news tomorrow, It's a bit late now.'

It was well after midnight and with no Kate around, Kerrien was in for a busy day tomorrow. There were all sorts of things that would need to be settled, not the least transport. Kate had taken the second car and Ashton needed his car all the time. Transporting the children to school and kindergarten could present a few problems but for now Kerrien needed sleep. The problems would have to be dealt with the next day. As she was going through the door, Ashton touched her arm.

'Thank you so much Kerrien,' he murmured softly. She smiled, unable to speak through the racing of her heart at his touch. She turned to look at him, wanting him so very much that it hurt and trying not to let it show in her eyes. Did he feel nothing for her? Apparently not. He was a doctor who was touching people all the time. Naturally, he was used to giving reassurance and his touch on the arm was just that. Reassurance. His velvety eyes looked into hers and she felt herself drowning in her own love. Perhaps she *should* just give herself completely to this man, as Kate thought she'd been trying to do from the time she arrived. Was it such a crime? Did it really matter that she was clinging to the old-fashioned idea that she would give herself to the man she intended to marry? Surely she should give herself to the only man she would ever love . . . and that was Ashton. But even if he did go along with it, would he hate himself and possibly her as well afterwards? Would she despise *herself* afterwards for being so weak? Before she could give in to her desires, Kerrien quickly turned and fled into her room. She shut the door firmly behind her. For once, Ashton could look in on his own children. She would take the whole night off from her duties and she would not leave her room again tonight. There were too many temptations around.

The next few days passed peacefully. Without Kate to boss everyone around and make her own inimitable comments about every situation, the whole household was remarkably harmonious. Ben and Jodie managed to smile again and behave like the happy children Kerrien had come to know and love. Ashton came home and went to work; he was obviously spending his

193

evenings with Martine but said very little about the plans for the wedding. In fact, there were times when Kerrien managed to forget all about it and live life pretty much as they had when she'd first arrived in Australia. With the onset of the cooler weather, the opportunity for long chats on the veranda with Ashton had passed. The chilled Chardonnay had given way to warming cups of tea which suited the chilly evenings. She watched more television and caught up with some of her old favourite soaps from England. They were several months behind here, but it was comfortable to renew her friendship with the characters in *Coronation Street* and *Eastenders* and the rest.

Ashton had organized a team of helpers from the practice to collect some of the shopping, when they needed a mid-week top up and another friend shared the school runs. He often dropped Jodie off on his way to work. It was decided that they would get another car to ease the problems and Ashton promised Kerrien that they would all go together at the weekend to choose one. No one, it seemed, knew anything of Kate's whereabouts. She seemed to have disappeared from the whole State, as far as anyone knew. If Ashton was at all worried, he was not sharing his feelings with the children or Kerrien.

The children were very excited at the thought of going to the garage to help choose a car for Kerrien to use. She had insisted that they should be in on the outing as they would be using the car to go to school each day.

'I want us to have a red car,' Jodie insisted.

'Blue,' Ben piped up. 'But you can have red seats if you like.'

Ashton laughed. 'I want us to have a yellow car. That's the safest colour.'

'Good idea,' Kerrien agreed. 'We want everyone to see us coming, don't we?'

'Yes, but it won't go with your red shorts, Kerrien,' the little girl protested.

'I do wear other things,' she laughed. 'And I've got a red and yellow tee-shirt!' she added. Ashton's face was a picture. He rarely enjoyed the chance to interact with his children, except on the slightly superficial level after his working day, or to be a part of the loving relationship Kerrien had built within the small family unit.

At the garage, there were lots of cars to choose from and the children skipped excitedly from one to the next, rejecting some of them for all manner of odd reasons and falling in love with others for equally odd ones. Finally, a little yellow car seemed to be the top favourite. Jodie liked it best because it had a furry teddy stuck to one of the back windows. Ben liked it because his beloved daddy liked it and because men always had to stick together.

'If you'd like to bring your wife back in a couple of days, we'll have it all ready for her to drive away,' the salesman said cheerfully.

'Fine,' Ashton agreed with a grin.

'You're *not* Daddy's wife, are you Kerrien?' Jodie asked puzzled.

'No, but it doesn't matter that the salesman thought

195

I was,' she replied. *If only*, rang through her mind.

'Martine is going to be his wife, isn't she? But she will never be our mummy,' Jodie insisted.

'No, 'cos you're our mummy, aren't you Kerrien?' Ben added.

She was spared further comment, as Ashton came back and climbed into the car.

'That was all very satisfactory,' he said, pleased with the afternoon. 'You did find the new car easy to drive, didn't you?' he asked Kerrien.

'Brilliant,' she confirmed. She had taken a test drive round the roads nearby, while Ashton waited with the children. They didn't have their special car seats and it wasn't worth transferring them for so short a journey. Ashton had tried the car himself and felt confident it was a reasonably good buy. Things were definitely coming together nicely.

'You weren't planning to go out this evening, were you?' he asked when they returned home. 'Only, I haven't seen Martine for a couple of days and we have a few things to talk through. I planned to go into town but she could come over here if you want to go out.'

Kerrien assured him that she was staying in and knew that she would prefer to do that than have Martine sleeping, or worse, in the room next to her own. She had not forgotten the pain she felt, when she had overheard the engaged couple talking one night. However brave she was trying to be herself, it was painful to see Ashton dressed in his smart suit and going out to meet Martine. She would not have been human if she hadn't wished just a little, that she was

196

the one who was being taken out by the man she adored. Somehow, by burying her longings deep within herself, she was managing to cope. She knew that she could go out with Brett almost whenever she wanted to, but it was not the same. Brett was nice enough but however nice, it wasn't the same as being with the man she loved.

While Kerrien was busy bathing the children that evening, the phone rang. With dripping hands she went to pick it up. She was most surprised to hear Kate's voice. Ashton's sister sounded happy and relaxed and said she was calling to let them know she was all right, if anyone was interested, she added. Before Kerrien could speak a word, Kate put the phone down. Evidently, it was not to be a long conversation, if it could even be described as a conversation. She smiled to herself. Typical Kate. A one-sided diatribe aimed at making everyone feel guilty that they hadn't been out searching for her, she supposed. Still, Ashton would no doubt be relieved to know that Kate wasn't suffering unnecessarily. Kerrien had voiced her suspicions to Ashton about Kate possibly having an affair with some married man, but he had made little comment. But why else would Kate be so secretive about what she was doing and who she was seeing?

Kerrien made herself a cup of tea and settled down in front of the television. It was nice to relax and have no demands on her time, other than seeing the children were all right. Once she was involved in her viewing, she could forget the stresses that surrounded

197

her and immerse herself in the film. At eleven o'clock, she locked the doors and went to bed. If Ashton came back late, he would let himself in and if he didn't, she wouldn't know. This was indeed, the best way of coping. If she didn't think about him and Martine together, she didn't grieve quite so much. Life could be tough, she decided. She wondered if everyone always wanted something they couldn't have or some-one who was not available. She could remember girls at school having crushes on particular boys and the anguish they seemed to feel when they couldn't have the one they wanted. In those days, anyone might ask them out and they would usually go willingly, always anxious to be seen to have a boyfriend and thus be the same as everyone else. That their chosen one didn't reciprocate, never seemed to matter so much. Such opportunities had rarely come Kerrien's way. Mostly, she had to return home immediately after school to look after her mother. She never mentioned anything about it to anyone but most of her friends instinctively sympathized and seemed to understand. When she had finally started to go out with someone, she *had* taken him home for her mother to meet. They had continued to see each other for a while but the relationship had fizzled out because Kerrien was never available when he wanted to see her.

'I have an afternoon off tomorrow,' Ashton an-nounced a few days later. Kerrien's heart jumped. What was he going to suggest? A trip out perhaps?

'You are going to have the afternoon off too and go out somewhere. I insist.'

'Wouldn't you like to go somewhere with the children?' she asked.

'I'll decide that later but *you* are going out on your own, no children to look after, nothing. Go and enjoy yourself. In fact, go and buy yourself something nice.' He handed her a couple of folded dollar bills, closing her hand over them, so that she shouldn't comment on the amount. When she glanced down there was five hundred dollars clutched in her fingers.

'I can't take all this,' she protested. 'You pay me well enough and I hardly ever spend very much.'

'Don't be silly. It isn't a fortune. I'm sure you will find something nice, something you want. Go on. Think of it as a little bonus for all you've done for us. Since Kate left, you've done everything I've asked of you and with much better grace than Kate ever did.'

'But I don't think my cooking comes even close to your sister's,' she murmured wryly, remembering several culinary near disasters.

'You're cooking is coming on nicely,' he laughed, then he became serious. 'You'll make Brett a wonderful wife.' His voice was husky as he spoke, almost as if he was trying to hide some deep emotion, Kerrien thought, not bothering to correct his assumption about her relationship with Brett.

Kerrien made the most of her free time. She went into town early and scoured the shops for bargains. With the extra gift from Ashton, she spent a lot more than she had intended, stocking up on clothes for the new season. She bought little presents for the children

199

and a box of hand-made chocolates as a present for Ashton.

She'd been saving hard for several weeks now, in case she had to cope with a period of unemployment later on, after the wedding. She passed a bridal shop and saw the array of white froth and tulle, feeling a pang as she thought of the imminent wedding. She ought to look for something to wear but wanted to leave such purchases till much nearer the time. Who could know what might happen before then? She may have been sent packing by then and the clothes would be wasted. In fact, thinking about it, Ashton had got no nearer setting the date than when Martine first organized their engagement. Perhaps he was stalling and she wondered why Martine was allowing such delaying tactics. Kerrien glanced at her watch. Four o'clock. She didn't need to hurry back but felt tired of shops and shopping. The reminder of the bridal wear display had quite dampened her enthusiasm. She went back to the car to deposit her shopping bags. She remembered that she had never visited the art gallery everyone raved about and decided to spend an hour or two looking round what Brett had described as one of the best in the country.

There was a cool breeze blowing down by the river and she didn't wait around to look at the architecture. She would surely visit again in better weather. The light, airy spaces showed the exhibits to their best advantage. Though not all the pictures were to her taste, it was a fascinating place. There was a special information pack for children, with a sort of adventure trail to follow and questions to answer. She wondered if Ben and Jodie would enjoy a trip there, planning to suggest it to them on her return. There were a few other people wandering round but it was generally a quiet time to visit. She sank onto a bench to rest her aching feet. Several hours walking round shops followed by the gallery was enough to tire anyone.

A couple of women passed her, one of them very familiar. She was about to call out the woman's name and a greeting but the words died on her lips as Kate turned to look at her companion. She was a pretty girl, around the same age as Kerrien. She had dark curly hair and a dazzling smile. She tucked her arm into Kate's and leaned closer to the older woman. She whispered something and Kate laughed, a warm, loving laugh that Kerrien had never heard from her before. They moved away from the picture they had been studying and arm in arm, went into the next room. Kerrien sat as if frozen to her seat. The affectionate exchange she had just witnessed said only one thing. Kate was not having an affair with any married man. Her chosen companion was another woman. Kate was gay.

CHAPTER 10

Kerrien sipped a cup of hot chocolate in the cafeteria, her hands wrapped round the comforting mug. She hoped that Kate and her friend didn't have the same idea. Kerrien had no prejudices about people's right to choose their sexual partners but somehow, Kate's whole attitude to life suddenly seemed to have become clearer. All these nasty, sometimes spiteful remarks were probably made because Kate didn't know how to cope with the cards that life had dealt her. She did genuinely seem fond of the children but perhaps felt that Ashton would be less than understanding if he knew that his sister loved another woman. It took some getting used to but Kerrien was convinced that she was not mistaken. The way the two women had looked at and spoken to each other showed quite clearly that they shared a deep relationship. It may also explain why Kate was so resentful of Kerrien. Her easy going manner with people was something of a contrast with Kate's own more restrained nature.

She wondered if Ashton could have known all along.

He had been unwilling to talk about Kate's supposed relationship with the mythical married man when Kerrien had suggested the possibility. But surely, he would have said something, if he had known, made some comment? She had to decide when and how to broach the subject. It was not an easy decision to make, in the circumstances. But for now, the immediate problem was to find her way out of the city and back home.

She arrived back around seven-thirty. It had taken her longer than she expected to drive through the evening traffic and she got home well after the children's bed-time. Ashton had put them to bed and seemed more than a little edgy when she went into the family room.

'I'm sorry I'm late but the traffic was something I didn't bargain for. Have you eaten?' she asked as lightly as she could manage. How did she tell him about Kate's relationship? What would his attitude be? She was spared from further conjecture, when he announced that he was going out for the evening and would leave her to mind the children. It was all rather hurried and his unusual shortness of temper suggested that he was irritated at being kept waiting. If she had realized he was intending to go out, she might have made an effort to return a little earlier. This was clearly not the time to break the latest piece of news concerning Kate.

Her brain was teeming with thoughts. The main problem was not Kate but Kerrien's future with Martine in residence. She had gone round and round in circles, one moment thinking that she would easily cope and the next knowing she couldn't bear to be in the same house as the other woman. That strange feeling she had sensed when they first met had flashed through her mind on so many subsequent occasions Kerrien shivered. Perhaps the evil she felt emanating from the woman was simply a recognition of the threat she posed to everything Kerrien herself held so dear. Feeling a desperate need to talk to someone, she telephoned Margaret.

'Hello, dear,' the kindly woman said, pleased to have the chance to speak to her young friend. 'I'm afraid Brett's out. Funny, I thought he said he was meeting you?'

'That was last night,' she laughed. 'Who knows where he is tonight? Can't be seen with the same woman two nights running, it would be bad for his image.'

'He could do a lot worse than settle down with you. You know – and he knows – I'd be delighted.'

Kerrien held her breath and then let it out slowly. She didn't want to hurt anyone's feelings but Brett was certainly not the marrying kind. She had enjoyed his company most of the times they had been out together but keeping their relationship light and superficial was the only way. Somehow, she couldn't quite get round to talking about the main subject on her mind; the subject of Kate and her sexuality. She was not expecting any form of opinion about it but wanted help with her decision of whether to tell Ashton or not. This seemed to be impossible. As

Kerrien realized that Margaret was unlikely to be of any help to her. After chatting for several minutes, Kerrien knew that she wasn't going to be able to confide in the older woman and drew the conversation to a close, making the excuse that she thought she could hear one of the children calling.

She wandered restlessly around the room, unable to settle. Hunger pangs reminded her that she had missed dinner and she went to make some toast. She poached an egg and sat with her simple meal on a tray in front of the television. How Kate would have disapproved, she thought and then smiled. Kate would never be able to disapprove of anything Kerrien did from now on! To her surprise, Ashton returned home quite early. His earlier bad mood seemed to have worsened into something of a temper. Kerrien did not venture to ask the cause. If he wanted her to know, he would no doubt tell her in his own good time.

'Shall I make you some coffee?' she offered.

'Is there anything to eat? I didn't get dinner after all.'

She offered him poached eggs – if he wanted something more substantial she could forage in the freezer. After a slight grimace, he chose the eggs. Doubtless he was comparing the offer to one of Kate's beautifully cooked meals – and not very favourably. Kerrien studied him as he ate. He looked tired and bone weary, almost as if he was tired of life itself. His normally powerful body was sagging, as if he was carrying a burden he could not cope with. The intelligent, alert face she knew and loved seemed to be drawn with strain and the inner glow which always called to her emotions seemed dim, as if the essential element which made Ashton Ashton had been turned off.

'Is something wrong?' she ventured when she could stand the chilly silence no longer.

'Problems, problems. I was supposed to meet Martine this evening but she left a message at the restaurant to say she couldn't make it after all. As you can imagine I was *not* pleased after hauling right across town. She said something had come up. She said it was important and might affect our future together. I'm just wondering what she's planning now,' he sighed wearily. 'Do you know, I almost think I've had enough of people trying to organize my life for me. Just because I made the mistake of marrying Jane, do I have to pay for it forever?'

Kerrien didn't quite know how to answer.

'You wouldn't have those two wonderful children of yours, if you hadn't married her.' His expression scared her. Ashton continued to stare into space, almost as if he was regretting even them. But he couldn't possibly wish they had never existed, not Jodie and Ben. She definitely couldn't broach the subject of Kate tonight, after all.

She stacked the few dirty dishes in the dishwasher and went towards her room. Ashton followed her.

'You know something?' he said softly. 'If I could start all over again, I wouldn't do any of the things I've done. From now on, I think I shall do what I want and damn the rest of the world.' He went into his own room and slammed the door shut.

'And we'd never have met in the first place,' Kerrien murmured. She stiffened, almost as if she was hearing her mum telling her to snap out of it. Suddenly she knew it was right . . . she had to stop all this mooning around. Life was for living and she had been failing to live it. Mum would never have forgiven her for wasting so much time. She was going to enjoy things again and if she couldn't cope with Ashton and his problems, she would find something else to do with her time. Feeling almost excited at the prospect, she turned on the shower and washed away her misery along with the dust and grime of the city. So what if she had fallen in love with a man who was unavailable? There were plenty of others around and she would no doubt eventually find one she could love enough to settle down with. Oh, she'd never feel the passionate attraction she felt for Ashton but many marriages were based on mutual respect and shared interests and the couples concerned seemed serenely content. By the time she had finished her serious talk to herself, she was almost believing at least half of it.

Kerrien kept to her resolve most of the time and the next few days passed pleasantly, with comfortable family meals and Ashton coming from and going to work as usual. He was out on several evenings but rarely mentioned where he was going. Kerrien realized that if she didn't spend time thinking about what he might be doing, she couldn't waste time in wishing things were different. When Brett asked her out on a date, she had no hesitation in accepting and drove out in what was now known as Kerrien's car. The little yellow vehicle suited her perfectly and Ashton had insisted she use it whenever she wanted to and not just for ferrying the children around or shopping. A small compensation, he explained, for the extra work she was always being asked to do. She had arranged to meet Brett in the centre of town and they would decide what to do later.

His car was already parked and waiting, when she arrived and she joined him in the front seat. He leaned over to kiss her on the cheek and she responded more enthusiastically than she had for ages. They drove to a new restaurant, one which was filled with young people and offered dancing in one of the rooms. Kerrien was determined that they were going to have fun. She flung herself into the group with an enthusiasm Brett found hard to cope with, let alone match.

'Whatever has come over you?' he asked after they had sat down, on his insistence. He was quite worn out with the energetic movements.

'Life is for living,' she laughed. 'Come on lazybones . . . or are you too old for such hectic dancing?'

'Cheek,' he said and leapt up again. 'I'll show you what real energy is!' At the end of the next dance, they both collapsed laughing and breathless into their seats and took long swigs of cold juice. They both had to drive home eventually, so neither was drinking alcohol.

'That was fun,' she said when, both exhausted, they finally gave up dancing and were returning in Brett's car to where she had parked her car.

'You surprised me, for one,' Brett answered her. 'I didn't realize you were so energetic!'

'It's all the swimming I was doing through the Summer. And I've been walking quite a bit, not to mention the housework and kids to mind. Life as a nanny is hectic but never more so than now. At least it keeps me fit.'

'And do you intend to stay on with the esteemed doctors when they're married?' Brett asked with a suspiciously innocent air.

'What makes you ask that?' she said, curious about the nature of the question.

'Well, you seem happier and not as worried as the last time we went out. I thought you may have changed your mind.'

'I might. Don't know yet. Oh damn, I've dropped my bag,' she muttered, scrabbling on the floor for several escaped bits and pieces.

When they reached the car park, she got out and tipped up the seat, making sure there was nothing vital lurking under it. Her hands touched a soft piece of fabric. It was silky and she sniffed enquiringly as a familiar scent rose from whatever it was. She pulled at the cloth. As it emerged, she could see it was green in the light from the street lamps. A long green, silk scarf. The perfume was the same as that worn by Martine and the older woman had worn an identical scarf on one of her visits to the Philips house. She dumped it on the seat she had vacated.

'You'd better return this to its owner,' she said tetchily.

'And you'd know who that is, I suppose?' Brett asked.

'Certainly. It wasn't difficult. She usually wears it when she drives and the perfume is quite unmistakable. Just what were you two doing together? How on earth did you come to have her scarf in your car?'

Brett looked uncomfortable.

'I . . . she asked if we could meet. She wanted me to persuade you to stay on after they're married. Don't know why she thought I have that sort of influence on you but, it seems she's scared. In fact, she's terrified at the thought of looking after the two children. She thought if I could persuade you, her life would be easier.'

'And how do you fit into her scenario?' she asked, her suspicions now fully alerted.

'She knows everyone who's worth knowing in the medical world. She can put some business our way. I have great plans to expand and she can help.'

Not wishing to jump to any conclusions, as Kate might have done, Kerrien looked him straight in the eye.

'Just business then?'

'Might as well combine the two, don't you think? Come on now Kerrien. This is on your terms remember . . . no strings. You can't be jealous because you don't want to get too involved, if I remember your words correctly. As to how the scarf was left in the car, I have no idea. I didn't even know it was there.'

'When was this little assignation?' she asked, remembering the night she had phoned his mother and he'd been out. He confirmed it had been the same evening. The night that Martine had stood up Ashton, because she'd had so-called business to discuss with some mysterious person. The two had gone out together and somehow, she had managed to leave her striking, easily identified scarf in his car. If she'd dropped it on purpose to make Kerrien jealous, it hadn't worked. Well, not really but she *was* angry. Angry on Ashton's behalf.

'She's some woman!' Brett sighed.

'Bit old for you, I'd have thought.'

'Miaow,' he smiled, staring at her for a clue as to how she really felt. 'Are you jealous?'

'Not jealous. Concerned for Ashton. He's as straight as anyone could be, so I guess I'm worried for him.'

'Think you might be in line to offer him comfort, do you?' he asked.

'Don't be silly. How could I compete with a woman like that? No, I just don't want him to be hurt any more.'

'You wouldn't of course. Oh come on, don't let's spoil a nice evening. See you again soon? We should go dancing more often It was fun.'

She waved goodbye as she drove out of the parking lot, her thoughts still milling around the strange meeting between Martine and Brett. She wondered if Ashton knew of it and if he did, why he hadn't mentioned it to her? She still hadn't said anything about seeing Kate and planned to have a long talk with him at the first opportunity. Should she also mention Martine and her meeting with Brett? She didn't want to be guilty of jumping to conclusions, but anything Martine did immediately raised her suspicions. She sensed instinctively that the woman was not to be trusted.

At breakfast the next morning, she broached the subject of needing a serious talk. Ashton looked worried.

'I was thinking, perhaps I needed to raise your salary. You've taken on so much more since Kate left. Will that help solve the problems, if problems there are?'

'It isn't that. Look, let's leave it for now. We can have a latish dinner after the children have gone to bed.'

'Please can we come?' Jodie asked.

'Not this time, darling,' Kerrien said softly. 'But I promise that one day soon, when Daddy isn't too busy, we'll have another take-away. Would you like that?'

'Yes . . .' they yelled in unison.

'Right then. That's agreed but only if you get yourselves ready for school in the next five minutes, Chop, chop.' They got down from the table and scampered off to the bathroom.

'You are so good with them, you know. And they adore you,' Ashton said.

Kerrien blushed with pleasure. She hoped he was right and it was good to hear him say it, even if he didn't include himself in the picture of 'Happy Families.' He caught her hand and the familiar shock ran up her arm.

'Please don't leave us. Think again. If that *is* what

212

you want to discuss.' The strained look crept round his eyes once more and the velvety pools became cloudy.

'Don't worry, it isn't that,' she smiled, comfortingly. 'See you later. I must get the children off to school.'

He stared after her. She had become so important to him. Could he really go through with marrying Martine, feeling these emotions for someone else? But Kerrien was also practically engaged, according to Kate and she did seem to be happier lately. No, Kerrien was not available to him and he had agreed to marry the eminently more suitable, Martine. Who knew where her contacts could lead him? His future was probably looking very rosy. So why wasn't he happy?

Kerrien decided that she would do her very best to produce a special meal that evening. Her cooking was not up to Kate's high standards but she could turn out a reasonable, plainish meal. She knew she did not have to impress Ashton particularly but it would make the discussion less of a strain if it were accompanied by good food and wine. She made a spicy sauce to go with some fresh pasta and prepared a salad to be tossed with a dressing just before they ate. The chocolate pots were an old recipe of her mother's and simple to make. A bottle of rich red Shiraz was uncorked on the sideboard, allowing it to breathe. The table was set with the best cutlery and plates and she had even put candles in the holders. She bit her lip, hoping she hadn't gone too over the top or that Ashton would misunderstand her motives. Too bad if he did, she decided.

Once everything was ready, she showered and changed out of her usual working clothes and put on a light sweater and full skirt. She looked fresh and neat and completely natural. She was pleased with the effect, knowing that she couldn't have presented more of a contrast to Martine. The children were safely tucked in and now all she needed was for Ashton to come home. He was late. When it reached eight o'clock, she began to worry. At eight-thirty she telephoned the surgery but only the answerphone was on, giving contact numbers for emergencies. When he hadn't returned by nine o'clock, she cleared the table. It was unusual for him to be this late and even more unusual for him not to have phoned. She cooked a little of the pasta and poured a generous portion of sauce over it. She also poured herself a large glass of the wine before recorking the bottle. She hadn't put the dressing on the salad and so left it in the fridge to use another time.

Kerrien's outward appearance may have been calm, but inside, she was blazing with anger. How could he treat her this way? Who did he think he was? She supposed that Martine had summoned him and he had been too busy to let her know. Obviously, he had to jump when Martine called, just as he had always jumped when Kate lived here. After all, who was she but just the nanny? She uncorked the bottle of wine and poured another glass. Some of these Australian reds were excellent. She continued her thoughts. She didn't have any rights over her employer and certainly no right to dictate what he should do. Even so, it was plain bad manners on Ashton's part, knowing she would be cooking dinner, even if it had only been eggs and bacon! How was he to know she had done something special?

It was after midnight when Ashton finally came home. She stood up, avoiding her empty plate which was still on the floor, beside her chair. The almost empty wine bottle stood beside it. She drew breath, ready to speak her mind about his rudeness and inconsiderate behaviour.

'Sorry about this evening,' he said wearily. 'Did you get the message?'

'And what message would that be?' she snapped.

'That I was called to the hospital? One of my elderly patients was taken in as an emergency.'

'Oh yes?' Kerrien said, the disbelief evident in her voice.

'One of the nurses said they'd phone and leave a message.'

'The phone has been totally silent all night. I've been here the entire time, with a special dinner waiting but don't let that worry you.'

'I am sorry Kerrien, but the nurse said she'd left a message. What else could I have done?'

'We don't have an answering machine, remember? you know Kate wouldn't allow one as she preferred to answer all calls herself. How could anyone have left a message?' She picked up her plate and stormed into the kitchen. What sort of fool did he take her for? It seemed quite obvious that he'd wanted an excuse to avoid talking to her and he'd been out with Martine instead. She avoided his eyes, knowing that his powers of persuasion and ability to get her sympathy would start the moment she gazed into those soft pools. The vulnerable expression she was sure they held was capable of swamping her completely. But she was determined he was not getting away with using her like this.

'Kerrien, listen to me. I've had a pig awful day. I *have* been working until now, whatever you choose to believe and what's more, I have just lost an old patient, a very dear old lady has just died. Whatever it is you think I've been doing all evening, I don't care. Just get off my back and allow me to go to bed! I've said I'm sorry about the meal and the chat. We'll have to postpone it till tomorrow. Now I'm going to bed. Goodnight.'

He strode out of the room and Kerrien heard him slam his bedroom door. She stood alone, contemplating her ruined evening and felt ashamed of herself. Poor man, he *did* work much too hard and took on too many worries. But he hadn't let her know he wasn't coming home and that was bad enough, but lying about it was ridiculous! After the strain of building herself up all day and planning what she would say, everything had gone wrong. She still nursed her secret about Kate and she still had the business of Martine and Brett's relationship to sort out. At least she would have no difficulty in sleeping for what was left of the night. The wine she'd drunk would see to that.

'Will you be in tonight?' Kerrien demanded to know at breakfast the next day.

Ashton still looked quite exhausted, as if he hadn't slept much. That was probably the case, Kerrien thought, but couldn't bring herself to comment on his appearance.

'Promise. I don't think I could stay awake anyway. I'll be home early and if you are still cross, I apologize again. But I did *try* to get someone to phone.'

Once she had the house to herself again, Kerrien decided to spend some time cleaning. She didn't like this sort of work much but Ashton had promised to try and get someone to come in to take over as soon as things had been sorted out regarding the future. Whatever else she might have felt about Kate, Kerrien had to admit that Ashton's sister had kept everything spotless.

Ashton phoned around ten-thirty. Despite all her resolutions, Kerrien felt her heart turn over, simply at the sound of his voice. He told her there *had* been a message, but left on the answerphone at the surgery, explaining that he was kept late at the hospital. There was a touch of *told-you-so* in his voice.

'Just wanted you to know. Bye for now,' he said, plopping the phone down before she had time to say anything! So, he had tried to let her know. Pity he hadn't given the nurse the correct number! Kerrien was still annoyed with him and still concerned about their impending discussion. She went to plug in the vacuum cleaner as the phone rang again.

'G'day Kerrien, honey. It's Margaret. Got time for a natter?'

'Hi,' she replied, glad to have an excuse to put off the dreaded cleaning. 'How are you?'

'Just taking a break for morning tea and well, I had to call, to see if it's true.' Kerrien shook her head silently. If what was true?

'Brett tells me things are going really well between the two of you and I wanted to check it with you. Oh I can't tell you how happy I should be if you two, well, got it together!' Kerrien was totally confused. What on earth could he have been saying to his mother?

'Well, yes, things are OK, but . . .'

'Oh that's wonderful,' she burst in. 'Lennie will be over the moon when he knows. Really took to you, he did. So different from the usual empty headed bimbos Brett hangs around with. So, when will you be making the big announcement?'

'Margaret . . . just stop, please. Listen. I don't know what he's been saying to you but we haven't decided anything. Really. We're just friends. No strings, nothing more. Besides, he has lots of women friends. Why, he's even been out with Ashton's fiancée!' As soon as she said it, she wished she hadn't opened her big mouth. However sweet Margaret was, she had no need to have said all that. She didn't even know what had made her say it.

'I see. Chip off the old block I guess. But whatever you think, Brett is very keen on you. I know my boy. I haven't seen him like this ever before. Mooning around he is, except when he knows he's going to see you.' Margaret's words echoed round in her mind. She had to see Brett quickly, before he led Margaret

218

on any more. There was nothing between them but friendship and if he was encouraging his mother to believe there was more, then he needed to be stopped.

'I must talk to him, Margaret. I want to know exactly what he's been saying. Can you ask him to call me?'

'Why don't you come over this evening? I'm going out but you and Brett could spend the evening together, have a really good chat about things. I know he'll be here because he said he wanted dinner tonight. I was going to leave him something in the oven. What do you say?' Kerrien's mind raced. She bit her lip thoughtfully. She had planned to talk to Ashton tonight but the need to see Brett had suddenly become urgent. He had to be stopped before he totally convinced his mother that they were about to get married. If Ashton could stand her up the previous night, she could deal him the same treatment tonight.

'OK. If you're sure it won't be any trouble. I should be able to get away as soon as Ashton gets in. He may not like it but it's important to me.'

She felt rather ashamed of her tit for tat attitude. It was little childish but her motivation was entirely based on the need to find out what on earth Brett thought he was playing at.

CHAPTER 11

'I thought you had something vital to tell me,' Ashton said at lunch. 'Something that couldn't wait a moment longer.'

'Perhaps I've got things in perspective a little better,' Kerrien replied, twisting her fingers together in her anxiety. 'What I have to talk about is important but something has come up that I must deal with and quickly. I have to see Brett and the sooner the better.'

He stared at her, peering into her eyes as if he could read something in them, as if he could somehow see into her mind to know what she was thinking. She was an enigma to him. One minute bursting with some news she needed to discuss urgently with *him* and the next, planning an evening out with her boy-friend. He had no doubt as to the reason for her sudden need to meet Brett. She had to give him an answer to the vital question and having made her decision, she obviously couldn't wait to tell him.

'Look, I know it isn't really my evening off but things have been hectic lately and I am still owed some time off.'

'Of course,' he said coldly. Obviously he felt curious about the mysterious discussion she wanted with him but he wasn't going to let her see that he was worrying about it. He had enough problems of his own. 'Take all the time you need. There's a programme I wanted to watch on television, anyway.'

'Thanks. I do appreciate it,' she said a trifle stiffly. She didn't want him to know the nature of the planned evening's discussion. 'I'll leave you a meal ready. There's a salad left from last night. The sauce will heat through and there's fresh pasta to cook, so that will be easy for you.' Somehow, talking about simple, practical things took her mind off the reality. Could Brett have really told his mother they were getting engaged? If so, he was jumping the gun just a bit! A night out dancing was one thing, getting engaged was another. This wasn't some silly game they were playing; marriage was a serious business in her book.

'I'll be home in time to put the kids to bed.' Ashton folded his napkin and got up to leave the table. 'I did mention that Martine was coming on the weekend, didn't I? You can have one of the days off and we'll cope with things.'

Kerrien's heart started pounding. Would Martine mention her evening out with Brett? Was it merely business or could there be something more between them? The prospect of another difficult weekend did not appeal to Kerrien one bit. It would be a test though, a test of whether she was going to be able to cope with staying on after the wedding.

Ben was irritable for much of the afternoon, tired after his morning at kindy. He didn't sleep during his usual afternoon rest and he and Jodie seemed unusually quarrelsome after she got home from school. Kerrien felt distracted, worrying about the evening ahead and felt quite exhausted by the time Ashton came home. She took a quick shower and changed. By six-thirty, she was driving out of their road and heading across town, her brain buzzing with the things she intended to say to Brett.

'Hi there! This was a nice surprise,' he said as she arrived at their home in Raby Bay. He reached over to kiss her on the lips but she turned her cheek towards him. He looked mildly disconcerted for a second but held the door open for her. 'Mum says she's sorry not to see you but sends her love. She's gone out to one of her evening classes.' Kerrien smiled cynically, remembering Kate's supposed visits to evening classes. At least they could believe what Margaret said. She had no need to fib.

The large house was comfortably furnished with every labour saving device possible. But, as the family business was concerned with the electrical trade, Kerrien supposed she should have expected it.

'I don't know much about your business,' she said suddenly. 'What exactly do you do?'

'We have a couple of stores selling electrical stuff for the home. Fridges, washers, all the usual,' he replied.

'But there's more to it than that, isn't there? I mean you mentioned some projects to do with medicine.'

'We do have a lab and a small manufacturing unit.

We've been doing some specialist work for the hospital. But I'm sure you don't want to know about all that and I sure don't want to talk about it now. Can I get you a drink?' He was obviously quite determined to end this line of conversation and went to the kitchen to pour drinks. Kerrien wandered round the room, noticing, for the first time, a photograph of Brett wearing a cap and gown. Obviously it had been taken on his Graduation Day. Well, well, she thought. Something else she had discovered. Brett had a degree. He wasn't quite the beach bum he tried to pretend he was. She suspected the family business was also something more than she had been led to believe. She wondered why Margaret had never mentioned Brett's degree. She talked so much about everything else that it seemed strange that she wouldn't have made the most of this aspect of her son. But then, she talked very little about the family's shop, making light of that too. Kerrien had already discovered there were two shops and now she knew there was some sort of manufacturing unit so perhaps Margaret and her family were considerably richer than she had realized. Not that it would influence her in any way, but it did explain Brett's rather expensive taste in cars and women and some of Kate's snide comments.

'Here we go,' Brett announced, carrying in two long drinks laden with fresh fruit, tacky cocktail umbrellas and chinking with ice cubes.

'Wow, they look exotic,' Kerrien smiled. 'But I am driving don't forget.'

'Guaranteed, non-alcoholic. Actually, you've prob-

223

ably noticed I hardly ever drink much. Usually too busy driving somewhere! I'm always getting called out at night.'

'You didn't tell me you had a degree,' she said, indicating the picture.

'Don't talk about it much. Ruins my image as a surfy! Only at the local Uni, so the experience was tempered by Mum's careful eye and excellent cooking. Never was a starving student in some garret. It was good though. Also made sure the old man listened to what I said, occasionally.'

'Talking of your mum. Whatever did you say to her to make her think you and I were, well, thinking of getting engaged?'

Brett looked uncomfortable. 'I . . . er . . . oh hell, I said we'd been seeing a lot of each other and that things were going really well. She assumed the rest.'

'Is it fair? I mean, we both know how keen she is to see you settled but to give her false hopes like that . . .'

'You evidently don't know my mum well enough,' he said uncomfortably. 'Thinking something makes it so, in her book. She had you all lined up for me, the moment you sat next to her on that plane. Look, I'm sorry if I embarrassed you but she had to be told something. She doesn't approve of me going out with so many different women and it's sometimes easier to let her think it's always you I'm seeing, than try to explain. End of story.'

Kerrien studied his face for a few moments. The

pale blue eyes stared back at her. They looked impenetrable, a shiny steel shutter that kept the inner man hidden from public scrutiny. So different from the dark mysterious pools of Ashton's eyes that worked the opposite way, drawing Kerrien deeper into the essence of the man's very soul. Brett's tan had barely faded from the summer and his even white teeth contrasted sharply with the brown face. His shock of blond hair had grown too, sun-bleached at the tips, just the effect some expensive hairdresser might try to achieve with chemicals. She genuinely wished she could feel love for him but her mind seemed to be constantly filled with the unattainable. She was inexperienced and her mother's old-fashioned ideals were somehow too deeply ingrained for her to accept what this man offered. Perhaps she should try letting down her guard, just a little.

They tucked in to the delicious meal that Margaret had left for them. There was chicken pie and fresh vegetables which Brett had cooked perfectly.

'And he cooks as well,' Kerrien teased. 'Is there no end to the man's talents?'

'You ain't seen nothing yet!' he retaliated, serving her a generous portion.

The conversation was light and easy but all the time, Kerrien knew that she had to discuss the serious subject of their future, whatever that was. When they reached the coffee stage, Brett suggested they move to the comfortable sofa. She perched uneasily on the end, hoping Brett would take the hint. But he sat down closely beside her and when both cups were empty, he took her hand and looked at her with a very serious expression. She almost giggled at that expression, largely, she realized, through nervous tension.

'I know you were worried about my so-called date with Martine. I genuinely did believe she might help me with contacts, for the business. I'm ambitious, I admit, and want to drive us in new directions. Dad has always been happy with the shops but I want more in my life than selling washing machines. Martine phoned me last week and asked if we could meet. She only made you the excuse, I think. She seemed to assume I had some influence over you but I told her she was wasting her time, once I got her round to talking about it.' Kerrien smiled. She could see the picture and felt slightly more forgiving towards Brett.

'Only then, it became obvious that she saw me as some sort of stud.'

Kerrien gasped. What was he saying? Martine? She could hardly believe it.

'She's some woman, that one,' Brett continued. 'Wow! Talk about coming on strong.'

'You mean she tried to . . .?'

'She certainly did.' He smiled in his lazy, sexy way and leaned back, his long body stretching along the sofa. 'She practically took me to bed right in the middle of the restaurant. Metaphorically speaking of course.'

'And afterwards?' Kerrien asked timorously, not sure whether she really wanted to hear any more. 'Was that metaphoric too?'

'It's more than any man can do to resist her,' he

226

smiled. He saw the expression of intense hatred that flicked through Kerrien's eyes and stopped. 'I was teasing you. What do you take me for? I saw through her little game immediately and no, I didn't sleep with her. Why would I? But I admit, I was tempted, I'm flesh and blood after all.'

Kerrien sat staring into space. She wouldn't have put it past him, given his track record, but Martine? How could she be so two-faced? Why was she so intent on pursuing Ashton if she preferred the younger, unencumbered, Brett?

'Kerrien? Are you listening to me? I said I didn't follow through. She may have fancied a brief affair but however curious I was, I didn't do anything.' The girl still looked unconvinced. Brett couldn't know that she wasn't concerned about *his* relationship with Martine. She was troubled for Ashton's sake. She wanted most of all to protect him but how could she ever tell him this latest bit of news? He would think she was simply stirring up trouble, trying to make him think badly of his fiancée, for whatever motive.

'Kerrien, darling, I don't know why, what it is, but you really have got to me. I care for you.' His voice seemed husky with deep emotion but she knew that all he was trying to do was soften her up. She was a challenge to him. She'd overheard him boasting to one of his mates, that first Sunday when she'd visited Margaret for the barbecue. 'I can make it with any-one' he'd said. It seemed like centuries ago. She'd certainly grown-up a bit since then, even if was only a few months ago.

'Brett, I don't know what to say. I do like you a lot, but . . .'

'There is always a *but*,' he said softly. 'Kerrien, come here.' He leaned over and drew her close to him. Very gently, he pressed his mouth over hers. He felt her relax and pulled her closer. She was not fighting back this time. His lips caressed hers more firmly, forcing them apart. Kerrien closed her eyes tightly shut, thinking that if she could only get over her own hang-ups, she might one day grow to love this handsome man who was apparently showing her real passion and affection. Her own body responded to the stimulation of his hands. She felt a tingling sensation in her breasts as he gently stroked them. She recognized the desire for closer physical contact and tried to make herself enjoy his expert caresses. He turned to press his body against hers and she felt him hard against her. It felt good but not like the time Ashton had held her close, the time she had known she was falling in love with him. Brett pulled away and looked into the blue, clear eyes as she blinked them open. It wasn't Ashton pressed close to her this time.

'I haven't felt this way about anyone before,' Brett said. She drew a quick gulp of air and her reeling senses came back to earth.

'And you've had plenty to choose from, I suppose.' The harsh words hit him like a slap across the face.

'I've never tried to pretend anything different,' he defended, a hurt expression in his eyes. 'Look, you may be innocent or try to give the impression of being innocent but I know a true response when I feel it. Yes, OK, call it experience. Tell me, do you intend going through your entire life celibate and end up a sour spinster?'

'I think I'd better go,' she said, bristling at his accusation.

'Kerrien, I'm sorry! I didn't mean it. I *want* you Kerrien, on whatever terms you insist on making. Think about it. I can offer you everything you've always wanted.' His face looked almost child-like in its pleading, like Ben or Jodie begging for just a few minutes longer, before going to bed. She almost smiled at the thought. They may want to stay up longer, Brett couldn't wait to get her to bed!

'Brett, I don't know what I can say. Of course I like you and I know my body seems to respond to yours but my heart doesn't. I can't explain it. I suppose that I physically have needs, just as everyone does but I just can't go further with this, with you.'

'You're just plain scared I reckon. Is that it? You haven't had sex before and you're scared. You needn't be. I can help you. I know what it's all about.'

'How dare you? I suppose you think it would be fun, teaching a virgin what to do? Your surfy mates would just love it. I can see you now, telling them all about the little English, sorry, Pommy Virgin, you screwed. Tight-assed little spinster, but the great Brett Matthews won her over!' Her eyes filled with tears and she turned to look away.

Angrily, Brett leapt off his seat and grabbed her hands roughly. His eyes flashed cold and hard as steel.

He turned her to face him and she felt suddenly terrified of the expression she saw on his face.

'How dare you, you stupid woman! Don't you recognize the truth when it stares you in the face? You're hanging on to some soap opera idea of romance. You see your precious doctor with moony eyes, as if he's some story book prince waiting to sweep you off your feet. Life isn't like that babe, and it's time to face reality. Ashton is about to marry one helluva sexy woman. Most men would give their eye teeth for a female like that. This is nearly the twenty-first century, not back in the dark ages. Real women, women like Martine go out and grab what they want. None of this pussy-footing around. She sets out to take what she wants and she makes sure she gets it. You, on the other hand, are wrapped up in some romantic dream of love and happy ever after. That's just not what life is all about. Get real. Wake up to yourself.'

Kerrien didn't know what to say. She stared at him. Perhaps he was telling the truth. He was, after all, a self-confessed womanizer. What he said about her was true. She did have romantic ideas of love and marriage but she also knew rather too much of the difficulties when marriages go wrong. She couldn't remember her own father but she had memories of long evenings of heart-ache her mother had suffered, trying to bring up a child on her own. She worked at anything she could, to make sure that Kerrien had everything she wanted. She had often been lonely, but never complained. When her health began to fail, Kerrien had become aware of an entirely different sort of suffering, and they'd had to face it alone with no one else to support them. Marriages that didn't work were a nightmare. *She* would not be trying the institution until she was absolutely certain she knew what she was doing. She had to look no further than at Ashton himself. He seemed to resent his entire life because of what Jane had done. Romance? Was there any such thing, outside silly women's stories? Why did everyone in the world expect so much out of life? The movies, television, books, everyone painted a false picture. There was no such thing as true love. One man for one woman. Brett was right. She should play the field a bit. Get some experience. Go out and enjoy herself. Wasn't that exactly what she had promised herself, only a few days ago?

'Brett, I'm sorry. I should never have spoken like that. I'm a romantic at heart and I know I'm stupid about some things. I know you wouldn't really boast about women, especially me, but I suppose I have some stereotyped ideas of men and what they're like. I think it might be best if I leave now. Thank your mum for the meal. It was lovely. Look, if you can still bear the sight of me, how about going out somewhere on the weekend? I have a day off and the dreaded Martine is coming over, so I'd quite like to get out of the way.'

He stared at her, obviously turning things over in his mind. His face was expressionless. He continued to stare and said nothing. Feeling a little like a specimen being studied under a microscope, Kerrien blushed.

'Perhaps you'd rather call it a day, right now,' she

231

challenged. 'Can't say I'd blame you if you did.' After
what seemed like an age, he drew in his breath.

'OK. We'll do something on the weekend. I don't
understand it. Any other chick would have been sent
packing long ago after the way you've treated me.
But you *are* different. You do have something
special . . . a way of getting under a bloke's skin.
Perhaps it is your damned purity, your *won't do
anything till we're married*, routine.' He compressed
his lips and sighed. 'You are a pain in the butt, do
you know that?' She stared up into his face, as if
trying to find some explanation for his words. Then
his expression crumpled into a smile and the hard
steel of his eyes melted. He reached out for her and
crushed her slender body into his strong arms. He
planted a kiss on her forehead and said, cheerfully
smacking her rump, 'Get home with you, baggage.
I'll call you on Friday night and we'll decide what to
do with our day. It'll have to be Saturday. Can't
manage Sunday.'

Kerrien smiled at him.

'Thanks,' she whispered. 'I'm sorry I'm such a pain
to you. Perhaps you should make it clear to your mum
what you really think of me!' She turned and went out
to the little yellow car, waving a casual hand as she
drove away.

'I certainly won't tell my mum what I think of you,
Miss Kerrien Clark,' he breathed. 'She could never
cope with all my fantasies about what you and I could
be doing together.' He shut the door firmly behind
him and went to clear up the dishes, However old he

was, he knew that his mother would not tolerate a mess!

Ashton was in bed when Kerrien returned home. Her mind felt clearer in a strange way, despite the fact that she and Brett had had a sort of row. It was comforting to know that she had faced up to some reality, even if she didn't really want to believe all the things Brett had said. She was still positive about her intention to try to enjoy life, even knowing deep inside that without Ashton, there would always be a huge emotional gap. Brett *could* evoke some sort of response in her, so perhaps it might not be too difficult to grow to love him. She worked hard to convince herself of the possibility and put her negativity down to her own inexperience. Perhaps all humans had been conditioned at some time, to believe in the one love for life theory. One look at the divorce rate proved that wasn't true! Surely, no-one, when they got married believed it wouldn't last? Growing-up, love and life were all too complicated. Poor Ben and Jodie. What problems would their future hold?

The next morning was sunny and warm. There were magical colours in the trees as they got near to shedding their last leaves. The dryness of the summer earth had been replaced by green and the lawns had been cut the final time for the season. The pool was emptied and cleaned and covered in plastic to keep the leaves out. Unlike being in England, Kerrien felt no sense of loss at the end of summer. Besides, the weather was still much hotter than many days in an English summer. She was not yet used to the difference in seasons between her old and new homes. It was just difficult to remember that it wasn't soon to be Christmas. Once the summer sales were over back at home, the shops immediately seemed to turn their attention to Christmas stock and the build-up seemed to get earlier each year.

'Kerrien, Kerrien, Daddy says we might be able to have a dog,' Jodie squeaked, rushing into the kitchen in her pyjamas.

'Don't get cold, darling. Go and get dressed, quickly and then come and tell me all about it.' Since Kate's departure, the rules had been changed about the children not getting up until called. Usually, they got themselves up and dressed as soon as they could hear someone moving around. What had Jodie said? A dog indeed, Kerrien thought. And whose idea might that have been? The pair had often begged for a dog but Kate's pride in a clean and tidy home would never have allowed it.

'We're getting a dog,' Ben burbled as soon as he came into the kitchen. 'Daddy says we can. Soon.' His smiling face was evidence of his pleasure and Kerrien could only grin herself. Her worries of the previous night seemed far away as she listened to their excited chatter.

'Come on now, it's nearly time you were getting ready to leave. Is Daddy awake yet?' she asked.

They scampered back to the bathroom, their minds totally focused on the possibility of a dog. She hoped it hadn't been a casual promise Ashton had made in the heat of the moment, to keep them quiet. They would never forgive him if he let them down. She went to supervise their preparations and found them arguing about names.

'I always wanted a dog called Holly,' Jodie was saying.

'That's 'cos of *Neighbours*, and it's a stupid name,' Ben announced firmly.

'No it isn't,' Jodie protested. 'It's a lovely name.'

'Come on now,' Kerrien intervened. 'When you get a dog, it may already have a name. If you don't get off to school, there won't be any sort of dog, whatever its name might be.'

When she returned, there was still no sign of Ashton. She knocked gently on his door, but there was no response. She wondered if he was unwell and knocked again, pushing the door open and calling his name. She looked at the bed but it was empty. The duvet was rumpled, so at least she knew he had slept there. He must have gone out early, before anyone else was awake. She drew back his curtains and tidied the bed. She went to see if his car was missing, but it was parked in its usual place. Very strange. He couldn't have gone out the previous night, not when she was out and the children were in the house. She called a few times but there was no reply. He was nowhere to be found. By eleven o'clock, she had allowed herself to become worried and telephoned the surgery. The receptionist told her that Doctor Ashton had called in early, saying he was taking the day off sick. She had assumed he was at home and that Kerrien would have known all about it. Kerrien made some feeble excuse

235

about having been out and that the doctor was probably still in bed. Most peculiar, she thought. It was definitely not like him to take a *sicky* without good reason.

When the phone rang, just as she was about to collect Ben from kindy, she snatched it up.

'Kerry, my dear. May I speak to Ashton please?' Martine's languid drawl set her teeth on edge.

'He isn't here,' Kerrien said shortly. She still felt angry with the woman for going out with Brett, not for herself, but for the ever trusting Ashton. 'And it's Kerrien!'

'But his office said he was off sick. You wouldn't be trying to stop us talking would you? Trying to get in the way, would you?'

'Don't be silly,' Kerrien retorted, rather more snappily than she intended.

'Then where is he?' the woman demanded.

'I have no idea. His car is still here but there's no sign of him anywhere. To tell you the truth, I'm a little worried. It isn't like Ashton to go off without a word.' Kerrien glanced at her watch. She really needed to leave to collect Ben.

'Look, Martine, I'll get him to call when he returns. I have to go now and collect Ben from kindy. He'll be worried if I'm any later. Goodbye.' There was no further comment from the other end and she replaced the receiver. She rushed out and drove quickly to the little boy's school. As she parked the car, one of the supervisors came out.

'Hello, Kerrien,' she said in surprise. 'Doctor

Philips came for Ben. Quite early, he was. Around half eleven. Hope everything's all right.' Kerrien didn't wait to ask any more questions but drove quickly back along the road. Whatever was Ashton playing at? Why hadn't he said anything to her if he had intended fetching Ben? Besides, the little boy would never manage to walk that distance. It was over two miles from the Philips house to the kinder-garten.

She drove along all the possible routes that Ben and Ashton might have taken but there was no sign of them. Could Ashton have had some sort of accident? Why was he behaving in such a peculiar manner? She drove back home again and let herself into the house. She called their names but there was still no reply. She became nearly frantic with worry and wondered if she ought to call the police. She knew what Ashton's response would be to that and decided on discretion.

When Martine phoned for the second time, Kerrien snatched at the phone, desperately hoping to hear Ashton's voice. She was so disappointed that it must have showed.

'You do sound genuinely worried,' Martine said. 'I suppose they couldn't just have gone off on a boys' day out?' she suggested.

'But why, without telling me? Ashton must have known how worried I'd be. And why go off without his car? Ben can't walk all that far.'

'Leave it with me. I'll make a few calls and let you know if I come up with anything.'

'Thanks,' Kerrien responded distractedly as she dropped the phone back into its cradle. She wandered round the house, thinking she might do some cleaning but not wanting to put the vacuum on in case she missed his call. She lifted the receiver several times, just to reassure herself the phone was working. When it was time to fetch Jodie from her school, still she had heard nothing. She didn't want to worry the little girl and tried hard to appear cheerful and make light of her brother's and father's strange disappearance. Driving back, Jodie was curious to know why her brother had failed to accompany Kerrien.

'He and your daddy have gone out somewhere for the day. It was a surprise.' And how, she thought silently. As the little yellow car stopped, Jodie yelled excitedly,

'Daddy's home! His car is there.'

'Jodie dear,' Kerrien began but she stopped suddenly. Standing by the window were Ashton and Ben, both full of smiles. They waved and Jodie leapt out of the car, rushing into the house.

'Where've you been? Kerrien said you were out. Why couldn't I come too?' she demanded.

'It was a bit of a surprising day for all of us!'

Kerrien stood silently near the door. She felt a mixture of annoyance at the worry she had been caused, tempered with relief at seeing them again, safe and sound.

'We saw some lovely doggies,' Ben offered. 'Lots of them. Daddy says we can have one soon.'

'It's my dog as well, I wanted to go to the kennels

and choose one,' protested Jodie, full of righteous indignation.

'Kerrien, how are you?' Ashton asked full of mock jollity. 'Did you have fun last night? Got any news for us? I must say, you hardly look as excited as I thought you would.' If she hadn't known better, Kerrien could have sworn he was drunk.

'Where on earth have you been? I've been worried to death. When Ben's kindy teacher said you'd fetched him earlier, well, I just didn't know what to do.'

'We had fun, didn't we Ben?' Ashton said, still sounding ridiculously cheerful.

'Why didn't you think to let me know. You might have known I'd be worried. Even the surgery thought you were ill and Martine, well she's probably got half of Brisbane out looking for you, right now.'

'What's she got to do with it?' he asked, sounding genuinely mystified.

'She wanted to speak to you and had tried everywhere else. Said she'd make a few calls and get back to me if she found anything out.'

'When are we getting the dog, Daddy?' Jodie wanted to know.

'Maybe at the weekend but you'll have to wait and see. Now, perhaps I'd better phone Martine and tell her we're all safe and sound. Can't think why everyone is in such a tizz about a measly day out.' Kerrien glared but said nothing. If they were indeed getting a dog, she would have liked to have been told about it. She knew exactly who would be expected to take it for walks and do most of the work connected with it. She was secretly rather pleased at the prospect, having always wanted a dog herself but had never been able to, because of her mother's illness.

'How was lover boy then?' Ashton asked brightly after dinner. 'Did you get all the answers you were hoping for?'

'Yes, thanks,' Kerrien replied, trying her best to sound cheerful.

'So when's the great day to be? Hope you're not planning on stealing our thunder, or perhaps you're hoping for a double wedding!'

'I'm sure, I don't know what you are talking about,' she said coldly.

'Whoops. Put my foot where angels fear to tread, have I? How about some wine to thaw the frost?'

'Look, I don't know what you've been doing all day, where you've been or why. I've been worried out of my mind, mostly about Ben of course, but seeing your car still in its place, I couldn't begin to know what was happening. I just don't know where I am any more. And no thanks. I don't want any wine and if you are as drunk as you sound, perhaps you shouldn't drink any more either!'

'Finished?' he asked grimly, when she paused for breath. 'I've been out with my son to look round some kennels for a dog that both my children want so very much. Ben asked if we could go on a bus, so I left the car behind. I'm sorry if I was supposed to ask your permission and failed in my duty. You may remember I told you I'd decided that my life was to become my own again? Well, I made a start today. But I'm back now and if you want to go to your worthless lover, you'd better go now!' He lay back on the sofa and closed his eyes, appearing to promptly fall asleep.

Kerrien stared at him and gently, shook her head. What was all that about? she wondered.

CHAPTER 12

Sleep was impossible and Kerrien paced her room for much of the night. Ashton was evidently going through some personal crisis which seemed to exclude both herself and the children. What was he talking about with her and Brett? News? Excited? He could only think that they were getting engaged. She wondered where he had got that idea. It was the very last thing she would have wanted him to think, when all the time *she* desperately wanted *him*. She also wished that his future with Martine was less certain. Double wedding indeed!

Ashton said little the next morning before rushing off to work. She caught him staring at her a couple of times, as if looking for some clue in her face. If he believed something special had recently happened to her, he did not voice his thoughts.

'I won't be home for lunch and don't wait dinner for me tonight. I may be out. Have you decided when you're going out at the weekend?' he asked.

'Saturday, if that's OK,' she replied. 'I'll organize

things before I go. Is there anything special you need me to buy? For meals, I mean.'

'No thanks. Saturday is fine. We'll go out, I expect and then probably have a take-out meal for supper.'

'Yeah,' yelled Jodie. 'We like take-outs best, don't we Ben?'

'If Kerrien's here we do,' Ben said firmly.

'You'll enjoy yourselves with Martine, just you wait,' Kerrien prompted automatically. They did not look convinced.

'You'll soon get to love her as much as I do, I promise,' Ashton said, getting up from the table. He was looking directly at Kerrien as he spoke, as if trying to test her reaction. He could not have failed to see the pained flicker that passed across her face and he smiled in satisfaction. She said nothing, afraid that she might hurt herself even more if she tried to tell him what she really felt about his beloved Martine. It seemed the happy couple were actually getting nearer to naming the day and her heavy heart dragged her into a state of depression that was hard to hide. Somehow, she had to find a way to cope and still keep up a cheerful front for everyone, most of all the two little children she loved so very much.

For the next couple of days, Kerrien kept herself busy with a flurry of cleaning and cooking and preparing for Martine's visit. Much as she hated cleaning, she was not going to have the woman finding fault with anything or saying that standards had deteriorated since Kate's departure. By the time Brett called

243

to discuss plans for the next day, she felt quite exhausted and could make no sensible suggestions.

'Leave it to me, then. I have a few ideas. I'll come and collect you soon after nine,' he promised. It couldn't be early enough, she reflected, to make certain she didn't have to come face to face with Martine.

'Will you be staying over?' Ashton asked. 'You can if you like. As long as you're back for Sunday. Martine and I have a lot to decide and discuss, so I'll need you around to take care of Ben and Jodie.'

'Thanks, I might. If I do, I'll be back early on Sunday morning,' she agreed, thinking it would be a relief to avoid having to listen to any noises they may be making during the night. The prospect of listening to passionate moans or bed-creaking did not appeal! She certainly wasn't going to follow Kate's routine of putting clean sheets on Ashton's bed, 'just in case', as she used to smirk suggestively. If Martine chose to share his bed she'd have to put up with the sheets he'd used all week! She gave a shudder at her own thoughts, covering it by pretending she needed to check on the sleeping children.

Ashton followed her into the corridor leading to the bedrooms. He stood watching as she looked in on first Jodie and then Ben. Her tenderness when she looked at the sleeping pair, was obvious. What a splendid mother she would have made for them, he thought. He sighed, knowing that she was no longer available to him and wishing he'd been brave enough to say something earlier. Damn Kate. It was all her fault, pouring scorn on 'the nanny' all the time. She had propelled him towards Martine and though he admired the woman, he didn't feel a real deep love for her. He always said that he knew love was impossible to define. He had thought he loved his first wife but now he knew that they had both been too young and immature. Whatever thoughts crept into his head about resenting the children, he knew deep inside, that he owed his own survival to them. He would have given up on more than one occasion if he hadn't recognized his responsibility to them. But it was pointless wishing for the moon. He wouldn't spoil Kerrien's chances of happiness with Brett. If he enthused about his own forthcoming marriage a little, it might make her feel better. She might even confide in him about her own plans. Whatever happened, he wanted to keep her here with the children. Martine might come round a little in the end but she would never look after them like Kerrien did. Maybe the surprise plan they had cooked up for tomorrow would help make the children feel happier with his future wife.

'All sleeping soundly?' he asked brightly as she came back into the family room. 'Come and have a glass of wine with me.'

'No thanks,' she said. 'I think I'm getting a bit too fond of wine these days. I hardly ever drank before I came here.'

'It's good for you, as long as you don't drink too much.'

They sat companionably, chatting about inconsequential things. Suddenly, Kerrien felt the blood draining from her face and an involuntary shudder passed through her body, as Ashton started on a new topic.

'We're hoping to fix the date for the wedding, this weekend. Make some final plans and begin to get organized properly.'

Kerrien stared into space, feeling a noise like the wind rushing past her ears. She thought she might faint. At least she had a proper doctor in attendance to revive her, she thought grimly. She even took the fantasy a stage further, imagining his arms around her as he lifted her and the concern she would surely see in his eyes. He gazed at her expectantly, waiting for some reaction.

'That's nice for you,' she managed to whisper feebly.

'Once you've finalized your own plans, we can decide how things will work in the future.' His voice contained a slightly odd questioning tone, as if he was expecting her to say something more.

'I could do with an early night,' she blurted out, getting up. 'I have an early start in the morning.'

'Martine is coming mid-morning, with a surprise for the children.' Kerrien stared at him. What were they planning now? she wondered, but her pride wouldn't allow her to ask. No doubt she would bring some expensive present, hoping to buy a little affection, Kerrien thought uncharitably. She said nothing but a simple goodnight as she left the room. Ashton did not move. He sensed that she had finally slipped

246

away from him and didn't like the gap he felt deep in his innermost soul.

Brett arrived in good time and opened the car door for her in an unusually, gentlemanly manner. Ben and Jodie watched them depart, standing forlornly by the door, both with thumbs tucked into their mouths. Despite her assurances that she would soon be back, they looked unconvinced and very sad. Kerrien wondered whether to suggest that they came too, but knew that part of the plan for the weekend was that Martine should learn to get on with them. One day quite soon, Kerrien herself would no longer be a part of the little family. The thought made her want to weep.

'Right,' Brett said, once they were under way. 'Today we are starting at the top and working down.' Kerrien looked puzzled.

'Once, many years ago, this area was a volcano and we're starting with one of the craters.'

'I didn't know that. It isn't active is it?'

'My dear girl, I am talking centuries, millennia even, back in history. It's a rather splendid view from the top in fact and that's where we are going first. It's a park area now. After that, I thought we'd do a little shopping and finally, Mum has insisted we go back for dinner. She's protesting that you only spend time with me these days and she's missing out. What time do you have to be back?'

The view from high above the town was spectacular, even at ten-thirty in the morning. It was a warm, dry day and they could see for miles. They sat on a seat, relaxing as the winter sun poured over them.

'Kerrien,' Brett said rather tentatively. 'We spoke about the future when were together last time. Have you given it any more thought?'

'Brett, I don't know what to say,' she whispered unhappily. 'I just don't know. I mean I like you well enough and I'm proud to have you as a friend.'

'Marry me, Kerrien,' he burst out suddenly.

'Marry you?' Her voice rose in pitch as she spoke, shocked by the suddenness of his proposal.

'It isn't such a strange thing to ask, surely? Please say yes. I think I love you. Yes I do love you, I'm certain.' His voice was hesitant.

'Who are you trying to convince? Me or you?' she asked with a hint of a smile. Brett's blue eyes froze for a moment.

'I told you the other day, there's no such thing as this romantic love everlasting stuff. I do know I'd much rather spend my life with you, than anyone else I have ever met.'

'But would you still feel this way if we'd already made love? It isn't just because you want me to give in to you and I won't?'

'Don't be silly. Of course I want you. What man in his right mind wouldn't? You're pretty, you have beautiful body, a good mind . . .'

'And I'm kind to animals and small children,' she finished for him.

'I do love you, Kerrien. I'm certain of it and not just because you said "no". If you want to wait until we're married before we have sex, I'm willing to wait. I'll take the risk!' He smiled, his eyes full of warmth, passion and maybe, Kerrien wondered, just a little love? She liked him more than she had ever liked any other man, Ashton apart of course, but was it fair to go ahead with a marriage she didn't entirely believe in, just because she loved someone else in a different way? Perhaps that particular love was because the children came with the deal and she was possibly misinterpreting her true feelings.

'Say yes, damn you woman. Do I have to go the whole hog and sink onto one knee? I don't have flowers or champagne or the ring hidden in my pocket. Marry me Kerrien?' and grinning, he dropped onto one knee in the time-honoured tradition.

'I promise to think about it and I'm not saying no at the moment.'

'You are driving me insane, woman, do you know that?' His face was softened by a rare expression of almost tender longing.

'I'll give you an answer by the end of today. I promise.'

He looked momentarily relieved that he had not been rejected out of hand.

'You drive a hard bargain for a real beaut girl, as Mum calls you,' he laughed. He took her hand and kissed the long fingers gently. She was aware of his warm breath blowing over the back of her hand. He put his arm round her shoulder and planted a kiss on her soft lips. She drew in her breath, not unnoticed by the man. He may not be thrilling her the way that Ashton did, but he was really very special in his own way. She might not feel as if she'd suddenly come to

249

life every time Brett touched her fingers or the shock of emotional electricity if she brushed his arm. Not like with Ashton. But she remembered the thrills of excitement she had acknowledged when Brett had caressed her breasts, knowing instinctively that they were connected entirely with her own desires for fulfilment. It had been a totally involuntary response, one that she had found no difficulty in controlling. Had it been Ashton in his place, she doubted whether she could have stopped things going further, couldn't or wouldn't, she didn't know.

Before she was forced to make further comment, Brett had leapt from the seat and was pulling her up after him.

'Come on,' he said. 'We've go things to do. Places to see.'

They spent the rest of the morning exploring an area down near the river. They looked up at the graceful arch of the huge bridge, towering high above them. The traffic drove to and fro, unaware of the people watching them from somewhere far below. They walked past the art gallery and Kerrien remembered with a pang of guilt that she still not talked to Ashton about Kate. She resolved to do it at the first opportunity, before he found out in some less pleasant way.

As they walked, Brett casually took her hand. Occasionally, he tucked it possessively into his arm. They laughed a great deal. He was determined that they should not waste the day in serious talking, which might eventually lead them nowhere. Life was for having fun and he meant to show her just that.

Whatever she gave as her answer, at least he would know they had shared a good time.

They went into the shopping centre during the afternoon. They wandered aimlessly round, until Kerrien noticed that Brett was leading her towards a large jewellery store.

'We could just have a look at some engagement rings, in case you do say yes. Give me some idea of what to look for.' She was speechless. She had never given a moment's thought to buying rings and couldn't begin to think of what she might choose.

'I can't, Brett. I mean, it isn't the right time yet. I am thinking, I promise, but please don't try to pressure me like this.'

His face fell.

'I wasn't,' he protested. 'I wasn't trying to put pressure on you. I just want to do everything right and when we do get engaged, I want to buy the ring and present it to you. Isn't that what they do back in the UK? Pull out the little box and present it over a romantic meal. I want to try my best to make you feel it's all been done properly and comes up to your expectations. I may be an old cynic in some ways, but I can prove that your genuine Aussie has a little romance in his heart after all.'

Suddenly, Kerrien knew she was hearing not Brett's words but those of his mother. She felt a blush sweeping over her. Margaret had put him up to this, she was certain. But logic told her that he was certainly not a man to follow his mother's wishes, unless he wanted to. She was flattered to realize that

Margaret really did, genuinely want her to join the family. She could do worse, she believed. The family seemed well-off and Brett was certainly something of a catch. She would never have believed this would influence her but the temptation to have a settled, comfortable life was almost too much. At least Jodie could be her bridesmaid, whatever she thought about the wedding itself. A flood of pain swept through her body. Ashton and Martine were making plans, probably at this very moment. Kerrien's wedding would surely be an anti-climax for Jodie, even if she was a bridesmaid again. It all seemed so final. Her chance with Ashton was gone. Had it really existed except in her own imagination? It was too late now.

The expectancy on Margaret's face could hardly be missed. She rushed out of the house almost before the car had stopped. She was wiping her hands on a flowery apron and pushing back escaped wisps of hair from her face, so anxious was she to hear some news. Kerrien was aware instantly, that she had known Brett's intentions for the day, all along.

'G'day Kerrien, my darling girl, had a nice time?' She was nodding and smiling encouragingly but Kerrien could say nothing.

'Lovely day, thank you. It's good of you to feed me again,' she added.

'Come on in. Make yourself at home,' she urged.

'Must use the bathroom, if I may,' Kerrien asked.

Brett shoved his mother out of the room and Kerrien could hear the whispered voices rising and falling.

'For heaven's sake boy, do I get the champagne out or not?'

'I don't know Mum, she hasn't given me an answer yet.'

Kerrien listened in growing discomfort. She was beginning to feel coerced, trapped. If she said yes, it was going to be for all the wrong reasons. If she said no, she might just be acting foolishly out of some misplaced sense of romanticism. She went slowly back to the family room, where Brett was waiting for her.

'Do I get my answer yet?' he asked. The blue eyes were shuttered and she could read nothing from them.

'Yes Brett, yes I will marry you.' She wondered why she didn't feel a thrill of excitement when she spoke. She had no time for further thoughts as Brett flung his arms round her and Margaret and Lennie came rushing into the room, carrying a tray of champagne glasses and an ice bucket containing a bottle of Krug Grande Cuvée in honour of the occasion. Kerrien guessed that they could have had several bottles of an Australian sparkling wine for the same price!

'Congratulations my dears. Can't tell you how thrilled we are,' Margaret effused. Kerrien smiled and gave her a hug.

'You'll stay over of course. Then we can all get down to some serious celebrating,' she went on.

The whole evening became a strange sort of blur to Kerrien. She felt as if she was watching some bizarre movie in which she was the lead actress but no one had given her the script. Because they all seemed to be so excited and happy, she went along with everything, listening to the plans they all seemed to be making.

'Well, Son,' the usually silent Lennie began. 'Now you seem to be settling down a bit, I think it's time we went for some of those plans you're always suggesting. I've seen a great little unit over near Wellington Point and there's some nice houses near by. What say me and your mum set you both up? Call it a weddin' pressie if you like. I'll still expect you to pull your weight in the shops occasionally but mostly, you can spend your time developin' all that mumbo jumbo stuff you're always on about. What do you say?'

'Wow! Thanks Dad, thanks a lot. You're real beaut. You know it's just what I've always dreamed of. What do you think, darlin'?'

Kerrien was still recovering from the length of the speech from Brett's father. She had not entirely understood the implications, apart from grasping he was offering to buy them a house.

'It's very generous of you. I don't know what to say.' Her voice had become husky and didn't seem to be responding as she expected. Luckily, everyone assumed it was because of the highly emotional nature of the evening. Brett was sitting on the arm of her chair and kept putting his arm round her, in a mixture of possessive and protective gestures. Margaret's flow of words grew stronger and stronger.

'You don't have to say anything, love. Didn't I tell you my Brett would be after you the moment he clapped eyes on you? I can hardly believe it! To see him settled at last. It's something I've dreamed of but with all his flitting about all the time, I'd begun to think he'd never settle at all, let alone with a great girl like you.'

Kerrien felt worse and worse as the evening went on. She couldn't feel the ecstatic happiness that the rest of them seemed to be experiencing and gradually began to feel she may be making a colossal mistake. She despised her own decision as being purely mercenary. She knew her action may be subconsciously designed simply to make Ashton notice that she was about to slip away. She began to hate herself but couldn't extract herself now, not when everyone was so happy and in the middle of a celebration. She drank rather too much wine but as the others were in the same state, no one really noticed.

It was well past midnight before Margaret and Lennie left them alone. Lennie was about to open yet more wine but his wife nudged him, whispering so loudly that they all heard quite clearly!

'Show a bit of sense, love. These young folk want to be on their own.'

'Oh, yes. Right. What do you mean, love?' She sighed and almost bulldozed the large man from the room, calling out goodnights as they went.

Brett pulled Kerrien down beside him on the large comfortable sofa. He put his arms around her and pulled her close. Immediately, the hairs on her neck rose and she stiffened.

'Don't worry, darling, I'll remember my promise. No sex till you've truly got me hooked! I'll admit, it's going to be tough but, a promise is a promise. You know, it does make you something pretty special.' He leaned over and kissed her again, gently, undemandingly. She responded automatically, feeling a numbness throughout her entire body. She felt he could do almost anything to her tonight and she probably wouldn't even notice. She felt bile rising into her throat.

'I think I've had a bit too much to drink,' she muttered finally. 'Actually, I think it was a lot too much. I'm sorry, Brett . . .' she said as she leapt off the sofa and rushed to the loo. For whatever reason, she was violently sick. Deep inside, she knew it wasn't because of too much wine. Feeling ghastly, she stuck her head round the door of the lounge.

'Brett, I'm really sorry but I must go to bed. I have to get back early tomorrow and I feel awful.'

'You look awful. I'll get you something to settle your stomach. Must be all the excitement,' he suggested.

'I guess so,' she allowed.

Her heavy eyes the next morning were proof of a sleepless night.

'Must be all the excitement,' Margaret suggested.

'I guess so,' Kerrien agreed.

'Brett hasn't surfaced yet. You haven't seen him, have you?' The unsubtle question didn't pass her by. Obviously, Margaret had expected them to spend the night together and she was mildly surprised, given Brett's reputation, that they hadn't. Kerrien thought about her own mother's attitudes and knew that she and Brett really were worlds apart.

'I have to get back early. Ashton wanted to go out today so I promised I wouldn't be late. Do you think Brett will mind taking me?'

'You could take my car if you like. I don't really need it and then you can bring it back in a couple of days and he can drive you home afterwards. We need to sort everything out, for the wedding and all.'

Without waiting to see Brett again, Kerrien accepted the offer and made a hasty exit before anyone tried to change her mind. She thanked Margaret, genuinely grateful for the care and friendship Margaret had shown her. Kerrien only wished that she herself felt as happy about everything. They kissed affectionately and she left.

'Come and see us soon,' Margaret called after her as Kerrien drove carefully out into the quiet road. The car was larger than she was used to and she drove more slowly than usual. It was after nine by the time she drew up outside the bungalow. Martine's car filled the entrance to the drive so she had to leave Margaret's car parked on the roadside. She noticed a new piece of wire netting had been placed across the side of the house, preventing access to the back garden. She let herself into the quiet house, assuming everyone was still in bed. A tide of noise erupted from the back and looking into the garden she saw Ben, Jodie and Ashton hurtle across the lawn in pursuit of a large puppy. It was a deep russet colour and had huge, fluffy paws. She opened the screen door and went into the garden. The puppy saw her and leapt up to her immediately. It was all legs and flapping ears and a huge pink tongue flopped out of its mouth.

'Kerrien, Kerrien, we've got a dog!' Jodie squeaked excitedly.

'So I see,' she laughed.

'Got a dog and it's ours,' Ben informed her.

'He was very naughty in the night,' Jodie went on. 'Daddy had to sit with him nearly all night 'cos he kept howling.'

'And howling and howling,' Ben assured her.

Kerrien was amused. She wondered how Martine had taken that. It must have quite put an end to any expectation she might have had of passionate love-making. It wouldn't have mattered after all, Kerrien thought, if she had been there. Then she realized that *she* would probably have had the chore of sitting up with the puppy.

'He's a setter,' Jodie said proudly. 'He's called Lloyd.'

'That's an unusual name,' Kerrien said. 'Who thought of that?'

'Martine did,' Ashton said, speaking for the first time. 'Lloyd was her idea. We went to collect him yesterday. She'd arranged it all through a friend who breeds them.'

'That was nice of her,' Kerrien said politely, gritting her teeth as she tried to sound pleasant. 'And did she help you sit up with him, all night?' Ashton glared. It was unlike Kerrien to sound catty. He knew that Martine's sole purpose in organizing the dog, was to encourage the children. By giving them something

258

they wanted, she hoped she could become closer to them. So far, it had been a disaster. The setter puppy had wet on her shoes, a pair of designer Italian leather sandals. Just before that, he had torn her long flowing skirt that she assured Ashton was made of Thai silk, fiendishly expensive and specially made for her by a little dress-maker friend. Ashton wondered why she had worn something so unsuitable for the occasion but realized that she never really gave any thought beyond how elegant she looked, regardless of what might be happening. Kerrien in her leggings was more much sensibly dressed.

The puppy rolled on its back in front of Kerrien, waiting for his tummy to be tickled.

'You're a beauty, aren't you little dog? Great ploppy paws and waggy tail.' She rubbed his tummy and was rewarded with a lick on her nose before he leapt up and raced off round the garden again. The two children streamed after him, calling his name over and over. It was not a name they would have chosen, but then Martine would only tolerate a designer type name to go with a pedigree dog. Thinking about it, his fur was a similar colour to her hair. They would make a handsome pair, Kerrien thought smiling at the prospect.

'Martine not up yet?' she asked innocently.

'She was exhausted after her day with the children so she's having a lie-in. We had a Chinese for supper and I don't think it was entirely successful. It wasn't Cantonese enough for her and anyway the children hated it. Actually, they were rather naughty about it

259

and kept saying it wasn't like "your things." Don't think Martine was too impressed.'

Kerrien gave a secret smile. She knew it was really being bitchy but she was delighted that the children had seen straight through Martine's attempts at bribery.

'Look,' Ashton went on, 'She's so exhausted that I promised to take her somewhere nice for lunch. Saves you the bother of cooking for everyone.'

'Oh right,' Kerrien said, adding wickedly, 'and you're taking the children too?'

He blushed slightly.

'We want to discuss our plans. We didn't have the chance yesterday, what with one thing and another.'

'Martine really gave Lloyd heaps when he wetted her shoes,' Jodie said almost conversationally. Kerrien chuckled.

'I bet she did. I can imagine you didn't have much time for talking. Setters are notoriously difficult to train. Your time will be fully occupied with Lloyd, I expect.'

'You do like dogs, don't you Kerrien?' Ashton asked suddenly.

'Oh yes. I love them, but I wouldn't want to get in anyone's way. Obviously, Martine will want to be involved in the training. She will be the mistress of the house won't she?' Without saying a word, they both knew immediately that Martine's idea of being the mistress of the house would stretch no further than parading two well-behaved, well-dressed children and an immaculately behaved setter at some orchestrated event. The rest of the time, someone else would be expected to look after them, feed, care for and love them.

'Did you have a nice time?' Ashton asked, changing what was becoming a painful line of thought.

'Yes thanks,' she said, trying to sound casual. 'Bit too much to drink last night. Actually, Brett is still sleeping it off. I came back in Margaret's car. It's still parked in the road as there wasn't enough space in the drive.'

'Special occasion was it?' he probed.

'As a matter of fact, yes it was. Brett and I got engaged.' She spoke the words unemotionally, her voice flat and only a trifle wobbly.

The deep pools of Ashton's eyes clouded. He felt his heart miss a beat and a cloud of deep despondency settled over him. It had happened at last, just as Martine and Kate had said it would. Why should he feel like this? After all, he was about to go out with the woman he was to marry, to make arrangements for his own wedding. Summoning all his strength, he put an arm round Kerrien and kissed her on the cheek.

'Congratulations, Kerrien,' he mouthed. The words were indistinct and his voice husky. 'Only five months in Australia and you're going to be a true blue Aussie, if only by marriage.'

'Marriage?' came a languid voice from behind them. 'Who is getting married?' Martine leaned against the door, clad only in the briefest of negligees. The puppy rushed up to her and began to leap up at her.

261

'Get him off me can't you? Wretched beast is scratching my legs.' The children rushed over, grabbing at the excited puppy quite unsuccessfully. Kerrien leaned out and caught him as he rushed past her and took him tightly by the collar.

'Sit, Lloyd,' she told him firmly, pushing on his rump as she spoke. Instantly, the little animal squashed its bottom on the floor and sat panting.

'Kerrien made him sit, Daddy,' Ben said quite unnecessarily.

'Your Kerrien is quite the wonder woman,' Martine drawled.

'Kerrien and Brett are engaged,' Ashton said in a calm voice. He had regained control of his emotions.

'Does that mean you're going to leave us, Kerrien?' wailed Jodie, tears springing to her eyes.

'I'm not sure yet. Probably not,' Kerrien assured her hastily.

'Why don't you marry Daddy instead, then you won't have to leave us ever?' asked the little girl.

'Because Daddy is marrying Martine,' she said, hoping Martine hadn't heard. She looked at the other woman, searching for some indication of the woman's reaction.

'I *should* go and dress. We're going to Lennons for lunch. We're considering using it for the reception.'

Having sat still for a couple of minutes, Lloyd gave a wriggle and escaped from Kerrien's restraining hand. He dashed across the garden but this time Jodie did not follow.

'Even Lloyd doesn't like her,' she mumbled. She took hold of Kerrien's hand and pressed it to her lips. 'We want you to stay with us, Kerrien. Not Martine.' For once, her nanny didn't try to stop her comments about their father's fiancée.

CHAPTER 13

However much she tried, Kerrien could not feel as happy and excited as most women should when they have just agreed to marry someone. The whole time, her heart was telling her it was a mistake. It was a gloomy trio who sat down for lunch. Ben and Jodie didn't want to eat and spent much of the meal time grumbling about the way Martine had made them try chop-sticks, taking it all much too seriously. It made a sharp contrast with the similar but hilarious meal they had shared with Kerrien and Ashton.

'She's so boring,' Jodie complained at last.

'But she bought you Lloyd. He's the sweetest puppy ever, isn't he?' Kerrien snapped in exasperation. She was heartily sick of defending the woman and basically, shared their views, though she knew she could never have admitted it in front of the children.

'I wanted to call him something else but Martine said he had to be called Lloyd because it was all to do with his proper kennel name. I do think he is lovely though, even if she did bring him,' Jodie conceded. 'I specially liked it when he peed on her posh sandals.

You should have seen her face, Kerrien. It was excellent.'

'Exlunt,' Ben agreed.

'Why didn't Daddy take us all out for lunch?' Jodie asked.

'They have things they need to talk about,' Kerrien replied, feeling waves of nausea in the pit of her stomach. They should be about up to discussing dresses, flowers and all the other trimmings Martine doubtless expected on her great day.

It was four-thirty by the time they returned. Martine's good humour was fully restored and she was bursting with the news that they had chosen 30 April as the date for their wedding. Just a few weeks away, Kerrien thought dismally.

'If you've chosen the same date, you can always change it,' Martine announced briskly.

'Or you, yours,' Kerrien muttered under her breath. Smiling sweetly, she said that they had not yet fixed anything but that they would keep it in mind so they didn't clash.

'I shall put announcements in the main papers, then the people we actually invite will be fore-warned. I think we must limit it to two hundred guests don't you darling?' she told, rather than asked, Ashton.

'Sounds like about one hundred and ninety too many,' Ashton muttered.

'Nonsense, darling. It will be difficult enough to cut it down to two hundred. It will be quite splendid. I am so looking forward to it. We wanted to ask you Kerrien, you will be staying on won't you? We shall certainly need you to take care of the children while we're on honeymoon if you can manage that. We can discuss long-term later. Do you still fancy the Caribbean, darling, or shall we look at something nearer . . . the Far East or Bali? No, Bali's totally overrun with tourists nowadays. Quite spoilt.' She went on and on about clothes, flowers, the people who should or should not be invited. Ashton had become quite glassy-eyed and was responding automatically, whenever it became clear that she was waiting for an answer. Kerrien and the children went out for a long walk with the puppy.

At last, Martine left, promising to phone very soon to keep Ashton up to date. From the expression on Ashton's face, it was quite clear that he was not interested in the elaborate plans. He couldn't help but feel out of his depth in the midst of such enthusiasm. He could see that Kerrien was equally uncomfortable. She looked pale and strained. He assumed it was as a result of her party the previous evening, when she had admitted she had drunk a little too much. That, followed by coping with the children and the lively new pup, must have taken its toll on her. He tried to cheer her by asking about her own arrangements but as they were only in the early stages, she had no real responses.

'*You* won't have long to organize everything,' Kerrien suggested.

'I shall leave everything to Martine. She seems to have it all worked out.' His voice was flat and unemotional. It seemed that both forthcoming marriages had failed to make either of them happy or excited participants.

Wednesday was Ashton's free afternoon. He asked Kerrien if she wanted to go out on her own but she was seeing Brett later that evening, when she returned Margaret's car and she declined his offer. She was certain he must have a lot to do. With a wedding of such grandeur to arrange, she was sure that he would need every available moment. He seemed totally disinterested in the whole affair. They all played in the garden with the puppy when the children came home from school. Lloyd really was a delightful little puppy and his antics lightened everyone's mood. They were making so much noise that none of them heard the telephone ring. They had installed an answering machine since Kate's departure, as the house was often empty particularly when Kerrien fetched the children from their schools.

The flashing light indicating a message was noticed first by Jodie. She had learned which buttons to press and came bouncing out into the garden.

'Daddy, Kerrien, Aunt Kate rang,' she announced. 'She's on her way over.' Ashton and Kerrien stared at each other with a sense of shock. Guiltily, they realized that no one had mentioned Kate for a couple of weeks. She certainly had not been missed.

'How do you know, darling?' Ashton asked.

'I pressed the buttons and heard the message.'

They all went into the house and listened to the message. Kate's voice filled the room. She sounded irritated and her comments about the answering machine made it quite clear what she thought of its introduction.

'Ashton,' Kerrien began. 'There's something I think you should know, before Kate arrives.' She could put it off no longer.

'You look serious. Is something wrong?'

'Not exactly. I don't quite know how to tell you. I'm not sure what your attitude will be.'

'Now you have got me worried. Come and sit down.' Ashton looked concerned, wondering what on earth Kerrien's news could be. Noticing the children were hanging onto every word, Kerrien paused.

'Why don't you go back into the garden with Lloyd?' she suggested. 'Leave Daddy and I to talk for a few minutes?'

'We want to know as well,' Jodie said.

Further conversation was interrupted as the door bell rang, followed by the sound of a key in the lock. The door into the room opened and Kate came in. At the same moment, Lloyd chose to dash across the floor, dragging a cushion he'd managed to capture from the sofa.

'Kate,' Ashton said feebly. 'What a surprise.' His face took on a grim expression, as he remembered the last occasion they had spoken, before she had stormed out.

'What's that creature doing to the place?' she demanded, indicating Lloyd who had now settled down quietly to chew his cushion.

'He's our dog,' Ben said firmly. He sounded defensive and it was obvious that he preferred the new regime to that of his aunt.

'Dirty, nasty creatures. I hope you are taking the proper precautions to ensure the children don't contract toxocariasis. Very nasty that can be. You surely don't approve of them having this creature?' she snapped at her brother.

He stood in the middle of the room with the slightest hint of a smile on his otherwise impassive face.

'I suppose this was your idea?' she accused Kerrien.

'Martine gave him to us. He is called Lloyd and he's a dog, not a creature. And he hasn't got any of that whatever you said was nasty. He's a dear dog and you can't make us stop having him.' Jodie's brave words suddenly became too much effort for her and she collapsed into tears, running to bury her head against Kerrien.

'Perhaps you'd be kind enough to take the children and that thing outside so I can talk to my brother. I have a number of things to discuss with him.'

Without a word, Kerrien took the children's hands and led them out. She went back for Lloyd and removing him and the cushion together, shut the door firmly behind her. However much she wanted to hear what was being said, there was no way she would allow the children to be exposed to the two adults having a blazing row. It was getting dark outside but Kerrien had put coats on the two children.

'Shall we take Lloyd for a little walk?' she suggested. 'It'll be fun in the dark, won't it? We'll just go a little way. Perhaps Auntie Kate will have finished her talk when we get back.'

'We aren't allowed to call her Auntie. She says it's childish. We have to say Aunt Kate.' Jodie was already showing the same sullen, withdrawn expression she had when Kerrien first arrived.

'She isn't coming back is she?' asked Jodie anxiously.

'We'll have to wait and see,' Kerrien replied. She hoped that whatever was going on inside the house, wouldn't take too long. She was supposed to get over to the other side of town to return the borrowed car. She glanced at her watch. Whatever Kate intended to say to Ashton, it would have to be postponed or done in front of an audience. She couldn't be expected to keep the children outside for much longer. It was dark and beginning to get cold. Besides, they were waiting for their tea and she still had things to do before she went out. Clutching the children firmly by their hands, the dog lead held in between herself and Jodie, she turned them back into their own drive. She put her key in the lock, drawing breath to announce their arrival when the sound of raised voices reached the little group.

'You really are a selfish bastard,' she heard Kate shout.

'Selfish? You dare to call me selfish? You think only of yourself. All your martyrdom, caring for the children, giving up your own career, it was for yourself. You had nothing in your life except interfering with other people. We only moved here to get away from you but you insisted on following us, then moving in. I think you actually drove Jane away you know.'

'That mealy mouthed little worm? She was nothing more than a spoiled brat . . .' Kerrien could stand it no longer. The pair of them were digging up every old complaint they could think of. It could do no good. It served no useful purpose to go on screaming at each other this way. They would both end up saying things they might regret for ever. She knocked hard on the door and went into the room.

'I'm sorry but it's too cold and dark for the children to stay outside any longer. We have come in and will wait in the dining room until you've finished. I must get the meal ready in about five minutes. Are you staying for tea Kate?' She smiled at the woman and was consoled by the flicker of discomfort in her eyes.

'I won't stay where I'm not welcome,' she snapped. 'I only came to offer my services for the wedding. I read about it in the paper. Pinned you down at last, has she?' Kate suggested with a sneer curling her lips.

'I'd have thought you'd have been pleased,' Ashton retaliated. 'It *is* what you always wanted after all.'

'It would have been nice to have been told personally, rather than having to read it in the paper.'

'Perhaps if we'd known where you are living these days?' Ashton suggested.

Kate gave a loud sniff.

'Congratulations anyway,' she said but the sincerity in her voice was non-existent. She was obviously disappointed that he had managed something without her intervention, Kerrien decided.

'Do stay for tea, Kate. Then you can continue your conversation. You can reassure yourself that the

271

children are well and being properly cared for.' Kerrien tried hard to sound welcoming but she was even more uncomfortable with the woman now, than when she had first met her. She'd forgotten how much more restful life was without Kate's intervention.

'We're only having fish-fingers and oven chips,' she added wickedly, knowing Kate's opinion of such food. It was worth the criticism that followed, just for the sake of seeing the expression of disgust cross her face.

'Aren't you going out tonight?' Ashton asked her suddenly. 'Don't make yourself late.'

'I'll phone and cancel it. I can go tomorrow, no worries.' She walked out of the room, not waiting to give him the chance of disputing her decision. She wouldn't miss the chance to put forward the truth as she saw it. Kate was not going to bully them any longer.

Brother and sister continued to shout at each other, despite Kerrien's warnings that the children could hear. She stuffed the rather less than healthy meal into the oven, made her call to Margaret and went back to the children. They were sitting with thumbs in their mouths, huge eyes peeping out of white scared faces. Ben was sobbing gently and Jodie looked frightened.

'Come on. What's wrong?' Kerrien said putting her arms round the two little ones.

'Daddy never shouts,' Jodie said in a flat voice.

'He's just cross with Aunt Kate for leaving us and then coming back unexpectedly.'

'Don't want her back,' Ben announced firmly.

'She always makes us do things and doesn't tell us nice stories,' Jodie added.

'But she loves you both. Very much. She only wanted to do her best for you.' Kerrien had slipped back into her role of making excuses for people. It made her feel somehow disloyal to herself and the children, having to stand up for things she actually disapproved of. Even Lloyd was sitting with his tail down and his head firmly on his paws, as if he understood that things were not quite right.

When Kerrien went back into the family room, the conversation ceased suddenly and she knew they had been talking about her. Kate started to collect her things, a coat she had discarded and her handbag.

'Don't you think of leaving yet. I haven't finished,' Ashton commanded in an unusually loud voice. Kate put her things down, glaring at her brother. She was not used to being spoken to like this. She looked uncomfortable, as if she was annoyed that everyone was managing without her. She even stayed for tea, a meal eaten with few words spoken. The children were withdrawn and even sullen. They picked at their food, usually a favourite meal which they only had as rare treat. Ashton and Kate left most of theirs, the tension of the occasion being too great to allow any politeness or civilized conversation.

At the end of the meal, Kerrien took the children through to the bathroom, deciding an early night was the best solution to the tensions. By the time she went through to join the others, their raised voices had calmed. They were discussing plans in a more sensible way, though Kerrien noticed that Kate still constantly interrupted with her own views.

'I think it would be better for me to return for a while, when you're away. I don't believe this girl should be left in sole charge of two small children. How do you know she won't bring that beach bum here the minute your back is turned?'

'Her fiancé, you mean?' Ashton said with a cynical smile curling his lips.

'So she's got him at last has she? His money too much of a temptation, I suppose?' Kerrien drew in her breath but managed to control the protest she had been about to make. After all, perhaps Kate had a point. She pondered that line of thought herself at times.

'She's no less suitable to care for my children than you are,' Ashton stated calmly.

'What? When she runs after anything in trousers all the time? Don't be so naive.'

'Excuse me,' Kerrien burst out, unable to maintain her composure any longer. 'Just because I happen to enjoy male company makes me no less suitable than you, who prefer female company!' There. She had said it.

Kate blanched. She looked at the girl murderously.

'You don't know what you're saying,' she snarled.

'No more do I,' Ashton said coldly. 'Perhaps you would be kind enough to explain what you mean, Kerrien.'

She didn't know how to begin. Kate could so easily dismiss what she was saying as mere conjecture. Suddenly, she felt inexplicably afraid. Suppose she wasn't correct? Suppose what she had witnessed at the

274

art gallery was nothing more than two friends together, sharing an interest. She'd often accused Kate
of jumping to conclusions. Wasn't that exactly what
she was doing right now? She took a deep breath.

'I saw you with your companion at the art gallery
one afternoon.'

'What do you mean Kerrien, *companion?*' Ashton
asked in a voice as cold as steel. He rose to his feet and
stood looking out of the window, as if he couldn't bear
to witness the truth. Kerrien longed to put her arms
round him and hug him, protect him from what was
happening.

Her eyes sought Kate's. There was an almost
desperate light in them. She could almost see Kate
begging her not speak. But that was nonsense. She was
becoming fanciful, imagining things.

'No big deal,' she said in a casual voice that belied an
inner trembling that would scarcely stop. 'Kate's
chosen companion is another female. Being gay
doesn't mean she is unsuitable to look after children, any more than being heterosexual makes me
unsuitable.'

'Gay? Is this true Kate?' Ashton's voice sounded
like thunder.

Kate lowered her gaze. She looked desperate. She
obviously wished herself anywhere but there. Then
she gained some sort of composure.

'As she said, it's no big deal.' Her voice sounded
steady and she had regained her old confidence.

'But why did you never say anything? Why didn't
you confide in me?' Ashton was shocked at the

revelation, not because of its implications but because he hadn't known. He'd believed that he knew his sister and his own lack of observation had failed to tell him something so fundamental.

'How could I?' she asked. 'How could I when you were always so busy? You didn't want to know about me or anything I cared about.'

'Who is this person?' he asked, suddenly curious. She had rarely met other people as far as he knew but then what *did* he know?

'Emma.' Her voice was flat and without any emotion.

'Who's Emma?' Kerrien asked.

'Only the previous nanny. The one whom *Kate* decided was unsuitable to look after the children and told me to get rid of. What a devious, manipulative woman you are Kate. I'm ashamed to have you a sister.'

'Now you realize why I could never confide in you,' Kate said dangerously calmly. She picked up her bag and coat and quickly left the room.

'Kate,' Ashton called after her but it was no good. She was closing the door behind her.

'It isn't her sexuality that bothers me, not one bit,' he tried to explain. 'It's her deviousness. She could have told me instead of engineering Emma's dismissal.'

'Perhaps she couldn't cope with living under the same roof and keeping up the pretences,' Kerrien suggested.

'It's her everlasting holier than thou attitude. She

was being so two-faced. Always critical of everyone else and all the time leading a double life. When was it you saw them?' he asked.

'A couple of weeks ago, I suppose. I could never quite pluck up the courage to tell you.'

'That's what you wanted to say that famous night when everything went wrong, wasn't it?' His voice was softer now that his anger had dissipated.

'Yes. But I wasn't sure how you'd take it. Just as Kate had no idea and she's known you all her life. She's still the same person, don't forget,' Kerrien said gently.

'But all that endless criticism. Running you down, and Emma come to that. If she is supposed to love Emma, why did she insist on her dismissal? Doesn't make sense to me.'

The phone rang and the answerphone cut into the ringing. They heard Brett's voice.

'Kerrien? I was worried honey. Everything all right? Please call me back when you can. Bye.'

'Go and phone him,' Ashton insisted. 'I and my family have messed you around enough for one day.' He got up and went into his room. 'Goodnight,' he called out. With a sigh, Kerrien picked up the phone and returned Brett's call.

Something woke her in the middle of the night. She put her light on and lay, hardly breathing, waiting to hear the noise again. It was a strange sound, a long moan. It was the sort of noise children make when they are trying to scare each other with ghost stories. She got out of bed and went out into the corridor. The moan came again, from Jodie's room. Softly, Kerrien went into the room, calling Jodie's name. The moaning continued and she crossed to the bed.

'Jodie? What is it love?' The child suddenly gave a heart-stopping scream and woke up. She was sobbing violently and put her arms round Kerrien's neck, hanging on so tightly that it almost hurt.

'Don't let Daddy shout any more. Don't let Aunt Kate come and make Daddy cross again. I'm frightened. I don't like anything any more. Everything is changing and I hate it all. I want to go back to when it was just us.'

'It's all right, darling. Go back to sleep now. I'll stay with you for a while. Would you like that?' Kerrien whispered.

'Yes please. Will you come in my bed with me. Just for a little bit?' She was racked with sobs so that each word came out in a gulp. Kerrien cuddled up to the little girl, lying on top of the covers. Somehow, she too felt strangely sensitive and vulnerable in view of Kate's visit. Soon, Jodie's breathing became deeper and more even. Certain she was asleep, Kerrien carefully slipped her arm from under Jodie's head and quietly left the room. She peeped in at Ben to make sure that he was still asleep. He was too little to realize the implications of all that had been going on, she thought with relief.

She felt heavy eyed and had a blinding headache the next morning. It was easily explained by all the tension that had been surrounding her, not to mention the disturbed night. Luckily, Jodie seemed to remember little about her traumas and appeared almost her usual self. Ben had dark rings under his eyes and was obviously feeling the stress in his own little way. Ashton too, looked as if he had hardly slept and grabbed a cup of coffee the moment he came through the kitchen door.

'Everyone all right today?' he asked with forced brightness, of no one in particular.

'We don't like you shouting, Daddy,' Jodie announced. 'I woke up in the night and cried a lot. Didn't I, Kerrien?'

'You did, but it was soon all right again, wasn't it?' Kerrien was mistaken if she had thought it was all forgotten.

'I'm sorry. I didn't hear anything,' Ashton muttered guiltily.

'It was because of you shouting at Aunt Kate. We don't like it when you shout. And we don't like Martine. She doesn't get on with children, I heard her say so.' Jodie spoke in a petulant voice, quite unlike her usual gentle manner.

'Now you're being rude,' Ashton warned. 'You never used to be rude, whatever else you were.'

Jodie looked rebellious and her bottom lip curled out, settling firmly beneath the top one in a gesture that plainly said, *think what you like, I've had my say*.

'What is it you don't like about Martine?' Ashton demanded. 'She does try to make you like her. And she did bring Lloyd for you.'

'She smells all scenty,' Ben complained, exactly the

way Jodie had first said it to Kerrien. She smiled, waiting for the next bit.

'And she keeps calling us *dears*,' Jodie came in scornfully, right on cue. 'She doesn't really care about us and expects us to be quiet all the time. I don't think she really knows how to *play* anything.' Kerrien stared at Ashton waiting for his reply. The children were perfectly correct in their assessment and she wondered how their father was going to reply. His face looked grim.

'You are being rude and unfair. Martine has never had much to do with children and she's trying very hard.'

Who's he trying to convince? Kerrien wondered. The children were right, Martine saw them as inanimate objects who inconveniently needed attention at times. She seemed to expect them to be well-behaved, clean and quiet all the time. Not unlike Kate's wishes, she thought ruefully but at least Kate loved them and did try to please them, just a little. The time Martine had spent with the children trying to get to know them, had been short and she'd relied mostly on Kerrien to keep them occupied and attend to their needs. However much she had come to love the little pair, there was no way Kerrien could bear to live with the family when Martine moved in. She could foresee endless conflicts, battles about what they should and should not do. It could never work, even if the love she felt so deeply for their father had never happened. She was engaged to Brett and even when they were married, she knew that the sight of Ashton and

Martine as a married couple would be a constant reminder of what she had lost.

'Go and clean your teeth,' she told the children and once they were out of earshot, she told Ashton of her decision. For the children's sake only, she would stay till the wedding and subsequent honeymoon was over and then she would leave. She made the excuse that she and Martine were never going to see eye to eye over their up-bringing. She also told him that the upset to Jodie in the night, had been entirely caused by the row that Kate and Ashton had had the previous day. She said that *she* felt that Jodie should not be exposed to such conflict and therefore it would be best if she left.

Ashton was tight-lipped. Inside, he knew that everything she was saying was true. Martine was not going to find it easy to take over the ready-made family but she had been very much the driving force behind the match. He did not pretend to know her motives but he knew that, flattered though he was, he didn't truly love her. How could he when he had given his heart to the English girl standing before him, lecturing him on his short-comings. But he must never tell her. He must not spoil her future. She was soon to be married herself and to a handsome, no doubt exciting younger man and one who could provide a secure, if undemanding future for her.

'We shall, of course, be very sorry to see you leave. The children love you and . . . well, you will be very difficult to replace.' His voice was low and he was struggling with emotions he dared not show. For one heart-stopping moment, Kerrien thought he was going to say he loved her, just as the children did, but he had stopped and said something quite different. It was hopeless. She collected the car keys and called the children for school. Luckily it was kindy day for Ben so she would have time to herself to think, later.

The children were desperately upset when their father told them that Kerrien had decided to leave once he and Martine were married. Their sobs distressed him more than he could have imagined. He had chosen to break the news while she was out with Brett, on their date postponed from the night before. Whatever he said to comfort them had made no difference.

'We thought she loved us,' Jodie sobbed.

'I'm sure she does,' Ashton replied, giving his daughter a cuddle. 'But she is going to be married herself soon and she has to leave us to start her own life.'

'We love Kerrien,' Ben said firmly, 'and she loves us better than Brett.'

'Why don't you marry Kerrien instead of Mrs Smelly?' Jodie asked rudely.

'Kerrien doesn't want to marry me. Now, you two. Off to bed. I don't want to hear any more nonsense about all of this. I'm sure we'll be able to find you a new nanny soon.' They knew when they were beaten. If they said any more, Daddy would get cross and they hated him to be unhappy with them. Holding each other's hands, they slowly left the room and Jodie put Ben into his bed, clinging to him unhappily as if she thought they might be wrenched apart at any moment.

Ashton made a decision. Martine was going to come over and try her hand at looking after the children on her own. He would find some excuse for Kerrien to be out of the way and to contrive his own absence on some pretext, once Martine was here. He smiled to himself, pleased with his plan. It would surely give him an idea of the true nature of the relationship his fiancée hoped for. He telephoned her and invited her to share the weekend once more. Immediately, she began rattling off lists of things they should discuss, things they must make time for. He said nothing of his plans to her, the children or Kerrien. He would suggest to the latter that she should go and stay with Brett's family, much as he disliked the thought of pushing them together under the same roof. But, it was a situation he had to accept and he was sure she'd be pleased to have some extra time off. She too, had plans to make, after all.

When Martine arrived on Saturday morning, Ashton and the children were playing in the garden with Lloyd. It was cold and they were wearing coats. Almost as soon as she arrived, Ashton went in to answer the phone. He had left a message with Margaret for Kerrien to ring him on some pretext, when she arrived. On cue, the call came. When he returned to the garden, Martine was looking uncomfortable, fighting off the lively pup who wanted to play at tug of war with anything he could get hold of. In this case it was her soft leather handbag. The children were laughing at the spectacle of the little dog and the elegant women sharing a battle of wills. Martine grimaced, trying not to show how she detested the hilarity and trying to retain some composure. Stifling his grin, Ashton called to them.

'Bad news, I'm afraid. I have to go out on a call. One of my older patients who refuses to see the duty doctor. Sorry, but I'll try not to be long. I expect there's something in the freezer you can cook for lunch if I'm not back. See you later.' And without further explanation, he got into his car and drove away.

'Get this animal off me,' Martine immediately demanded. Jodie went over and grabbed his fat little rump. She pulled him off and he finally relinquished his hold on the handbag, but not before he had ripped a sizeable hole in the leather.

'Damn,' she exploded. 'You have no idea how much this cost, have you, dog?' She smiled sweetly at the two children who were watching the spectacle intently.

'Shall we see what we can find for lunch?' she suggested.

'We only like roast chicken,' Jodie announced.

'Yes,' Ben agreed. 'With roast potatoes.'

'And we don't eat cabbage or carrots,' Jodie continued, noting the contents of the vegetable rack. None of it was true, of course, but those seemed like the most difficult things she could think of on the spur of the moment.

'Right,' Martine said uncertainly, 'you two go out and play with Lloyd and I'll see what I can do.' She took off her tailored suit jacket and rolled up the sleeves of the cream silk blouse she wore beneath.

'You can borrow Kerrien's apron if you like,' Jodie

284

suggested, passing her a plastic one with *Best Cook Ever* emblazoned on the front. She made a slight move of disgust and put it on.

'We can't go out 'cos it's raining,' Ben announced cheerfully. He was beginning to enjoy this game. 'I'll let Lloyd in 'cos he's getting wet.' As Ben slid the screen door back, the soaking puppy scampered into the room. He shook and rolled on the floor, making large wet patches. Ben rushed after him, making Lloyd wild with excitement and then both of them slipped over and crashed into the bookcase. It teetered and finally toppled over. The tangle of legs, wet puppy, books and a desperate Martine trying to separate them, reduced the former order to total chaos.

'The sink's overflowing,' Jodie said in a matter of fact voice. Martine had put a frozen chicken in the sink with water running over it. There surely couldn't be much to roasting a chicken, she thought, providing she left it to thaw.

'Damn,' she snapped, leaving the mêlée on the floor.

She finally sent both children to their rooms; tied the dog outside on the veranda, where he howled pathetically, and began to tidy the books back onto the shelves. She put the chicken into the microwave and left it to get on with cooking itself.

'I need a drink,' she muttered, delving into the cupboard to find something. She poured herself a glass of wine and sipped it gratefully. She gritted her teeth and made a renewed effort to organize lunch. She wasn't going to be defeated by a badly trained dog and a pair of kids. Damn Ashton for landing her with all this. She had expected an ordered household with Kerrien either cooking or leaving a prepared lunch and Ashton talking to her while keeping an eye on the children. Really, it was too bad of him.

He phoned, leaving a message for them to continue lunch without him. He said he was going to be delayed indefinitely. Martine, juggling with potatoes and vegetables, didn't manage to reach the phone before the message cut out.

'Is lunch ready yet?' Jodie asked, peeping round the door. 'Only we usually have it at one o'clock and it's nearly half-past.'

'Not quite yet,' Martine said, as calmly as she could. 'Shouldn't be long.'

'Only Ben's wet himself and I can't find any clean pants for him.'

'Why didn't he go to the toilet?' Martine asked.

'You said we had to stay in our rooms,' Jodie answered smiling sweetly.

By the time Ashton returned around four, he found Martine lying on the sofa with a moist flannel over her forehead. The children were sitting on the floor, thumbs in mouths, watching a cartoon on television. Lloyd was sprawled flat out between them, exhausted by his earlier prolonged barking.

'Had a nice day?' he asked cheerfully.

'No,' said both children, without removing their thumbs.

Martine lifted a corner of the flannel and shook her head.

286

'I'm sorry darling but I've developed a migraine. I shall have to lie down in my room. Thank God you're back.' She rose and tottered out, clutching the door for support as she went. Her cloud of perfume was mingled with smells of cooking and, could he also detect just a hint of burning? Or perhaps that was from somewhere else, he wondered, noting a blackened pan sitting in the sink.

'How about telling me exactly what's been happening?' he asked the children. They scrambled up beside him on the sofa and began to recount the day's events.

CHAPTER 14

'When Kerrien gets married to Brett, can me and Ben go to live with them please?' Jodie asked one morning during the following week.

'Jodie, don't be silly,' Kerrien said in horror. Whatever would Ashton think of such a suggestion?

'Why do you say that, Jodie?' he asked.

'Well, you want to live with Martine and get married to her and we don't like her 'cos we like Kerrien best, so you must like her more than you like us, so it seems the most sensible thing to do.' The mixture of childish logic and understanding was almost laughable in its simplicity.

'Jodie, I could never love anyone more than I love you and Ben. It's a ridiculous suggestion. Love doesn't work like that. You don't suddenly stop loving someone when another person comes along. I didn't stop loving you when Ben was born. I was able to love you both, just as much. It's like having a balloon without any air in it. When you blow it up a bit, the balloon stretches. You can then blow it some more and it stretches again. This balloon is so big, you can never fill it quite full. Love is like that. It sort of stretches.' The little girl seemed to accept the explanation but then her expression changed.

'If you keep blowing it up for ever, the balloon bursts,' she said. 'I think your balloon must have burst and all the love fell out.' She left the table and went into the other room.

Ashton looked down. He felt tears burning at the back of his eyes but couldn't let anyone see them. He felt as if his world was falling apart. A while later Kerrien left the table to find Jodie. In the hall-way, a stream of water greeted her.

'Jodie? Where are you? What's happening?' she called. In the bathroom, Jodie was standing in the growing stream of water. She had both the sink taps turned on full and began to dance in the water, jumping up and down, splashing everywhere.

'It's fun isn't it, Kerrien? Ben, Ben!' she shrieked suddenly. 'Come and have some fun Ben.'

Kerrien turned the taps off, horrified at the mess and the cause of it.

'What on earth has come over you?' she demanded. The little girl looked sullen. 'Come on, I'm waiting for an explanation.'

'Nothing come over me, except the water. It's fun. I like being naughty.' She laughed, almost hysterically and dashed from the bathroom, trailing water from her sopping slippers.

'Ben, where are you?' she shouted. 'Come and see what I've done.'

Kerrien shook her head. The action was so unlike

anything Jodie had ever done before. With a sigh, she lifted the dripping mats from the floor and put them in the bath. She collected a mop and bucket and set to work drying up the mess. Ashton came in and fumed. He was very angry and bellowed at Jodie. She stared defiantly at him, the two pairs of identical deep greeny-brown eyes glaring at each other.

'Answer me. Why?' he shouted at the child.

'I wanted to,' she shouted back. 'It was fun.'

'Let's see if you think it's such fun when you're the one who has to clean it all up,' he snapped, flinging a towel at her. 'Get on with it. Start drying, now.'

'I'll be late for school,' she scowled.

'Tough. *You* can have the pleasure of explaining why you're late.' Then he spoke to Kerrien, 'I'll drop Ben off. No reason for him to suffer.'

Jodie made a poor show of her task. The carpet in the corridor was so wet it would probably have to be professionally dried, Kerrien thought. Once the worst of it was cleaned up she would try leaving a heater on but she knew that it probably wouldn't work. She told Jodie to get ready for school and that she would try to finish off the drying later. By the time she went out into the drive, Jodie was already sitting in the car. She looked pale but her eyes still flashed with deep seated anger. Suspecting she already knew the answer, Kerrien asked Jodie to tell her why she had done such a naughty thing.

'I wanted Daddy to know how very much I don't love him any more.' The jumbled answer would have made her smile at any other time.

'You know that isn't true. You do love your daddy, of course you do. You just feel angry, don't you?' The child nodded. 'Is it Martine?' She nodded again.

'You were pretty awful to her the other day. Fancy saying you only eat chicken. She's seen you eat other things before, so that was a silly thing to do, wasn't it?'

'But she isn't nice to us. She thinks we're a nuisance. And I don't want to be a rotten bridesmaid. She'll only moan that I'm holding the flowers wrong or my tummy sticks out.' Kerrien stifled another grin. Jodie had the woman well summed-up. Martine's priorities were definitely not child orientated.

Jodie's teacher was cross with her for being so late but she had to assume it was not her fault, as she was always driven to school by Kerrien or Ashton. After the poor start, Jodie's behaviour apparently became worse. Kerrien was distressed to receive a phone call during the afternoon, saying the little girl had been very naughty again and asking if there was something wrong, some reason for her extraordinary behaviour. Kerrien did not feel it was her place to make any comment and so said that Ashton would call them later. She knew it was a case of passing the buck but it didn't seem unreasonable. Kerrien sighed. She knew exactly why Jodie was behaving this way but she was quite unable to say it to Ashton. Besides, if she said anything, he would think it was sour grapes on her part, simply because she disliked Martine.

It was a strained and tense evening when Ashton finally came home. He was late. He had problems with various things at work and was obviously very tired.

Kerrien hated having to draw him into another set of problems but these would not go away. He took Jodie into her room and they talked quietly for some time. When he finally came through, his body seemed to be sagging with weariness. His beautiful eyes were clouded and the long lashes were swept downwards as if he couldn't bear to look directly at anyone. Silently, Kerrien cleared away the last few dishes and made some coffee. Almost speaking to himself, Ashton muttered, 'It's not as if I have ever truly failed them. I've done everything in my power to give them the best life I could. I thought having Martine permanently around would be the perfect answer.'

Kerrien longed to take him in her arms and hug him, just as she would hug Ben when something went wrong. Instead, she placed a mug of coffee near to him, gently taking his hand and putting it on the handle. He looked up at her.

'What have I done wrong, Kerrien?' he asked. She hesitated, How could she say anything, even though he was asking her directly? His fingers were clutching her arm and causing a fire that seemed to be spreading through her body. She realized with a start that subconsciously, she had been avoiding any contact with him, remembering how she reacted to his physical presence. Even this tiny touch was enough to make her burn inside. Why didn't she feel like this with Brett? If she did, there would have been no question of waiting for marriage before they made love. If anything, she would have been the one who needed holding off! She felt her own eyes grow misty with the deepest feeling of love she had ever known. Her particular balloon was almost full to bursting just with love for Ashton! She dragged herself unwillingly back to earth. He was almost a married man! She prised his fingers off her arm, feeling a sense of loss as their grip slackened. His eyes held an intensity that she didn't understand. The colours seemed to be swimming together green, brown merging into cloudy pools of great depth. She opened her mouth to speak but found she could make no sound. It was altogether too dangerous to be close to this man.

'I need a large brandy with this,' he muttered. He pulled himself up and went to the drinks cupboard. He took out a new bottle of cognac, a present from a patient at Christmas and never touched until now. He poured a measure into a brandy balloon and took a long swig. He coughed slightly as the liquid burned down his throat.

'Help yourself,' he offered, pushing the bottle towards Kerrien.

'I don't think this is a good idea at all,' she said quietly.

'Don't be a spoilsport. Come on. Try a drop or two or three.' He emptied his own glass and poured himself a second drink. He took out another glass and poured a measure for Kerrien. She sipped at it cautiously. She never usually drank spirits but enjoyed the sensation of the burning liquid trickling down her throat. The coffee following it tasted hotter than usual and she felt the warm glow spreading over her body once more, only this time for a different reason. Perhaps this was why people drank such drinks, to reproduce the glow that others could get from sexual contact with another person.

Ashton seemed to be getting quite morose. The down-side of too much to drink, Kerrien told herself primly. He should have known better.

'Perhaps you should think of going to bed,' she suggested.

'Can't *stop* thinking of it!' he muttered.

'You'll soon be married, Ashton, then all your wishes will be granted.' She tried desperately to keep her tone light.

'Not sure I can wait much longer' came the gruff voice. Kerrien felt her heart grow heavy in her chest. Tight bands of pain seemed to clamp themselves around her, making her breathing grow restricted. Was he trying to tell her something that his drunkenness prevented him from explaining properly?

'I'm in love, Kerrien,' he was mumbling. 'I'm so much in love.'

'Yes,' she answered, hating this conversation. 'I know you're in love, that's why you're getting married.' She began to try and help him up, steering him towards the corridor and his bedroom.

'You're wrong you know,' he went on. 'You've got it all wrong. I'm in love with the wrong person,' he said at last. 'What d'you think of that? The wrong person.' But Kerrien wasn't listening to what he was trying to say. His almost dead weight was too much for her. She was strong enough for most things, but the weight of a drunk man standing over six foot tall, was too much for her. He slumped forward and they both fell into a heap on the floor of the corridor, still wet from its morning soaking. She wriggled to get out of the tangle of limbs and he put his arms round her, seeking comfort from the depths of his stupor. However much she had longed for this moment, the reality was all wrong. If he had been sober, perhaps she might have enjoyed it. In his present state, it was quite obvious that he was totally unaware of what he was doing and the person he was with. What did he mean, he was in love with the wrong person? He was obviously upset about something but he simply didn't know what he was saying, she told herself. After much heaving and struggling, she managed to drag his inert body to his own room. She somehow dumped him on his bed and covered him with a duvet. Doubtless he would have one king-sized headache the next morning. She snapped off the light and went back to the family room. She took Lloyd out for a last run in the garden and shut him in the laundry room, where they had decided he could do the least harm. The little furry body shook with pleasure as she gave him a cuddle. Must be nice to have such an uncomplicated life, she thought, putting him gently into his bed. She looked in on the sleeping children, wondering how they would fare in the future when she was not there to protect them and give them the love they needed. Ashton did love them, it was obvious, but he seemed surprisingly uncertain of himself, considering his profession. Perhaps he was able to compartmentalize his life, giving so much to his work that there was very little left for home. She shut their doors and silently wished them goodnight. She looked in on Ashton one last time. He seemed to be sleeping peacefully, snoring gently. She wondered if such excessive drinking was a usual occurrence when he was with his fiancée, and how Martine felt about that little weakness. Kerrien hoped she hated it.

With an almost guilty start, she realized she hadn't once thought about Brett, the whole evening. For someone who was supposed to be in love enough to get married, she was a complete failure. She shared Ashton's conviction: she too was in love with the wrong person. She still wondered what he meant by it but decided it could have been nothing more than drunken mumblings. Perhaps he really did have a drink problem. Hadn't she read somewhere that doctors were one of the most vulnerable groups? Surely, though, he was too intelligent to let it get out of hand? Could that be the real reason his first wife had left? But surely not – this was the first time Kerrien had seen him the worse for drink and he obviously had a lot of problems to cope with at the moment. 'Oh well,' she sighed and took herself off to bed.

Both children were very subdued the next morning, much to Kerrien's relief. She didn't want a new conflict to begin when Ashton woke up with the hangover he must surely be suffering. Hopefully, she would be able to get the children to school before he emerged and they wouldn't need to know anything about the previous night. Lloyd had been good and was very pleased to see everyone, as he went rushing into the garden. He was gradually getting the idea of being house-trained and was becoming less trouble.

'Be good today,' Kerrien called as Jodie got out of the car at her school. The little girl waved and skipped in through the gates. Perhaps yesterday had simply been a difficult day for her too. She dropped Ben off at nursery and went back to face Ashton. Miraculously, he was up and dressed and finishing a cup of coffee, looking fresh and relaxed.

'Morning,' he said, fairly cheerfully. 'I don't remember the last bit of last night. As I was in my clothes when I woke up, I can only assume I made a bit of a fool of myself. Sorry.'

'Apology accepted,' Kerrien smiled. She felt relieved that she did not have to face another scene.

When the phone rang later in the morning, Kerrien waited to hear the message rather than lift the receiver. She had an instinctive, bad feeling about the call and her worries were immediately justified. It was Jodie's teacher again. She requested that either Kerrien or Doctor Philips should go to the school and collect her. Jodie was being quite impossible and seemed very distressed about something. She asked that her father should deal with the problem, as it was obviously something home-based. Kerrien set off immediately, once she had phoned the surgery. It seemed important that Ashton should know about the problems as he should be involved. Again, she shut the unwilling Lloyd into the laundry room. There was nothing else she could do and she promised the pup a long walk later. His mournful eyes indicated that he did not understand what she said and his sad expression added to the feeling of gloom that had begun to descend once more.

Jodie was tight-lipped and rebellious when she came out of the school, though she clutched Kerrien's hand tightly.

'Why, Jodie? Why are you doing this?' she asked. 'It isn't like you to be so naughty.'

'P'raps I'm not really me any more. P'raps someone came and swapped me in the night.' Then she clamped her mouth shut and refused to speak again.

'I promised Lloyd an extra long walk today to make up for having to be shut up for so long. Shall we both go with him this afternoon?'

Jodie shrugged her shoulders and gave a non-committal grunt.

Ashton came home for lunch in a furious mood.

'What is going on?' he demanded of his daughter.

'You're shouting again, Daddy,' she said with a supercilious look, not unlike Martine's expression.

'What do you expect when you behave like some yob,' he snorted. 'How do you think it makes me feel to hear you are sent home from school because you're too naughty to stay? Honestly. What has come over you?'

She stared her father directly in the face.

'Martine,' she said simply.

'I don't know what you mean,' he replied in a voice that was so clipped and tight that the words were almost spat out.

'If you marry Martine, I don't think I can ever be

good again.' Her voice sounded surprisingly adult and carried a venom that came from somewhere deep inside.

Ashton went white. How dared she? This was his own six-year-old daughter trying to run his life. What did she know about anything?

'Come on darling, I think you should stay in your room for a while,' Kerrien urged diplomatically. The way things were going, one or both of them would say something that could destroy their relationship, possibly forever.

'Can Lloyd come in with me for a bit?' the little girl asked, very close to tears.

'Just this once,' Kerrien allowed, 'but keep an eye on him if he misbehaves.'

In the family room, Ashton's face was clouded. He sat with his chin resting on his hands, staring into space once more.

'What should I do, Kerrien?' he said at last. She shook her head.

'If I marry Martine, I could lose my daughter, possibly forever. If I don't marry her, I may be losing my own last chance of happiness.'

'Perhaps you should delay the wedding for a while,' Kerrien suggested. 'Give Jodie time to get more used to the idea.' A tiny flicker of hope shone in her mind.

'Impossible,' he said. 'Martine's too far into organizing everything. She wants to move in here, to get the kids used to it. I've resisted so far but I think it's the only way. Jodie might come round if Martine's here every day.

The tiny flicker of hope drowned in the torrent of dismay that washed down into the depths of Kerrien's soul. The situation was getting worse by the minute.

'I must get back to work,' Ashton said leaping up suddenly.

'But you haven't had any lunch,' Kerrien protested. In the midst of all the drama, she hadn't even started to prepare anything. He shook his head and left the house. She would scramble some eggs for the children and cook a proper meal later, she decided. She called them both through when the simple meal was ready but neither of them replied.

'Ben? Jodie? Come on, your meal is ready.' She could hear no sound from either bedroom and went through to see what was happening. Not even Lloyd was to be seen. They must have gone out through the rear laundry door and, hopefully, just into the garden. She went outside to look but there was no sign of them. She called again, her heart beginning to constrict with anxiety. She looked into the cubby house and there, a small huddled group of two children and a wriggling dog were sitting in the dimness. She crept in after them.

'What are you doing hiding in here?' she asked, squatting down on the floor beside them. Lloyd wriggled free of Jodie's restraining arms and greeted her like a long-lost friend.

'See?' Jodie cried triumphantly. 'Even Lloyd likes you best. He peed on Martine's shoes but he likes you. Dogs are never wrong.' Kerrien smiled.

'I'm quite sure it was an accident when he ruined

Martine's shoes. Puppies are like children, they don't always mean to wet themselves. Accidents just happen. Now, why didn't you come when I called?'

'Jodie didn't let me,' Ben said firmly.

'Tell-tale,' Jodie teased him. 'We're having a protest. We're having a sit-in.' She was quite adamant in her intentions.

'Where did you learn about such things?' Kerrien asked curiously. It seemed a strange thing for such a little girl to say.

'Telly,' she said briefly.

'I see. And what are your terms for ending this sit-in?'

'For Daddy to marry you instead of Martine.'

Kerrien felt tears springing to her eyes. If only . . . There was nothing she would like better but Ashton loved Martine and there was nothing she could do about it.

'Listen to me. You can't tell grown-ups what they should or shouldn't do. When you grow up, you wouldn't want Daddy to tell you who you should marry or what you should do about anything. Believe me, I know.'

'Don't you love us?' Jodie asked.

'You know I do. I love you very much.'

'And Daddy? Don't you love Daddy?'

Kerrien was quite floored. She did love their daddy. She loved him passionately, intensely and with all her heart and soul but much good it did her.

'Of course. He's your daddy isn't he?' She hoped she had twisted the emphasis sufficiently for when

301

they inevitably repeated this to their father. 'Now, I have made a bowl of scrambled eggs and if we don't go in now, they'll be spoilt. Are you hungry, Ben?'

'Starving!' the little boy replied.

'We can't let him starve, can we Jodie? Bet you're hungry too and Lloyd must need to go outside as well. Are you coming?'

'Told you. It's a sit-in.'

'If you insist. But Ben and Lloyd and I are going to have something to eat. You can come if you like.'

Stubbornly, the little girl sat firmly on the floor, her legs curled up round her. She didn't want to lose face but her tummy was rumbling very hard. Perhaps she should postpone the sit-in till after lunch. Besides, if she started it later, Daddy would be home to see it as well. She scrambled to her feet and ran inside after the others.

As they took Lloyd for his long walk, Kerrien tried to make Jodie talk as much as she could. She wanted Jodie to try and come to terms with the huge changes in her little life and somehow persuade her that it was for the best. Ben went along with whatever Jodie said. He accepted things that happened without rancour, perhaps without understanding the true implications. Whoever their father had chosen to marry, it would mean a lot of changes for the two children. For Jodie, however much she wanted a new mummy, almost anyone would do, except Martine. How ironic then, that she was the one that Ashton had chosen. Kerrien knew she had never really seen the best of the woman she considered her rival. She had only experienced the

302

established doctor talking to one of her 'underlings'. Kerrien was a paid employee as far as Martine was concerned. Somewhere deep inside the superficial veneer, the woman must have qualities that made Ashton love her. She was undeniably beautiful and had wonderful taste in clothes, and men, Kerrien added ruefully. Kerrien was reasonably pretty but could never compete with the other woman. She was only a nanny, nothing like in the same league, despite the teachers at her old school desperately wanting her to take up a University place she could so easily have gained. Training to be a nanny had meant she could stay at home and look after her mother and begin to earn money much sooner. She fantasised about the future that might have been, had she followed her studies. Perhaps she too could have become something important in the medical profession. But then, she would never have come to Australia and never met Ashton. She had forgotten her intentions to talk to the children and had spent most of the walk dreaming about herself.

'We'd better go back now,' she said at last. 'We'll cook something special for tea. Daddy missed his lunch, so we need to make up for that. What shall we have?'

'Frogs' legs on toast,' suggested Jodie.

'No frogs,' Kerrien retorted.

'Chocolate pie,' suggested Ben.

'No chocolate,' Kerrien capped.

All the way home, the children made ridiculous suggestions, their minds so busy thinking of silly things they had quite forgotten their worries by the time they got back. It was good to hear them laughing again and Kerrien's black mood lifted a little. She got the children involved in helping with the dinner preparations. Jodie peeled some of the potatoes and under strict supervision, Ben chopped the carrots.

'You will tell Daddy I made the carrots, won't you?' Ben asked anxiously.

'Of course,' Kerrien promised, stroking the little boy's dark curls. Innocent blue eyes stared up at her. He was so unlike his father and sister.

'And I did the potatoes?' Jodie piped up. She was trying hard to make up for her earlier bad temper. By the time Ashton returned, the mood was altogether brighter. He looked relieved. He played with the children while Kerrien finished the cooking and laid the table. He bit his lip, hating the thought of spoiling this happier atmosphere with his news. He had called Martine and they had agreed that she should move in at the weekend. Permanently. He had other things to face besides telling the children and Kerrien. He had his own personal problems that he had not yet over-come. Somehow, he had managed to avoid letting Martine sleep in his bed, until now. He knew that she would expect, probably demand to share his bed when she moved in. He was not sure how he would cope. What the world saw as a confident doctor, an attractive single man, was very different from the real man he knew lurked inside. The final unhappy years married to Jane had completely convinced him. He *knew* he was a rotten lover! Martine was so overtly sexual, she would expect so much more. He could never understand why she seemed so enthusiastic about marrying him, when she could have had any man she desired. But if she was happy with him, who was he to argue? If he couldn't have the woman he wanted, Martine was surely a wonderful second best?

He decided he would wait to break his news until after dinner.

CHAPTER 15

Things seemed almost normal during the cosy family meal. The children were much more relaxed and obviously happier. They played with the little pup after the meal, rolling round the floor and laughing at his antics. Ashton watched them, taking pleasure in watching his children and Kerrien fooling about. Somehow, he could not picture Martine romping around on her hands and knees like Kerrien was doing. At last, Kerrien stood up protesting.

'We'll have indigestion all night. Let's sit and do something quiet now.' Ashton drew in his breath. It was time.

'Actually, I have something to say to you all,' he began. 'This is as good a time as any.' Kerrien lowered her eyes. She could guess what he was about to say and she didn't like it, not one little bit.

'Martine is going to move in here soon. On Saturday, actually. It seems like a good idea for you to have the time to know her better before the wedding.' Stony silence greeted his statement.

'She will bring her all things over on Saturday and

get them sorted out properly. Then she'll stay. Not go back home,' he went on, desperately trying to fill the widening gap in the conversation. 'You'll enjoy seeing all her pretty things, won't you? Perhaps she'll let you help her to find places for everything.'

'No thank you, Daddy,' Jodie said quietly. 'I'd rather not have anything to do with her.' Silently, she rose from her seat and went through to the bathroom. Sounds of washing and teeth brushing reached them and finally she went into her bedroom and shut the door firmly.

Kerrien broke the silence in the family room by suggesting to Ben it was time for him to go to bed as well. He made no protest and said nothing to Kerrien as she got him ready. She looked in on Jodie but the light was out and there was no sound. She crossed to the bed and leaned over in the darkness, wanting reassurance that the child was indeed there and had not just left a pillow strategically laid under the covers.

'Goodnight, darling,' Kerrien whispered, knowing she was not yet asleep. She heard no response and sighing gently, left the room. If Jodie wanted to be alone and quiet, she would not intrude.

Ashton was already pouring himself a brandy when she went back. He had settled down in front of television, though he was obviously not watching the programme on household repairs. She cleared the dirty dishes away and set the dishwasher to work. The tension was unbearable and the atmosphere so oppressive that Kerrien decided to go to her own room and read. She could not bear to see the man she loved so very much, drinking himself into another stupor. If he wanted to abuse himself this way, she didn't have to watch.

'Goodnight,' she said suddenly. 'I'm going for an early night as well. Hope you don't mind.' She knew she would still have gone, even if he did mind. He could put himself to bed tonight and if he did get drunk again, he would be pleasing himself and impressing no-one. She heard him go out a little later and hoped he had left Lloyd somewhere safe. She didn't fancy the idea of a distressed puppy keeping everyone awake all night. She fell asleep, worn out with the emotions of the day.

The memory of Martine's imminent arrival came back to settle over her like a dark cloud, when she woke the next morning. She wondered when and if Ashton had gone to bed. A shower woke her fully and she prepared herself for another day. In just two days, her life would change as much as the children's and she wasn't sure how she would handle it. Ashton was fast asleep on the sofa when she went through. His face was unshaven and he was still wearing the clothes from the previous day. He looked unkempt, vulnerable and almost child-like. She felt a wave of tenderness sweep through her, wishing fervently that she could scoop him up and wipe away his worries. A squirming bundle wriggled out from his arms. The little dog had fallen asleep with his master. Ashton must have taken him for a walk when he went out last night. The bottle of brandy was firmly corked on the side and, as far as she could tell, no more drunk from it. Ashton must have been too tired to go to bed. He yawned and stretched. He felt stiff from the cramped position and watched as Kerrien put the pup out into the garden.

'Didn't have you to oversee my bed-time rituals last night,' he grinned. 'Sorry to give you the shock of seeing me like this. I'll go and change and shave, before the kids catch me out as well.' Kerrien smiled, relieved that he had stayed on the sofa through tiredness alone and not because he was too drunk.

The children were quiet during breakfast and Jodie seemed especially thoughtful. They went to school without any protest and Jodie walked sedately up the school path. Kerrien hoped there would be no repetition of the previous day. Ashton had spoken to the teacher and tried to give some sort of explanation. Drearily, Kerrien went home and cleaned the house. Soon, she would no longer be in charge and memories of Kate's bossy regime, almost forgotten now, came pouring back. Martine would be quite a different prospect and would doubtless make sure that Kerrien knew who was the boss. Nor, did she suppose, would Martine try her hand at cooking again, after the last series of disasters. But, she decided, there were limits to what she would do for the woman and she knew she would have to make sure her duties were made clear, right at the start of the new arrangement. She was, after all, a trained nanny and not the chief cook and bottle washer she had been since Kate's departure. Her main obligation was to the children and their care and welfare. Anything else she had been doing, was through her own goodwill and definitely not part of her official duties.

At breakfast on Friday morning, the two quiet children were munching their cornflakes with an air of gloom. Suddenly, Jodie put her spoon down and asked,

'Please can we have a take-out tonight? It's our last evening alone together and it would be a sort of final celebration party, before everything changes.'

Kerrien looked from the little girl to Ashton. His mouth tightened, before he spoke.

'You make it sound a bit like the last supper,' he tried to joke. The serious expression on Jodie's face did not alter.

'It's the last time we'll all be here together, just us as a family. Everything is going to change tomorrow when *she* comes.' Obviously, in Jodie's mind, nothing had changed her attitude towards Martine and she saw this as a last happy fling before her own misery set in forever.

'I think that would be a lovely idea, don't you Ashton?' Kerrien said, noticing a flicker of relief crossing Jodie's face.

'Fine,' he agreed, 'but it isn't the end of everything when Martine comes. It will be the start of all sorts of new things to enjoy.'

'It might be for you but not for us. Don't forget Kerrien's leaving when *she* comes.' The adults exchanged glances. It seemed pointless to continue the conversation.

'Indian or Chinese?' Ashton asked.

'Take-out,' Ben shouted. They all giggled, lightening the otherwise, growing tension.

'Chinese, please,' Jodie chose.

'Right. I'll call for it on my way back. Around six OK for everyone?' He wondered for an instant whether to invite Martine to share the meal but decided against it, in view of Jodie's comments. Besides, she would be busy packing her possessions for the move from the other side of town. Somehow, he did not feel the enthusiasm he had expected to feel. He was too concerned about his own problems. But, if the children wanted a little celebration, who was he to complain? When Martine called during the day to ask him to come over to help her with the packing, he said the children were having a little party but he would come if he could. Once the children were in bed, there would be no need for him to stay at home. Perhaps he might even be able to limit the number of belongings she was planning to bring over. There was little enough empty space, he realized, without an extra person in the house. There was always Kate's room, which had been left as it was, untouched since her sudden departure but he didn't want to change anything there, in case she did ever need it again.

Kerrien was determined it would be a happy evening, however miserable they were all feeling inside. She found some of the shiny paper left from Christmas and made little crowns for them all to wear. She blew up some balloons to add to the festivities and hung them over the dining table. It may have seemed silly but she wanted the children to enjoy themselves and remember the evening with pleasure. Even if she cried all night when she went to bed, no one else need know how unhappy she felt.

Ben and Jodie watched her efforts with great excitement. Their mood was lighter and they seemed to have accepted the situation. Ashton arrived right on time with the collection of foil boxes and spread them out on the hot tray to keep warm. His mood, too, seemed good and he was obviously excited at the prospect of the woman he loved coming to share his home. Kerrien pushed the thought away. She would let nothing spoil this evening. They all tried eating with chop-sticks, hilariously tossing them aside for spoons and forks when they decided they might starve otherwise. They played word games, sitting at the table, Ben and Kerrien against Jodie and Ashton. There was a lot of laughter and every now and then, Jodie gave Ben a wink. After half an hour, they called it a draw. Jodie leaned over to Ben and whispered something. The boy nodded and both asked if they could be excused.

'We're tired. We want to go to bed now and we'll put ourselves to bed. Goodnight.' Jodie seemed strangely excited and almost conspiratorial. Ben trotted behind her obediently doing everything he was told as usual. Kerrien moved to get up and follow but Ashton put his hand on her arm restraining her. Surprised, she looked at him.

'They're planning something,' he whispered. 'Don't spoil it, whatever it is.' Kerrien relaxed, as much she was able, with his hand still resting on her arm. She felt the familiar rush of blood tearing round her body at his touch. He smiled at her and she felt every inch of her body turn to warm liquid. How could the man have such an effect on her and yet seem so completely in control himself? The sounds of the children cleaning their teeth, followed by doors shutting, interrupted her thoughts.

'Perhaps *I should* see what they're doing?' she questioned as silence followed. Both bedroom doors were shut tight and the children had obviously settled themselves for the night. She opened Ben's door quietly and peeped in. 'Goodnight Ben,' she whispered and was rewarded with a tiny snort of laughter. She smiled, sending her own invisible waves of protective love over the little boy. She called goodnight to Jodie, softly and gently, loving her as much as she did her little brother.

'There's something for you in the fridge,' the child whispered. Then she snuggled down and would say no more. Kerrien was intrigued and went to the kitchen where Ashton was already loading the few dirty dishes into the dishwasher.

'Are they OK?' he asked. 'Can't think what's come over them. They never go to bed voluntarily like that. Not for me anyhow. Shall I put the coffee on?'

'Jodie says there's something for me in the fridge. I never noticed anything, did you?' They opened the door and sitting in the rack was a bottle of champagne. It had a large envelope attached to it, tied on with a bit of ribbon.

'What on earth . . .?' Kerrien began. 'How did she get hold of this?'

'I think it may have been from the box in the garage. I hope so anyway. Shouldn't like to think of her going to the shop on her own and them serving her! I have several crates of wine out there but you must have noticed them. What's in the envelope?'

Her fingers trembling slightly from emotion, she pulled out the card.

'*Dear Daddy and Kerrien, Congratulayshuns on getting engayjd. We love you both. Love From Ben and Jodie*' The writing was large, crooked and done in various coloured crayons.

'I don't understand. What do you think she's getting at?' Kerrien asked.

'Isn't it obvious? Wishing makes it so. It has been very clear what they wanted for a long time.' Ashton's voice was soft and thick with emotion. 'They think perhaps we needed a push and this was their way of giving it to us. Hadn't you better open it? Shame to waste all their efforts.'

'You do it. I'll get the glasses,' Kerrien mumbled. She was still confused about the message it contained. Could the children think she and Ashton were engaged after all? No, they couldn't possibly, not after all the problems of late. The cork shot out with a loud pop. They both laughed, suddenly shy. It was almost as if they had only just met for the first time. Was it her imagination, or did she hear the faintest sound of laughter outside the door? She smiled. She wouldn't spoil the children's fun by going to look.

Ashton poured them a glass each and lifted *his* glass for a toast.

'To the future and two of the best kids a dad ever had.'

'To the future, whatever it holds,' Kerrien drank. The slight noise outside the door came again. She looked at Ashton, who shrugged. They sipped the cold champagne and she wondered again, how Jodie had organized it all and what she hoped to gain. It was too late to make any changes now, Ashton himself had said so.

She sat down, feeling relaxed despite her whirling thoughts.

'Wonderful stuff this champagne. Think I could get hooked on it,' she said at last.

Ashton moved to sit beside her and poured her another glass. She smiled at him, a smile that was trying to say how much she loved him.

'Shall we drink to us?' he whispered.

'Why not,' she agreed, emboldened by the effects of the wine.

'To us,' they said, twisting their wrists round each other's so they moved very closely together as they drank.

'Kerrien, oh my dearest Kerrien,' he said suddenly. She started. What was he saying? 'I love you, Kerrien.'

'You can't. I mean, Martine! Brett!'

'I'm sorry. I shouldn't have said that. You're engaged to be married.'

'So are you. Did you mean it?'

'What? That I love you or that I shouldn't have said it?'

'I love you too, Ashton. I seem to have loved you forever.'

'But what about Brett?'

'Self-defence I suppose. You got engaged and I knew I'd lost you.'

'You got engaged first. I only agreed to marry Martine when I thought it was too late to ask you.' They stared at each other and burst out laughing.

'Poor Martine,' Kerrien exclaimed.

'Poor Brett,' Ashton echoed and they laughed again. 'Come here you amazing woman,' he ordered reaching out for her. He put his arms round her and drew her close to him. His hungry lips sought hers and together they plunged into the deepest wildest kiss either of them had ever known. His tongue probed her mouth and she responded. His body pressed against hers and the fire became molten desire, each longing to fill and be fulfilled by the other. He pushed her away and stood up. She felt suddenly bereft and hurt. What had she done wrong? But she need not have worried. He put his hand out and pulled her to her feet. Again he pressed their bodies closely together so that she could feel his hardness against her own body. His desire was clearly as strong as hers.

'Not in here,' he whispered. 'Not in front of the puppy!' She smiled at the little dog. His tail wagged, as he sensed someone was on the move. He rushed to the door hopeful of another walk but neither of them took any notice of him. The mood was shattered by the

phone shrilling. Martine's petulant voice came over
the speaker as the answering machine cut in.

'Darling? Where are you? I'm desperate for your
help. I need at least half a dozen more suitcases. Call
me back immediately.' She plopped the phone down
with a bang. Kerrien stared at Ashton. What was he
going to do?

'Thank heavens for the answer phone. Shame I
didn't hear her message till too late. Now, where
were we?'

He drew her close again and led her to the door.

'My place or yours?' he whispered.

'Yours is further from the children,' she smiled. Her
body was shaking with the longing. Was this really
happening or was it just another dream? They walked
hand in hand along the corridor to his room. Though
she had cleaned it and made his bed nearly every day,
it seemed a different, unfamiliar place here in the
darkness. He switched on the soft bedside light and
held her away from him so that he could look at her.

'I want to undress you slowly, so I can look at every
inch of you and explore your beautiful body, a little at
a time.' He began with the pale blue silk blouse she
had worn in honour of the little party. He unbuttoned
it, revealing a white lacy bra. Greedily, his mouth
sought and found the raised nipples, through the lacy
fabric. He teased them, awakening desires she hadn't
known existed before. His hands holding her arms
pressed deeply into her flesh as their mutual desire
grew, producing its own exquisite pain. He drew away
and she waited impatiently for her next pleasure centre

to be unwrapped and teased into life. He unzipped her
trousers and pulled them away. He caught his breath
with pleasure as he gazed at the newly exposed flesh.
He kissed her everywhere but left the very centre of
her being alone and untouched till the very end. He
pressed her down onto his bed and she relaxed,
anticipating his body covering hers and wanting to
feel his entire length against her own. His eyes, deep
pools of passion looked into hers, plumbing the deep
blue depths of her inner soul.

'Beautiful Kerrien. Love me back, just a little, my
darling.'

'I do love you, Ashton.' To her shock, he rolled off
her and lay on his back. He was still fully clothed and
waiting for her to uncover his body. She realized what
he wanted and began very slowly to unbutton his shirt.
She smelled his musky male scent and felt as if she
might faint from sheer pleasure. He wriggled impatiently as she found her way down to his trousers. Still
painfully slowly, she unzipped him and gradually
pulled out his shirt from the restraining waistband.
She ran her fingers over the soft blond hairs covering
his chest, bending to kiss his nipples. They too
responded, hardening until a low moan escaped from
his lips. He moved to grab her, but she pushed him
down again. He smiled up at her, the love deep in his
eyes. How much he had longed for this moment, never
believing she would ever be his. She pulled his
trousers off roughly, caressing his long firm legs as
she removed them. Then she pulled down his briefs.
He was beautiful – hard and straight and ready for her.

He lay back, waiting for the woman he loved to caress him. He opened his eyes again and watched in disbelief as she left the bed and went to the door. She surely couldn't have teased him this far, and not intended to make love with him? He leapt up, suddenly angered.

She turned at the sound.

'What's the matter?' she whispered.

'What do you think?' he snapped.

'I'm just making sure the door is locked. I couldn't face being interrupted by the children.' He fell back onto the bed, laughing in relief.

'Oh Kerrien . . . I thought you'd changed you mind for one desperate moment.'

'Oh dear me no. This time, you are not getting away!' She almost ran back across the room to the bed. He raised himself on one elbow and pulled her to him. He pressed her back against the pillow and once more began his exploration of her. Her released her rounded breasts from their imprisoning lace covering and stimulated them into erect buds with his tongue. He let his tongue travel down her entire torso to the top of the lace pants. He bent to the centre of her crotch and blew gently onto the lace. She felt his warm breath as a gentle caress and felt a deep longing stirring from the base of her spine down to her heated centre of pleasure. She wanted him. She wanted him deep inside her, plunging into her deepest soul. He tugged at the panties, pulling hard to remove them and she shifted to help. He pulled again, wanting to tear the flimsy fabric away from her.

The destruction excited her, excited them both. He kneeled on the bed above her, staring in wonder at the vision before him. He had no doubts about what he would do. There was no question about him not being able to perform this act of love. Whatever his ex-wife had made him think about his virility it was clearly not true. He kissed her all over and a low moan escaped from her lips. If this was what love meant, she wanted more and more and more. Never-ending moments of pleasure like this. He raised his mouth once more to meet her breasts. The nipples responded sending waves of heat rippling uncontrolled unchecked through her body. His mouth pressed against hers again and at last, his body was covering hers. She wrapped her legs around his waist, pulling him closer and exposing her own desire in order to receive him better. She gasped as he entered her. The pain was exquisite. The feeling of his engorged masculinity pushing deep, deep inside her dissolved her very bones into pulsating jelly, liquid fire that burned with sensuous pleasure. His rhythm quickened and she matched his movements with a perfection that sent them both soaring to dizzy heights. She felt her orgasm with a powerful beating of her heart, pounding to meld her whole being with this man. He climaxed, just as she was starting her climb down, sending her once more spinning quite out of control. He fell back sideways, panting with exertion and covered in sweat.

'Tell me something Kerrien. Was that really your first time?' She stared back. How had he known?

Wasn't she very good at it? She lowered her lashes.

'I'm sorry. Did I disappoint you?'

'Disappoint me . . . how could you think that? No darling, of course not,. You're quite wonderful. It's just than when I entered you, well, I could tell. I thought you'd had sex with Brett and suppose I just assumed . . .'

'Was I as good as Martine?' she asked, slightly hurt that he knew her so little.

'Better, I'm sure. Whatever you may have thought, I haven't been to bed with her either. In fact, since Jane, there hasn't been anyone.' She stared in disbelief. The sophisticated Martine had actually intended to marry him, untried? Untested?

'Forget the rest of the world Kerrien, it's just us now.' He kissed her again, long and slowly. Unable to hold back, she pressed herself to him again and soon he was ready once more. The second time was altogether slower, less urgent and they could relax and enjoy more of the new dimensions of their love.

They fell asleep, limbs entwined, as closely as they could, as if each was afraid the other might try to escape. When she awoke, Kerrien looked immediately for proof that she had not been dreaming. Ashton was staring down at her, his head supported on one hand.

'Hallo, you,' he murmured.

'What time is it?' she asked, suddenly afraid the children might be awake.

'Still the middle of the night, to all intents and purposes and speaking of intents it is my intent to take you again, right now!'

'You can't take something that is freely given and given with love,' she whispered. He smiled down at her. His desire rose again and once more he caressed Kerrien's breasts, moving along her slender body until he found her pleasure centre. His fingers probed the soft moistly warm heart of her, raising her once more to heights of sensuous pleasure. She reached her orgasm, feeling a slight sense of disappointment that Ashton had not shared it. Shyly, she caressed him, gently stroking and teasing, until he lay moaning and breathing hard and fast. Through clenched teeth, he hissed at her to stop. She drew back, shocked and waited. He opened his eyes, grinning and pulled her over him. She sat astride his torso and he lifted her onto his throbbing organ. He grasped her breasts and held them in his hands, all the time, his hips moving to match her own rhythmic movements. She gasped again at new sensations and rode with him to a new, more thrilling climax.

'Wow,' she gasped when they finally lay back, exhausted. 'I am so glad I waited for the right man. I shall always remember my first time. I love you so much Ashton.'

'I love you Kerrien,' he replied. 'My kids seem to have been the only ones with any sense around here.'

She lay back smiling, relaxed and happier than she ever remembered. What was it she had said about this sort of love and passion only existing in silly stories or women's novels? Now she knew differently.

There was so much to talk about. He asked about her mother's last months and felt tears welling up in his own eyes, as she told him how much her mother would have loved him. He asked about Brett and why they had never made love. She asked about Martine and he told her his own deeply personal worries. He told her about the wife who had scorned him with such intensity that he had believed he was unable to satisfy a woman, any woman. Thanks to Kerrien, this worry had been dispelled because of what she'd done for him.

'You've probably restored my sanity,' he said with a smile. Then his expression changed. He looked anxious and suddenly worried.

'What is it?' Kerrien asked.

'Some fine doctor I am. I take it that as this was your first time, you haven't been taking any precautions?' She looked away. How could he be so unromantic as to talk about contraception at a time like this?

'I suppose I thought you were all prepared, the pill or something but I should have realized. I'm not only thinking about babies of course. Even if you were thinking of having sex only with Brett that must have its hazards.'

She felt angry. If he thought she was capable of having sex with just anyone . . . even the fact of him thinking it, was bad enough.

'What do you mean by hazardous?' she demanded.

'Well, I guess Brett gets around a bit, doesn't he? Can't imagine he's one to sit at home all his life waiting for the right woman to come along.'

'You mean like Martine did?' she asked, a little cynically.

'She's a woman of the world,' he said as if that explained everything.

'Did you know she was seeing Brett?' she asked casually. He stared in disbelief.

'Before or after your so-called engagement?'

'I'm not certain. I'm not sure whether they actually slept together but it wouldn't surprise me.' Ashton looked tense. He knew that he couldn't rely on Martine for many things, but he had believed in her loyalty at the very least. It was going to be a difficult day tomorrow. But for now, Kerrien was occupying his mind, his love and his body. She may have been inexperienced to start with but she was learning fast!

'Forget the rest of the world, my dearest Kerrien,' he murmured as he pressed himself against her, feeling again the wonderful flood of passion as he once more began to love her beautiful body. A brief memory of his wife flashed through his brain. Despite having two children together, there had never existed between them a love like he was feeling for Kerrien. He had never felt so aroused, so masculine and so much in control of the pleasure he was giving and receiving from his love. He pushed her legs apart and nuzzled the inner softness of her thighs. He gently scratched his fingernail across the white flesh, sending tiny pulses of anticipation deep into her body. He moved to stroke her intimate areas again, very gently teasing the fine covering of hair just enough to make her groan with pleasure and excitement.

'Come into me again,' she pleaded, moaning gently as she spoke.

'You have to wait,' he smiled. 'Turn over,' he commanded. She rolled on to her front and he covered her back with his long body. His hands slipped under her breasts, cupping them gently. He moved across her back, gently caressing all of her with his own body. She felt the ecstasy of passion flowing once more and moaned with pleasure. It seemed that whatever he did to her, wherever he touched her, the effect was to make her feel as if she was drowning in pleasure. He slipped away from her and gently turned her again.

'Are you ready for me?' he whispered, his voice soft and thick with emotion.

'Always. I shall always be waiting for you.' And he plunged again, deep inside her. She knew she was experiencing everything she had ever dreamt of and with Ashton, those dreams had come true.

It was after seven when she finally awoke. Kerrien sat up, smiling at the sight of Ashton, wrapped in a piece of duvet he had managed to rescue. She leaned over and kissed the back of his neck. Slowly, he uncurled and reached for her. She leapt out of his reach and dodged round the bed avoiding him. He chased her, pushing her back down onto the bed with a laugh.

'You don't escape so easily woman. Lie still and take what's coming to you.'

'Not now Ashton . . . the children will hear. Let's wait till everything is sorted out properly.' He looked disappointed but sat back, letting her free.

'Go on then. Away with you, woman. I need a

325

shower.' He rose and went into the en-suite while she grabbed her clothes and holding them in front of her, she rushed along the corridor to the safety of her own room. Quickly she showered, almost hating to wash away the scent of Ashton that was clinging to her skin. She glanced at herself in the mirror to see if she looked any different. Her eyes were bright, almost looking intoxicated but there were lines under them. She looked as if she was a little short of sleep, which wasn't far from the truth. It was her grin that gave everything away. She simply couldn't stop grinning. She felt like shouting from the roof-tops . . . proclaiming to the world that the man she loved, loved her too. With a light heart, she bounced into the children's rooms, calling good morning as she went to wake them.

CHAPTER 16

The children had almost finished breakfast by the time Ashton came through. He was dressed in a dark green shirt and lighter green trousers. The colour suited him perfectly and Kerrien complimented him on his good taste.

'Martine bought them for me one day,' he said casually. The words stung Kerrien and she regretted mentioning the clothes. She tried to tell herself she mustn't be sensitive about such things. After all, they both had a past of sorts. It was the past that made them into the people they were today, the very ones that each of them had fallen in love with.

'Did you have a nice evening?' Jodie asked, the very picture of wide-eyed innocence itself.

'Lovely thank you. It was nice of you to give us your surprise,' Kerrien said, looking hard at Ashton for his support. He said nothing. Jodie was looking hard at them both, trying to see if she could read a clue in either of their faces. Kerrien began to feel slightly uncomfortable at Ashton's silence. Why didn't he say anything? At least give them a sign to tell them something of what had happened. His eyes were masked with an unreadable blankness. He avoided all eye contact with Kerrien.

'Is Martine still coming here?' Jodie asked at last, unable to bear the suspense any longer. Kerrien waited for his denial, thinking that perhaps he might have rung her by now, to put her off.

'Of course she is. Why wouldn't she be?' he said in a clipped voice. 'Excuse me, but I have a lot to do.'

Kerrien sat in stunned silence. Martine was still coming? After all they had said to each other, all they had done together? There must be some mistake, surely there must? She followed Ashton to his room where she found him busily stripping the soiled sheets off the bed. He avoided her gaze and bundled the sheets to take to the laundry-room.

'What are you doing?' Kerrien spluttered.

'Changing the bed. Even you must agree that it needed changing.' His voice was flat and unemotional.

'But you never change your own sheets. Ashton! What is it? Is something wrong? Have I done something to upset you?' she demanded to know.

'I need clean sheets. I'm getting them. End of story. I don't know what all the fuss is about.' He left the room and went into the laundry, shutting the door behind him. In a daze, she organized the children and the dog and sent them into the garden to play. What was going on?

Martine arrived at nine-thirty. She was in a bad mood because, Ashton had not called her back the previous night. He had been much too busy with other things,

Kerrien remembered fondly but her smile faded. *Seducing me, it seems. Not falling in love as I believed.*

'I was hoping he would come over and collect some of my stuff. His car is so much bigger and will save me lots of journeys. Where is he?' she asked.

'I think he's still in his room,' Kerrien mumbled, still suffering from shock. After the previous magical night, she'd hoped never to see this woman again, let alone have her in the house.

'Make some coffee would you? I have a throat like a birdcage this morning.' Martine swept out in her usual cloud of expensive perfume, carefully shutting the door so Kerrien could not follow. Still operating on some sort of automatic pilot, she put the kettle on. She was waiting, hoping, to hear the shouts of complaint when Ashton told Martine that he had changed his mind about the wedding and her and everything . . . but nothing, not a sound was heard. She opened the kitchen door and listened. There was no sound from anywhere. She crept along the corridor and dived into her own room as she heard someone coming out of Ashton's room.

'Darling, we're going to have such fun. This is the right decision. Getting everything sorted out well before the wedding is much the best idea.'

Martine, a smile on her face, wandered back to the kitchen.

'Did you make me some coffee?' she demanded as Kerrien returned.

'I put the kettle on for you,' she replied as calmly as her shaking heart would allow.

'I can't drink that awful instant stuff. Haven't you got proper coffee? Oh dear, that's something else I'll have to get changed. We must have a decent coffee machine and decent coffee.'

What was going on? Kerrien wondered. Had she been dreaming last night? Ashton had said he loved her. He had certainly acted as though he loved her. She had bared her soul to him and could never believe she had been mistaken. So what was happening now, with Martine? The woman had gone out to her car and was carrying the first of her many suitcases into the house. She went through to Ashton's room and left them in there.

'Not much point my putting them in the guest bedroom, is there?' she said, as she swept past Kerrien. Ashton came to his door and took the bags from her. What was he doing? Kerrien felt sick. She felt as if the air was rushing past her ears, almost as though a gale was blowing right through her, tearing out her heart as it went. With disbelief she watched, like someone watching a horror movie, with no power to turn it off.

'Is she really moving in,' came Jodie's voice from the doorway.

'Seems like it,' Kerrien managed to say.

'Right,' Jodie said, her voice implying something like, *we'll see about this*.

Before Kerrien could utter a word, Jodie walked through the house carrying a bucket of water. She opened the front door, crossed the drive to Martine's car and poured the contents of the bucket over the red leather seats. She made certain that she caught some of the suitcases in the deluge obviously hoping to ruin some of the woman's clothes in the process. She had a satisfied smile on her face as she came back, never uttering a single word. Kerrien's jaw had dropped as she realized that Jodie had done exactly what she herself would have loved to do. She stifled a laugh and followed Jodie outside again.

'Jodie? Come here this minute,' she shouted. The little girl turned and Kerrien could see sheer desperation in her eyes. 'What were you thinking of?'

'That woman can't come here. I won't let her! She can't marry Daddy. I wanted you to marry him and I thought it was all going to be all right after last night, But it isn't. Daddy still wants her here and it's awful.' She promptly burst into floods of tears and disappeared into the cubby house. Ben began to cry too, in sympathy. He didn't really know why but if Jodie thought it was bad enough to cry about, then he was not going to be left out. In her own grief and despair, Kerrien felt helpless. She wanted to put her own head down and weep but she knew that would not serve any purpose.

A feeling of nausea crept into her stomach and along with it a thought insidiously wormed its way inside her. She paled and sat down heavily, the impact of realization hitting her like a ton of bricks. Ashton had confessed that his wife had told him he was a useless lover. So he had played an elaborate game with Kerrien, just so that he could take her to bed to make sure he didn't really have a problem. Before he would risk making love to Martine, he had to know he was capable of performing properly. All that talk of love had meant nothing. Why, even his questions about contraceptives, rather too late to do any good, must have been to ensure that she didn't become pregnant and spoil things for him. After all, most men who are about to get married don't sleep with the nanny, not the night before the prospective bride moves in! She felt sickened, used and worst of all a totally gullible fool. All the things he'd said and the fact she had believed him made her feel worse with each moment.

She had to get out. She would not stay under the same roof as either of them. With a pang, she thought of the children and what would happen to them. But there was no way she could stay. Grabbing only her handbag and keys, she ran out of the house and got into the little yellow car. She would arrange to return it later but she had to get away before Martine asked for explanations. She couldn't bear to see Ashton again, not ever. He had used her in the most shameful way, taking her most precious gift. She had always promised herself that she would only give herself to the man she intended to marry. She thought that was exactly what she had been doing the previous night. What was it he had said? *he wanted to take her*. Ingenuously, she had told him he could not take that which was being freely given. How he must have laughed at her naivety. Why even now he and Martine might be sharing the joke!

Her heart weighing like a ton of bricks, she switched on the engine and started the car. She drove off as

Martine and Ashton came out of the house. They watched her drive away, Martine with a sense of relief that this difficult woman was leaving, for however long it might be. Ashton felt a deep sense of loss, tinged with slight anger that Kerrien clearly had not trusted him. He shrugged and went back inside. He looked for the children but could not see them. Had she taken them with her? He could not believe she would do that without telling him, but they were nowhere to be seen. Damn it, he had quite enough to do without all of this. Martine was even now waiting for him to drive over to her house to collect more of her things. How could Kerrien and leave them all when everything was so chaotic?

'Jodie? Ben?' he shouted into the garden. He looked round the house but there was no sign of them. He shouted again and finally went to look inside the cubby, knowing it was a favourite hiding place. The pair were sitting in a dark corner, huddled together.

'Why on earth didn't you come when I called?' he demanded to know.

'We're having a sit-in,' Jodie said. 'We won't come out as long as Martine is here.'

'You'll have a long wait then,' he snapped, thoroughly out of temper. 'Come on out now,' he said. 'I have to drive over to Martine's and Kerrien's taken it into her head to drive off somewhere. Do either of you know where she's gone?'

'We are on strike. Nothing to say.' Jodie closed her mouth tightly and refused to utter another word.

'Ashton? Where are those damned kids of yours!

333

Just come and see what they've done. Trying to ruin my car and everything in it. I hope you're going to punish them.' Martine was an angry woman.

'Is this true?' Ashton shouted through the door of the cubby. 'Get out of there now.' Ben began to cry and Jodie put a comforting arm round him.

'It'll be all right Ben. Don't worry.' She tucked his grubby thumb into his mouth and hugged her little brother to her. It wasn't easy to be on a sit-in strike when she was only six!

Ashton's head was beginning to throb. Wearily, he went back to Martine to explain that he couldn't leave the children and that she would have to go alone, even if it took her umpteen trips and the whole day. He needed to think.

Kerrien drove down towards the beach. She parked the car and walked along the sands. The wind was blowing from the South East, chilling the air and making her shiver slightly. It began to drizzle, the damp, miserable weather matching her mood. She had come out without a coat and she began to shake, partly with cold, partly shock. She was feeling as if she had reached the depths of despair. Tears coursed down her cheeks and she blushed with shame, thinking of how easily she'd been taken for a fool. Wishing makes it so, leapt into her mind. She had wanted Ashton, she had wanted him so intensely, so completely that she had been easy prey. She was devastated to discover that he wasn't the man she had thought him to be. The trustworthy, honourable man was no more than a figment of her imagination. The reality was despicable and she should waste no more time thinking of him, grieving over him.

She need never see him again. She *would* never see him again. He could pack up her things and send them on. Where was she to go? There was only one other family she knew in the whole of Australia. She was supposed to be engaged to their son. She knew with certainty now, that she did not love Brett and that she could never marry him. It might make it impossible to visit her friend in the future but now, she must go to Margaret one last time, just to break off the engagement that never was. She owed it to all of them, Margaret especially. Wrestling with a conscience that told her she must go and a cowardly heart that told her not to, she got back into the car. She drove slowly to Margaret's house and parked. She sat in the car for several minutes, trying to pull her resources together so that she could knock on the door.

'That you, Kerrien love? G'day my dear. What are you doing out here? Were we expecting you? Brett didn't say anything. Come on in.' Margaret pulled open the door and helped her out.

'What the hell's happened to you love? You look terrible. What you need is a nice drop of brandy to warm you up. Why for heaven's sakes, you're almost frozen to death.' The large, comfortable woman led Kerrien inside the house and placed her on the sofa. She pulled a rug over her and went to make a hot drink. Kerrien closed her eyes and once more felt tears burning at the back of her eyes. She hoped Brett wasn't around. At this moment she wanted nothing but the oblivion of sleep. Why had she ever come to this dratted country?

'Have you had lunch?' Margaret was asking her.

'Lunch?' she repeated stupidly.

'It's nearly three o'clock and you look as if you haven't eaten all day. I'll get you some soup but drink this first.' At the first sip, Kerrien choked. It was coffee, laced with a hefty dollop of brandy, making it so hot that her eyes watered. It coursed through her cold and weary body, like a river of warmth.

'Brett?' she asked.

'Out. Gone to see someone over Birkdale way. Said it was business but what people want with business on a weekend, don't ask me. He'll be back later. Do you want to talk about anything? Gees love, there's obviously something very wrong with you. Might help you to talk, love.'

How could she talk to Brett's mother of all people? Margaret was the driving force, Kerrien was certain, behind this mockery of an engagement. Luckily, Brett had not bought her a ring yet so at least he hadn't gone to any expense on her behalf, she thought practically. The hot coffee and brandy were doing their work and she sat up, feeling better.

'Sorry Margaret, but things got on top of me. I'm feeling better now. I'm sorry to turn up suddenly like that.'

'That's all right love. What friends are for. I'll go and warm you a drop of soup now. You look like you could do with something hot inside you. Bet you *didn't* have any lunch did you? Hope you can stay a whiles, have some supper with us. Don't know what Brett was planning to do tonight but he can always change his plans, don't you think so?' Kerrien was not really listening but she couldn't help but smile at the woman's enthusiasm. It was almost infectious. She wondered how much consternation her absence from home had caused. If Ashton was fully occupied with Martine, he would only have noticed in as much as he'd have to organize lunch for them all. They could always phone for a pizza or something. She wondered how she could manage to be so darned practical, even at a time like this! It wasn't her problem any more.

The soup Margaret was heating smelled wonderful, reminding her that she really did feel ravenously hungry. She wandered through to her friend's kitchen and sniffed appreciatively.

'You're always feeding me,' she remarked.

'Don't be silly, love. You're already one of the family.'

Kerrien drew her breath to make her speech. She didn't know how she was going to explain how she felt to Margaret, of all people. She had to postpone the moment, when the telephone interrupted them.

'Might be Brett now,' Margaret said, rushing through to answer it. Kerrien held her breath. She could hear Margaret's excited voice talking to her caller. There were several mentions of the wedding, with excuses made for the lack of news.

'I've got Kerrien here with me right now. I'm hoping for a woman to woman chat and we shall get everything sorted . . . dates, reception and everything.

337

Yes. I'll be sure to let you know as soon as I do. Yes. Bye now.'

She breezed back into the room.

'My sister. Wants all the details of the wedding. Said I'd have to call her back, once we've talked it through. You haven't decided on the date yet, have you?'

This was awful, Kerrien thought. She hadn't even had time to talk to Brett yet and Margaret was making all sorts of demands on her.

'I thought you and I should sit down together and sort a few things out. Those men of mine couldn't organize anything if they tried. What do you say? We'll sort it all and tell them what we've decided. Now, I'm not having a word of protest from you. Lennie and me, well, we decided we should provide you with everything you need. We're treating you to the dress and flowers, reception, the lot. No, dear, don't say anything, we insist. You haven't got parents of your own to pay for things and we've got more money than we'll ever need. It's the least we can do.'

At last, Margaret ran out of steam and Kerrien's could get a word in. She hardly knew where to begin but she couldn't let this dear lady carry on believing that everything was wonderful. Far from it.

'Margaret, you must listen to me.'

'I thought I said I wanted no arguments. I meant what I said.'

'Please listen,' Kerrien begged desperately. 'I'm so sorry but I don't think I can marry Brett after all. I know I shouldn't be telling you first, but I haven't had the chance to tell him yet'

'Not marry him? But I thought . . .' Margaret's voice trailed off and she looked blankly at the girl.

'I really am so sorry but I know now that I don't really love him. I know it's hard, especially as he's your son and you've been a wonderful friend to me. I feel awful about it but it's best this way.'

Margaret sat down heavily. She looked incredulously at Kerrien, as if staring hard enough could somehow influence her to change her mind.

'How do you mean, you don't love Brett? He's a good lad at heart, even if he's been a bit wild at times. He'd be good to you, love. I'd never let him cause you any harm or problems. I promise you, any trouble and I'd really give him heaps. He's not a drinker and I know he's got a good head on his shoulders.' She shook her head in disbelief. She knew he'd always been one for the women but he would never hurt Kerrien, she just knew it. If he did anything to let her down, why she would never let him forget it.

'It's not Brett's fault, it's all mine. I think I knew all along it wasn't quite the right thing to do. You made me so welcome here and have been such a good friend, I think I went along with the plan because I didn't want to hurt your feelings. I'm sorry,' she finished lamely. 'I expect you'll want me to leave, but I'd be grateful if I could stay long enough to see Brett. To talk to him.'

'Is there something you're not telling me?' Margaret demanded.

'I've fallen in love with someone else but it didn't work out. I'm seriously thinking of going back to

339

England. I think it's for the best.' Despite her brave words, their full implication suddenly hit her and she became aware of tears once more trickling down her cheeks.

'There there, love. Don't you cry. I'm sure everything will work out for the best. Do you want to phone your doctor and tell him you want to stay over?' she asked kindly. 'I think you should stay here for tonight at least. Get yourself sorted out.'

'He won't worry about me,' she replied in a small voice. 'I think he might guess where I am.'

The older woman stared at her. She seemed to be searching every nuance of her expression, seeking some explanation for her behaviour. Light dawned in her eyes.

'You don't mean this other man is the doctor? You haven't gone and fallen for your doctor?' She laughed out loud.

'It doesn't matter who it is,' she gasped. 'The plain truth is, I don't love Brett and it isn't fair to go ahead with plans for marriage, knowing that. I do hope you understand.'

'Isn't he supposed to be getting married to some other doctor at the hospital?' Margaret asked.

Kerrien nodded, unable even to speak Ashton's fiancée's name. She wanted to shout, *yes, he's marrying that awful woman but not before he took my own love, took my virginity*. He did take it, she knew now, even if she had wanted to give it freely to him. She shuddered at the thought of her own stupidity, promising herself that she would somehow erase it from her memory when it was a little less raw. She would stop hurting one day. One day, she might remember all of this with some sort of amusement. How she had fallen for a handsome Aussie doctor and allowed herself to be taken in.

'And he didn't return your love, I take it?' Margaret was asking. 'How about his kids? What do they think about all this?'

The thought of the two dear little children made Kerrien bite her lip in renewed anguish. She'd been so busy thinking of her own misery, she'd given no thought to them. They must be feeling desperate. The last thing she remembered was the bucket of water in Martine's car. She recounted the incident to Margaret, who roared with laughter.

'Think that about says it all, don't you? I'd have loved to have seen the woman's face.'

Kerrien grinned for the first time since her arrival.

'Guess it might have been something to enjoy in this whole sorry mess.'

Margaret went to put the kettle on. She called through to say that Brett had just driven into the yard. He came bounding up the steps and flung his arms round Kerrien.

'This is a surprise. Thought you were working today? Snook out did you? Couldn't have been a better time. Mum tell you where I was this avo?'

'No,' said Kerrien, 'she just thought you were doing some business deal.'

Brett's eyes gleamed with triumph.

'Not often I put one over on the old girl. I've got a

341

surprise for you.' He put his hand in his pocket and pulled out a little box. A ring box. Kerrien's heart sank. It seemed like it was too late.

'Go on, open it,' he urged.

'I can't,' Kerrien protested. 'We have to talk Brett.'

'I insist you open the box first and then we'll talk.' Kerrien gave a shrug and lifted the lid. As expected, it contained a ring, an engagement ring. The sapphire and diamond ring flashed with hidden lights, a stylish, modern design, resting in a blue velvet-lined box.

'Well? Say something. Don't you like it? I had it made especially for you. Old mate of mine from college. Lives over in Birkdale. That's where I was this avo. I chose the stone to match your eyes. Beautiful blue.'

'Brett, it's gorgeous but I'm sorry, I can't accept it.' His face fell.

'But it's an engagement ring, your engagement ring,' he said stupidly.

In a halting voice, Kerrien tried to explain to him. It seemed so insubstantial, her reasons seemed so flawed. His face paled with anger and he almost shouted at her to stop being so silly. His temper was running white hot and Kerrien became almost frightened by his words.

'Don't you mess me about Kerrien,' he warned through clenched teeth. 'No one makes a fool of me.'

Margaret came back into the room carrying a tray of very normal looking tea. She spoke softly.

'This gets us nowhere Brett.'

'You mean you knew? She told you? She told you

before she told me? Kerrien, what do you have to say? How dare you speak to my mother before you tell me?'

'That's my fault Brett. I made her tell me what was wrong. You should have seen the state she was in.'

'I'm sorry, Brett. I should have talked to you first but it just happened this way.'

She drew a deep breath and began to try to explain. She told him that she was in love with Ashton but that now Martine had moved in, she felt unable to share the house. She omitted the intimate details, especially concerning last night! She was determined to return to England, to get back to her own country.

'You have more guts than that, love,' Margaret announced.

Kerrien stared. Guts was not one of the qualities she would have considered a strong point in her make-up, especially at this moment.

'I'll leave you two to get on with your chat,' Margaret said, leaving the room and shutting the door behind her.

'So, Martine has moved in, has she?' Brett said thoughtfully. 'That will put a stop to her little games, won't it?'

'What little games?' Kerrien asked innocently.

'She's quite a devious lady that one. I hope Ashton knows what he's doing. She could manipulate the devil himself, if the mood took her,' he said with a wry smile.

'And did she manipulate you?' Kerrien asked, wondering what he could possibly mean.

'Very nearly. I almost got trapped in her web but

343

managed to extricate myself in time. I was tempted. It's not every day a woman like that sets her cap at you. I was almost intrigued enough to take up her invitation to go to bed with her. But I thought better of it, knowing how much store you set by this sex and marriage thing. I decided I'd keep myself pure and wholesome, just for you.' He grinned as he spoke but the smile died on his lips as he remembered why she was there, sitting in his parent's home. 'Ironic eh?'

Kerrien blushed. Her own shame at what she had done, especially after all she'd said about love and marriage, hit her hard. She'd lost the one gift she had promised he should be the first to receive. Even though it was over, her guilty feelings stabbed at her soul.

But Martine. What game was she playing? She questioned Brett further and finally persuaded him to explain. It seemed the woman had promised him a contract with her own medical department, to produce some electronic parts for a special machine. Once developed, the machine would be cheaper than any other similar appliance on the market. A fortune could be theirs. Along with the competitive price, she had certain expectations of a rather more personal nature.

'I guess I shouldn't tell you this in the circumstances but she did say that Ashton was a little, what shall we say? . . . lacking excitement in the sex department. She seeks her gratification elsewhere and I was targeted as one of her possible alternatives. I would guess that she'll need an evening out without her husband, at the very least, once a week.' His voice held a certain amount of venom as he spoke.

'And did you get her contract?' she asked.

''fraid not. I didn't quite come up to scratch either. Pity in the circumstances, especially as I only turned her down on your account.' He shrugged his shoulders, dismissing the subject.

'So why the heck is she so keen to move in and marry Ashton?'

'All to do with status in the hospital. Evidently the *Head of Everything* practically demands his staff are married and settled down, if they are to be really useful to him. An undemanding man with a ready-made family seems perfect for Martine's purposes and she doesn't even have to take time out to produce the kids. Evidently, in the hospital rule book, kids are essential to make a stable marriage!'

'I can't believe anyone could have such old-fashioned thoughts, not these days. Martine's done all right for herself, hasn't she? Marriage or no marriage.'

'Seems she's worked her way through most of the staff there already and there have been a few complaints. All unofficial, of course. She sees this as her chance to gain irrefutable respectability.'

'Wow. And how do I tell all this to Ashton without seeming like the original sour grape in the bunch?'

'Perhaps you shouldn't. It's all moved out of your control now.'

'But I can't let her loose on him and those poor children. I just can't stand by, whatever my own personal feelings.' Kerrien felt a deep surge of anger replacing some of the pain. Whatever Ashton had done to hurt her, she couldn't let the children suffer. She had come to love them so much, more, possibly, than if they'd been her own flesh and blood.

'I'm so sorry, Brett,' she said, closing the box that held the lovely ring and handing it back to him. 'You're a wonderful man but I can't marry you. You'll soon find someone else who'll be much more of a wife to you than I ever could. Don't hate me for it.'

To her great relief, he laughed. He put his arm round her shoulder and kissed her on the nose.

'No worries. I guess I feel a sort of relief. I don't believe I'm cut out for this marriage lark, though I must confess, I was more than a little intrigued about you. Have you truly never slept with anyone?' Kerrien hesitated. What could she say now? When she had seen him last she had never slept with a man, but that was before yesterday. She looked down.

'When I told you I'd never slept with anyone, I wasn't lying.' She hoped he wouldn't probe further.

'You are an unusual woman, Kerrien. One of a kind. Friends?' He held out his hand for her to take.

'Friends. I'd like that, if your mum will ever let us just be friends!' They both smiled and shook hands. At least she didn't have to lose every friend she had, after all.

'You're a lovely man, Brett,' she smiled.

But now, she had to face another problem. What should she say to Ashton and would he believe her?

She had been hurt very badly but she didn't want to
see him destroyed by that evil woman and nor did she
want the children to suffer any more upsets in their
lives. A flood of anger seemed to rush through her
body. She had to take some action.

CHAPTER 17

Margaret assumed that Kerrien was going to stay over, whatever was happening between her and Brett. For once, and quite out of character, she did not pry into their affairs. She saw that they were smiling at each other and seemed to be on good terms. A slight flicker of hope was kindled but remained deep inside.

'It's so important to be friends,' she remarked, thinking of her own relationship with her husband. Brett and Kerrien smiled at each other.

'We're certainly staying friends, Mum,' Brett told her.

'And the wedding?' she asked tentatively, knowing the answer before she asked.

'It's off, I'm afraid,' Kerrien said softly. 'I'm sorry but it's better now than later.'

'I guess you're right love, but I'm well gutted. You were just what this lad of mine needed. A sensible girl who has her head firmly on her shoulders. I suppose there's no chance of . . .? No, course not. Have a few more potatoes, love. Build yourself up a bit.'

Kerrien laughed inside. Margaret was incorrigible.

She would hate to have to say goodbye to them all. Even though they'd only known each other for a few months, their openness was amazing. None of the traditional British reserve and holding back real feelings that she was used to.

'You've all been so good to me,' she said at last. 'I shall miss you all.'

'You plannin' on going somewhere, then? Thought you'd given up them thoughts.'

'I have to find some sort of work and I'm certain Ashton is never going to give me a decent reference, not after I walked out on him. Can you imagine what Martine would have to say about it if he did?'

'Strikes me that woman is a real mongrel. Can't think how she manages to stay in her job, Miss High and Mighty doctor.' Margaret had obviously been listening to some gossip.

'I suppose she's good at her job,' Kerrien forced herself to say.

'Shouldn't like her as my doctor, from what I hear. Rumour has it she only got where she is by lyin' on her back.'

'You have a wonderful choice of words, Mother,' Brett teased.

'Go on with you. I speak as I find.'

Kerrien was infuriated by what she was hearing. How come Ashton didn't know about her reputation? Evidently his prowess as a lover had been the least of Martine's worries; she had that well organized elsewhere. All she needed was his name and his respectability. How could an intelligent man like Ashton be

349

taken in by her? How could he have said all those things to Kerrien last night? How could he have said he loved her with such warmth and passion, only to dump her the next day? She felt a new wave of anger at her own stupidity.

'You look like you're planning some sort of revenge,' Brett said, staring at her. 'What do you have in mind?'

'Don't know yet. There's not much time, but I'm damned if that woman is going to harm those little children. I don't mean physically harm them of course but emotionally. I don't think they can take much more. After Kate and now Martine, poor little things need to be really loved and properly cared for.' Anger burned deep inside her yet the blue eyes flashed with an icy calm.

'Go for it, Kerrien,' Margaret urged. 'I don't pretend I hadn't got high hopes for you and this lad of mine but I'd rather you were both happy apart than fighting like cats and dogs together.'

'Thanks Margaret,' she said gratefully. 'This way, we all stay friends. But I shall have to plan what I'm doing very carefully.'

They chatted through the various options; everything from leaking news to the gutter press, to confronting the hospital manager with complaints. All their ideas were discarded as being impossible and impractical. They did, however, have a bit of fun discussing it and Margaret noticed some of the strain lines had eased from Kerrien's pretty face.

'Let's sleep on it,' Margaret suggested. 'We'll talk

350

some more tomorrow and see if we can't come up with something.' She went off to bed, leaving the couple alone.

'You know something? Now everything is out in the open, I feel so much happier being here with you, Brett. Somehow, I'm more comfortable, knowing I don't have to pretend or fight you off.'

'Don't bet on it,' he laughed and made as if he was going to grab her. She laughed and punched him a positively fraternal way.

'You know, I do love you, Kerrien,' he said softly. 'Not the way I've loved other women. I guess you're the daughter my mother never had and that must make us brother and sister.'

'Funny. That's more or less what was going through my mind,' she admitted.

'Come on now, bed.' He pulled her off the seat and dragged her out of the room.

'Now there's a sight, ripe for misinterpretation,' she smiled.

She slept late on Sunday morning, despite thinking that she would never sleep at all. She had woken several times during the night, on each occasion, remembering the previous night of love and passion that now seemed a lifetime away. She thrilled to the memories, cherishing the tenderness and deep, deep love she had felt towards Ashton. That was before she had realized his true intent. Although she was no nearer a solution to her problems when she awoke, at least she was reasonably well rested.

After a leisurely breakfast, she was gradually convincing herself that she should go over and see Ashton and Martine. She even managed to convince herself the main purpose was to check on the children and to remove her possessions from the house. It would take all her strength and courage to face this new regime. By early afternoon, she was certain she would be able to cope. Brett and Margaret had both offered to accompany her but she knew that she had to face this task alone. If she didn't make every effort to save the man and the children she loved from this evil, manipulative woman, she would never forgive herself. As for her own future, she would have to wait and see.

'That's my girl,' Margaret encouraged. 'Make sure you come back here after you've finished. I shall want to hear all the details but most of all, I want you to know you have a home with us for as long as you want it.'

Kerrien hugged the woman gratefully.

'You're the best friend anyone could have, Margaret. And you too, Brett. As good as a big brother any day.' He grinned at her, half wishing he was going with her to protect her as a decent brother should.

She climbed into the little car and drove away. Yesterday's drizzle had continued and the roads were slippery and wet. She drove carefully and slowly not only to avoid skidding but to give herself more time to plan what she would say when she arrived. The roads were quiet as most of the residents of the city relaxed after Sunday lunch. She realized with a shock that this place had truly become home to her. After so short a time, she knew that she didn't want to leave it, whatever happened in her own personal life. Perhaps she had been in too much of a hurry to want to settle down. Some inner drive that wanted her to put down new and permanent roots in a country far away from her own home with its memories of her mother and all the suffering she'd known in her final months. Somehow, the new country had exorcised her own fears and guilt, however misplaced that guilt had been.

Back in her own familiar suburb, she drove into the road which had been her home for the past few months. Her heart was thumping as if it were trying to escape from its cage. Her knees felt weak. She took a deep breath to steady herself and turned into the drive. Neither Ashton's nor Martine's car were parked there. *Damn*, she told herself. *Why didn't I think of phoning first, to make sure they were in.* Frustrated anger swept through her body. She had steeled herself for this moment and now the opportunity was lost. She had a sudden vision of them all enjoying a family outing together and felt an irrational jealousy surge through her. She stopped the car, wondering whether she should, after all, go in and collect her belongings. She still had her key of course and all her things were inside. With a shaking hand, she pushed the key into the lock and went inside.

The house was silent. She called out the names of the children, just in case someone was there. There was a slightly uncanny feel to the place which she could not quite work out. The children's toys were on the floor of the family room, unusually left strewn around. Even Ashton usually demanded that they were put away before they went out. She looked in the kitchen. Dirty dishes from the previous day were lying on the side benches. He had not even put them in the dish-washer, another diversion from the normal routine. He was fussy about hygiene in the house. Curious, she went through to the bedroom corridor and despite knowing there was no-one there, knocked on the door to Ashton's room. She pushed it open tentatively, a sense of dread filling her mind.

Unlike the rest of the house, this room was positively pristine in its tidiness. The pile of suitcases and bags brought by Martine had all been tidied away. Hating herself for prying, she pulled open Ashton's wardrobe. His suits and shirts hung in their usual neat rows. No trace of Martine's vast collection of clothes. Maybe she had left them in the spare room, after all. Kerrien pushed open the door of that room. It looked as tidy as when she'd last seen it. No sign of any extra bags and the cupboards were quite empty, just as the other room had been. Her heart gave a surge and the blood rushed to her head, making her feel slightly dizzy. Had Martine's move been cancelled after all? Could Ashton have sent her packing? How she hoped so. She would never understand why he'd let the woman continue with her proposed move. But where was everyone? The house was deserted for some reason and it was clear that it had been left in some haste.

She heard the phone ring and half expecting Brett or Margaret, she rushed through to the kitchen to listen.

The answer phone cut in and a familiar voice boomed out.

'Anyone there? Martine? Kerrien? Someone pick up the phone if you're there.' It was Kate and she sounded quite desperate.

Hesitatingly, Kerrien lifted the receiver. After their last encounter, she wasn't sure she really wanted to talk to Ashton's sister.

'Hello? Kate?' she said.

'Kerrien. Thank heavens you're there. How are they? The children, I mean?' Her heart sank. She had known deep inside there was something terribly wrong.

'What do you mean?' she asked, her whole body shaking in anticipation of what she might hear.

'Don't you know about the crash? You haven't heard? Wherever were you? It was on the local news this morning. No names of course, but I recognized the car.'

Kerrien slumped down onto the stool near the phone. She felt her very life blood draining out of her body. The room began to spin. She pulled herself together sufficiently to speak.

'I haven't heard the local news today. I was staying with friends. What accident?' she forced herself to say.

'Ashton and the children were involved in a dreadful car crash, late last night, apparently. I've been trying to get hold of someone who could tell me where they all are. The news said they had been taken to the Princess Alexandra Hospital but they said they'd had to move them and didn't seem to be able to help. The press have been hounding them for details following the news broadcast. They won't give out information on the phone. Whoever you say you are.'

'What about Ashton?' she managed to whisper.

'I don't know. Serious I believe, but I haven't got any details. They said he was in surgery and there wouldn't be any news for several hours. Said it was pointless my going there, as I couldn't see him.' Kerrien felt relief wash over her. At least he wasn't dead.

'Do you know what happened?' she asked.

'Skidded on wet roads. Lorry went into them and smashed the car to nothing. It looked awful on the TV. Made me feel quite ill. Look, let me know as soon as you hear anything. I shall stay by the phone.'

'Yes, OK,' Kerrien mumbled after taking Kate's number, still in a state of shock. The children. Were the children still alive? They must be or Kate would have said something more. Automatically, she dialled Margaret's number. She briefly passed on what scrap of news she had before putting the phone down, not waiting for Margaret to answer. Her mind was racing. Whatever had happened here at home to make them all leave in such a hurry? Martine had clearly gone, taking all her possessions with her. Where then, did the family fit into the events? She looked through the phone book and found Martine's number. Curiously, she had never known it and never dreamed she would ever have the need to call the woman. She dialled and waited. Martine's answer phone began its message, the languid voice managing to sound suggestive, even there. Kerrien hung up. If she wasn't home, there seemed little point in leaving a message.

She looked up the various hospitals in the phone book and began to dial. The Princess Alexandra Hospital were of little help. Doctor Philips had been taken to the Royal Brisbane but they could give no further information by telephone, just as Kate predicted. They said they knew nothing of his children. This was ridiculous, Kerrien thought. Someone must know what had happened. She called the Brisbane Royal, who finally did tell her that Ashton was out of surgery and in recovery. She phoned Kate to update her and put the phone down, intent on driving straight to the hospital. Perhaps they would tell her about the children when she got there in person. For now, she had to assure herself that Ashton would recover. Whatever injuries he might have sustained, she had to be there with him. If Martine was there or even in charge of him, she didn't care. She, Kerrien, loved him to distraction and if he died, her own love would die with him. She planned to do everything she could to fight for him, to help him.

She drove carefully along the damp roads. She was unsure of the way but eventually picked up signs that directed her. She found somewhere to park and walked what seemed like miles to the main reception. She asked at the desk for directions. She needed to see first Ashton and then the children. To her immense relief, she was told that both Ben and Jodie were there, in the children's ward. They had been trying to get hold of someone but all the children seemed able to say, was that Kerrien had gone. She rushed to intensive care, hoping to see Ashton first, praying she would have good news to take to the children.

She was not allowed into his room and was forced to peer in through a window. He lay on a narrow bed, not moving. Scars and bruises covered his face, making him almost unrecognizable. His eyes were closed and a vast array of tubes and monitors seemed to be attached to every available part of him. She could only look, longing to touch him, any part of him, even his hand would do. She knew it might be some time until she was allowed near him. Strangely, she felt no tears. The same strength that had filled her through her mother's final days, returned to her and she knew that her inner resources would carry them all through the crisis. She stared, willing him to sense her presence, to feel her strength flowing into his inert form as it lay there. She became aware of someone standing beside her and turned to see Kate. The woman slipped her hand under Kerrien's arm and gave it a squeeze.

'Don't worry too much. It always looks much more frightening than it really is,' she whispered.

Kerrien smiled at her gratefully. Kate looked well, much more relaxed than when they had last met, despite this horror that had overtaken them all.

'Did they tell you anything?' Kate asked.

'Not really, The usual hospital platitudes. As well as can be expected. The crisis will last for the next few hours. We can only wait.'

'And the children? How are Ben and Jodie?'

With a jolt, Kerrien remembered that she had not yet been to see them.

'Poor loves, they're in the children's ward. I was going to see them as soon as I had seen Ashton.'

'You'd better go along then,' Kate said softly. 'They will be longing to see you.'

'Aren't you coming too?' Kerrien asked.

Kate shook her head and motioned her away.

'They will be better with you alone at the moment. They shouldn't have any extra stress at present. The last time I saw them, it all ended in that blazing row. I want to stay here. I have to know that Ashton will forgive me. In case, you know . . .'

Kerrien noticed there were tears in Kate's eyes and she gave her a comforting squeeze before she left her staring through the window at the battered body of her brother.

The children's ward was bright and noisy after the silence of the room she had just left. A few of the children were out of bed, playing with the huge array of toys. Others were in cots of various sizes. At the nursing station, she asked where Jodie and Ben were, quite unable to see them among this mass of people. She was directed to a side ward where there were only four cots. Squatting in the middle of his, the inevitable thumb plugged firmly in his little mouth, sat Ben. He had a bandage round his head and a couple of plasters on his face but otherwise looked unscathed. His face lit up in delight, as he saw Kerrien. Even the thumb was removed temporarily as he stretched his arms out to her to be picked up. She leaned over the side and gave him a quick hug before turning towards Jodie. The little girl was lying down, her arm encased in plaster and also with a bandage round her head.

'Kerrien, you came back,' she sobbed. 'I missed you.'

'And I missed you two. I couldn't ever have gone and left you for good.'

'Martine's gone as well. There's just us now, When we get home, Daddy will marry you, won't he? Then we can be a proper family and I can be a bridesmaid.'

'We'll have to wait and see but don't worry, I have no plans to go anywhere else.' She knew now she could never leave Australia and this little family she had become so much a part of. Despite all the problems, the highs and the lows, this was where she wanted to be.

'When's Daddy coming to see us?' Ben demanded. Kerrien bit her lip.

'Daddy is very poorly. He has to stay in his bed for a while, but I'm sure he sends his love to you both.' Her voice was steady and calm and she reassured them as best she could.

'Wish I had my monkey,' Ben said.

'Where is he?' Kerrien asked. 'I can get him and bring him in for you tomorrow.' The stuffed toy had been Ben's favourite companion for years, especially necessary at bed time.

'In the back of Daddy's car. Daddy's car is all bashed up. The ambulance men came and pulled us out but they didn't get Monkey.'

'I'll have to see what I can do,' Kerrien promised,

knowing she might have to find a replacement. If, as Kate said, the car was a total wreck, there could be no chance of recovering the child's toy. 'Would you like me to see if there's a lonely bear or something in the main ward?' Ben nodded and she went to collection of toys in the other room. She selected a panda and took it to the little boy.

'This one needed a cuddle,' she said, handing it to the child. He took it and pulled it close. His thumb was returned to its usual place and he looked sleepy. Gently she laid him down and he soon fell into a doze. She turned back to Jodie and sat beside her bed.

'Daddy is going to be all right, isn't he?' she asked in a trembling voice. 'You would tell me if he wasn't, wouldn't you?'

She tried to reassure the little girl, hoping she sounded more convincing than she felt.

'Where's Lloyd?' Jodie asked suddenly. Kerrien's heart jumped. He hadn't been in the house when she'd been back and she had no idea.

'Where did you leave him?' she asked, fearing the worst.

'He came in the car with us. He was in the back with us, sitting like a really good dog.'

'I'll have to ask someone. I don't know where he is but I'm sure someone will be able to help.' Again she hoped she sounded more convincing than she felt. She told Jodie that Aunt Kate was with Daddy and asked her if she would like to see her when Kerrien returned to sit with Ashton.

'Will she shout at me?' Jodie asked.

'I shouldn't think so for a minute,' she smiled. Jodie nodded her agreement and Kerrien got up to leave.

'I'll send her along then and I'll see you soon. Don't worry, I won't be going away from the hospital.'

She went quickly back to Ashton's ward. Kate sat staring through the window at the inert form on the bed. She shook her head and Kerrien gasped. He couldn't have died, not now, not when she wanted to tell him everything was all right. One of the machines was still bleeping and she realized she had misinterpreted Kate's signal.

'There are internal injuries they have not been able to assess yet. I just spoke to the doctor. He has a broken leg and multiple lacerations, as you can see.'

'When will they know?'

'He has to recover from the shock before he can stand any further examination. They won't know about long term effects until he regains consciousness. He took several bangs on his head. What about the children?'

'They seem OK. Badly shaken of course but nothing life-threatening. Jodie has a broken arm and they are both concussed. They would like to see you, if you want to go.' Kate's face was a picture. Her expression had softened into one of great relief. She looked so delighted that Kerrien herself felt like smiling. They hugged each other and Kate's face broke into a radiant smile that came from deep within.

'Thank you, Kerrien. And I'm sorry I was such a bitch to you. I suppose I was insanely jealous of the way you just walked in and seemed to be accepted by everyone. The children loved you immediately while I always seemed to have to work so hard at it. My life hasn't been easy, hiding the truth about myself. It took me many years to come to accept it myself. Even in these enlightened times, being gay seems to carry some sort of stigma.'

Kerrien returned her attention to Ashton, lying there so still. Apart from the machinery bleeping away, she thought, there was no other indication that he was still alive. The thoughts were too awful to contemplate. Suppose the head injuries had damaged his brain. Would she be able to cope with him if the worst happened?

For the children's sakes, she would also have to try and get some news about Lloyd but it did not look good for the little pup.

CHAPTER 18

It was two days later before the crisis ended. Kerrien was allowed to sit by Ashton's side and she was able at last, to hold his hand. It lay cool and limp, the slow pulse barely noticeable. Her days had been filled with amusing the children who were rapidly recovering and becoming their normal, lively selves. Kate had been magnificent, visiting every day and staying until the little ones were asleep for the night. They had shared the bedside vigil of Ashton, Kerrien was almost torn apart with the longing to be at Ashton's side *and* wanting to give the children her time and love. She dreaded that he would come round when she was not there. She so desperately wanted to be the first thing he saw, when he finally opened his eyes. There were moments when he seemed to near the surface of consciousness but at other at times, he looked so still and pale that she wondered if she would ever again, truly see the Ashton she loved. She became friendly with the nurses and they brought her cups of tea and coffee, not strictly allowed but they saw her so often that she was almost becoming part of the staff. They suggested that she should talk to Ashton in case he could hear during the brief moments he seemed nearer the surface of consciousness. A familiar voice could help his battle.

She was almost dozing, worn out after more than two nights without sleep. She jolted awake suddenly. Had she dreamed it or had she felt a slight movement? She was instantly fully awake, peering at the patient for some sign of life.

'God, I'm thirsty Kerrien. Can you find me some nice cold wine?' The voice was a husky whisper. His eyes were still tightly shut.

'Ashton,' she breathed. 'Oh Ashton, you're back! Oh my love, I've been so worried.'

His eyes flickered and opened briefly for a moment. They closed again and she pressed the buzzer for the nurse.

'He spoke to me,' Kerrien whispered, her eyes bright with tears. 'Asked for a glass of wine.' She laughed almost hysterically, with the relief. His prime care nurse gave her a delighted hug. Then she returned to her professional self, bustling round and calling the doctor. Ashton, still very weak, smiled at Kerrien, holding onto her hand with a baby-like grip.

'Not letting you go again,' he whispered.

'Not going again,' she countered. 'Except to go and see the children and to tell Kate the good news.' He nodded his agreement and, unwillingly, she left him as the doctor arrived at his bedside. The children were both fast asleep, so the news would have to wait until the next day. Kate had gone home for a rest, once the children were safely tucked up for the night. She planned to return early the next morning and had insisted that Kerrien should herself take a rest. Although they had spent little time together over the past two days, they had become closer, sharing this desperate fight for the life of person they both loved so deeply. Once emotions had been explored and the reasons for past antagonisms accepted, the barriers to their friendship no longer existed. They now had a common bond, a common purpose.

Kerrien dialled Kate's number, knowing she would want this latest piece of news, whatever the time of night.

'Oh, my dear,' Kate sighed, when she heard the good news. 'Thanks heavens. Give him my love, won't you? I'll be there first thing. Try to get some rest yourself now. You must be exhausted.'

Happier than she had felt for several days, Kerrien returned to Ashton's room. The doctor had been in to examine him and was satisfied that the worst was now over. As far as internal injuries were concerned, it seemed that apart from the massive bruising, there was nothing seriously wrong. Ashton was lying with his eyes closed when she went into the room. He looked at her and gave the ghost of a smile. She sank back onto the chair she felt had almost become part of her body. She reached for his hand. His hair was lank and clung to his forehead in damp strands. His eyes opened, now looking green against the pillow.

'What happened?' he whispered. 'I can't remember anything except driving from the house with the kids in the back of the car. Can't remember why or where I was going.'

'Don't try to talk too much and don't think about what happened. There's plenty of time ahead of us for that.' Kerrien was just so grateful that she was here and that he had returned to her. The fears of brain damage seemed to be unfounded, thank heavens.

'I think you should go home and rest now,' said a voice behind her. The nurse put her hand on Kerrien's shoulder. 'Get some sleep and come back tomorrow. He will sleep now. You both need lots of rest, ready for the days ahead.'

Kerrien felt bone weary. All the stress of the past few days suddenly caught up with her and she could scarcely lift herself from the chair. When she did finally manage to stand, she almost fell again, unable to support herself.

'Whoa, there,' the nurse said. 'Do you have far to drive?' Kerrien could hardly remember even where she had left the car. She shook her head.

'I think maybe, you had better have a bed here. You're in no state to drive tonight. I don't want to have two of you to look after.' She bustled out of the ward and returned later to lead Kerrien through to a small room nearby. It was usually kept for relatives but had been fully occupied the past few days by some anxious parents waiting for news of their son. She lay between the crisp white sheets and closed her eyes. Sheer exhaustion and relief knocked her into unconsciousness immediately and she slept for the first time in days. When she finally awoke, she

367

couldn't remember where she was. Then relief swept over her and she got up quickly, anxious to see Ashton and learn how he was progressing. Kate was already sitting by his bed and she turned as Kerrien went into the room.

'Sh,' she warned. 'He's asleep again.'

The two women sat beside him, watching every flutter of his eye lashes, waiting to hear him speak. Kerrien knew she should go to see the children but she could not bear to leave Ashton's side. She almost wished that Kate would go to them instead, leaving her free to sit beside the man she loved so deeply.

'I'd better go and see the children,' Kerrien said. 'They don't even know that he's come round yet.' It had been difficult to know what to say to them, not to worry them but at the same time trying to explain why they hadn't had a visit from him.

'Kerrien, Kerrien, the doctor says we can go home,' Ben shouted as she came into the ward. They had been moved into the larger ward now they were almost recovered. The bandages had been removed from their heads and apart from Jodie's plastered arm, they both looked pretty normal. She knew she would never forget the looks on their faces when she told them their father was going to be all right. Ben smiled a little slow smile and Jodie gave her own great big grin.

'When can we see him?' she wanted to know.

'When he gets a little bit stronger and doesn't need quite so much sleep,' she promised. The ward sister called Kerrien into the office.

'I understand you have responsibility for Ben and Jodie?' she asked.

'I suppose so, yes. As you know, their father is in intensive care, so I suppose it is me and their aunt. Is there something wrong?'

'Not wrong exactly, but we can't keep them here any longer. They don't need hospital care now and we need their beds. Obviously, if they can return to their own home it's for the best or we shall have to make arrangements for them to be fostered.'

'Heavens no, they must come home. I can't pretend it will be easy but I'll manage somehow.'

'Thanks you, Mrs . . . er Miss . . .?' Kerrien was tempted to say that she would soon be their new mummy, but knew that would be wrong. After all, the last time she'd seen Ashton before the accident, they had parted on very bad terms. Fortunately, he did not seem to have remembered.

It was good to return home, after so many days spent away. Once the children were settled, she wandered round the house, almost as if seeing it for the first time. She peeped into Ashton's room, remembering the last night she'd spent here. It seemed like a century ago now, yet it was less than a week. A sudden noise interrupted her reverie. A door slammed shut and she rushed through, anxious in case one of the children had fallen. In the family room stood Kate, suitcase in one hand and a couple of plastic carriers of shopping in her other.

'Hallo,' she said. 'I'm back. I'll just put the food in the fridge and then move back into my room. I suppose it is still empty?'

Kerrien didn't know what to say. Undoubtedly, Kate's presence in the house would be a help, under the circumstances, but she wasn't sure she was entirely happy with the thought of her taking over once more. Still, for the moment, it would at least mean that she would be able to spend time visiting Ashton.

'Of course. Your room is just as you left it. Nothing's changed.' Kate gave a small sniff.

'I can see some things have changed and not for the better. There is an awful lot of junk food in this freezer. Still, I suppose it won't take long to get things back onto a proper footing.' She picked up her bag and went into her room.

'I don't want Aunt Kate to start bossing us all round again,' Ben announced.

'And I still want fish-fingers and chips sometimes,' Jodie added.

'We'll just have to make sure she understands,' Kerrien assured them. 'Nothing is going to change again. I promise.' She would let Kate settle in and then she'd explain how *she* liked things to be done, nowadays. She would be grateful for a little help, but she would not tolerate Kate making a new takeover bid for the house.

She was able to visit Ashton again, later in the afternoon. She walked along the impersonal corridors to his ward. To her amazement, he was sitting upright, chatting to one of the nurses.

'Kerrien,' he said. 'Hi there. How are you? It's so long since I saw you.'

'All of five hours,' she grinned. He stared at her.

'Five hours? It's weeks. Before my wedding, I think.' Kerrien glanced at the nurse, as if she could give some sort of explanation just by looking at her.

'But, I was here this morning. I've been here all the time you were unconscious. Don't you remember? I took the children home today. They're better now, almost fully recovered. Kate's staying with them.'

'It's good of you to help us out like this. I expect my wife will be home soon. I'm not sure where she went, do you know?'

Kerrien felt sick. Whatever had happened to him, since this morning? He had seemed to be perfectly normal when she left. Now he was treating her as almost a stranger. And all this business about being married. Who was he supposed to have been married to? There was still something very wrong with him. She excused herself, trying to signal to the nurse that she needed to speak to her, outside the room.

'What is he talking about?' she demanded. 'Is there something wrong with his memory?'

'I don't know. I thought he was talking normally. I understood his wife had left him, that he was divorced. Perhaps he's forgotten the years in between. Sometimes being unconscious plays strange tricks.'

'He was going to marry someone else, but that was cancelled. I think, I thought . . . I mean, well I thought, *we* were going to get married. We had a row just before the accident. I suppose, I don't really know what will happen now.'

'Try to take things easily, one step at a time. He may be confused for some time. Try to go along with what

371

he says and remember that he doesn't always know what is the truth and what he's dreamt about. Give him time.'

Kerrien sighed. It wasn't over yet. There were still many miles to go before this particular path reached its end. She was so disappointed, distressed about this new turn of events but knew it would be up to her to keep reminding him of what was happening, of the truth.

'I don't understand why my wife hasn't been in to see me. She must be very busy. She's a doctor you know.' Kerrien listened, biting her lip and trying not to let her feelings show too much. By the end of visiting hours, she felt worn out with all her efforts.

She tried to explain to Kate, when she finally arrived back at the house.

'It's as if he's forgotten everything that happened recently and has gone forward in time, according to the original plans.'

'Perhaps you had better explain yourself to me as well,' Kate suggested. Kerrien realized that, of course, Kate knew nothing of the various happenings just before the accident. She did not know that Martine's brief engagement had come to an end, nor that she had been in the process of moving in, when the accident had happened. She must have wondered about Martine's absence from her fiancé's bedside but it had not been mentioned by either of them. There was a lot of catching up to do. She did omit details of the night that she and Ashton had spent together! The very thought of it was enough to bring back floods of memories, memories that might, in view of today's new developments, be all she would ever have.

Back in her own familiar bed in her own room, Kerrien slept little. After the exhaustion of the previous night, her mind was much too active to let her rest. She ought to speak to Margaret and Brett again and then she remembered with a shock that she had done nothing to try and find out what had happened to the little puppy. Lloyd seemed to have disappeared without trace.

By the time she finally fell into a restless sleep, it was almost morning. When she went into the kitchen, Kate was already making coffee and putting out cereals for the children. Feeling rather dopey, Kerrien reached for the phone.

'Must ring to see how Ashton is.'

'He's making reasonable progress. Had a comfortable night,' Kate informed her. She had beaten her to the phone and made the call before Kerrien had even woken up.

'I'll go and see to the children,' she suggested.

'I've told them to stay in their rooms until we're ready for them,' Kate said. Kerrien felt a sense of déjà vu. However brilliantly Kate had supported them through this trauma, she would never really change. She would automatically try to take charge again and doubtless Kerrien would fall into the role of the paid help once more. But what could she do? For the time being, she had to rely on Kate if she was to spend any time at all with Ashton.

'I shall go to the hospital this morning and you can go later, this afternoon. Does that suit?' Kerrien nodded. There was nothing else she could say. At least she could catch up on a few calls this morning, see how the rest of the world was getting on without her.

She used Ashton's room to make the calls about Lloyd, so that the children didn't hear if the news was bad. It seemed the little dog must have been in the car before the crash, but there had been no sign of him afterwards. She spoke to the police and the paramedics who had attended the scene. No one had seen any sign of the little setter puppy. Perhaps he had jumped from the wreck and disappeared into the darkness. No one had even reported finding a dog or seeing one in any other accident. It seemed he was lost forever.

When Kate returned from her visit to the hospital, she seemed strangely subdued.

'Daddy sends his love,' she said, almost automatically to the children. To Kerrien, she said nothing. 'Fine' was all she would offer, when she had inquired about Ashton's progress. Kerrien couldn't wait to get to see him herself and left as soon as she could during the afternoon.

He had been moved out of intensive care and she was directed to his new room by another nurse.

'He does have a visitor, but as long as you don't get him too excited, it should be all right for you to go in.' She seemed more formal after the friendly relationship Kerrien had built with the nurses from Intensive Care. She knocked on his door and went in, wondering who the other visitor would be.

'Oh, it's Mary Poppins herself,' the familiar voice called out. 'That's nice for you, darling. I shall have to

374

be on my way, I'm afraid.' Martine rose from the seat next to Ashton's bed and crossed to the door. 'Mary Poppins' was seething gently, not pleased either to see the woman or to hear her affected voice. To her surprise, Martine beckoned her to the door again.

'Poor dear seems to think we're married! I think you of all people, know that isn't true, nor likely to be after that last debacle. Can't think how this has happened. All too dreadful. I don't wish the poor man any harm, but I really can't do with all this emotional stuff. See you.' And she swept out of the room, waving lightly to the patient and leaving her trail of perfume to compete with the usual hospital smell.

'Ashton, how are you today?' Kerrien asked as gently as her fury allowed. How could he believe he had actually married that woman?

'Kerrien. You are being good to me to keep visiting like this. Are you living on this side of town now?' he asked conversationally. She felt completely out of her depth, simply not knowing what to say or the best way to deal with the situation.

'Did you see my wife? Lovely isn't she? I'm a lucky man.' He smiled fondly at the door through which he had watched Martine disappear.

'The children send their love,' she muttered feebly, thinking she would have to try to ignore what he said and continue with her own conversation.

'Oh, you've seen them, have you? Martine is such a good mother to them Treats them as if they were hers. I was married once before, you see. They aren't her children.'

'How long have you been married?' she asked suddenly.

'Not long. We had a splendid wedding, in the Cathedral. I think you were there weren't you? I know you were supposed to be. I think we had a row about it but I said you would look after the children best.'

Kerrien listened to his ramblings for as long as she could bear. She had heard enough of the fabulous Martine and all her virtues and decided her time would be better spent with the children. How would they take this new turn of events? If they thought things were back on with Martine, who could tell what effect it might have on them?

She excused herself from his company and left the hospital. It was going to be long haul. She longed to see again the man she loved, to have the original Ashton back. She also had the problem of the newly established Kate to sort out. Perhaps she would like to spend the rest of the day back with Emma. It might improve her mood a little, when Kerrien told her a few of her own rules. It had been quite an eventful few months, she reflected. What was it she had thought as the plane landed? Something about the start of a whole new life? She wondered if she would still have come if she had known what lay in store. One look at the children, lying asleep in their beds was enough to convince her.

Kate leapt at the chance to return to her new home for the night.

'I hadn't expected you back so early,' she said.

'He isn't himself, is he?' Kerrien asked. 'He's so muddled.'

'Perhaps Martine will come good for him,' Kate suggested.

'She was there when I arrived. She isn't interested, not now he's no longer of use to her. She more or less handed him over to me.' She tried not to sound bitter but she knew she was making him sound like shop soiled goods being passed around.

'I'll get off now then,' Kate said when they finished talking. 'I'll be over in the morning.'

Kerrien sat with a glass of wine in her hand. She twisted the stem in her long fingers, wondering what she should do. Ashton was home lying in bed in his own room and she was gradually wearing herself out, trying to cope with all his demands. She had been warned that doctors often make the worst patients. Once his medical needs had been satisfied, there was no need for him to remain in hospital. The doctors had decided that his home environment might best help his memory to return to normal. He was still finding it more comfortable to stay in bed for most of the time, until the plaster could be taken off his leg.

Finally, in desperation, she had removed the telephone from his room to try and stop him phoning Martine. The woman had made it quite obvious, to everyone except Ashton, that she didn't want to know. She was slighted that he had called her bluff, that dreadful day when she had nearly moved in with him. She'd got her things almost installed when he had told

377

her exactly what he expected of his future wife. She could not believe he could have turned round so completely. Someone had obviously been talking about her own foibles, spreading malicious rumours. When he finally announced that he intended to marry his little Mary Poppins, that had been the final straw. She had left. Moved everything out again. She was glad, though, that she'd had nothing to do with his crash. In fact, she had no idea it had even happened until that tiresome sister of his had phoned her the next day.

Ashton had been home for over a week now. His memory for many things had returned to normal but for the one fact. He still believed that he had gone through with marriage to Martine and made excuses most of the time for her prolonged absence. She had become an internationally renowned heart surgeon, kept busy flying round the world to operate; she was an expert on something else and speaking at conferences. Nothing anyone could do or say would persuade him differently. For Kerrien, it was the greatest test anyone could ever have made of true love. She gritted her teeth and got on with life, hoping and waiting for Ashton to return to his old self.

Jodie had gone back to school and Ben was going to his kindergarten most mornings. It gave Kerrien a little respite, time to try and catch up on everything, particularly as Kate came in several times during the week and mostly sat with Ashton while Kerrien played with the children. They repeatedly asked for news of Lloyd, but the little dog had vanished without trace.

They pleaded for another dog but under the circumstances, she did not feel able to cope with even one more thing added to her days. There seemed to be no progress, no improvement. She was only sustained by her love for Ashton and the children, always hoping for the return to the life she had longed for.

One morning, a huge basket of flowers was delivered to the house. It was addressed to Ashton and bore a card, sealed in an envelope. She carried it through carefully, and put it down on his dressing table.

'Just look at this,' she said, longing to know who had sent it.

'Wow. Someone loves me, for sure. Pass me the card.'

Kerrien ripped it off the holder and handed it to him.

'*Best of luck for the future. Offered a job I can't refuse in Singapore. Off tomorrow. Martine.*'

His face blanched.

'She's leaving me,' he said, disbelief in his voice. Then to Kerrien's horror, he went very pale and began to shake. She bent over him, putting her arms round his body, comforting him with a swaying motion, just as she might comfort Ben. His body shook violently for a time, terrifying Kerrien. She dared not leave him to call for a doctor. Was he having some sort of fit? His body relaxed and stayed still for several minutes. She moved away from him slightly, trying to see his face. Silent tears were running down his cheeks. Suddenly, he gave one final jerk and sat bolt upright. He stared at Kerrien, as if seeing her for the first time.

'My God,' he said in the strongest voice she had heard since the accident. 'What the hell has been happening to me, Kerrien? I feel as if I've been ploughing through the jungle for a month.'

'Perhaps you have,' Kerrien replied, fresh tears in her eyes. This time, they were tears of joy. Ashton had finally come home.

CHAPTER 19

The whole house bustled with activity. The two children were excited and seemed to be rushing around squealing every few minutes. For once, the normally unruffled Kerrien was getting a little short tempered with them.

'Please, go out and play in the garden. There are millions of things I have to do and I need a little bit of peace,' she begged.

'It's no fun without Lloyd,' Jodie protested.

'You only had Lloyd for a very short time so you must have been used to playing for years without him.'

'Can't we have another dog? Please, Kerrien?'

'Please, Kerrien?' Ben added.

'We'll see after the wedding and when we come back from holiday.'

She sighed. The disappearance of the little dog was the only mystery that remained unsolved after the dreadful accident, now nearly three months ago. Even the rather battered, blood-stained toy monkey, so dear to Ben, had been recovered from the wreck.

Ashton had made an almost complete recovery, still limping slightly from the effects of his broken leg but now back at work and loving every moment of it. The children had never looked back once they realized that Kerrien was at last, going to be Ashton's wife and more importantly, their own new mummy. Ashton had finally told her the whole story behind his actions that fateful day. He was determined to teach Martine a lesson she would never forget. People had told him things about her that he hadn't wanted to believe but had known inside made sense. He wanted to show her once and for all, that she could not manipulate people, thinking she could use her looks to get what she wanted. Kerrien had laughed, when he recounted his demands of his future wife: no career; selfless dedication to himself and the children; at least three more children; no social activities that didn't include him. It was perhaps the final demand that broke her, Kerrien had suggested.

'And she believed you?' Kerrien had asked incredulously.

'It's the truth. What I expect. Why wouldn't she believe me?' he had said. For a moment, Kerrien almost did believe him and drew breath to make her own protest.

'Come here my darling. I shall never have to make any demands on you. You are my idea of the perfect wife, just the way you are.' He kissed her fondly before continuing his tale.

Once Martine had left, he had spent the day thinking and planning their future together, if only

Kerrien would come back to him. He had treated her badly, he realized but had not dared to say anything to her of his plan as he knew it wouldn't work unless she was kept in the dark. Now he knew it had been a mistake. He had not bargained for Kerrien rushing away as she did and it had been later in the evening he had known that he must go and search for her. He had bundled the children and dog into the car and drove out to find Margaret's house, guessing that was where she would be. There had been a bad storm earlier and the roads were very wet. The lorry had come out of a side turning and swiped his car off the road, almost flattening it in the process. Kerrien shuddered, thinking of how close she had come to losing all of them.

Now, in just three days' time, they were to be married. Her simple, well-tailored suit hung in the wardrobe. It was blue, Ashton's favourite colour. Jodie's bridesmaid's dress was a deeper blue and Ben was to wear a denim suit with a waistcoat, '*the bestest clothes I ever had*', he declared. It was to be a simple wedding, at the nearest registry office, followed by a small reception for a few close friends back at home. Kate was in her element, organizing the buffet.

'Can't have you serving up your old fish-fingers,' she joked. Kerrien was relieved to have the task taken away from her and was delighted to give her future sister-in-law the free run of the kitchen for a few days.

The door bell rang and a package was delivered. She

signed for it, noting with a slight sense of dread it was post-marked Singapore. There was only one person she knew who lived in Singapore. Martine. She turned it over in her hands and despite it being addressed to Ashton, she tore it open. There was a bundle of papers inside and she looked curiously, wondering what on earth the woman could have sent. Then she breathed a sigh of relief. It was the registration document for Lloyd. Evidently she had discovered it among her other papers and thought they may as well have them. Kerrien looked through them, feeling sad. *Lloyd of Meadowgold Caspar*, his official name stated. Poor little pup. Turning over another sheet, she felt a shiver of excitement. The hairs on her arms suddenly prickled.

'*Identichip Number*,' followed by a string of numbers and letters. The little dog had an electronic tag! It was a long shot after so much time but she knew she had to try to follow this small lead. She dialled the company and they passed on some information. The dog had been picked up wandering along the roads, late one night. He had been taken to the pound, because there seemed to be no one available at the registered address. As far as they knew, he'd been kept there. They could tell her no more.

'You should realize though, they don't keep dogs forever at the pound. If no one claims them, they have to be put down.'

Fingers crossed, Kerrien called the pound. They were pleasant enough but could only confirm that Lloyd was no longer there. Nor were they able to

384

say what had happened to him. She put the phone down and bundled the papers away into her handbag, in case the children saw them. It wouldn't do to have their hopes raised, as hers had been.

'I have to go and see the florist,' she called to Kate. 'Can you keep an eye on the kids or shall I take them?'

'They can stay, if they're good. I'm much too busy to spend my time sorting them out.' She was in the middle of baking endless vol au vents, enough, Kerrien believed, to last them for months.

She drove out, having warned Ben and Jodie that she wanted only good reports of their behaviour from Kate. They were so happy and excited this week that she knew they would be no problem. Once her errands were done, she sat in the car, thinking again about Lloyd. It would really put the tops on the whole wedding if she could trace the little dog. She went round to the dog pound, sad to see so many hopeful animals stuck in cages, desperate for any owner that might release them from their fate. At the desk, she asked if they kept records. The young girl asked her name and then smiled.

'I was going to phone you back. I mentioned your call to one of the others and she remembered the dog. It was obviously a pedigree and very young and one of our officers decided to give him a home, once we had done all the necessary searching. No one had connected it with that accident as it hadn't been reported missing.'

'With all the upset, I completely forgot about him

for several days.' Kerrien felt desperately guilty, at what she saw as her own negligence.

'Anyway, our Mr Davies still has the little fellow. You can try asking him but I guess the pooch has become part of his family by now.'

Kerrien took the man's number, her hopes raised. Surely, in the circumstances, he must at least give her request some consideration?

She said nothing to the family and after dinner, she asked Ashton if they could all go for a little trip. They looked at her in great surprise.

'At this time of night?' Ashton questioned.

'I wouldn't ask, but this is something very special. I have the address but I'm not sure where it is. I know you'll be able to find it more quickly, Ashton.' With a shrug, he rose and they all went out to the car. Ben and Jodie were full of questions but Kerrien still wouldn't say a word. As she was smiling, they knew it must be something nice and kept pestering for an answer.

'Is it to do with the wedding?' Jodie asked.

'Sort of,' was all she would say.

They stopped outside the little house and Kerrien made them stay in the car while she went in first. She appeared in the lighted doorway and beckoned. When the children reached the door, they stopped and screamed,

'A new dog. Just like Lloyd, only bigger. Isn't he lovely. Is he for us?'

'Sit Rusty,' the man said and he squatted down obediently. 'Lloyd, you called him?'

'We lost our little puppy in a car crash,' Jodie said, her eyes looking moist as she remembered. 'He ran away.'

'Reckon this little fella might just be the one you're looking for,' he said kindly.

'This is Lloyd?' Jodie said, wonder in her voice. 'But he's massive. Lloyd was only a little puppy.'

Everyone laughed.

'They do grow, you know, especially at this age. He's just a bit older now, but I reckon he's the same one.'

'Lloyd, Lloyd,' Ben called. The pup lifted its head, as if searching for some lost memory. He leapt up and tail wagging furiously, he ran from one to the other of the children, who were squeaking with joy.

'I guess that clinches it,' the man said. 'Can't pretend I won't miss the little mutt but he's obviously yours.'

'Thank you, thank you,' Jodie cried. She had her arms tightly round Lloyd's neck, not wanting to be separated from him for a moment.

'Can we offer you something towards his keep for the past months?' Ashton suggested.

'Nah,' the man said. 'Make a donation to the pound. They can always use a few extra bucks.'

Around a dozen or so friends stood round the magnificent cake that Kate had produced, as Ashton and his new wife plunged the knife in. They all applauded and then the group broke up to chat, as Kate cut the cake to pass it round. Brett was looking handsome in his dark

suit and seemed fully engrossed with his new girl-
friend, a pretty dark haired girl. Margaret shook her
head at him.

'Don't reckon he'll ever change, Kerrien, do you?
Never get to see him married in my life time.'

'You never know,' she laughed. 'He's a good man.
Someone will snap him up before you know it. Thanks
for being such an amazingly good friend,' she whispered. There were tears in Margaret's eyes as she
replied.

'Just don't forget who your old friends are. I shall
expect to see you very often and if the Doc does
anything to upset you, I'll send Brett round to sort
him out.' They both laughed.

Emma, Kate's friend, was pleased to see Ben and
Jodie again. She hadn't seen them since her dismissal
but she felt no resentment, especially as Kate had
now moved in to share her home. She was good with
both of the children and Kerrien made a selfish
mental note that she could be useful as an occasional
baby-sitter!

The little family sat together on the beach in the
early spring. The setter puppy scampered madly
round, barking at the gulls who teased him by dive
bombing and soaring back into the blue sky.

'I'm glad you let us come on your honeymoon,'
Jodie whispered, nestling up to Kerrien.

'How could we have left our very own family at
home?' Ashton smiled.

'Can I go in the sea now, Mummy,' Ben said,
grinning at his new word.

Tears of joy filled Kerrien's eyes, also at his new word, as she nodded.

'Come on Rusty Lloyd,' he shouted as he bounded off into the waves, Jodie running behind him.

'Love you,' Ashton whispered.

'Love you too,' she replied.

'It was a long path to love, but we made it in the end.'

THE EXCITING NEW NAME IN WOMEN'S FICTION!

PLEASE HELP ME TO HELP YOU!

Dear *Scarlet* Reader,

As promised, I have some excellent news for you this month – we are beginning a super Prize Draw, which means that **you could win 6 months' worth of free Scarlets!** Just return your completed questionnaire to us (see addresses at end of questionnaire) before 31 July 1997 and you will automatically be entered in the draw that takes place on that day. If you are lucky enough to be one of the first two names out of the hat we will send you four new Scarlet romances every month for six months, and for each of twenty runners up there will be a sassy *Scarlet* T-shirt.

So don't delay – return your form straight away!*

Sally Cooper

Editor-in-Chief, *Scarlet*

*Prize draw offer available only in the UK, USA or Canada. Draw is not open to employees of Robinson Publishing, or their agents, families or households. Winners will be informed by post, and details of winners can be obtained after 31 July 1997, by sending a stamped addressed envelope to address given at end of questionnaire.

Note: further offers which might be of interest may be sent to you by other, carefully selected, companies. If you do not want to receive them, please write to Robinson Publishing Ltd, 7 Kensington Church Court, London W8 4SP, UK.

QUESTIONNAIRE

Please tick the appropriate boxes to indicate your answers

1 Where did you get this Scarlet title?
Bought in supermarket ☐
Bought at my local bookstore ☐ Bought at chain bookstore ☐
Bought at book exchange or used bookstore ☐
Borrowed from a friend ☐
Other (please indicate) _____

2 Did you enjoy reading it?
A lot ☐   A little ☐   Not at all ☐

3 What did you particularly like about this book?
Believable characters ☐   Easy to read ☐
Good value for money ☐   Enjoyable locations ☐
Interesting story ☐   Modern setting ☐
Other _____

4 What did you particularly dislike about this book?
_____

5 Would you buy another Scarlet book?
Yes ☐   No ☐

6 What other kinds of book do you enjoy reading?
Horror ☐   Puzzle books ☐   Historical fiction ☐
General fiction ☐   Crime/Detective ☐   Cookery ☐
Other (please indicate) _____

7 Which magazines do you enjoy reading?
1. _____
2. _____
3. _____

And now a little about you –
8 How old are you?
Under 25 ☐   25–34 ☐   35–44 ☐
45–54 ☐   55–64 ☐   over 65 ☐

cont.

9 What is your marital status?
   Single ☐   Married/living with partner ☐
   Widowed ☐   Separated/divorced ☐

10 What is your current occupation?
   Employed full-time ☐   Employed part-time ☐
   Student ☐   Housewife full-time ☐
   Unemployed ☐   Retired ☐

11 Do you have children? If so, how many and how old are they?
   _____
   _____

12 What is your annual household income?
   under $15,000 ☐ or £10,000   ☐
   $15–25,000   ☐ or £10–20,000   ☐
   $25–35,000   ☐ or £20–30,000   ☐
   $35–50,000   ☐ or £30–40,000   ☐
   over $50,000   ☐ or £40,000   ☐

Miss/Mrs/Ms _____
Address _____
_____
_____

Thank you for completing this questionnaire. Now tear it out – put
it in an envelope and send it to:

Sally Cooper, Editor-in-Chief

USA/Can. address
SCARLET c/o London Bridge
85 River Rock Drive
Suite 202
Buffalo
NY 14207
USA

UK address/No stamp required
SCARLET
FREEPOST LON 3335
LONDON W8 4BR
*Please use block capitals for
address*

PALOV/3/97

Scarlet titles coming next month:

MASTER OF THE HOUSE   Margaret Callaghan
Ella has just started a new life as housekeeper to the wealthy, newly engaged Fliss. But when Fliss's fiancé comes home, Ella's troubles really begin! For Jack Keegan is Ella's ex-husband – the only man she's ever loved . . .

SATIN AND LACE   Danielle Shaw
The last proposal Sally Palmer expects to hear from her boss, Hugh Barrington, is 'Will you be my mistress?' Surprising even herself, Sally embarks on the affair with consequences which affect everyone around her!

NO GENTLEMAN   Andrea Young
When Nick comes back into Daisy's life, she's convinced she's immune to his charm. She's going to marry safe, handsome and loving Simon. So let Nick do his darnedest to persuade Daisy that it's excitement *not* security she desires. She's already made her choice, and nothing will change her mind . . . or will it?

NOBODY'S BABY   Elizabeth Smith
Neither Joe Devlin nor Stevie Parker tell the truth when they meet. He thinks *she's* a writer, she thinks *he's* in PR. After a wonderful night together, Joe leaves with no explanation. So Stevie takes her revenge . . . then Joe plots his!